Mary Ellen Porter
and
Becky Avella

Strength and Valor

Previously published as *Into Thin Air* and *Targeted*

HARLEQUIN® LOVE INSPIRED®CLASSICS

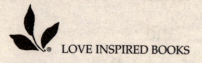

LOVE INSPIRED BOOKS

Recycling programs for this product may not exist in your area.

ISBN-13: 978-1-335-14769-1

Strength and Valor

Copyright © 2018 by Harlequin Books S.A.

First published as Into Thin Air by Harlequin Books in 2015 and Targeted by Harlequin Books in 2015.

The publisher acknowledges the copyright holders of the individual works as follows:

Into Thin Air
Copyright © 2015 by Mary Ellen Porter

Targeted
Copyright © 2015 by Rebecca Avella

www.Harlequin.com

Printed in U.S.A.

CONTENTS

INTO THIN AIR   7
Mary Ellen Porter

TARGETED   245
Becky Avella

Mary Ellen Porter's love of storytelling was solidified in fifth grade when she was selected to read her first children's story to a group of kindergartners. From then on, she knew she'd be a writer. When not working, Mary Ellen enjoys reading and spending time with her family and search dog in training. She's a member of Chesapeake Search Dogs, a volunteer search and rescue team that helps bring the lost and missing home.

Books by Mary Ellen Porter

Love Inspired Suspense

Into Thin Air
Off the Grid Christmas

INTO THIN AIR

Mary Ellen Porter

Many are the plans in a man's heart,
but it is the Lord's purpose that prevails.
—*Proverbs* 19:21

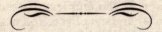

To Eldridge, for always believing in me,
even when I doubted myself. Your love, support
and unfailing encouragement are
the foundation of all my achievements.

To my children, Skylar and Trey. No mother could
be more proud than I am of you; you make me smile
every day. May you find God's special purpose for
your lives within your hopes and dreams.

And to my sister, Shirlee McCoy,
whose ten years of persistent and "gentle" prodding
resulted in this book. Smart. Talented. Tenacious.
Stubborn. A definite combination for success. It's
finally my turn to say "me, too." Thank you for
never letting me forget my dreams. This one's for you.

Chapter One

It was a passing glimpse, no more. A young teen walking slowly along the edge of the darkening side street, a violin case tucked in the crook of her arm, her face illuminated by her cell phone screen as she furiously texted, aware of nothing but the phone in her hand.

The van made even less of an impression, the driver all but invisible as the vehicle passed Laney Kensington's Jeep Wrangler.

Both should have been easy to ignore, but they nagged at Laney's mind—made the hair on the back of her neck prickle. Laney told herself it was just her imagination getting the best of her—but she couldn't simply drive on.

Call it intuition, call it divine intervention—Laney called it never wrong.

She'd never ignored it on a search. She wouldn't ignore it now.

She glanced in the rearview mirror, pulse jumping as the van swung a wide U-turn and headed back toward the girl. Laney did the same, stepping on the gas, her Jeep surging forward.

The slowing van closed in on the girl. She finally

looked up, eyes widening as a figure jumped out and sprinted toward her. The violin dropped from her arms and she tried to run.

Too little, too late.

The man was on her in a flash, hand over her mouth, dragging her toward the van. In seconds they'd be gone. One more child missing. One more family broken.

Not today. Not if Laney could help it.

Although it had been years since she'd last prayed, Laney found herself whispering a silent plea to God, begging Him for help that deep down she knew would never come. She'd learned a long time ago that the only one she could depend on was herself.

Putting her trust anywhere else was just too risky.

The van was right in front of her, and there was only one thing Laney could think to do to stop the kidnapping. She braced for impact, ramming the front of the van with her Jeep in the hope of disabling it. In the back seat, Murphy yelped at the jarring stop; there was no time to comfort the dog.

Leaping from the Jeep, Laney threw herself at the would-be kidnapper. His weight off-balance from the struggling child, he tumbled over. The girl went with him, her high-pitched scream piercing the still air. Laney snagged the girl's hand, yanking her to her feet.

"Run!" she shouted, but the kidnapper was on his feet again, snatching a handful of the girl's shirt and dragging her back.

"Back off!" he commanded, his voice chilling.

Laney slammed into him again, this time with so much force they all fell in a tangled mass of limbs, pushing and grabbing and struggling. The kidnapper grunted as Laney kneed him in the kidney. His grip on the girl loosened, and Laney shoved her from the heap.

But the kidnapper would not let his prey go without a fight. He reverse punched Laney, propelling her backward. She tumbled onto damp grass, her head slamming into hard earth. She had a moment of panic as blackness edged in. She could *not* lose consciousness. She willed herself up, lunging toward the struggling pair as they neared the van. Laney yanked the guy's arm and slammed her foot into the back of his knee. He cursed, swinging around, the girl between them.

"I said *back off*!" he growled, his dark eyes filled with fury, his hand clamped firmly over the girl's mouth.

Laney eased around so that she stood between him and the van. She saw that the girl was still fighting against his hold, but her efforts were futile. She met Laney's eyes, the fear in her gaze something Laney knew she would never forget.

It's okay, Laney wanted to say. *He's not going to take you. I won't let him.*

"Let her go," Laney demanded.

"I don't think so." The man glanced just beyond Laney's shoulder, a cold smile curving his lips.

The girl stilled, her eyes widening.

Laney knew without even looking that someone was behind her.

Her blood ran cold, but she turned, ready to fight as many people as it took for as long as she had to. Eventually, another car would come, someone would call the police, help would arrive. She just had to hold the kidnappers off long enough for that to happen.

A shadowy figured jumped from the van's open door. Laney had the impression of height and weight, of dark hair and cold eyes, but it was the gun that caught and held her attention. Although the gunman was shorter and more wiry than his stocky partner, the firearm in his hand made him far more lethal.

"Don't move," he snapped, the gun pointed straight at Laney's heart.

Laney stopped in her tracks, hands in the air in a display of unarmed surrender.

She wanted him to think she'd given up; she needed him off guard. She had to get the gun out of his hands, and she had to free the girl.

"Get the kid in the van before someone else comes by," the gunman ordered his accomplice.

"What do we do with the woman?" the other man asked as he dragged the child around Laney, grunting and tightening his grip as the girl's sneaker-clad foot caught his shin.

"Get rid of her. She's a loose end. No witnesses, remember?" The words were spoken with cold malice that sent a wave of fear up Laney's spine.

No cars coming, nothing to hide behind. No matter what direction Laney ran, a bullet could easily find her. If the girl was going to survive, if *Laney* was going to, the gunman had to be taken down. Laney braced herself for action, waiting for an opening that she was afraid wouldn't come.

Please, she prayed silently. *Just give me a chance.*

The girl grunted, trying to scream against the hand pressed to her face. They were close to the van door, so close that Laney knew it was just a matter of seconds before the girl was shoved in.

"Bite him!" she yelled.

"Shut up!" the gunman barked, glancing over his shoulder to check on his accomplice's progress. That was the opening Laney needed. She threw herself at his gun hand. He cursed, the gun dropping to the ground.

They both reached for it, Laney's fingers brushing cold metal, victory right beneath her palm. He slammed his fist into her jaw and she flew back, her grip on the gun lost in a wave of shocking pain. A dog growled, the harsh sound mixing with the frantic rush of Laney's pulse.

Murphy! She'd not given him the release command, yet he raced toward them, teeth bared.

The man raised the gun. Laney tried to scramble out of the way as he pulled the trigger. Hot pain seared through her temple, and she fell, Murphy's well-muscled body the last thing she saw as she sank into darkness.

Grayson DeMarco rushed through Anne Arundel Medical Center's fluorescently lit hallway, scanning the staff and visitors moving through the corridor. He'd been working this case for almost a year. He'd dogged every lead to every dead end, traveling from California to Boston and down to Baltimore, and he'd always been a few steps behind, a few days too late.

Sixteen children abducted. Four states. Not one single break.

Until tonight.

Finally the abductors had made a mistake.

A young girl was missing. The police had received her parents' frantic call less than thirty minutes after a woman had been found shot and unconscious on the sidewalk, a violin case and cell phone lying on the grass near her. The case had the missing girl's name on it.

Grayson had been called immediately, state PD moving quickly. They felt the pressure, too; they could see the tally of the area's missing children going up.

Like Grayson, they could hear the clock ticking.

They'd found a gun at the scene, spattered with blood, lying in the small island of grass that separated the sidewalk from the street. Grayson hoped it would yield useable prints and a DNA profile that could possibly lead him one step closer to the answers he was searching for.

He prayed it would, but he wasn't counting on it.

He'd been to the scene. He'd peered into an abandoned Jeep, lights still on, driver's door open. He'd opened the victim's wallet, seen her identification—Laney Kensington, five feet three inches and one hundred ten pounds. He'd gotten a good look at the German shepherd that might have been responsible for stopping the kidnappers before they were able to kill the woman. He'd pieced together an idea of what might have happened, but he needed to talk to Laney Kensington, find out what had really gone down, how much she'd seen. More importantly, he needed to know exactly how valuable that information might be to the case he was working.

Time was of the essence if Grayson had any chance of bringing these children home.

Failure was not an option.

A police officer stood guard outside the woman's room, his arms crossed over his chest, his expression neutral. He didn't move as Grayson approached, didn't acknowledge him at all until Grayson flashed his badge. "Special Agent Grayson DeMarco, FBI."

"Detective Paul Jensen, Maryland State Police," the detective responded. "No one's allowed in to see the victim. If that's why you're here, you may as well turn around and—"

He cut the man off. "We don't have time to play jurisdiction games, Detective. As of tonight, three kids are missing from Maryland in just under six weeks."

"I'm well aware of that, but I have my orders, and until I hear from my supervisor that you're approved to go in there, you're out."

"How about you give him a call, then?" Grayson reached past the detective and opened the door, ignoring the guy's angry protest as he walked into the cool hospital room.

The witness lay unconscious under a mound of sheets and blankets, her dark auburn hair tangled around a face that was pale and still streaked with dried blood. Faint signs of bruising shadowed her jaw, made more evident by the harsh hospital lights. A bandage covered her temple, and an IV line snaked out from beneath the sheets. She appeared delicate, almost fragile, not at all what he was expecting given her part in the events of the night. Fortunately, as fragile as she appeared, the bullet had merely grazed her temple and she would eventually make a full recovery.

Unfortunately, Grayson didn't have the luxury of waiting for her to heal. He needed to speak to her. The sooner the better.

He moved toward the bed, trying to ignore the pine scent of floor cleaner, the harsh overhead lights, the IV line. They reminded him of things he was better off forgetting, of a time when he hadn't been sure he could keep doing what he did.

He pulled a chair to the side of the bed and sat, glancing at Detective Jensen, who'd followed him into the room. "Aren't you supposed to be guarding the door?"

"I'm guarding the witness, and I could force you out

of here," the detective retorted, his eyes flashing with irritation and a hint of worry.

"What would be the point? You know I've got jurisdiction."

The detective offered no response. Grayson hadn't expected him to. Policies and protocol didn't bring abducted kids back to their parents, and wasting time fighting over jurisdiction wasn't going to accomplish anything.

"Look," he said, meeting the detective's dark eyes. "I'm not here to step on toes. I'm here to find these kids. There's still a chance we can bring them home. All of them. How about you keep that in mind?"

The guy muttered something under his breath and stalked out of the room.

That was fine with Grayson. He preferred to be alone with the witness when she woke. He wanted every bit of information she had, every minute detail. He didn't want it second-or third-hand, didn't want to get it after it had already been said a few times. He needed her memories fresh and clear, undiluted by time or speculation.

Laney groaned softly and began to stir. Just for a moment, Grayson felt like a voyeur. It seemed almost wrong to be sitting over her bed waiting for her to gain consciousness. She needed family or friends around her. Not a jaded FBI agent with his own agenda.

He leaned in toward Laney. Though only moments ago she had appeared to be on the verge of waking, she had grown still again.

"Laney?" he said softly. "Can you hear me?"

He leaned in closer. "Laney?"

She stirred, eyes moving rapidly behind closed lids. Was she caught in a dream, or a memory? he wondered.

"Wake up, Laney." He reached out, resting his hand gently on her forearm.

She came up swinging, her fist grazing his chin, her eyes wild. She swung again, and Grayson did the only thing he could. He ducked.

Chapter Two

"Calm down," a man said, his warm fingers curved around Laney's wrist. She tried to pull away but couldn't quite find the strength. Her head throbbed, the pungent smell of antiseptic filled her nose, and she couldn't manage to do more than stare into the stranger's dark-lashed blue eyes.

Not the kidnapper's eyes. Not the eyes of his accomplice. She wasn't lying on the pavement in the dark. There was no Jeep. No van. No struggling young girl with terror in her eyes. Nothing but cream-colored walls and white sheets and a man who could have been anyone looking at her expectantly.

"What happened? How did I get here?" she asked, levering up on her elbows, the hospital room too bright, her heart beating an erratic cadence in her chest.

"A couple of joggers found you lying on the sidewalk," the man responded. "Do you remember anything about tonight?"

Anything?

She remembered *everything*—heading home from Murphy's training session, seeing the girl and the van, struggling and fighting and failing. Again.

"Yes," she mumbled, willing away nausea and the deep pain of failure.

"Good." He smiled, his expression changing from harsh and implacable to something that looked like triumph. "That's going to help a lot."

"Help who?" Because her actions tonight certainly hadn't helped the girl or her family. Overwhelming sadness welled up within her, but Laney forced it back. She had to get a grip on herself. She had no idea how long she'd been unconscious, what had happened to Murphy, or most importantly, if the police even knew a child had been taken.

"I'm Special Agent Grayson DeMarco with the FBI," the man explained. "I'm hoping you can help with a case I'm working on."

"I'm not worried about your case, Agent DeMarco. I'm worried about the girl who was kidnapped tonight." She shoved the sheets off her legs and sat up. Her head swam, the pain behind her eyes nearly blinding her, but she had to get to a phone. She needed to tell Police Chief Kent Andrews what had happened. They needed to start searching immediately if there was any chance to save the child. And there *had* to be a chance.

"The girl *is* my case—and several other children like her," Agent DeMarco responded. "The local police are at the scene of the kidnapping. They're gathering evidence and doing everything they can to locate her, but she's not the only victim. If you've been watching the local news, you know that."

Because he seemed to expect a response, Laney nodded, realizing immediately that was a mistake as pain exploded through her temple. Her stomach churned.

"Lie down." Somehow Agent DeMarco was standing, his hands on her shoulders as he urged her back onto the pillows. "You're not going to do anyone any good if you're unconscious again." The words were harsh, but his touch was light.

Laney eyed him critically. She'd been working around law enforcement—local as well as Secret Service and DEA—for much of her adult life. She knew how the agencies operated. The FBI wouldn't be called in on an isolated, random child abduction.

"I'm fine," she muttered, pushing the button on the bed railing until the mattress raised her to a sitting position.

"You came within an inch of dying, Laney. I wouldn't call that fine." He settled back into the chair, his black tactical pants, T-shirt and jacket making him look more like a mercenary than an officer of the law.

She gingerly fingered a thick bandage that covered her temple and knew Agent DeMarco was right. "Murphy must have thrown his aim off."

"Murphy is the dog that was found at the scene?"

"Yes, I need to—"

"The local police have him. I was told he was being brought back to the kennel."

"Told by whom?" she asked. Agent DeMarco was saying all the right things, but she didn't know him, hadn't seen any identification, still wasn't a hundred percent convinced he was who he said he was.

"Chief Kent Andrews. He'll probably be here shortly. He's still overseeing the scene."

"I'd like to speak with him." She and Kent went back a couple of years. She often worked with the Maryland State Police K-9 team, correcting training issues with both the dogs and their handlers in an unofficial capacity.

"You will, but I need to ask you a few questions first."

"How about you show me some ID? Then you can ask your questions."

The request didn't surprise Grayson. He'd been told that Laney knew her way around law enforcement and that she wasn't someone who'd blindly follow orders. While working with the state K-9 team as a dog trainer, her skills with animals and the trainees alike had garnered the respect of the police chief and his men. More than that, Grayson got the distinct impression that Kent Andrews really liked Laney as a person and wasn't surprised at all that she would put herself in danger to help another.

"Sure." Grayson fished his ID out of his pocket, handed it to her.

She studied it, her wavy hair sliding across her cheeks and hiding her expression. She didn't trust him. That much was obvious, but she finally handed the ID back. "What do you want to know?" she asked.

"Everything," he responded, taking a small notepad and pen from his jacket pocket. "All the details of what happened tonight. What you saw. Who you saw. Don't leave anything out. Even the smallest detail could be important."

"I was on my way back from Davidsonville Park with Murphy when I saw her."

"Was she alone?"

"Yes. She was walking by herself. I always hate seeing that. I can't even count the number of kids my team and I have searched for who were out by themselves when they disappeared." She pinched the bridge of her nose and frowned. "Sorry, I'm getting off track. This headache…" She shook her head slightly and winced.

"Want me to call the nurse and get you something for the pain?" He would, but he didn't want to. He needed her as clear-headed as she could be.

She must have sensed that. She rested her head on the pillow. "That would be nice, but I'm not sure I'll be any good to anyone filled with a bunch of painkillers."

"Don't suffer for your cause, Laney. If you need pain medication, take it."

She smiled at that, a real smile that brightened her eyes and somehow made the smattering of freckles on her cheeks and nose more noticeable. She was pretty in a girl-next-door kind of way. He tried to imagine her taking on a guy with a gun. Couldn't quite do it. "I hate taking narcotics," she muttered. "I'll ask for Tylenol later."

He wasn't going to argue with her. "You saw the girl walking alone," he prompted her.

"Yes. I was headed home. A van was coming toward me in the opposite direction. We passed the girl at nearly the same time."

"Passed her?" He'd assumed she'd driven up as the girl was being abducted.

"Yes. The van made me think of the news reports of other abductions in the area. I glanced in the rearview mirror and saw the van U-turn. I did the same." Laney looked away as if unable to meet his gaze. "Unfortunately, it reached her first. She was texting and didn't even see them coming."

"Could you see the color of the van?"

"Not initially, but I got a good look at it when I rammed it with my jeep. It was a dark charcoal gray. My front fender probably scraped off some of the paint.

It will have a fresh dent on the front passenger side…" Laney's voice faltered.

"Did you see the person who grabbed her? Can you describe him?" he asked, every cell in his body waiting for the answer. If she saw the guy, if she had a description, if there was DNA on the gun, they'd finally have something to go on.

"I had a pretty clear view. There were streetlights and the headlights from my Jeep."

"Tell me what you remember. Don't hold anything back." Grayson urged.

"He was about six-foot-one with the build of an ex–football player—beefy but not in great shape anymore. His hair was dark brown and cropped close, like a military cut. He was wearing jeans with a black hooded sweatshirt and black work boots. He had brown eyes and an olive complexion. I saw part of a tattoo on the back of his neck, sticking out from the collar of his sweatshirt, but I didn't get a good look at it." She paused, frowned. "He wasn't alone. There was another guy in the van. He came out to help. He was shorter— I'd guess about five-foot-ten. Thin—like a runner's build. His hair was light brown, nose slightly crooked. He was the one with the gun."

Grayson scribbled notes furiously. "What about their ages?"

"Early to mid-thirties. Both of them."

"Did either speak?"

"Both did, but they didn't call each other by name."

Too bad. That would have been another lead to follow.

"What about accents?"

"None that I could distinguish."

"Did the girl seem to know her kidnappers?"

"If she knew them, it didn't show. As far as I could tell, she was an arbitrary target, but the way the van was parked would have made it nearly impossible for anyone on the street to see the kidnappers. It seemed random…but not."

"How so?"

"Like they were trolling the streets looking for someone, but once they picked a target their actions were deliberate—no hesitation—like they'd done the same thing before. If I hadn't been there, the girl—"

"Olivia Henley. She's thirteen. She was on her way home from her weekly music lesson. Her parents reported her missing shortly after the joggers found you." He wanted Laney to have a name to go with the face. He wanted her to know that there was a family who was missing a child. Not because he wanted her to feel guilty or obligated, but because he wanted her to understand how serious things were, how imperative it was that she cooperate.

"Olivia," she repeated quietly. "If I hadn't been there, she would have disappeared, and no one would have known what happened." She paused, her face so pale, he thought she might lose consciousness again. "If only I had done something differently, maybe she wouldn't have been taken."

"You did what you could, which is more than most would."

"But it wasn't enough, was it?" She leveled her gaze at him, surprising him with the depth of anger he saw reflected in her eyes. "That little girl is gone, Agent DeMarco. Her bed will be empty tonight."

Grayson recognized and understood her frustration. So many children went missing every day, and not all of them would make it home. He knew that better than most. "Not because of you, Laney. Because of the kidnappers."

"That's no consolation to her parents." Laney closed her eyes. "I wish I could have saved her."

"You still might be able to. If you're up to it, I'd like you to meet with a sketch arti—"

"I'm up to it. Let's go." Before the words were out of her mouth, she was up from bed, the white cotton sheet draped around her shoulders like a cape as she wobbled toward the door, the IV pole trailing along behind her.

"I didn't mean now," he said, taking three long strides to beat her to the door and slapping his palm against it so that she couldn't open it. "And I didn't mean you should walk out of here with an IV line attached to your arm, either."

"Then bring the sketch artist here." She turned to face him, swaying a little in the process. "The sooner you have an image of these guys, the sooner everyone can be on the lookout for them. If you really think Olivia can be saved, there's no time to lose."

She was right, of course. About all of it. There was only one problem with her plan, and it was a big one.

"We're not bringing the sketch artist here," he said, leading her back toward the bed. "You'd better lie down before you fall down."

She dropped into the chair instead, her face ashen, her eyes a dark emerald green against the pallor. "Why *not* bring the sketch artist here?" Her voice had lost some of its strength, but she hadn't lost any of her determination. "We're wasting time talking when we could be—"

"As far as the kidnappers know, you're dead, Laney," he said, cutting her off.

"What?"

"Dead. Deceased. Gone."

She rolled her eyes. "I know what you meant, Agent. I want to know *why* they think I'm dead."

"You were shot. Murphy might have distracted the shooter, but you went down. You were bleeding enough to make anyone think you'd been mortally wounded. The joggers who found you were a couple of teenage girls. They panicked, called 911 and reported a body. No one knows who you are or that you survived except the first responders and the hospital staff treating you, and they've been asked to keep it quiet. As far as the media and the public are concerned, Jane Doe was shot and killed on Ashley Street at approximately seven-thirty this evening. I'd like to keep your identity quiet for as long as possible."

Laney frowned. "Protecting my identity is the last thing we need to worry about."

"I disagree."

"Maybe you should explain why."

Grayson hesitated. Andrews had assured him that Laney was as good as they came, loyal and trustworthy. Even so, Grayson was reluctant to divulge too much. He was used to working alone. Putting his trust in God and his own abilities above all else. He had this one perfect lead, and he didn't want anything to keep it from panning out. "For now, I need you to trust that I'm making the best decisions I can for you and Olivia."

"For now," Laney agreed, struggling to her feet. "But you need to know that I'm not going to spend much time sitting around this hospital room while you make decisions for me. That's not the way I work."

She jabbed the call button on the bed railing, and he had visions of her walking out of the hospital in the mint-green hospital gown, the bandage on her forehead a glaring testimony to her injury. If the kidnappers were hanging around hoping to hear rumors confirming Jane Doe's death, they might catch a glimpse of Laney and follow her home. That was the last thing Grayson wanted.

He was all too aware that his biggest hope just might lie on the slender shoulders of Laney Kensington. If she could identify the kidnappers, he would be one step closer to saving Olivia—and the other children. He needed her help. And to get it, he had to give her some measure of trust.

"Then tell me how you *do* work," he offered. "And, let's see what kind of a compromise we can reach."

"I'm not looking for compromise. I need to know what's going on. Let's start with what you've got on these kidnappings."

It went against his nature to give her the information. He'd been keeping everything close to the vest. The less media coverage about the kidnappings, the better, as far as he was concerned. He was closing in on the perps. He could feel it, and he didn't want to risk scaring them off. He needed them to feel comfortable and confident. Their cockiness would be key to bringing them down.

On the other hand, he couldn't risk having Laney go maverick on him. If what the police chief had said about her was true, she knew enough about search and rescue and about police work to be dangerous. He had no doubt that she understood she could walk out of the hospital and away from him altogether. He had nothing on her and no legal means to keep her where she was. And if the kidnappers caught even a glimpse of her, the damage would be done. She'd gotten a good look at the kidnappers. He could only assume they'd gotten a good look at her, too. Once they knew she was alive, how quickly could they find her if they put their minds to it?

"Okay," he finally said. "Just have a seat and I'll tell you as much as I can."

She hesitated, her face drawn. Finally she complied, dropping back into the chair and fixing all of her attention on him.

"Well?" she prodded.

He pulled a chair over and sat.

They were knee to knee, the fabric of his pants brushing against the sheet she'd wrapped herself in, the IV pole just to the side of her chair. She looked young and vulnerable, her life way too easy to snuff out. That thought brought memories of another time, and for a moment, Grayson was in different hospital room, looking into another pale face. He hadn't been able to save Andrea, but he was going to do everything in his power to make sure Laney survived.

Chapter Three

❧

"What I am about to tell you is sensitive," Agent DeMarco said. "I need your word that you'll keep it confidential."

"Of course," Laney agreed.

"Good, because you're the only witness to a kidnapping that is connected to the abduction of two other children over the past six weeks."

"That's not a secret, Agent. It's been in the news for a few weeks." In fact, those abductions—one outside of DC and the other in Annapolis—had been nagging at her when she saw the van on Ashley Street.

"There have also been similar clusters of child abductions in two other states."

She definitely *hadn't* heard that before. "How many children are we talking about?"

"Thirteen others, so far. Not including the three from this area."

"Sixteen kids missing? I'd think that would be all over the news."

"It has been. Regional news only. The first seven disappeared from the Los Angeles area over a four-month period. The next six disappeared from the Boston vicinity in just under three months. In many cases, there were reports of a dark van in the area around the time of the abductions."

"Just like the van tonight."

He nodded. "Your description is the most detailed, but other witnesses mentioned a dark panel van. Unfortunately, no one has seen the driver. You're the first witness we have who's seen everything—the van, the missing child, the kidnappers. It's the break I've been waiting for, and I don't want anything to jeopardize it. We need to keep the fact that you survived quiet for as long as possible. The less the kidnappers realize we know, the easier it will be to close in on them."

"I understand. I won't tell anyone."

"It's not as simple as that. The kidnappers are aware that you were shot. They could have followed the ambulance to the hospital. They could be waiting around, hoping to hear some information that will confirm your death or refute it."

"Why would they bother? I saw them, but I don't know who they are."

"You've worked with law enforcement for years, Laney. You understand how this works. They tried to silence you to keep you from reporting what you witnessed. If they see that they failed, they may try again."

"But is sticking around to kill me really worth the risk when they could just skip town with the kids and disappear?" That's what she thought they'd do, but she wasn't sure how clear her thinking was. Her head ached so badly, she just wanted to close her eyes.

"This trafficking ring is extensive," Agent DeMarco explained. "We've had reports that the children are being transported overseas and sold into slavery. This is a multi-tier operation that isn't just being run here in the United States. There are kids missing in Europe, in Canada, in Asia, and each time, the kidnappings occur in clusters. Five, six, seven kids from a region go missing, and then nothing."

"Except families left with broken hearts and no answers," Laney murmured, the thought of all those kids, all those parents and siblings, all those empty bedrooms and empty hearts making her heart ache and head pound even more.

"Right." Agent DeMarco leaned forward, and Laney could see the black rim around his blue irises, the dark stubble on his chin. He had a tiny scar at the corner of his left brow and a larger one close to his hairline. He looked tough and determined, and for some reason she found that reassuring.

"Olivia's abduction makes the third in this area," Agent DeMarco continued, "but if their pattern holds, they plan to target more from the surrounding area before moving the kids."

"It seems a safer bet for them to cut their losses and move on," she said doubtfully.

"We're talking money, Laney. A lot of it. Money is a great motivator. It can turn ordinary men into extraordinary criminals."

"And kidnappers into murderers?"

"That, too." He stood and paced across the room. "This is a business for them, with schedules to keep and deliveries to make. I'm certain the children are being held somewhere while they wait for prearranged transport out of the country. Moving them to another location would also risk exposure. You were shot tonight because they can't afford any witnesses. They need to buy time to get their quota of children ready for delivery. With you dead or incapacitated, the immediate threat of exposure is gone."

"So as long as they believe I died, it's business as usual."

Agent DeMarco nodded, returning to his chair, and leveling his gaze on her. "The longer it takes for the kidnappers to realize you survived, the better it will be for everyone."

"Not for Olivia," she pointed out, that image—the one of the girl, her eyes wide, begging for help—filling her mind again. She'd failed to save her, and that knowledge was worse than the pain in her head, worse than the nausea. "She's terrified and alone. She doesn't care who knows what. All she cares about is getting home."

"You're wrong. It does matter for Olivia," Agent DeMarco responded. "There's a chance that we can reunite Olivia with her family, but only if the kidnappers aren't scared into moving early. All we have to do is find Olivia's kidnappers, and we'll find her. We'll find them all."

His words made her heart jump, and she was almost ready to spring up from the chair and start looking in every place they could possibly be. "Then why are we sitting here? Why aren't we out searching for them?"

"Chief Andrews said you'd ask that," he responded, a half smile curving his lips. "He told me to assure you that he has a K-9 team working the scene."

But Laney knew they'd not find much. Olivia had been driven off in a van. Even her retired search dog, Jax, who had been one of the best air scent dogs in the country, wouldn't be able to pick up her scent under those circumstances.

She recognized that, but still, she wanted to be in on the action in a way she hadn't wanted to be since the accident that took her teammates' lives. The accident that had prompted her to leave her search-and-rescue work behind and put Jax into early retirement. The thought stole some of her energy, and she sank back against the chair. "That's good. If there's something to find, they'll uncover it."

"That's what I've been told. You've been working with them for a while?"

She had. For nearly two years now. She volunteered her time to ensure high-drive, problem dogs were given the chance to succeed. She'd helped train several dogs that had been like Murphy—problematic but with obvious promise. Although Kent made repeated offers to make her role with the department more permanent, she was reluctant to fall back into the stressful life of a contract employee. Besides, her own clients kept her busy enough. "Unofficially. I own a private boarding and training facility in Davidsonville. Murphy is the most recent in a line of MPD K-9s I've worked with."

"Murphy." His smile broadened. "He's quite a dog."

"He's quite a problem child, but we're working on it."

"He came through for you tonight," he pointed out.

"Yes. Though technically, he's supposed to leave the vehicle only on command."

"Well, in this case, it's a good thing he didn't."

"I think seeing the gun set him off. We just started working with firearms last week, and he's making good progress." Better than she had hoped. She was pleased at how quickly Murphy was improving after being booted out of the MPD K-9 program once. He was a little high-energy and distractible, but he possessed the important shepherd traits—intelligence and loyalty.

Agent DeMarco smiled. "Andrews and the K-9 handlers certainly seemed happy the dog came through for you."

She forced herself out of the chair, every muscle in her body protesting. "Speaking of which, I need to talk to Kent. I don't suppose you have my things?"

"Purse? Cell Phone? House keys?"

"Yes."

"They've been collected as evidence. Your Jeep was impounded, too. And your clothes—" his gaze dropped from her face to the cotton hospital gown "—were also taken as evidence."

"I guess I'll be flagging a taxi in this hospital gown," she responded. She wasn't going to stay in the hospital any longer than necessary. Her business was thriving. That meant plenty of work to do at the kennel. She was hoping that would keep her mind off her failures. She didn't need to spend months mourning what she hadn't been able to do for Olivia. She'd been down that path before, and it hadn't led to anything but misery.

"Leaving in a hospital gown isn't going to work. It's a surefire way to get the wrong people's attention. When you leave, we're going to do everything possible to make sure no one notices you."

"That's going to be really difficult with—"

There was a sudden commotion outside the door, a flurry of movement and voices that had Agent DeMarco pivoting toward the sound.

"Stay there," he commanded, striding toward the door and yanking it open.

His broad back blocked Laney's view, and she moved closer, trying to see over his shoulder. A police officer stood in the doorway, back to the room.

"Ma'am, I told you no one can enter without permission," he said to someone Laney couldn't see.

"Ridiculous," a woman responded, the voice as familiar as the morning sun.

Great-Aunt Rose. Someone must have called her.

"Aunt Rose, don't—" Laney began.

Too late. Rose somehow darted through the blockade of masculinity, slipping past the officer.

Agent DeMarco stepped to the side, letting her by. Obviously he wasn't worried about a five-foot-nothing octogenarian. The officer, on the other hand, looked quite disgruntled.

"Do you want me to cuff you, ma'am?" he shouted.

"Don't be silly, boy. I'm too old. You'd break my brittle wrists." Rose smoothed loose strands of silver hair back into her neat bun, then brushed invisible lint from her beige slacks. Her gaze settled on Agent De-Marco for a moment before her focus shifted to Laney.

"You're awake! Thank the good Lord for His mercy!" she cried, hefting an oversize bag onto the bed.

"Yeah," the officer sputtered. "She's awake, and I'm going to lose my job."

"Now, why would you go and do something like that?" Aunt Rose asked, completely unfazed by the commotion she'd caused. Typical Rose. Always in the midst of trouble and never quite sure why.

"My aunt is notorious for getting what she wants," Laney cut in. "I'm sure Chief Andrews will understand the position you were in."

"He might, but I don't," the officer responded irritably. "But I guess as long as she's your aunt, I'll go back to my post."

He returned to the corridor, closing the door with a little more force than necessary.

"You've annoyed him, Aunt Rose," Laney said.

"And you've annoyed me. Getting yourself shot up and tossed into the hospital and interrupting a perfectly wonderful book club meeting," Rose responded. She touched Laney's cheek and shook her head. "What in the world happened? I mean, Tommy said you'd been shot...but I figured he's so old, he probably got it wrong."

"Tom is barely sixty, Aunt Rose, and you know it." Laney sighed. Her aunt and the deputy chief of police Tom Wallace had never hit it off. She'd have to remember to thank him for calling Rose. The poor guy tried to avoid Rose as often as possible.

"But he acts like he's a hundred, 'bout as fun as a stick in the mud. Remember that picnic at the kennel last year? He—"

"Aunt Rose, please. I'm not in the mood for trips down memory lane," Laney said, her head pounding with renewed vigor.

"Are you in the mood to sit down?" Agent DeMarco asked, taking Laney's arm and urging her to the chair she'd abandoned. "You look like you probably should."

She settled into the chair, watching with horror as Rose peered up at Agent DeMarco. If Laney's brain had been functioning at full capacity, she'd have found a way to refocus her aunt's attention. As it was, all she could do was hope that Rose didn't say anything she'd regret. Or, more to the point, that *Laney* would regret.

"You must be that FBI agent Tommy told me about," Rose said with a smile.

"Yes, ma'am. Special Agent Grayson DeMarco."

"Well, I'm too old to be remembering all those names and titles—what's your mama call you?"

Agent DeMarco smiled at that. "She calls me Gray."

"Well, then, Gray it is, and you can call me Rose. None of those niceties like 'ma'am'...that just makes me feel old." Rose plopped down in the chair Agent DeMarco had vacated only moments ago.

"How'd you get here Aunt Rose? I hope you didn't drive," Laney said. The thought of Rose speeding down Route 50 was not especially comforting.

"Of course not. You know my license was temporarily revoked after that unfortunate incident at Davis's Plant Emporium. Really, I don't understand why everyone was so upset—it was only a couple of bushes and some potted plants, after all...but that's neither here nor there." Rose shook her head and patting Laney's knee. "Tommy drove me. Kent sent him to pick me up. I imagine Tommy will be along soon." She lowered her voice to a decidedly loud whisper. "I made him drop me off at the door so no one would see us walk in together— that's how rumors get started. Before you know it, the whole congregation will be saying I was arrested or some such nonsense."

"Rose," Agent DeMarco said, "did Deputy Chief Wallace explain that we need to keep the details of this situation quiet?"

"Yes, yes. He explained. No need to worry about me. My mind is a steel trap, and my lips are sealed." Rose put a hand up as if waving away the agent's concerns, then turned to Laney. "So, how on earth did you get yourself shot?"

Was Laney allowed to mention the kidnapping? She didn't know, so she kept it brief. "I witnessed a crime and tried to intervene."

"I bet you weren't carrying that mace I gave you last Christmas, were you?" Rose frowned. "That stuff's supposed to be powerful enough to stop a bear in its tracks. A criminal would probably have a hard time aiming at you with that in his eyes. I've got my can of it right in that bag. Anyone tries to come at us, I'll take him down."

* * *

Grayson would almost have liked to see that.

Laney's aunt looked about as old as Methuselah, but she moved like a woman much younger. He could picture her reaching into the bag, yanking out the spray and taking down a kidnapper.

A quick rap at the door and a young female doctor walked in, followed closely by Deputy Chief Tom Wallace. Grayson had met him at the crime scene, and he'd liked the guy immediately. Though old-school and by-the-book, he didn't have any compunction about sharing information with the FBI.

"Agent DeMarco," Wallace said, "the chief said to let you know they've finished with the crime scene. He's going to the precinct to make sure the blood and finger prints on the gun are expedited for processing."

"Thanks, Deputy." So far he liked the way Chief Andrews handled things, and he wasn't surprised that Andrews was taking a very personal interest in the case. "I may head that way myself after Laney is discharged."

"*If* she's discharged," Wallace replied. "The *doctor* will decide that and *then* we can come up with a plan for getting her out of here."

They weren't going to do anything. Grayson had a plan, and he was sticking to it. He didn't bother telling Wallace that. The doctor was already leaning over Laney, flashing a light in her eyes, asking about pain level, nausea, dizziness. Laney answered quietly.

"We did an MRI when you were brought in. I'm happy to report that there's no fracture and no hemorrhage in the brain," the doctor said, tucking a loose strand of black curly hair behind her ear and pushing her glasses up on her nose. "You do have a concussion, and the effects of that can last for a while. Expect the headache to linger for the next few days. I can give you some prescription-strength Tylenol to take the edge off the headache, or something stronger if you think you'll need it."

"Prescription-strength Tylenol's fine."

The doctor marked something in her chart. "You were really fortunate, you know. If that bullet had traveled a different trajectory—just a half an inch in any direction—the outcome would have been very different." She tucked her pen in her lab-coat pocket and her clipboard under her arm. "There's really no need to keep you here overnight, assuming there's someone at home to monitor you."

"I'll be with her," Rose piped up.

The doctor looked over at Rose, then back at Laney, an almost indiscernible look of concern crossing her face. "Do you two live alone?"

"Oh, we don't live together," Rose responded. "I like my space. But I'm happy to stay with her for a few days."

"I see." The doctor frowned. "Maybe it *would* be best if you stayed here overnight, Laney." Her gaze jumped to Grayson. "Unless you two—"

"No!" Laney said quickly, cheeks reddening. "He's a—"

"Law enforcement." Grayson cut in.

"I see," the doctor responded. "It's no problem to let you stay here tonight, Laney. We can monitor your condition—"

"I'll be fine, doctor. I'm sure I'll sleep better in my own bed," Laney insisted.

"Well, if you're certain, the nurse will be in momentarily to remove the IV. She'll give you written wound-care instructions and your medication, then wheel you out."

"I think I can make it out without a wheelchair—" Laney began, but the doctor was already walking out of the room, with Deputy Chief Wallace close behind. Grayson figured they would discuss Laney. Though he was curious to know what they were saying, he was more interested in making sure Laney stayed safe, so he didn't follow. He just waited as Rose hovered over Laney, chatting incessantly, while a nurse arrived and removed the IV. Grayson spent the time counting the seconds in his head until he could get Laney safely home.

The nurse handed Laney discharge instructions and a bottle of pills and went to look for a wheelchair.

A few seconds later, Wallace returned. "Looks like you're clear to go, Laney. Once the nurse gets back, I'll roll you out and—"

"How about you take Rose, and I'll take Laney?" Grayson suggested.

"Now, wait just a minute," Rose protested. "I'm staying right here with my niece until she leaves this building."

"Rose," Laney interrupted. "Don't argue. Just do what you're asked so we can get things moving. I want to get out of here quickly, and I don't really care how it happens."

Rose's face softened. "Of course, love. But don't you worry. I'll have Tommy bring me to your house. I'll be there when you get home." Rose began to turn away but stopped. "Oh, I almost forgot, I brought you some clothes and your spare house keys. They're in the bag on the bed. Do you need help dressing?"

"I'll manage."

"Then I guess I'll see you at home. Come on, Tommy." She grabbed Wallace's arm and dragged him to the door.

"That's your cue to leave, too," Laney told Grayson quietly. She'd regained some of her color, but she still looked too fragile for Grayson's liking. He wasn't completely happy that she was being released tonight. He would have preferred she stay in the hospital under guard until they found the kidnappers, but since that wasn't going to happen, escorting her home was the next best option.

"I thought we agreed that we're going together."

"We may be leaving together, but I'm not putting on my street clothes while you're standing in the room." She reached into the bag Rose had brought and pulled out what looked like a huge pink sweater. "Great," she muttered.

"Don't like the color choice?"

She turned the sweater so he could see the front. A giant white poodle with fuzzy yarn fur stared out at him.

"Nice," he said, swallowing a laugh.

"If she brought me the matching leggings…" She pulled out bright pink leggings covered in white dog bones. "She did."

"A Christmas gift?"

"Birthday. Two years ago. Needless to say, I've never worn them. Typical Rose, bringing them for me when she knows I have no other option but to put them on."

Grayson smirked. He wasn't into fashion, but even he could see why a person would not want to be caught dead in that getup.

Then the smirk died on his lips, the thought sobering

him instantly. The truth was that if he wasn't vigilant, that is exactly what could happen to Laney Kensington.

"You have options," he said. "It's that or the hospital gown. Pick your poison."

"Right." She pulled the outfit to her chest. "I'll change in the bathroom."

It took her longer than it should have. She might have told the doctor she was feeling okay, but Grayson wasn't buying it. Her eyes had been glassy, her complexion still a little too waxy. If she passed out in the bathroom, he wouldn't know it.

"Laney?" Grayson rapped on the door. "You okay?"

"Fine." She opened the door, her body covered from neck to ankle in pink and white.

He shouldn't have smiled. He knew it, but he couldn't stop himself.

"Wow," he murmured as she met his gaze.

"And not in a good way, right?"

"You almost make it work."

She offered a wan smile and sighed. "I'm not worried about making it work. I'm worried about everyone in the hospital catching a glimpse of me in it. If we're trying to slip out of here undetected, this outfit isn't going to help."

"I can fix that," Grayson said, shrugging out of his jacket and setting it on her shoulders. She slipped her arms into the sleeves, and he tugged the hood up over her hair, his fingers grazing silky skin.

That he noticed surprised him. Since Andrea's death, he'd devoted himself to his job. There wasn't room in his life for anything else.

He stepped back. The jacket hung past Laney's thighs, the sleeves covering her hands.

"It's a little big," he said.

She scowled, pulling at the pink leggings. "Not big enough, I'm afraid."

He laughed. "Well, at least the poodle is covered."

"There is that." She grabbed Aunt Rose's bag from the bed. "Do you think if I press the button, the nurse will come any faster? I'm ready to get out of here."

"You can give it a try," he responded. He was anxious to leave, too. He had an uneasy feeling that said things weren't going to go down as smoothly as he wanted them to.

Laney jabbed the call button. "Really, I think a wheelchair is silly. I'm perfectly capable of—"

The lights went out, the room plunging into darkness. No light seeping in under the door. No light filtering in from behind the curtain. When he'd driven in, Grayson had noticed construction signs for a new wing—perhaps the power outage was related to that. Unfortunately, he couldn't afford to assume anything.

"What's going on?" Laney whispered.

"I don't know," he responded, grabbing her hand and pulling her close to his side. "But, I can tell you this. We're not waiting for the wheelchair."

Chapter Four

Laney's nerves were on edge, her vision adjusting to the darkness as Agent DeMarco guided her toward the door. It flew open as they reached it, and Detective Jensen barged in. The door slammed shut behind him. "What do you make of this, DeMarco?" His voice was low and tense. His hand rested on his holstered revolver.

"Could be a power outage from the construction that's going on or—" the agent glanced at Laney "—something less innocuous. It's hard to say, but I don't like it. We need to get Laney out of here."

"You have a plan for doing that without attracting too much attention?"

"Laney and I will leave now, through the hospital service entrance on the ground floor. I'll take care of getting her home. You call Chief Andrews and fill him in. We're going to need a couple of guys down here to investigate—we need to know for sure what caused this outage."

"Do you really think this power failure could be connected to the kidnapping?" Laney interjected. "It seems like that would be a lot of trouble to go through."

"How much trouble is too much trouble if it's going

to keep a multimillion-dollar operation running?" Agent DeMarco asked.

It was a good question. One that Laney couldn't answer. Agent DeMarco struck her as levelheaded and calculated, completely focused on the investigation. If he thought the hospital's power failure could be staged by the kidnappers, she wouldn't write off the idea.

"Are you sure you don't need me for backup?" Detective Jensen asked, brows furrowed in concern.

"I'd rather you stand your post. Act like you're still guarding the room. Make note of everyone that comes by—hospital employee, electrician, patient—everyone," Agent DeMarco replied.

"Will do." Detective Jensen pulled the door open, stepping out of the way, and Agent DeMarco pressed a warm hand to the small of Laney's back.

"Stay close," he said as he led her into the hall.

She didn't need the reminder. She planned on staying glued to his side until they exited the building. The emergency generator must have turned on. The hallway wasn't quite as dark as the room had been. A row of red lights illuminated the area, providing just enough light to see down the corridor to the dimly glowing exit sign.

A nurse made her way down the corridor, peeking into rooms as she went, calling reassurances to patients, inquiring about the occupants' welfare. Other than that, the hallway was empty, the stillness of the hospital unsettling. Agent DeMarco took Laney's elbow, urging her toward the stairwell.

"We're going to have to take the stairs," he said, wrapping his arm around her waist, pulling her closer to his side, the protective gesture somehow reassuring. "We're on the eighth floor, do you think you'll be able to make it?"

"Yes, I'll be fine." She didn't have a choice.

"If you need to take a break, let me know. If you get dizzy or—"

"How about we just go?" she cut him off, because the longer they stood around talking, the more her head ached and the less energy her legs seemed to have. They were on the eighth floor, which meant navigating seven flights of stairs down to the ground floor. She was fit and healthy. She had to be to train dogs the way she did. On most days, she could sprint up ten flights of stairs and barely break a sweat. This wasn't most days.

"Just remember," he responded, opening the stairwell door and ushering her onto the landing, "you pass out and I'll be carrying you out of here like a sack of potatoes, not worrying about maintaining your dignity."

"If I pass out, dignity won't be first on my priority list."

But neither of them would have to worry about it, because there was no way she was passing out in the stairwell like some damsel in distress. That wasn't her style. It was bad enough she was forced to make a covert escape from the hospital in tight, itchy leggings and a fuzzy poodle sweater. She wasn't going to do it lying over Agent DeMarco's shoulder.

Not if she could help it.

By the time they reached the fifth-floor landing, she wasn't sure she could.

Her head throbbed with almost every jarring step. She was dizzy and nauseated. The only thing that kept her on her feet was the horrifying vision of herself slung over Agent DeMarco's shoulder, her puffy sweater–clad torso slapping into his back as he jogged down the stairs.

Just five more flights of stairs. Four more. She

counted them off in her head, forcing herself to take one step after another. She'd do everything she needed to do to buy the FBI and the MPD some time if that meant there was a chance of finding Olivia and the other children.

Her feet seemed leaden, every step more difficult than the one before, but she kept going, because she didn't want the image of Olivia's fear-filled eyes to be the last one she had of the girl. She wanted to see photos of her being reunited with her family, wanted to see her smiling and happy and playing the violin she'd been carrying when she was abducted. She wanted this time to be different. She needed a happy ending for Olivia. An ending she'd not been able to offer her teammates' families…

She stumbled, her legs nearly giving out.

Agent DeMarco's grip tightened on her waist. "Do you need to sit for a minute?" His voice rumbled close to her ear, his breath ruffling the fine hairs near her temple.

"No. I'm fine," she lied, and kept walking.

Laney was lying, and Grayson knew it.

He wouldn't insist she sit down, though. He wanted her out of the hospital, and this stairwell, as quickly as possible. If that meant carrying her out, so be it.

Voices drifted into the stairwell as they neared the third-floor landing. Grayson tensed, wary of who might be approaching. He didn't believe in coincidences, and a power outage at the hospital while the key witness to a kidnapping was in it would be a big one. It was possible the construction crew had knocked out the power, but he wasn't counting on it. If the kidnappers were responsible for the power outage, they might be on a fact-finding mission, hoping to discover who Laney was and whether or not she was actually deceased.

If they already knew she was alive, Grayson had a new problem. Namely that someone who knew Laney had survived had leaked the information to the kidnappers. Though he hoped it wasn't the case, a leak could explain why the kidnappers always seemed one step ahead.

Laney stumbled again. He pulled her closer, steadying her.

"We're almost there," he murmured, leading her down the stairs as quietly as possible. By the time they reached the second floor, she was visibly weak, her hand clutching the railing as she took the final step onto the landing.

Even in the dim red light, he could see the paleness of her skin, the hollows beneath her cheeks. Her eyes were glassy, her skin dewy from perspiration. She might have the will to make it out of the stairwell, but he wasn't sure she had the strength.

He pulled the hood from her head and pressed a palm to her forehead. Her skin was cool and clammy, her breathing shallow and quick. "Maybe you'd better sit for a minute."

She backed away from his touch, squaring her shoulders and yanking the hood back up over her hair. "I appreciate your concern, but if we stop every time I feel light-headed or dizzy, we might not make it out until morning."

Her matter-of-fact tone left no room to argue, so he stayed silent. Now was not the time for a struggle of wills.

"Three more flights to go," he pointed out, and he thought he heard her sigh quietly in response.

It was taking forever to reach ground level, but then, Grayson wasn't the kind of guy who liked to do things slowly. He liked to have a plan in place and execute it with efficiency and as much speed as was prudent.

In this case, that meant going at a snail's pace.

It would have been quicker and easier to carry Laney the rest of the way down, but she wouldn't have appreciated it, and he needed her cooperation.

Somewhere above them, a door opened and shut with a bang.

How many floors above? he wondered. Four? Three?

Grayson stilled, listening. A quick shuffling of feet, then nothing.

Ten seconds passed.

Twenty.

The stairwell remained eerily silent. He didn't like it. Someone was up there, still and listening, and he had a hunch it wasn't a hospital employee. If he was right, his witness's identity had been compromised. Peering over the railing, he scanned the stairwell below, its dark corners untouched by the dim emergency lights. There were now only two flights between them and escape. Multiple doors that the enemy could enter. He and Laney were vulnerable here, sandwiched between whoever had entered above and anyone who might be waiting below.

If there had been any other way out of the hospital, he would have selected it over the stairwell. Experience had taught him stairwells were prime locations for an ambush. A gunman above, a gunman below, and a person could be taken out in an instant.

Caught between floors, they had no choice but to continue down. He doubted Laney would make it up even one flight of stairs. Meeting her eyes, he held a finger to his lips, then guided her quickly down.

On the ground floor below, another door opened. He could hear heavy footsteps coming their way.

Not good.

Grayson had no intention of being caught in the middle of an ambush. Better to go on the offensive—meet trouble one-on-one. Grayson urged Laney down to the first floor landing, gently pushing her into the shadows. Drawing his gun, he peered over the rail.

A shadowy figure ascended the steps quickly, the barrel of a gun glinting in the dim emergency lights. From above, footsteps echoed loudly as the second person rushed down the stairs.

Grayson needed to act now. And it wouldn't be by the book.

If he announced himself, he'd lose the element of surprise. If he took a bullet, Laney would be easy pickings.

There's no way that was happening.

He had to time it perfectly. The gunman slowed as he neared the landing, cautiously stepping around the corner, gun first. In one quick motion, Grayson cracked the butt of his service weapon on the guy's wrist, eliciting a startled howl of pain and sending the gun clattering down the stairs.

The guy turned back—whether to flee or retrieve his gun, Grayson couldn't be sure. Reaching out, Grayson grasped a handful of the guy's sweatshirt and brought his gun forcefully down on the man's temple. The blow sent the man crumpling to the ground in a motionless heap.

Grabbing Laney's arm, Grayson pulled her forward, ushering her around the fallen assailant. The unmistakable pop of a silenced pistol echoed in the stairwell, a bullet slamming into the concrete wall a foot from Grayson's head. He shoved Laney forward, placing himself between her and the gunman as they raced down the last few steps to ground level.

He shoved the door open, scanning the hallway and the open door of the room beyond. Backup lights illuminated the hospital's laundry room, the huge cavernous area the perfect cover for anyone who might be lying in wait. Footsteps pounded on the stairs above, the second gunman moving in quickly.

Grayson dragged Laney into the hallway, shielding her from any threat that might be waiting.

"This way." He motioned toward a glowing neon exit sign pointing them to their escape route. They ran toward the far wall, turning the corner as the stairwell door slammed open once more.

Grabbing Laney's hand, he sprinted toward the exit. He knew she was struggling to match his pace, but slowing down wasn't an option.

Right now he couldn't worry about anything but getting her to safety—as safe as any place could be for the only witness against a very large, very lucrative crime ring.

They barreled through the exit door into the employee parking lot.

"Come on," he encouraged her. "I parked my car out here."

Agent DeMarco didn't let go of Laney's hand as they ran through a near-empty parking lot. Silver streaks of moonlight managed to break through the intermittent cloud cover, providing some visibility beyond the shadows of the building. Too much visibility if their pursuer ran out of the building behind them. Laney shuddered at the thought.

She didn't want to be within sight of that door if it opened and the gunman appeared.

Her body was wearing down, though. No matter how much she wanted to keep sprinting along beside Agent DeMarco, she wasn't sure how much farther she could go. Her legs shook, every pounding step across the pavement making her head throb.

She stumbled, and his grip on her hand tightened.

"You can do this," he urged her.

Maybe she could.

If wherever they were heading was closer than a few steps.

They rounded the corner of the building, putting brick and mortar between themselves and the door. She wanted to feel safer because of it, but fear pulsed through her veins, churned in her stomach. They had no idea how many men were after them—or where their attackers might be lying in wait.

A sudden clatter from around the building, like a can kicked across pavement, had Agent DeMarco snagging the arm of the jacket she wore, yanking her behind a large metal Dumpster.

"Stay hidden. I'll be right back," he ordered before easing around the Dumpster and moving soundlessly into the night. She stood still, keeping as quiet as possible. Listening. She could hear nothing but the deafening rush of her own blood in her ears. Without Agent DeMarco, she felt exposed and vulnerable. Releasing the breath she hadn't realized she was holding, she tried to shake off that feeling.

She'd worked under stressful, even dangerous, circumstances in the past, and she'd never had to rely on anyone to get her through them. She couldn't allow herself to rely on Agent DeMarco, either. Playing the part of the victim just wasn't her style. After all, if something happened to him, she would have to take care of herself.

And she would. She'd been doing it her whole life.

She'd realized at age eight that her mom was powerless to protect either of them from her father's violent outbursts. Laney had been forced to take on that role. She'd learned to protect them both. This was no different. She needed to be ready. She needed to assess the situation herself. Plan her escape route should anything go wrong.

She eased out from behind the Dumpster, peering into the darkness. Nothing. The night seemed too still, the parking lot too dark. Dozens of cars were there, the streetlights off, the moon temporarily hidden by clouds.

A shadow moved at the edge of the lot, a deeper darkness in the gloom.

She jerked back, heart pounding wildly.

"Good choice," someone whispered, and she jumped, spinning toward the voice.

Big mistake. Blood rushed from her head, and she swayed.

Firm hands cupped her waist, held her steady as she caught her balance.

She looked into Agent DeMarco's face. "Where did you come from?" she whispered.

"I was circling around to get a location on him. I also told you to stay out of sight."

"I did."

"You didn't." His hands dropped away. "I had you in a position of cover. You walked out where anyone could see you."

"It's dark."

"Ever heard of night-vision goggles?" he asked. "Because someone who has money enough to run a kidnapping ring the size of the one we're dealing with has money for all kinds of things the average Joe might not have at his disposal."

She hadn't thought about that, but she wasn't going to admit it.

"Did you see him?" she asked.

"He's headed in the other direction—toward the visitor's parking lot, but it won't take him long to figure out we're not there and double back." He grabbed her arm, leading her toward the parking lot. "Come on. Let's not lose our head start."

Chapter Five

The investigation had been compromised, and Grayson needed to find out who was responsible. But first, he needed to get Laney as far away from the gunman as possible.

He'd already called the local PD. Officers would be on the scene soon. They could deal with the gunmen. Grayson would deal with protecting Laney.

"You live in Davidsonville, right?" Grayson asked, laying his cell phone in the center console.

"Yes." Laney glanced over at him. "The quickest way is Route 50 to the 424 exit—that road is a straight shot to my community."

"I don't think we'll go the quickest route," he said as he stopped at the darkened signal lights on Hospital Drive. He'd seen the gunman moving through the parking lot, could have taken a shot at him, but he had no idea how many others there might be, and he couldn't afford to take any chances.

"Why not? The sooner we get home, the happier I'll be," Laney responded, leaning forward in her seat, scanning the darkness as if watching could keep trouble from coming.

"I don't want to risk anyone following us." He turned left on the main road, heading away from her house.

She looked over her shoulder, eyeing the empty road. "I hadn't thought about that."

"Then, it's good we're together," he responded. "Because anyone who'd take a couple of shots at someone while she's with an FBI agent isn't going to hesitate to follow us."

"He might not have known who you were."

"Maybe not." But Grayson thought the perp did. Whoever the kidnappers were, they seemed well connected. Somehow, some way, they'd found out that Laney was alive.

"But you think he did?" she asked.

"I don't know, but I'm not willing to take chances with your life."

"What about Olivia's? If the kidnappers know I'm alive, they may move her now. If they're desperate enough, they may do worse."

He'd had the same thought. He didn't like it any more than Laney seemed to. "She's a high-priced commodity. I doubt they'll do anything that will compromise their bottom line."

"You doubt it, but you don't know," Laney said with a sigh. "I should have—"

"You should have stayed behind the Dumpster when I left you there." He cut her off, because he understood the regrets she had, the guilt. They wouldn't do Olivia any good. They wouldn't do Laney any good, either.

"We've covered this ground before," she responded wearily.

"And now we'll cover it again. I need you to understand what we're dealing with. You have to listen to the precautions I suggest and take them seriously."

"I understand…"

"I don't think you do. You're my only witness, Laney. The key to closing a case I've been pursuing for over a year."

"Wow," she said drily. "I feel so…special."

That surprised a laugh out of him. After speaking with Andrews, he'd known Laney was a force to be reckoned with. He hadn't expected her to make him smile, though. "You should. I gave you my coat. I'm taking you for a moonlit drive."

"You're saving my life," she added quietly.

"You saved your own life. Or maybe Murphy did. You'll have to thank him." He glanced in the rearview mirror. Nothing. No sign that they were being followed. He wasn't sure that meant anything. If the perps knew their witness was alive, they might also know her identity. He drove into a cul-de-sac, waited a few seconds, drove out again. Still no sign of a tail.

His phone vibrated, and he answered it quickly. "De-Marco here."

"It's Kent Andrews. I'm at the hospital."

"What'd you find?"

"No sign of either of the perps. The fire marshal is here assessing the damage from the electrical fire that caused the power outage. He's calling in the arson investigator. Looks like the wiring in the circuit panel was tampered with. Someone went through a lot of trouble to make it look like faulty wiring, but the fire chief isn't buying it. How's Laney doing?"

Grayson glanced at Laney.

She smiled, and something in his heart stirred to life, some gut-level, knee-jerk reaction that surprised him as much as his laughter had. "I'll let her answer," he responded.

* * *

That was Laney's cue to speak, and it should have been easy enough to answer Kent's question. The problem was, she wasn't sure how she was doing.

"Laney?" Kent prodded.

"I'm fine," she managed, and Kent let out a bark of laughter.

"You were shot in the head. You're not fine."

"In a couple of days, I think I'll be good as new."

"That's a relief," he said, "You had us all worried. Murphy was beside himself, by the way. Wouldn't let anyone near you, even the patrolman who responded to the scene. Luckily he was wearing his MPD collar, so a K-9 handler was called in. He backed down on command." Laney could hear the smile in Kent's voice. "He did real good tonight."

"Yes, he did." She smiled at the thought of the overly excitable dog, of the hours she'd spent working with him, determined to make him into the K-9 team member she thought he could be. She hadn't been sure it would work. Not every dog was capable of the focus required, and Murphy had already flunked out of the K-9 training program once. Now there was hope. All the hard work on both their parts was finally paying off. "Where is he now?"

"He's at headquarters being pampered. The guys bought him a huge steak and brought a dog bed into the office for him. He thinks he's a king or something. Never seen that dog look quite so proud of himself."

Laney laughed. "Good for him." Before tonight, you couldn't have paid a K-9 handler to work with Murphy. A couple more weeks and he'd be ready to enter the program again.

"We'll take good care of him until you're ready to have him back. Don't you worry."

"You can bring him by tomorrow. I don't want any breaks in his training routine. He's almost there."

"Are you sure? Wallace reported back the doctor's orders for you to take it easy for a few days." The concern in Kent's voice was obvious. The guy was gruff and abrupt most of the time, but he had a heart of gold.

"I won't overdo it. Riley and Bria both work tomorrow, so I'll have plenty of help at the kennel."

"You're not going there tomorrow," Agent DeMarco said so abruptly, she nearly jumped out of her seat belt.

"Going where?"

"To the kennel."

"Of course I am. It's my job."

"You think your job is worth dying over?" DeMarco responded, and Laney frowned, all her fatigue washed away by a wave of irritation mixed with anxiety.

"Of course not, but I have to live my life."

"Have your crew do the work at the kennel tomorrow," Kent cut in. "That will be the safer. As a matter of fact, maybe you should be in a safe house until we find the guys who are after you. What do you think, DeMarco?"

A safe house?

Laney hadn't even given that scenario a thought. She'd agreed she wouldn't take unnecessary chances, but she wasn't sure she was willing to put her life on hold. After all, if the kidnappers knew who she was, they could have just waited for her to arrive home rather than cause an elaborate power outage at the hospital.

"I think we can wait on that," Agent DeMarco responded. "If the kidnappers knew her identity, they would have waited at her place, taken her out there."

Hearing her own thoughts spoken aloud, imagining men skulking in the shadows of her house, made her blood go cold.

"Are you sure waiting is the best decision, De-Marco?" Kent asked.

"No. But I *am* sure there's a leak, and since I don't know if it's in my house or yours, I can't be certain Laney will be any more protected in a safe house than she would be at her own house, under guard."

"Okay. I'll send an officer over. He'll be there when you arrive.

"Thanks, Andrews."

"Laney's one of us. We'll do whatever's needed to keep her safe."

"Understood. When do you think you'll be wrapping things up over there?"

"About an hour. We're waiting for copies of the surveillance video and questioning the security guard."

"Did he see anyone in the area?"

"He says he didn't." Laney could hear the hesitation in Kent's voice.

"But you're not buying it?" Grayson asked.

"It's just a gut feeling, but no." Kent said. "We're going to make an excuse to get him down to the precinct for more thorough questioning."

"I think I'll get someone to run a background check on the guy. Can you email me his information?" Grayson asked.

"Sure, but the hospital does a thorough background check before they hire someone. I think you'll find that his record's clean."

"I'm more interested in the state of his bank account."

"You think he was hired to set that fire—or look the

other way?" Kent asked, his Boston accent thicker than usual. He'd transplanted from New England years ago, but Laney had noticed that the faster he talked and the more enthused he was about the subject, the thicker the accent became.

"I just want to be thorough," Agent DeMarco replied.

"And yet, you didn't ask me about his work record."

"I take it you checked?"

"Absolutely," the chief said, sounding almost gleeful. "His logs check out, but he's been reprimanded previously for sleeping on the job. Ideally the surveillance videos will give us a good look at what really transpired while he was on duty tonight."

"I like the way you think, Andrews," DeMarco said as he veered onto Route 50. "Do you mind if I drop by the precinct while you're questioning the guard?"

"That's not a problem."

"Then I'll head over after I get Laney settled."

"See you then." Kent disconnected, and Laney laid her head back against the seat, tempted to close her eyes just for a minute. She was that tired. So tired she didn't care that she might start snoring loudly while a good-looking FBI agent sat beside her.

"You still with me?" Agent DeMarco asked.

"Where else would I be?"

"Dreaming?"

"Good idea. I think I'll give it a try," she responded, and then she did exactly what she'd been wanting to do, closed her eyes, the pain still pulsing through her head as DeMarco sped along the highway.

Grayson found Wynwood easily, driving into Laney's well-established, affluent neighborhood and glancing in his rearview mirror as he turned onto her street.

Nothing. The road was empty. Just the way he wanted it.

Laney groaned softly, asleep, but obviously not pain-free.

He didn't wake her. Just followed his GPS coordinates down the quiet street. Grand brick homes sat far back from the street, their large lots sporting well-manicured lawns and decorative plants. Nothing wild or unkempt about this place. People who lived here were affluent and not afraid to show it.

It was a nice community. Pretty. Well-planned.

Laney shifted in her seat, and he glanced her way. She'd pulled his jacket close, her hands barely peeking out of rolled cuffs. It reminded him of a spring evening long ago, the scent of rain in the air, the refreshing coolness. Reminded him of Andrea, her senior year of college, his jacket around her shoulders as they lay on a blanket watching the sunset. He'd proposed to her that day, and she'd had the tiny diamond ring, the best he could afford, on her finger.

"Our access road is on the right, just after that set of mailboxes," Laney said, her voice rough with sleep. It jarred him from memories that he tried hard not to dwell on.

The past was what it was. He couldn't change it.

He could only move forward, do everything in his power to be the man God wanted him to be, do the work that had been set before him.

"Where?" He could see nothing but thick foliage that butted up against the narrowing road. This end of the neighborhood had fewer houses and was less polished, but there was beauty in the overgrown fields that stretched out on either side of the road.

"See those tall bushes?" She gestured to the left.

"And the mailboxes? Just slow to a crawl. You'll see the access road when you're almost on top of it."

He did as she suggested, barely coasting past the mailboxes until he spotted the road, a long gravel driveway lined with mature trees.

He drove nearly a quarter of a mile down the gravel road before the first house appeared. A quaint one-story cottage with white shutters and a wraparound porch, it was nothing like the other houses in the neighborhood. The moon had edged out from behind the clouds, its reflected light shimmering across a small pond set off to the left. Tall trees cast dark shadows across the gardens and neatly cut yard surrounding the building—perfect hiding places for an assailant. Despite his confidence that they'd not been followed from the hospital, Grayson wasn't comfortable with this setup at all.

"Perfect," he muttered under his breath, imagining all the ways someone could approach the house unnoticed.

"It really is," Laney agreed. Apparently she hadn't heard the sarcasm in his voice. "My great-grandfather built it. At one time, he owned all the land in the neighborhood. When my grandfather sold a portion of the land, he kept the cottage and the main house. Aunt Rose lives in the cottage. I'm at the main house."

"Which is where?" he asked. The location of the cottage wasn't ideal. Maybe the main house was in a less secluded spot.

"Just keep following the driveway. It veers past the cottage. The house is another quarter mile in."

The headlights of the sedan flashed across thick woods and heavy foliage as Grayson drove past the cottage.

The "main house," as Laney had called it, looked

to be a slightly larger version of Rose's cottage. Same wooden shingles, same white shutters and a very similar porch. Its single-story layout meant that all rooms of the house could be easily accessed by an intruder. Worse, it sat in the middle of a clearing that looked to be approximately twenty acres in diameter and was surrounded by woods on three sides, making it a surveillance nightmare.

Grayson pulled up to Laney's darkened home and turned off the engine. "What's in the back of the house?"

"The kennels, agility course and covered training pavilion." Laney tried unsuccessfully to suppress a yawn. "Would you like a cup of coffee before you head out?" she asked.

"I'll pass on the coffee, but let me take a quick look around the property while I wait for the officer to arrive."

"Sure. I'll turn on the outside lights for you."

"Hold on," he said, but she was already opening the door and stepping out of the car.

By the time Grayson had grabbed his flashlight from the glove box and exited his vehicle, Laney was halfway up the stone walkway to her house. For someone who'd nearly died, she moved fast, making her way up the porch stairs. He wasn't sure how long it would take her to realize she didn't have the bag her aunt had packed for her. Rose had said the keys were in it, so he grabbed it, heading up the porch steps after her.

She was patting the pocket of his jacket as he reached her side. The hood had fallen off her head, and her auburn hair looked glossy black in the darkness, her face a pale oval. "I hope I didn't leave my keys at the hospital," she said, plucking at the fuzzy sweater as if the keys might be hiding in there.

"Didn't Rose mention she'd put your spare set in the bag?" He held it out, and she took it, offering a smile that made her look young and a little vulnerable.

"Oh, that's right. Thanks." She dug the keys out, said good-night and walked inside. Seconds later, the porch light went on, casting a soft white glow across most of the yard. He saw the front curtains part slightly and wondered if it was Rose or Laney who peeked out.

He waved to whoever it was, then turned toward the yard. A large sign sat to the left of the driveway. He flashed his light across it, reading Wagging Tails Boarding and Training Facility. Flower beds around the sign and in front of the house were similar to those surrounding Rose's cottage. A cool breeze carried the faint scent of pine and honeysuckle. Above the sound of the rustling wind, Grayson detected the crunching of leaves and underbrush in the woods to the left of the house. He turned the corner of the house just in time to see the last of a small herd of deer returning to the safety of the woods.

He trained his flashlight back toward the house, inspecting the grass and mulch beds for signs of disturbance.

Nothing.

The window screens were all in place. Floodlights shimmered over the expanse of yard between the house and the kennels. He was impressed by the setup. There was a very large agility course with tunnels, beams, ladders, hoops, cones and platforms at various heights connected by tight netting. The kennel looked as if it could accommodate twenty dogs, with each dog having its own inside space and an exterior fenced-in run. The dogs were in for the night. One or two barked as he walked around the structure, checking doors. Everything was locked.

Next to the kennel, the covered pavilion was also fenced in. He walked around the training facilities, shining his flashlight into the darker corners of the yard and toward the woods. All was quiet. Peaceful. Almost idyllic.

Satisfied that there was no one lurking in the shadows, Grayson turned back toward the house. Laney was safe, at least for the moment. Yet he felt uneasy at the thought of leaving her alone, even for a quick trip to the precinct. He tried to shrug it off. She wasn't in protective custody. At this point, there were limits to what he could do to keep her safe. But Grayson was used to pushing the boundaries, and he knew that if he wanted to solve this case, bring the kids home, and keep Laney safe, he was going to have to think outside the box to do it.

He wasn't sure what that would mean, what it would look like, but he knew one thing for sure—he would do anything necessary to protect his only witness.

Chapter Six

Agent DeMarco was still outside. Laney could see his light bouncing along the tree line near the kennels.

Jax, her six-year-old Australian shepherd, and Brody, her ten-year-old Belgian Malinois, were too happy to see her to notice the stranger out in the yard. Both followed her through the kitchen, tails wagging as they waited patiently for her to acknowledge them. She took off Agent DeMarco's jacket, tossed it over the back of a wooden chair and called the dogs over. They sat in front of her, tails thumping as she scratched behind their ears, murmured a few words of praise. Both barked as a car pulled into the drive. Must be the officer Kent had sent over. That would mean that Agent DeMarco would be heading out soon.

Good. There was something about him that made her…uncomfortable.

Maybe it was the way he studied her, as if she were the secret to some great mystery he had to solve.

She almost laughed at the thought, because that's probably exactly what she was to him.

The only witness to Olivia's kidnapping, the one person who could identify the kidnappers and potentially help put them behind bars.

She tugged at the itchy sweater as she headed toward her bedroom. She needed to take off this getup. Now. Not only because it looked ridiculous but also because it was probably the most uncomfortable outfit she'd ever owned. There was definitely wool in the sweater. Perhaps if she threw it in the washer and then put it through the dryer on high, it would shrink so badly it that wouldn't be fit for anything but the Goodwill bag. She smiled at the thought, but who was she kidding? Even the homeless wouldn't grab this outfit off the rack. The dogs followed her down the hall toward her bedroom.

The door to the guest room at the end of the hall opened, and Aunt Rose popped her head out. "Oh, you're home, dear. Don't you look nice."

Laney ignored the compliment. Aunt Rose meant well, but she had questionable taste at times. "It's after eleven, Aunt Rose. You didn't have to wait up for me."

"I was just catching up on my devotional," Rose said. "Let me grab my slippers and robe and I'll be right out."

"There's really no need…" But Rose shut the guest room door before Laney could get her sentence out. She sighed, hurrying into her room before Rose could reappear. She immediately peeled off the offending tights and sweater, letting them drop to a heap on the floor, then changed into some comfortable yoga pants and her old University of Colorado sweatshirt. A glance in the mirror showed she still had a few faint streaks of blood on one side of her face, and the bruise on her jaw was starting to turn from red to blue. She carefully peeled back the bandage. A thin line of five staples started at her temple, disappearing into the hairline. Only about a half inch of the scar would be visible when healed. The rest would be concealed by her hair.

A shadow passed outside her bedroom room window, and Brody growled deep in his throat. Laney's pulse quickened—then she shook her head, chastising herself for being so jumpy. Agent DeMarco had probably decided to take another look around. She pulled back the curtain, peering out the window. There was no sign of him. Or anyone else.

"It's okay, boy." Brody had always had a protective streak in him—surprising since he had failed his temperament test for the Secret Service as a puppy. Too laid back, they'd said.

She'd been under contract with the company that supplied the puppies and had been given first choice for adoption. She'd seen the potential in him and had turned him into a top-notch search dog, cross-trained in both air scent and human remains detection. He was her first partner. In the years they'd worked together, they'd logged more than a hundred searches in the Colorado wilderness and had twenty-eight live finds to their credit. His hips forced him into early retirement at the age of six. By then, Jax was already trained and operational as an air scent dog. She'd worked exclusively with Jax then, only retiring him after the accident—and before he was able to complete his human-remains detection training.

She knew both dogs missed the work, so she regularly ran training exercises on the weekends with the neighborhood children. That training was all the "action" any of them saw these days. She hadn't been on a real search since that last find. The one that left three teammates dead.

Shaking off the thought, she went into her bathroom,

ran a comb through her hair and scrubbed traces of blood from her face.

The doorbell rang, and she hurried to the foyer. Both dogs barked three times and remained at her heel—their signal for a visitor. Laney pointed to the cushions in the corner of the family room, as customary when visitors arrived, and gave the command "place." The dogs immediately sat, eyes trained on Laney, waiting for the next command. She peered out the peephole, saw Agent DeMarco standing on the porch and opened the door. "I take it everything's clear?" she asked.

He nodded, his eyes scanning the room before his gaze settled on her. "You changed." He smiled, and she was drawn to the dimple at the corner of his mouth. "That look suits you." Her face warmed under his scrutiny. For once, a quick comeback failed her.

"Don't you have a security system out here?"

Laney gestured toward the dogs. "There's my security system."

"Dogs are a great deterrent, but I'd feel a whole lot better if you had a top-notch alarm." He turned, inspecting the deadbolt on the front door.

"It would be a waste of money, Agent DeMarco. Aside from some recent vandalism and petty theft in Wynwood, we've never had much crime out here. It's a long walk down that access road in the dark, and we'd hear a car coming up the gravel drive before it could reach us."

"A walk down the gravel driveway in the dark versus announcing their presence and a lifetime in prison? How do you think a criminal would weigh that?"

"Point taken."

Grayson turned his attention back to her. "I see the bandage is gone."

He closed the small gap between them.

"Do you mind if I look?" he asked, gesturing to her temple.

She shook her head, and then he was in her space, and she was breathing the fresh scent of the outdoors mixed with something dark and undeniably masculine. "Go ahead," she responded, her voice just a little rougher than she wanted it to be.

He gently lifted her hair, his warm fingers lightly brushing her forehead. Laney's cheeks heated as he studied the wound.

Finally, he let her hair drop back into place. "The scar shouldn't be very noticeable once it heals."

"I'm not worried about it. I'm alive. That's way better than the alternative."

"Agreed." He smiled, absently fingering the scar on his left brow.

Had he received it in the line of duty, or was it a battle scar from some childhood antic? She didn't know him well enough to ask, but neither scenario would surprise her. He seemed determined and relentless. Those traits were likely to get a kid into all kinds of trouble.

"But I've found that women can be a little more self-conscious about scars on their faces than most of the men I know," he said.

She shrugged. "We all have scars. Some just run deeper or are more visible than others."

She took a seat on the overstuffed, well-worn leather reclining chair that still smelled of her grandfather's cherry tobacco. She breathed in the scent. Felt herself calming at the memories of him. This home, and her grandfather, had often been her refuge as a child, avoiding her father's drunken rages and her mother's frequent bouts of depression. In her teens, she'd spent more time at her granddad's house, helping him with the kennels and the dog training, than she'd spent in her own home. His passing last year had left a void no one could fill.

Laney looked at the dogs, who were eyeing Agent DeMarco with interest. "The dogs want to say hello. Do you mind?"

"Not at all. I love dogs."

Laney gave a quick hand signal with the word "break." At her command, both dogs bounded off their pillows and headed over to Agent DeMarco, tails wagging. He smiled, rubbing them behind the ears.

"The Aussie is Jax, and the Mal is Brody."

"They're great."

"Thanks." Laney smiled. "They love attention—they'll sit there all night as long as they're getting petted. Do you have a dog?"

"No." Agent DeMarco smiled. "I've thought about getting one, but the truth is, I work too much. It wouldn't be fair to leave it home alone all the time."

"Dogs do need companionship."

"Laney!" Rose called. "Is someone here?"

She had to know someone was. Despite her age, she had perfect hearing. "Yes. We're in the living room."

"Who is it?" Rose asked, sashaying into the room wearing a fuzzy teal robe and a muted pink granny nightgown. Laney might have believed that she'd just rolled out of bed and hurried down the hall, but every hair on Rose's head was in place. She had powder on her cheeks and pink lipstick on her lips. She smiled sweetly as she spotted Agent DeMarco. "Oh, I didn't know you were here, Gray."

"I was looking around outside and decided I'd check in before I left."

"Would you like a cup of tea?"

"No, thank you. I'll be heading out in a minute."

"Maybe you could give Aunt Rose a ride back to her place?" All Laney wanted to do was get in bed and fall asleep. She definitely did not need Aunt Rose flitting about, making herself "useful." As much as she loved Aunt Rose, the woman had more energy than three people combined, and Laney wasn't sure she could handle that tonight.

"What?" Rose responded with a frown. "I'm staying here tonight, remember?"

"There's no need. I don't plan on doing anything but sleeping. I'm sure you'd be more comfortable in your own bed."

"Well, that's a thought, but it's not going to happen," Rose said, grabbing the bag from the foyer floor as she entered the family room. "You heard what the doctor said—you shouldn't be alone for a few days."

"The doctor was speaking out of an abundance of caution."

"She was speaking out of genuine concern for your well-being!"

"I agree with Rose," Agent DeMarco interjected.

"And that's supposed to make me concede?" Laney asked, shooting him a sideways look.

"I once knew a man who got knocked in the head by a piece of shrapnel," Agent DeMarco said. "He thought he was fine until he wasn't."

"If you're going to tell me he keeled over and died, I'm not going to believe you."

"I was going to tell you that he ended up in the hospital in a coma for two weeks, but your version is a lot more compelling."

If she hadn't been so tired, if her head hadn't been aching so badly, she might have smiled at that.

"That's settled, then," Rose stated matter-of-factly. "There is no way I'm leaving you here and having you fall into a coma. You look a little flushed. Have you taken your painkiller yet?"

"No, I haven't had a chance. I'll take some in a minute."

"You'll take some now." Rose rifled through the bag, pulling out the bottle of pills. "I'll get a glass of water. Stay put." She hurried off.

Which left Laney and Agent DeMarco alone in the family room.

That should have been fine. She was used to being around male law enforcement officers.

But it felt odd having him there, eyeing her somberly.

"What?" she finally asked.

"I got word that the sketch artist flies in at one-fifteen tomorrow. I'll have her here between two and three, depending on traffic."

"That seems a long time to wait..."

"She's worth the wait. The best in the nation." Agent DeMarco studied her. She felt her face flush under his scrutiny. "Are you sure you're going to be up to working with her?"

"I'd work with her now if I could."

"Just take care of yourself between now and then."

"You've got to make sure your key witness stays healthy, huh?" she joked. Only Agent DeMarco didn't look like he thought it was funny.

"I need to make sure *you* stay healthy," he responded. "You're important to my case, but you're also a civilian, and it's my job to make sure you stay safe."

"It's not—"

He held up a hand. "It's late. You need to rest, and I've got to meet Andrews at the precinct. Stay inside.

Don't leave the house for any reason—not to walk the dogs, not to run to the grocery store, not to check the mail. Not for anything."

Having never been one who liked to be told what to do, Laney tried to control her annoyance at his demanding tone. She'd been making her own decisions since she was eight and was accustomed to weighing her options and deciding the best course of action for herself. In the end, she was the one who had to deal with the consequences of her choices. "Agent DeMarco, I appreciate your concern, but..."

"Call me Grayson, or Gray. Your aunt already took the liberty, so it only seems fitting that you do as well."

"Fine, Grayson. I appreciate your concern, but let's not forget there's an officer parked right outside."

"Don't be lulled into a false sense of security. Remember, if someone manages to get to you, they'll get to your aunt, too."

He had a point, and she'd be foolish not to consider it. If something happened to Laney, if she was shot or wounded or attacked, Aunt Rose would run out to help. "Okay. I'll stay close to home." She had a few board-and-trains in the kennel, but that was a short walk from the house.

"Glad to hear it." His gaze jumped to a point beyond her shoulder, and he smiled. "You're just in time, Rose. I've got to head out of here."

"I found your jacket hanging over a chair in the kitchen." Rose handed it over. "And Laney's business card is in the pocket. Just in case you need to reach her."

"Aunt Rose!" Laney protested, but Grayson was already walking out the door, pulling it firmly shut behind him.

She crossed to the window and pulled back the curtain just enough to peek outside. She felt foolish doing it, like a teenager mooning over a secret crush, but she still watched him stop and chat with the officer before getting in the car, anyway. Her work cell phone buzzed, but she ignored it. Probably Kent checking in on her.

It buzzed again, and she sighed, letting the curtain drop and grabbing the phone from the coffee table. She had two text messages from a number she didn't recognize. Curious, she opened the first one. Get away from the window, and save this number in your contacts. Gray.

The second one said, See you tomorrow afternoon.

That made her smile. She was still smiling as she said good-night to Rose and headed to her room.

Chapter Seven

Laney usually slept with her windows open in the early fall, but after Grayson's warnings, she thought it best to keep them closed. It was nearly midnight by the time she pulled the comforter around her and lowered her head onto her soft down pillow. She closed her eyes against the dull ache in her temple. Even after Rose had retired to the spare room and the house had grown quiet, Laney found herself shifting restlessly in her bed, sleep evading her despite her exhaustion. It seemed like hours before she was finally lulled to sleep by the soft breathing of her dogs.

She woke with a start, blood rushing loudly in her ears with every beat of her heart. She lay still, trying to control her breathing, listening for some sign of what had yanked her from her sleep. The silence was deafening. Pale silver moonlight streamed in through a sliver of an opening in the curtains, casting its eerie glow across her bedroom walls and floor. The blue numbers on her digital alarm clock announced the time as two-fifteen.

Suddenly Brody emitted a low growl. Rising from his spot on the floor, hackles up, he walked toward the

window. Soon Jax was beside him, a silent sentry focused on the window. A small scraping sound caught
her attention—like a tree branch brushing softly against
the screen or the siding. But there were no trees outside her window. *Was someone there?* A dark shadow
outside the window blocked the moon's light for a brief
instant, and she knew. Something—or someone—*was*
there.

She grabbed her cell phone, hands shaking as she
found Grayson's number and dialed. He picked up on
the first ring.

"Grayson?" Laney whispered. "It's Laney."

"Laney." His voice was instantly alert. "What is it?"

"I'm not sure." Her voice trembled as she tried to
keep from being heard by whoever was out there. "The
dogs are growling, and I thought I saw a shadow pass
by my window." She paused, listening. "I'll admit I'm
a little on edge after tonight, so I might be overreact-
ing… It could just be the officer looking around. Should
I go check?"

"No," Grayson answered quickly, voice firm. "I'm on
my way. Stay away from the windows. Call 911, wake
up Rose, and turn on every light in the house. If it's the
officer, we'll sort it out in a hurry."

"Okay, I'll do that now—" A muffled thud interrupted her, followed by a sudden shout from down the
hall.

Aunt Rose!

"Oh, no!" She gasped, dropping her phone as she
launched herself from the bed with a yell. "I'm coming, Aunt Rose!"

Heart in her throat, she ran toward the door, grabbing her mace from the dresser and rushing down the
hall, the dogs at her heels. Flinging the guest room

door open, she barged in, mace at the ready, prepared for the worst.

The window was wide open, screen missing. The curtains flapped in the breeze. Bright silver illuminated the room.

And a man. Dressed in dark clothing and wearing a ski mask.

He advanced toward Rose who was backing toward the wall, mace in hand. Ducking his head, the intruder shielded his face with one hand to avoid the foam mace shooting out from Rose's special-edition breast-cancer-awareness canister. The mace did actually have as good a range as the canister, and Rose, had claimed. Unfortunately, Rose's aim was not as reliable. From the amount of foam on the floor, wall, and intruder himself, there couldn't be much left in the canister.

The intruder must have known it. He snagged Rose's nightgown, jerked her toward him. Something glinted in his free hand.

Laney's pulse jumped. A gun.

Without thinking, she rushed toward them, bare feet slipping on the hardwood floor slick with foam mace. The dogs followed her in.

"Halt!" Laney commanded the dogs to keep them out of the mace. The dogs stopped immediately at the emergency command. Both Rose and the intruder looked her way.

Aunt Rose ineffectively pelted the man with her small fist and the mace can, her face flushed and angry. Foam mace covered the left side of the intruder's ski mask. Though his left eye was squinted shut, he glared at Laney with his unaffected right eye. It was then he caught sight of the dogs behind her and hesitated.

"Brody. Jax. Danger." On her command, the dogs

growled. "Don't move, or you'll be dog food," she yelled, mace at the ready.

It was a bluff, a scare tactic. Jax and Brody were search dogs, and not cross-trained in protection. But their teeth were bared, their growls menacing. The man stilled. "Put your hands where I can see them and step away from my aunt." Laney's calm command belied her terror for Rose. Years spent working with dogs that were far more sensitive to moods than the average person had taught her to control her emotions.

The man released Rose, shoving her away from him and taking a step toward Laney, hands raised, gun still in his grasp. Glancing first at the door, then toward the window as if calculating his likelihood of a quick getaway, he took yet another step closer.

Could this be one of the kidnappers? If he was, Laney couldn't afford to let him get away. He could lead them to Olivia and the others. She needed to figure out how to detain him until help arrived.

"Drop the gun," she ordered, her gaze and the can of mace trained on him.

"That's not gonna happen," he sneered, teeth gleaming behind the ski mask as he stepped forward. Brody's growls turned to a menacing bark.

"Don't move another step," she warned him. "I mean it."

Behind him, Rose quietly sidled around the wall to the dresser. Grabbing a large vase of flowers and hoisting it over her head, she launched it with as much force as she could muster. Unfortunately she wasn't very strong, and the water-filled vase was heavy. It hit him near the base of the neck, covering him with flower petals and water as it deflected off his shoulder and smashed to the floor—shards of glass mixing with flowers, foam mace and water.

The man cursed, quickly turning on Rose. In a blink, she grabbed the empty mace canister and pitched it at the intruder. He deflected it easily, rushing toward her as she scrambled across the bed in an attempt to evade his reach.

She wasn't fast enough.

He grabbed Rose's ankle. She cried out, kicking him ineffectively with her other foot.

Not wanting to inadvertently spray Rose with the mace, Laney frantically scanned the room for something she could use as a weapon. Anything to give them a fighting chance until help arrived.

A lunge whip Laney used to evaluate play drive in puppies rested by the closet. Snatching it up, she furiously slashed at the man's head and hands with the heavy nylon cording. The last hit left a welt on the bare skin between his gloved hand and his sweatshirt sleeve, causing him to release his grip on Rose.

He angrily grabbed at the whip as it angled down toward his head, trying to yank it from Laney's grasp, but it was slick with foam mace.

Jerking it back, and ignoring biting shards of glass under her feet, Laney rushed toward the intruder. The only other weapon she had was the mace, so she brought the canister down with force on the side of his head and ear. Letting out a howl, he cursed again and came around swinging. Laney ducked. Scrambling backward, she narrowly avoided the blow. Her feet lost purchase on the slippery floor and flew out from under her. She landed on her backside, the jarring force sending pain shooting through her body all the way up to her aching head. She felt dizzy, sick, and then he was on her, one hand on her throat, the other pointing the gun. She lifted the mace, pointed and prayed.

Gravel crunched under the tires and pelted the bottom of Grayson's sedan as he sped along Laney's drive. It had been several minutes since Laney had called, and time wasn't on his side. It took only seconds for a life to be snuffed out. Grayson knew that all too well.

Pulling his car to an abrupt stop in the front drive, he noticed the officer in a heap by the open driver's-side door of the marked car—head bleeding, gun holster clearly empty. There was no time to check his condition.

Leaving his emergency lights flashing, Grayson rushed to the front door, the distant approach of another car on the gravel road giving him hope that backup was on the way.

The house was locked tight. He'd never be able to break down the solid oak door. Knowing that the sliding glass door to the kitchen was his best bet, he ran the length of the porch, vaulting over the railing and sprinting around the corner of the house.

"Laney! Rose!" he called out, racing toward an open window and the scuffling sounds of a struggle mixed with barks and growls.

"Gray! In here! Help!" Rose's voice.

Hoisting himself up, he dropped through the window, into the room.

Laney was on the floor, wrestling with a man for a gun. One of the dogs had a hold of the man's pant leg. The other dog was by Laney, barking and growling furiously. Rose was doing her best to help, pelting the intruder around the head and neck with a boot.

"Get back, Rose!" Grayson yelled, rushing forward

as the man wrenched the gun from Laney's grasp and rose to his feet, turning the gun on her.

The quiet click of the trigger, then nothing.

No bullet. No blood.

And no way was Grayson giving the guy a second chance. He rammed into him. Hard. They were both thrown off-balance as Grayson grabbed for the guy's gun hand, twisting it around until the perp had no choice but to drop the gun. It clattered to the hardwood floor.

"Aunt Rose—get the lights!" Laney called out.

Balling his fist, Grayson slammed it into the guy's ribs, then quickly followed that blow with an uppercut to the jaw.

The lights flicked on, and Grayson dodged a punch. Then another. His opponent was slower, half-blinded by mace. But Grayson still had the image of Laney at the barrel end of the gun in his mind. Still heard the click of the trigger. He had no mercy as he returned the attempted blows with an onslaught of punches to the perp's face and ribs.

The guy dropped to his knees with a grunt.

Grayson helped him the rest of the way to the floor with a hard shove, then pressed his knee into the guy's back.

Reaching for his cuffs, he saw Laney going for the gun. "Leave it," he cautioned her.

Laney stopped short. Dressed in black yoga pants and a tank top, her feet were bare and bloody. Smudges of mace lined her bruise-covered jaw. Her hair fell in wild, tangled waves around her face. "What do we do now?" she asked, worrying her bottom lip. Somehow she managed to look both tough and vulnerable.

"There's a police cruiser pulling up to the house.

You two meet the officers at the door and bring them back to me."

Ten minutes later, he and Laney were seated at the kitchen table while Rose busied herself making a pot of tea. Laney's foot was elevated. A paramedic used tweezers to extract small shards of glass. Grayson was certain it hurt, but probably not as much as being shot had. And she'd come close to having that happen again, close to dying.

She winced as a larger splinter of glass was removed.

"You holding up okay, Laney?" he asked, his eyes turning toward the suspect who'd been read his rights and brought to the kitchen to be cleaned up. His ski mask had been bagged as evidence, along with a glass-cutter and some duct tape. The only other thing he'd had on him was a folded piece of paper with Laney's address printed on it.

And the gun. He'd taken it from the patrol officer after he'd knocked the guy out.

"I'm great," she responded, and Grayson turned his full attention back to her. She had the greenest eyes he'd ever seen.

"You're lying," he replied with a soft smile.

"Maybe a little." She flinched as the paramedic dug another piece of glass from her foot.

One of the officers was none-too-gently wiping remnants of the mace from the intruder's face with a wash-cloth. Grayson wished he'd hurry. Having the guy who'd tried to kill Laney in the same room had to be disconcerting for her.

There was a flurry of sound from the foyer. Then Kent Andrews rushed into the kitchen with Deputy Chief Tom Wallace right behind him.

"What have we got?" Andrews asked Grayson. In his

early fifties, Andrews was a fitness buff who made the gym part of his job. Grayson had brought him into the case six weeks ago when the first Maryland victim, an eight-year-old girl from Annapolis, had disappeared. Since then, Andrews kept an open line of communication between the MPD and Grayson. Though Grayson was used to working alone, he appreciated another set of eyes on the case file and ears on the streets.

"White male. Possibly late twenties, early thirties. No ID on him, and he won't give his name." Grayson sighed. "He's lawyered up, not talking."

"Typical."

Grayson nodded in agreement. "The officers are cleaning him up. Quite a bit of mace squeezed through openings of the ski mask he was wearing. We're hoping either Laney or Rose will recognize him."

"Any signs of an accomplice?" Wallace asked.

"Not that I could see. He appears to be working alone. How's the officer?"

"He's conscious. Paramedics are loading him into the ambulance," Andrews said. "He's a little fuzzy about what happened, but we surmise the suspect staged a distraction and attacked after the officer got out of the car to investigate, obviously stealing the gun while the officer was down."

"It was fortunate the safety was on and the perp didn't have a clue," Grayson replied.

Andrews nodded. "Right now we're canvassing the area to see if we can tie a vehicle to him. It stands to reason he either lives or is parked somewhere in the community and came up the gravel road."

"That's my thought, too," Grayson agreed. "Though there's still a slight possibility he has a car and driver waiting for him, or a scheduled pickup time with an accomplice."

"Agreed. This property backs right up to Route 2, I've got two cars searching," Andrews offered with a glance at the suspect, whose back was to them. "But the underbrush is heavy this time of the year, and he looks way too free of thorns, burrs or dirt to have taken that route."

"Sounds like you've got all the bases covered. I was going to see if I could call in some agents if you didn't have men to spare."

"This case is our number-one priority right now. We'll do what needs to be done." Grayson recognized the sincerity and determination in Andrews's tone.

"I know you will." Grayson cast a glance at Laney. "And by the way, this wasn't a random break-in. He had a piece of paper with Laney's address folded up in his pocket."

"He's as good as he's gonna get, Chief, but his eyes are still a little swollen shut." The officer grabbed the suspect by the arm, yanking him toward the kitchen table. Grayson took a good look at the suspect. The officer was right. The perp's eyes were red and irritated. The mace had done a job on him. The punch he'd taken to the face hadn't helped, either.

Grayson stood up, grabbing the suspect's other arm and turning him toward Laney. "Do you recognize him?"

Laney shook her head. Sighed.

"No." She bit her lip, resting her head in the palm of her hand. Grayson could see Laney was as disappointed as he was. If this had been one of the kidnappers, they would have been one step closer to finding Olivia and the other children. Instead, they had another mystery on their hands. Who was this guy, and how was he connected to the case?

"Rose, how about you?" Grayson asked. Rose came around from the kitchen counter, walked right up to the suspect and gave him a once-over.

"He doesn't look familiar." Rose took one step closer, peering up at the suspect, and Grayson thought he felt the suspect twitch. "Nope. I've never seen him before."

"Get him out of here," Andrews said to the uniformed officers.

He then turned back toward Grayson. "What do you make of this, Agent?" Chief Andrews asked.

"It's got to be connected to Olivia's abduction."

Andrews nodded his agreement. "Can I speak with you in the foyer for a moment?" he asked.

Leaving Laney and Rose in the company of Deputy Chief Wallace, Grayson joined Chief Andrews in the foyer. "Here's what's bothering me about this. There have been a number of home invasions in the surrounding area lately. Same MO—a glass cutter and duct tape have been used to cut a pane of glass from a window so the robber can reach through to open the lock. We've kept the method out of the media."

Grayson hadn't been aware of that similarity. The implications were not good. He knew this break-in hadn't been random. If it had been, the perp would have aborted when he saw the uniformed officer outside. Besides, the slip of paper with Laney's name and address made it clear that she'd been specifically targeted. But someone obviously wanted the break-in to look like it was connected to the recent home invasions.

Someone with access to law enforcement files.

"I don't like this, Andrews."

"I know where you're going with this," Andrews

said quietly, "and unfortunately, I'm thinking the same thing. There's a leak somewhere, and whoever it is has access to MPD files."

"Can you pull the files from the break-in cases? We can review them to see who might have had knowledge of the abduction and shooting tonight."

"Yeah, I'll do that, but I know every man in the precinct, and I can't think of one who would want Laney hurt."

Grayson knew Andrews wanted to believe that his men were honorable, but unfortunately, things were not always as they seemed. "You could be right. I'd also like to send a forensic expert down here to triage your computer networks. It's possible that your networks have been hacked—that you have a leak, but it's not from one of your own."

"Your forensics expert can have full access. I'll let our IT guy know he's to cooperate fully."

"Thanks. I'll have my laptop triaged, as well." Even though Grayson hoped the leak wasn't in his own house, the fact remained there *was* a leak—either in the local PD or the FBI—and he had to check out every possibility. He'd kept his suspicions to himself, sharing them only with his supervisor, Michael King, and his friend and mentor, retired FBI profiler Ethan Conrad. Like Grayson, both men were reluctant to believe the leak was in the FBI. But they'd agreed he had to look at all scenarios equally.

"Has anyone taken statements from Laney and Rose?" Andrews inquired.

"Not yet."

"I'll do that now."

"Can you step up patrol in the area until sunrise?" Grayson asked. "I'm going to stay here until then if

Laney agrees. I've also asked Special Agent in Charge Michael King to authorize FBI protection starting tomorrow."

"There will be a car on this property until morning, Agent. With two officers," Andrews stated matter-of-factly, glancing into the kitchen, where Laney and Rose were quietly talking. "There's no way I'm leaving Laney's safety to chance."

"Then that makes two of us," Grayson said. And judging from the events of the night, he suspected that keeping Laney and her aunt safely out of trouble might be more of a challenge than Andrews thought.

Chapter Eight

An hour after the police carted the suspect away, Laney sipped a cup of now-cold tea and waited to be asked the same questions another fifty times. She was pretty sure that was how many times she'd already been asked them.

She wasn't annoyed by Kent's thorough interview. She was exhausted. She eyed the police chief as he paced across the room, pivoted and headed her way again.

"So," he continued, "what you're saying is that—"

"I've never seen the man before. I don't know why he broke into the house. I don't know what he wanted. Aside from the fact I tried to stop a kidnapping, I can't think of any reason why anyone would want to hurt me or my aunt."

Grayson snorted, and Laney was pretty sure he was trying to hold back a laugh.

He hadn't said much since the interview began, just leaned against the counter, nursing a cup of coffee and eyeing her intently.

She'd tried not to notice.

It had been difficult.

The guy exuded masculinity, confidence, kindness. All the things she'd have wanted in a man if she'd actually wanted a man in her life at all.

"Sorry to keep asking you the same questions, Laney," Kent said. "But sometimes things become clearer the more we go over them."

"I think this is all pretty clear," she responded, standing on legs that felt a little weak and walking to the sink. She washed her cup, set it in the drainer. She felt… done. With the questions, with the interview, with what seemed like an endless night.

She needed to sleep. She wanted to pull the curtains back from the window so she'd be awakened by the sun rising above the trees. Sunrise was always her favorite time of day. It reminded her of new beginnings, second chances.

"I think she's had enough," Grayson said quietly. No demands. No commands. But there was no doubt he was saying the interview was over.

She almost turned around and told him that she could take care of ending it herself, but she was too tired to protest. The past few years had been tough, digging out of the hole of mourning and guilt, rebuilding her life into something that resembled normal. It had worn her down. So had all the events of the past ten hours.

"I guess I have everything I need. You get some rest, Laney." Kent patted her shoulder, the gesture a little awkward and rough but strongly sincere.

"I will." She forced a smile and walked him to the door.

She thought Grayson would leave, too, but he just waited while she said goodbye to Kent, didn't even make a move toward the door as she waited with it open wide. The sky was dark, dawn's glow not yet peeking above the trees.

"You should probably go, too," she said, and he shook his head.

"I don't think so."

"What's that supposed to mean?"

"It means that he wants to help me with this crossword puzzle," Aunt Rose said as she looked up from the dining room table. "I'm stumped, and I've heard that FBI agents are very intelligent."

"I'm not sure that's true in my case," Grayson said with a smile. "But I'll be happy to help if I can."

Laney didn't have the energy to argue with either of them. Shutting the door, she retreated to the family room.

Not only was she exhausted, but her headache was returning, the dull throb making her stomach churn.

She dropped into her grandfather's chair and pulled one of the handmade quilts across her lap and shoulders. Grayson and Rose were discussing which five-letter word best fit Rose's puzzle, and she let her eyes close, let herself drift on the quietness of their voices, the gentle cadence of their conversation.

It felt…nice to have other people in the house. Paws clicked along the wood floor, and she opened her eyes to see Grayson crossing the foyer from the dining room into the family room, Jax and Brody at his heels. The dogs seemed to have taken a liking to the FBI agent.

"It's been quite a night," he commented as he sat on the couch across from her, the dogs taking their spots on the dog beds in the corner. "How are you holding up?"

"Pretty well, all things considered." She smiled.

"God was watching out for you and Rose tonight, Laney." Grayson ran a tanned hand through his hair.

Laney admired his conviction, but it was one she had a hard time sharing. She'd gone to Sunday school every Sunday as a child, had prayed every night for her mother to get better. To be stronger. To leave her father. And every day those prayers went unanswered. As she'd gotten older, she'd stopped praying and started acting. She'd had to rely on her own ingenuity and street smarts to protect them both from her father.

"We definitely got lucky," she agreed.

"I don't believe in luck. Everything happens for a reason. The good and the bad. All the events of our lives, big and small, shape us into who we are. Prepare us for our purpose." He fingered the scar over his brow absently, and Laney again wondered how he'd gotten it. It was definitely an old scar, its jagged ridges faded. It didn't detract from his good looks, but rather gave his face more strength of character. He looked real. Not like some politician, musician, or model. Like a man who would risk his life for what he believed in.

"I hope you're right," she said, because she wanted to believe the way he did. She wanted to think that everything she'd been through had brought her to the place she was supposed to be. That was hard, though, with the weight of guilt on her shoulders, the sorrow heavy in her heart.

"I'm going to bed." Rose announced, standing on threshold of the foyer and the dining room. "A good night's sleep is important to keep the mind sharp."

"Good night, Rose." Grayson remained seated on the couch.

"I need to get some sleep, too," Laney admitted with a yawn. She hoped he would pick up on her not-so-subtle hint as she headed toward the foyer to let him out. "I guess we'll see you in a few hours, then…"

"I'm not leaving." Grayson's voice was firm.

"I'm afraid I have only one spare room, and Rose is using it."

"I'll be fine on the couch. The sun will be up in a few hours, and I'd just as soon keep watch on the house until that happens."

"Well, I personally think that's a good idea," Rose interjected. "I'm a little too tired to take on another intruder tonight—plus my can of mace is depleted. I'll get the blankets and the extra pillows." Without waiting for Laney's response, Rose headed down the hall.

"Well, then, I guess it's settled," Laney agreed, not wanting to admit, even to herself, that she felt better knowing Grayson would be down the hall. "If you'll excuse me, I need to go grab the pillows from the top shelf before Aunt Rose takes it upon herself to get on the stepladder—we definitely don't need another trip to the emergency room tonight."

Grayson woke with a start.

He was up and on his feet in seconds, the pile of blankets Rose had given him falling to the floor. No sign of any danger, and the dogs weren't barking.

Something clanged in the kitchen. A pan or pot, maybe.

He thought it might be Rose, and he went to join her, stopping short when he spotted Laney standing at the sink. The early-morning sun cast gold and amber highlights through her silky hair as she put on the coffee and popped an English muffin into the toaster. Jax and Brody acknowledged him with brief glances, then continued sitting patiently by the counter, watching Laney's every move.

"Good morning."

Though he spoke softly, Laney gasped and turned toward him, clearly startled.

"I'm sorry," he said. "I didn't mean to scare you."

"It's not your fault. I was lost in my thoughts. I guess I'm a little on edge, that's all." She grabbed two dog bowls and a bag of food from the pantry. "Would you like a muffin or some coffee? I've just put on a pot," she asked while preparing the dogs' food.

"A cup of coffee would be great. And I'd like to grab a quick shower later this morning if you don't mind."

"Of course. Fresh towels and soap are under the cabinet in the hall bathroom. Unfortunately, I don't have any clean clothes that would fit you…"

"I keep spare clothes in a duffel in my car."

"Then you're all set. And feel free to help yourself to anything you need from the visitor kit I keep in the bathroom. Sometimes clients will stay overnight when they drop their dogs off, and I like to be prepared."

"That's not a surprise."

"What's that supposed to mean?"

"Just that you seem like the kind of person who prefers to have a plan in place."

"This from the guy that keeps spare clothes in a duffel in his car?" she retorted, placing the dogs' bowls down by the sliding glass door. Neither dog moved from its spot. Eyes trained on Laney, they watched as she crossed the room to the coffeepot and grabbed two mugs from the cupboard.

She glanced at the dogs. "Break," she commanded, and both went for their food.

"They're really well-behaved," he commented.

"Dogs need to understand their boundaries and limitations. Consistency in reinforcing those things is the key." She poured coffee into the mugs. "Milk or sugar?"

"Black is fine."

She leaned against the counter, sipping her coffee. Dressed in beige tactical pants, work boots and a white, long-sleeved T-shirt with the Wagging Tails Boarding and Training logo on it, it was clear she was ready to work. "Heading out to take care of the dogs?"

"It's what I do."

"Not without an escort."

"You're welcome to come along, but I've got some training to do, so I may be a while."

"How long have you been a dog trainer?"

"Professionally, since I was about nineteen—it helped pay my college living expenses—but I've been training dogs since I was eleven. I picked it up from my grandfather. He's the one who started this training facility. He mostly trained police dogs for protection work and drug sniffing back then. Some of my best childhood moments were spent in the kennels with the dogs." Her smile lit her eyes. "But then, what kid wouldn't like playing with dogs all day?"

She pulled her hair up in a ponytail, tying it off with an elastic band she'd worn around her wrist. She wore no makeup, the bruise at her jawline now a bluish green; the end of the red, jagged bullet wound and one staple were clearly visible at her temple near her hairline, but none of it detracted from her quiet beauty. She had an inner strength and calmness about her that he was sure was part of her success as a dog trainer. Grayson had always believed dogs to be perceptive about people's character and moods.

"I've got to head out. My staff will be here by eight to help open the kennels, and I have a potential new client coming at nine for a puppy evaluation—it should be interesting because I've never worked with a Leonberger before. Her name is Maxine."

Grayson had never even *heard* of a Leonberger. "Do we have time for me to grab my laptop? I've got some case files I want to go over."

"Can you do it in two minutes?"

"It's out in my car. I can do it sixty seconds."

"Challenge on," she responded, lifting her wrist and staring at her watch.

He made it back with the laptop in fifty seconds, because he was pretty sure she wouldn't wait the entire sixty.

She was still in the kitchen, the sunlight still playing in her hair.

He thought he'd like to see her outdoors, working with her dogs, doing what she did best.

And that wasn't a good thought to be having about his key witness.

"So what are you planning to tell your staff about your injuries?" he asked, because he needed to get his mind back on protecting Laney. Even though it seemed certain her connection to the case had been leaked, he still thought it wise to downplay her involvement, to keep the reason for her injuries quiet.

"I think explaining your presence, and that of the patrol car, could be just as difficult, actually. What would you suggest?"

"For now, let's blame your injuries and police protection on the break-in and call me an old friend."

"We can try it, but I'm not good at subterfuge. If they start asking questions, that story will fall apart quickly."

"Well, I guess you'll have to keep them too busy to ask questions."

"That part probably won't be much of a problem."

She opened the sliding glass door, letting the dogs out into the yard.

Grayson followed Laney to the kennels, where she busied herself filling water bowls with a two-gallon jug. She had released most of the dogs, about fifteen in all, into a fenced enclosure in the center of the kennel that appeared to be an indoor training area. The morning quiet was now broken with lots of barking, yapping, jumping and running around. He noticed one dog, a large Rottweiler, remained in its enclosure. "What's wrong with that one?" he asked out of curiosity.

"He's here as a board-and-train. He's a rescue, but he's dog-aggressive and hard to control on walks. He's improved since he's been here, but I don't trust him to play unsupervised yet."

"That's too bad."

"He's young, and he's smart. His new owners love him. He'll have a happy ending." She smiled.

A door opened at the back of the facility. A girl, about fifteen, came out, hands filled with two buckets overflowing with metal dog bowls. An older teen boy was behind her, pushing a cart piled high with dog food.

"Guys, I'd like you to meet Grayson DeMarco. He's an old friend. Grayson, this is Riley Strong and Bria Hopewell, my staff."

Riley stepped out from behind the cart, extending a hand to Grayson. "Nice to meet you," he said, pumping Grayson's hand just a little harder than socially acceptable. Not at all threatened by Riley's obvious territorial gesture, Grayson smiled.

"The pleasure's mine," he countered, returning the handshake. He had no doubt Riley knew he was no match physically for Grayson, but he appreciated the kid's protective posture and wondered if Laney recognized his obvious devotion to her.

Bria stepped forward, pushing her glasses up on her nose and extending her hand, as well. She was taller than Laney, about five-six, and way too skinny. Her natural blond hair was pulled up into a ponytail, the bangs falling into her eyes. She barely met Grayson's eyes as she mumbled, "Nice to meet you," before dropping his hand like a hot potato. Grayson had seen kids act like that before, and usually for a reason other than severe shyness. He made a mental note to ask Laney about Bria's story later.

"What's up with the cop car outside?" Riley asked.

"We had a break-in last night, and Chief Andrews thought it would be safer to leave some officers here." A red flush crept into Laney's cheeks. She was right. She was possibly the worst liar Grayson had ever seen. The kids didn't seem too perceptive, however, accepting her explanation and going about their task of feeding the dogs.

"You're welcome to use my office if you need a place to work, Grayson. Here, let me show you where it is."

"This is a nice setup," he commented, following her through the facility.

"I renovated when I took over the business from Granddad about two years ago."

Grayson noticed a sprinkler system in the ceiling, and cameras in the corners focused on the training ring.

"You have security cameras in your kennels but won't get an alarm in your house?" Grayson asked. It seemed to him that her money would have been better spent equally on the house and the kennel.

"The cameras are for recording training sessions

only. They're not set up for around-the-clock monitoring."

Grayson's phone vibrated on his hip. "Mind if I take this?"

"Why would I? You've got work to do, and so do I. My office is this way." She led him past the reception area, down a small corridor that ended at an office and storage area as Grayson answered the phone.

"DeMarco."

"Andrews here. The arson investigator is wrapping things up. He'll have the official report to us this afternoon, but the fuse at the hospital was deliberately blown. He confirmed his initial assessment of arson."

Just as Grayson had expected. "What about the surveillance video?"

"No one was in or around that area except the security guard. I've sent a patrol car out to his house to bring him to the precinct for further questioning," Andrews said.

"Good. We need to press him. Any ID yet on our perp from the break-in?" he asked, meeting Laney's eyes. She looked worried. She should be. It was obvious the kidnappers knew she had survived. There was no doubt the blown fuse, the intruder, all of it were connected with the intent of finding and silencing her.

"Prints were a match for Stephen Fowler," Andrews continued. "Two-time loser. Just released nine months ago after serving a four-year stretch for B&E. His car was parked at his parents' house in the neighborhood, but they claimed they'd not seen him since his release. Father seemed pretty angry over a stolen family car a few years back—claims he'd cut off all ties. Mom may be maintaining contact without telling dad, but

I don't think either had any knowledge of his actions last night."

"Fowler say anything useful?"

"No. He's still clammed up. It doesn't look like he'll be able to make bail. Maybe another night in jail will loosen his tongue."

"Maybe. We could definitely use a break. Right now I'm pinning all my hopes on Laney being able to ID a suspect," Grayson said.

"Do you think we should reconsider moving her to a safe house?" Andrews asked.

"The problem is, I don't know who to trust. I'd feel better if she was here, with a combination of police and FBI protection for the next few days."

"I'll support that. I'll rotate officers out front," Andrews said. "Any word on the FBI protection detail?"

"Best case scenario, tonight or tomorrow. I'll stay around until we get more people lined up."

"I'll be by in a few hours to drop Murphy off. You can let me know then if you think we need to take additional precautions."

Grayson checked his watch. "Actually, I've got the sketch artist flying in soon. If you're going to be here, I'll feel better about leaving Laney to pick the sketch artist up from the airport. My plan is to bring her directly here—the quicker we get the sketches done, the better."

"That won't be a problem," Andrews said. "You still planning to bring in that computer-forensics guy? Because if you're not, I'm calling someone in. If there's a leak in my department, I want to know it."

"She's coming, but she's not a guy. I called in a favor and got the leading cyber-forensics investigator in the country." He didn't mention that Arden was his sister.

No need for that. Andrews would figure it out soon enough.

"She's FBI, too?"

"No. She's brains for hire. An independent contractor. But I know I can trust her, and that's all that matters right now."

Grayson said a quick goodbye and disconnected.

"Well?" Laney demanded, her eyes deeply shadowed, the bruise on her jaw purple and green against her pale skin.

"I think you heard most of it. The arson team confirmed that the fuse box had been tampered with, and the perp from the break-in is still not talking. Kent's planning to bring Murphy..."

A sudden commotion in the kennels, followed by a reverberating crash and a piercing scream, had Grayson on high alert, hurrying toward the office door. "Wait here," he ordered Laney as he rushed into the kennels, pulling the door shut behind him.

Drawing his gun, he raced to the indoor training ring, scanning the facility for the source of danger.

He didn't have to look far.

Near the entry of the indoor training facility, a brown-and-black mass of fur on legs was excitedly pulling on its leash. It must have weighed a good seventy or eighty pounds. The poor owner was putting all his strength into holding it at bay as it wagged its tail excitedly and tried to reach Riley and the food cart. It had already managed to barrel over Bria, knocking her off her feet and scattering metal dog bowls all over the concrete floor. Riley was trying to pull her up, one eye warily trained on the furry menace.

Unexpectedly, the pup pulled free, launching himself in a ball of unbridled excitement toward the teens and the food cart. Grayson cringed, but it was like watching a train wreck about to happen. He just couldn't look away.

Footsteps pounded on the ground behind him, and he whirled around, ready for danger. Laney was there, wild auburn curls flying around her face, eyes wide with surprise. She held a long metal pole, her knuckles white from her grip on it.

"I guess," she said, as he turned back and saw the furry beast had its head in a bucket of dog food, "that is Maxine."

Chapter Nine

Maxine was a darling, but she was a wild one.

Laney barely managed to get her back into her owners' SUV after the evaluation was done.

They drove away, waving wildly, probably in gratitude that Maxine hadn't killed Bria or Riley.

Maxine stuck her head out the side window, her tongue lolling out.

"I can't believe that thing is only five months old." Grayson commented.

"She's cute, isn't she?" Laney asked.

"Cute? I don't think anything that big can be called cute."

"Beauty is in the eye of the beholder," she responded absently, turning to clean up the mess left in Maxine's wake.

"You shouldn't have come running out of the office. You know that, right?" Grayson asked, helping right the cart and scoop what was left of the food back onto it.

"What was I supposed to do? Cower in my office, hoping and praying that the screams weren't my staff members being slaughtered?"

"You thought they were being slaughtered, and you

came outside with this?" He lifted her grandfather's old catching pole, a tool used to control vicious, potentially dangerous dogs. It was a five-foot-long aluminum rod with a grip on one end and a retractable noose on the other.

She had never used one herself, and in all the years she had worked with her grandfather, she had never seen him use one, either. But when she'd prepared to leave the office to find the source of the screaming, it had been the only potential weapon within her reach.

"It made sense at the time." She shrugged, her hair sliding along her neck and falling away from the wound on her head. She'd almost died trying to save a stranger. It shouldn't surprise him that she'd come running to rescue her employees.

"It would have made more sense to stay where I left you. I have a gun, Laney, and I'm trained to take down criminals."

"And I'm trained to take care of the people who work for me. I'm not going to sit back and let them be hurt because I'm too afraid to act." Her voice shook—she hoped he didn't notice.

"Okay," he said, sounding less like he truly agreed and more like he simply didn't want to argue with her.

"What's that supposed to mean?" she asked, her voice laced with suspicion.

"It means you're exhausted. And you need some rest."

"I need to meet with that sketch artist."

"She'll be here this afternoon."

"But will that be soon enough? The kidnappers know I'm alive. They may move Olivia and the other children sooner rather than later."

"Moving them early would take a lot of coordination

and effort," he reminded her, but she heard the doubt in his voice. She knew he'd hoped to lull the kidnappers into a false sense of security by making them believe she was dead. Since that plan had fallen through, he had to be just as worried as she was that the abductors would decide to cut their losses and leave the area with the children they'd already taken.

"That doesn't mean they won't do it, and once the kids are out of the country, they may never be found."

"I suspect they have a quota of children to meet, and the kidnappers are not going to jeopardize their payday just yet. Not until they've exhausted all other options."

"As in tried everything to get rid of me?"

"Something like that. Come on. Let's go back to the house. You're looking a little pale."

She had a feeling he was being diplomatic. If the aching exhaustion she felt was any indication, she probably looked like five miles of rough road. "I'm feeling a little pale, too, but I have dogs to take care of."

"Your staff can handle it." He pressed his hand to her lower back, urging her to the house.

He looked even more worried when she didn't bother to protest.

They walked to the house silently, her steps slow and a little unsteady. The adrenaline that had shot through her when she'd heard the screams of her staff was fading, leaving her drained and hollow. When she'd heard Bria and Riley calling out, her heart sunk with the certainty that she had—once again—put the people who trusted her in harm's way. Now her mind was filled with dark memories and all she wanted was to crawl into bed and hope that sleep would push those memories away, at least for a little while.

"You know what?" she murmured without looking at him. "I think I'm going to lie down for a while."

She didn't give him a chance to say he thought it was a good idea. She just walked down the hall and into her bedroom, closing the door behind her.

Sunlight tracked along the ceiling, the house filled with noises. Rose's voice. Grayson's. The television blasting *The Price Is Right*. Dishes clanked, and the sweet smell of fresh baked treats filled the room. The dogs sniffed at the closed bedroom door. She could hear their quiet snuffling breaths, but she was too tired to let them in. She allowed herself to drift in that sweet place between waking and sleeping, that soft spot where memories didn't intrude and circumstances didn't matter so much.

Someone knocked on the door. "Laney," Rose called. "Do you want some tea?"

It was Rose's cure-all, and most times Laney would humor her aunt by having a cup. This wasn't most days, and she kept her eyes closed, pretending to be asleep as the door swung open.

"Laney, dear?" Rose whispered. The floorboards creaked as she approached the bed, and Laney caught a whiff of her aunt's lavender body wash. "Are you awake?"

"I'm trying really hard not to be," Laney muttered.

"Oh. Well, then, I'll just leave you to it. That good-looking FBI agent is sitting in the living room having one of my famous cinnamon rolls. I thought you might like one, too."

"First of all," Laney said, finally opening her eyes, "you know his name is Grayson. Second, your famous cinnamon rolls come from a can, so I'm not sure how you can even call them yours or famous."

"They *are* famous, Laney. The commercials for them are all over the television. I made them. Therefore, they are mine," Rose huffed.

"I'm sure several million other people have also made them." Laney sat up, her entire body achy and old-feeling. "You didn't just come in here to ask me if I wanted a cinnamon roll. What's up?"

"I'm worried about you," Rose admitted, sitting on the edge of the bed and placing a hand on Laney's thigh. "Since when do you lie around in the middle of the day?"

"Since I got shot in the head?"

"Don't try to be funny, Laney. This isn't the time for it."

"Really, Aunt Rose. You don't need to worry. I'm fine."

"The bruise on your jaw and the staples in your scalp would say differently."

"What they say, Aunt Rose, is that I survived. That's a great thing. Not something to make you worry."

"I always worry about you, dear. Ever since that unfortunate incident—"

"I think I *will* have one of those cinnamon rolls." Laney stood so abruptly, her head swam.

"You can't keep running away from it forever, Laney." Rose grabbed her arm, her grip surprisingly strong for a woman of her age. "Eventually, you're going to have to do the hard work of letting go."

"I have let go." She just hadn't forgotten, would never forget.

"Then maybe what you really need is to grab on to

something worth believing in." Rose planted her fists firmly on hips that sported bright pink running pants.

"I suppose you're going to tell me what that is?"

"*I* suppose that *you're* intelligent enough to figure it out yourself! But maybe not, since you've spent the past few years hiding in your safe little house, ignoring God's calling for your life!" She flung the last over her shoulder as she huffed out of the room.

Laney sank onto the bed, her muscles so tense she thought they might snap. She didn't like to talk about what had happened in Colorado. She didn't like to think about it. Of course, she still thought about it almost every day. How could she not? She'd lost three well-trained team members. Not just team members. Friends. All of them gone in a blink of an eye and the wild heaving of an avalanche. She rubbed the back of her neck, tried to force the memories away.

They wouldn't leave her. Despite what she'd said to Rose, she hadn't let go. She *couldn't* let go. She'd been responsible for her team, and she'd failed them.

There was nothing that could change that, nothing that could bring back the lives that had been lost.

Not even giving up search and rescue, a quiet voice inside reminded her.

She ignored it. She'd made the decision to retire Jax. It had been the right one to make. She was doing good things with her business, and she didn't see how that could be construed as ignoring God's calling.

Whatever that calling might be.

She frowned, eyeing the old family Bible that sat on her dresser. It had belonged to her grandfather, and he'd given it to her a few weeks before his death. She had opened it once, to read verses from it during his funeral. She touched the cover. Ran her fingers over the embossed letters that read *Travis Family Bible*. It was smooth as silk, decades of being handled and read leaving the old leather soft. She'd believed in God for as long as she could remember. What she hadn't believed was that He cared, that He had a purpose and a plan for her life.

Aunt Rose, though, was convinced otherwise.

So, apparently, was Grayson.

Laney wanted to believe it. She wanted to know everything that had happened would eventually lead her to the place she was supposed to be.

"Everything okay in here?" Grayson asked from the open doorway. He'd showered and changed into a clean set of black tactical pants and a black T-shirt with the FBI logo. Her breath caught as he smiled. He looked good. Great, even. And she'd have to be blind not to notice it.

"Yes."

"Then why did Rose stomp into the kitchen muttering something about stubborn nieces? You're not planning your escape, are you?"

"Not hardly." She laughed, her hand falling away from the Bible, the soft feel of its cover still on her fingers and in her mind. "She's just annoyed with me."

"Why?" He walked into the room, and it felt smaller, more intimate.

"Because I retired from search and rescue," she admitted, sidling past him and moving into the hall. The last thing she wanted was Grayson DeMarco in her bedroom.

"I read about that," he responded.

She stopped short, turning to face him. The hall was narrow, and they were close. She could see the stubble on his chin, the dark ring around his striking blue irises. "Where?"

"A local paper did a story about you a couple of years ago, remember?'

"Yes, but I didn't think anyone else did."

"I did a little research while you were resting and found it. I told you I planned to work this morning."

"I'm not sure I like that you were digging into my past. As a matter of fact, I'm pretty positive that I don't like it at all."

"I wasn't digging. I was doing background checks on everyone involved in the case."

"You need a background check on a witness?"

"Not every witness is an innocent bystander, Laney," he responded, eyeing her. "Now that I'm thinking about it, Rose was also muttering something about grumpy nieces."

"I am not grumpy!" Laney protested, even though she probably was.

"Sure you are. Sleep deprivation will do that to a person. Come on." He took her arm, his strong fingers curving around her biceps, their warmth seeping through her cotton shirt. "A little sugar will perk you right up."

"I don't need—"

"What you need," he cut her off, his expression serious, "is to let go and let someone take care of you for a while." He began leading her to the kitchen.

It was the second time in just a few minutes that someone had told her she needed to let go.

Maybe it was time, she thought, but she wasn't sure she knew how.

Chapter Ten

The cinnamon roll was surprisingly good, despite the slightly burnt edges. The conversation was better.

Grayson was funny and intelligent, and Laney would have been lying if she said she hadn't enjoyed spending time with him. But Grayson's easy banter couldn't belie his concern. He was reluctant to leave, even after Kent arrived with Murphy, who'd greeted Laney like a long-lost friend before eying Grayson suspiciously until introductions were made. Grayson had finally given her a stern reminder to stay in the house and left for the airport.

With Grayson gone, Laney tried not to watch the clock, counting the minutes until he'd return with the sketch artist. The armed officers in Laney's drive, plus the curtains pulled tightly closed throughout the house, were blatant reminders of the danger she was in. If that wasn't enough, the nagging headache and various aches and pains she had would have been.

She watched as Rose popped opened another container of cinnamon rolls. Despite her cheerfulness, she looked tired, her skin a little pale, her hair a little less bouncy than usual.

"Why don't you let me do that, Aunt Rose?" she asked, and Rose scowled.

"You think I'm too old to handle this?"

"I think that if I'm tired, you must be, too."

"Well, I am, but Grayson would probably enjoy a few more piping hot cinnamon rolls when he comes back, and you've never been all that good of a cook."

"This isn't cooking," Laney said, taking the can from her aunt's hands. "And you know that Grayson has only been gone forty minutes. If we bake these now, they won't be hot when he gets back."

"Truth be told," Rose admitted, "I want one. I stress-eat, dear. That's how I got these." She patted her hips, and Laney laughed.

"You've got nothing. Now, sit down. I'll take care of the rolls."

She helped her aunt to the chair, anxious to get her off her feet. The woman had more energy than most twenty-year-olds, but she wasn't twenty, and she could easily overdo it.

Once Rose had settled into the chair, Laney opened the container, peeled out the rolls and placed them in the baking dish. After sticking them in the oven, she did a half dozen other things that were everyday and easy. All the while, her heart slammed against her ribs. Her throat was dry. Every minute, she expected something to scratch against the kitchen window, someone to kick in the kitchen door.

Sure, they had armed police officers outside, but that hadn't made any difference the previous night.

As if thinking about it made it happen, the back door flew open.

She screamed, the sound choking off as she saw a police officer standing in the doorway.

"Sorry about that, ma'am," he said, his gaze shooting to a spot just past her shoulder. She glanced back and saw Kent on the kitchen threshold.

"What's going on?" he asked, his tone cold, his eyes icy. Maybe he thought the police officer was a threat. Whatever the case, the young officer swallowed hard, took a step backward.

"Mills Corner store and gas station has just been held up at gunpoint. Dispatch has called us in since we're the closest officers. You cool with us going to the scene, Chief?"

Kent hesitated, then nodded. "Go ahead. Call in to dispatch to have a couple of officers head out here to fill in, though. We don't want to take any chances."

"Will do!" He raced back outside. Seconds later, the sound of a siren blasted through the afternoon stillness.

"I don't like this," Kent said with a scowl, pacing to the front window and pulling back the curtain. Murphy, sensing his anxiety, was instantly at his side. "That gas station is so far off the beaten track, it's nearly impossible to find if you don't know where to look. It's too much of a coincidence that it just happened to be robbed today. Call those kids back from the kennel, Laney. I'm going to take Murphy with me and do a sweep of the property. Make sure everything looks clear. Let the kids in, lock the door and stay inside."

He snapped a lead on Murphy, issued a command and opened the sliding glass door.

As soon as he disappeared from view, Laney texted Bria and Riley, telling them to come to the house. The chief was right. The little gas station had been around for as long as Laney could remember, and as far as she could recall, it had never been robbed before. The mom-and-pop store offering cheap prices on junk food and milk didn't look like much. It certainly didn't look like much money could be found there.

Riley knocked on the sliding glass door, and Laney opened it, waving the teen inside. Bria was right behind him, her eyes wide. "What's going on?" she asked. "More trouble?"

"Not yet," Laney responded, keeping her tone calm. She didn't want to scare her employees.

"Meaning you're expecting trouble?" Riley asked. "Because if you are, I want to go home and get my hunting rifle."

'There's no need for that," she cut him off. "We're not even sure there's actually any trouble."

"Then Bria and I should go back to the kennel. We've got a lot of work to do." He opened the slider, stepping outside. One of the kenneled dogs barked, the frantic sound a warning that Laney recognized immediately. Trouble. Danger.

She met Riley's eyes. "Was everything okay when you left?"

"It was fine," he responded. "We were…" His voice trailed off as a wisp of gray smoke spiraled up from the corner of the kennel.

The scent of it followed, wafting into the kitchen, stinging Laney's nostrils.

"Fire!" she shouted. "Rose, call 911! There's a fire at the kennel."

Rose grabbed the kitchen phone while Laney raced out the sliding glass doors toward the kennel, Riley and Bria close behind. They needed to get the dogs out first and then worry about containing the damage to the kennels.

"You guys get the hose and meet me by the outdoor dog runs. We're about to put the emergency evacuation system to the test. Remember, under no circumstances do either of you go into the facility." Her mind racing, Laney knew she could be walking into a trap. As much as she wanted to get the dogs out safely, she could not endanger either Riley or Bria to do it.

Laney was at the kennel entrance in moments. She'd had an emergency release switch designed to open all the dog runs at once. She'd tested it after it was installed but had never needed to use it again.

Throwing the facility door open, she rushed in. Smoke billowed from under her office door. So far the flames were contained behind it. Laney knew the sprinkler heads would activate only with direct heat. There were two sprinkler heads in her office. She hoped they would contain the fire. She pulled open the dog run control panel and yanked down the emergency release lever. The grinding sound of the gates opening was an immediate relief. Now it was just a matter of getting into each run, putting a leash on the dogs and taking them to the outside training pavilion until help arrived.

A shadow passed across the open door.

Was someone there? "Kent?" she yelled, hoping the chief had finally arrived. The property was large, but there was no way he'd missed the thick cloud of smoke that was engulfing the area.

"It's Riley," the teen responded. "I thought you could use an extra set of hands."

"I told you not to come in the kennel," she snapped as Riley appeared at the threshold. She didn't want him to become an unintended target.

A sudden movement behind Riley caught her eye.

A man ran toward the entrance to the kennels, a baseball cap pulled low over his face, a tire iron in his hand.

"Riley! Look out!" Laney warned, rushing toward

him. Riley turned, ducking and bringing his arm up in an attempt to block the blow from the tire iron. Though his arm took the brunt of the blow, the tire iron still caught him on the side of the head. He crumpled to the ground in a heap.

"No!" Laney cried out as the man roughly nudged Riley with his foot, stepping callously over the body of the unconscious teenager.

She couldn't see the man's face, but something about him was eerily familiar. He had the same wiry frame and runner's build as the gun-wielding kidnapper. A familiar fear ran up Laney's spine as he advanced toward her, tire iron poised for attack.

Glancing around, she saw the catching pole resting against the front desk where she had left it that morning. Wielding it like a sword, she swung it at him. He dodged back to avoid the blow. She swung again, the tip of the pole hitting his hand.

"You're going to pay for that!" he growled.

He lunged forward, the tire iron arcing toward her head.

She ducked, swung the pole again. He grabbed the end and tried to rip it from her hands.

"Laney! Where are you?" Kent called from the other side of the kennels.

"Here, Kent! Quick! Help!"

At the sound of Kent's voice, the man dropped the catching pole and darted toward her. The tire iron whizzed through the air.

She felt it glance off her arm as she ran toward Kent's voice.

She thought she'd feel it again, slamming into the back of her skull or the side of her head. She was sure that at any moment, the man would be on her.

Instead, she felt nothing. Heard nothing. She glanced over her shoulder and saw him disappearing into the woods.

She was safe.

But she didn't feel safe.

She felt terrified.

Kent called out again, and she managed to respond, her heart in her throat as she turned back and knelt beside Riley. He groaned, his eyes fluttering open. He was alive. She was thankful for that. She had to keep him that way. Keep Rose and Bria safe.

A task that seemed to grow more difficult by the hour. If something happened to any of them, she'd never forgive herself. She was all too familiar with that scenario. Her failure to protect them would haunt her dreams. And her waking hours.

A fire truck, an ambulance, two police cruisers and a K-9 unit were still in the yard when Grayson navigated the gravel road. Andrews had called and briefed him on the attack and Grayson's mind was racing as he parked quickly, jumping out of his sedan and opening the passenger door for the sketch artist.

"Slow down," Willow Scott demanded, her curly blond hair pulled into a loose bun, the hairstyle matching her no-nonsense business suit perfectly. "Rushing isn't going to change what's already happened," she said, her long stride easily keeping up with his as he jogged toward the house.

"Moving slow isn't going to keep more from happening," he growled, frustrated with himself, with Kent, with the two officers who'd left their post to respond to the falsified report of an armed robbery.

The door flew open as he jogged up the porch stairs,

and Kent Andrews appeared, a streak of soot on his cheek and a scowl deepening the lines in his face. "This the sketch artist?" he asked, gesturing to Willow.

"I am," Willow responded, moving past him and into the house, adjusting a bag of art supplies she had slung over her shoulder. "Where's the witness?"

"In the kitchen. She thinks the guy who was out here today might be one of the kidnappers from last night."

"How'd he get away?" Grayson asked.

"I'm pretty sure he had an accomplice parked out on the highway. Murphy and I scoured the woods. No sign of anyone, though Laney clearly saw him disappear into the trees."

"That's unfortunate. I really want to ID these guys quickly," Grayson responded.

"Well, if Laney is as good a witness as you think she will be, we'll be able to run a sketch through the system before the day is out," Willow interjected. "If the partial prints or DNA profile from the gun recovered at the scene pan out, your case will be airtight—and if either of the kidnappers is in the system, we'll have a positive ID in no time."

Grayson was banking on it. The FBI's new facial recognition program was able to compare surveillance images and even sketches against the FBI's national database of mug shots in minutes. That's why he'd brought Willow in. She'd had a hand in developing the system and the highest hit ratio of any artist using it. "Let's hope both perps have criminal records."

"There's a good probability they do. You don't get involved in this type of crime overnight. I'm betting these guys are career criminals."

"Let's get this done, then." Grayson said, leading the way to the kitchen.

The house bustled with activity. Firefighters, police and ambulance personnel were all milling around, eating freshly baked chocolate chip cookies that Rose was passing around on a platter. Despite the cookies, the air was still ripe with the scent of smoke, the sliding glass door open, cool air tinged with a hint of moisture drifted in.

He scanned the room and found Laney seated in a chair at the table. She caught his eye and smiled. She looked young, her hair scraped into a ponytail, her eyes shadowed. "You made it back," she said.

"Better late than never, I guess." He took a seat beside her, the acrid stench of smoke heavier there. Though her clothes were smudged with soot, her face and hands looked freshly scrubbed.

"You're not late," Rose cut in. "You're just in time for a cookie." She handed him one, and Grayson ate it.

It tasted like dust. Or maybe mud.

"Good?" she asked, beaming as she held out the platter. "Have another."

"Thanks, but we've got a lot of work to do. Maybe you could—"

"Say no more!" she interrupted. "Bria and I will check on the dogs, but we'll go see Riley first. He's conscious but the paramedics want him assessed at the hospital. His parents just arrived and they're planning to head over there with him. Bria, grab that platter of cookies in case anyone needs a snack."

Seconds later, Kent had cleared the rest of the room, then joined firefighters and police outside. Willow took a seat on the opposite side of Laney, smiling as she introduced herself. She was good at what she did. Great at it, and part of that gift was in her ability to make the witness feel comfortable and confident.

She emptied her bag of supplies onto the kitchen table.

Grayson had seen her in action before, but he pulled up a chair and watched, anyway. He needed this sketch to match something in the database. Despite the police presence, he was worried. Laney had been attacked again. Both times she'd been under the protection of the MPD. Both times, he was not around.

Had the attacker known Grayson would be at the airport picking up the sketch artist? The timing of the fire seemed to indicate that, but only a few people had known when Willow would arrive.

Was the leak in the FBI or in the local PD? It was a question Grayson needed answered. Until then, he'd be taking extra precautions. And unless it was absolutely necessary, he wouldn't be leaving Laney's side.

He'd confirmed the FBI protection detail had been processed and should arrive before the day was out. It couldn't come quickly enough for Grayson.

His phone vibrated, and he glanced at his caller ID. Ethan Conrad.

Good. Grayson needed to run a few things by him.

Though retired, Ethan remained an influential and well-connected force in the FBI. He had lobbied for Grayson to be assigned the kidnapping ring case when the Boston field agent stepped down. He'd been Grayson's sounding board during the past few months, helping him weed through and make sense of dozens of reports and reams of information from field offices in California and Boston.

Grayson didn't bother excusing himself, didn't want to interrupt the flow of Willow's work. Instead, he stepped out the sliding glass door. "Grayson here. What's up?"

"Just making sure Willow arrived as scheduled. I spoke with Michael this afternoon, and he's antsy to get a sketch of the perps into the system."

"Same here," Grayson responded. "Willow's working with Laney Kensington now. The sooner we can identify our suspects, the better. There've been additional attempts on Laney's life."

"I thought you requested twenty-four-hour protection."

"I did. MPD's been covering so far and FBI is on the way. But our perps seem to know my schedule, and they use it to their advantage." He explained briefly, and Ethan sighed.

"Your theory seems accurate, then. We've got a leak. In the bureau or in the police precinct."

"I'm inclined to think it's in our office. Who else would have known what time Willow would arrive?"

"Anyone with access to airport databases can search for a name and find out when that person's flying in or out of a city. Willow is one of the most sought-after sketch artists in the country, and this kidnapping ring is savvy enough to pinpoint who you'd likely bring in and follow that person's activities. It would be easy enough to figure out what time she'd be arriving."

He was right, but Grayson couldn't shake the feeling that the leak was somewhere in the FBI's house. "I've got Arden coming in to take a look at the computer system at the local police department. If any information is being filtered out or in there, we'll know it."

"You've got that right." Ethan chuckled. "She won't miss anything."

"Do you have time to look through some case files for me, see if there's something I missed?" Grayson asked.

"Send the files to me over the FTP site. I'll grab them from the server and start reading through them tonight."

"Thanks. And Ethan, let's keep our suspicions quiet. If the leak *is* a federal agent, we don't want to give him a chance to cover his tracks."

"You know me better than that. I'll call if anything jumps out at me from the files. In the meantime, stay focused. This kidnapping ring has got to be stopped before any more families are destroyed."

Disconnecting from the call, Grayson paced the length of the back deck. He didn't want to believe the leak could be one of their own. But he couldn't afford to bury his head in the sand. *Someone* was leaking information to the kidnappers. There might be a computer hacker accessing the online systems, but the information the perps had went deeper than that. They seemed to know who would be where, and when. There was no way for them to know so much without an informant.

Worse, Grayson was beginning to believe the head of the child trafficking ring might be hiding behind an FBI badge. The cases spanned three states and international waters. It was possible someone in the state PD was on the payroll, but there was no way that person was the mastermind. It had to be a nationally connected source, and the FBI was the only agency working this case. The thought wasn't a reassuring one, and Grayson wanted to ignore it.

He couldn't. Children's lives were at stake. Families were at stake. Laney's safety was at stake.

He walked back into the kitchen. Laney was still at the table, eyes closed as she said something to Willow. Was she visualizing the perps? Trying to bring their faces into better focus?

Maybe she sensed his gaze. She opened her eyes,

glanced his way and offered the kind of smile that seemed to say she was glad he was there.

She was a strong woman, determined, hardworking, energetic and obviously willing to sacrifice her safety for the safety of others.

So why had she retired from search and rescue? His cursory search of national databases hadn't revealed much. She'd retired early from her work, but the article he'd read hadn't said why. He wanted to know. Not because it would help with the case, not because it mattered to the outcome of his investigation, but because he wanted to know more about Laney.

He wasn't sure how he felt about that, but it was a truth he couldn't deny, one that he carried with him as he crossed the kitchen and settled in the chair next to her.

Chapter Eleven

Laney tried to focus on Willow Scott's work as Grayson took a seat beside her.

It shouldn't have been difficult. Her elegant hands deftly moving across the paper, Willow was bringing Laney's description to life. The work was fascinating, her questions as detailed as her drawing.

Yes. Laney definitely shouldn't have had any trouble keeping her eyes on Willow and her sketch. Unfortunately, Grayson was difficult to ignore. Especially since he'd pulled his chair a little closer, his arm brushing hers as he leaned in to get a closer look at the sketch.

She met his gaze, her heart doing a strange little flip when he smiled.

"So," Willow said, turning the drawing pad toward Laney and forcing her to refocus her attention. "How's this match with what you saw?"

Laney's breath caught in her throat. The charcoal drawing looked like a black-and-white photograph of the gun-wielding kidnapper.

"Wow, that's him." Laney didn't think it could be any more perfect—down to the small scar on his left cheek and the slightly crooked nose. Willow had captured him perfectly.

Grayson leaned over to look at the drawing, his closeness oddly comforting. "I'll run this through my scanner and feed it into the facial recognition system while you work on the sketch of his accomplice."

Carefully tearing the page from her pad, Willow handed it to Grayson. "Let's stretch and grab a drink of water, Laney. Then we'll do the next sketch."

"There's probably some homemade raspberry iced tea in the fridge if you're interested," Laney offered, her focus still on the sketch. The guy looked mean, and she could almost picture him slinking through the kennels, setting fire to her office. Had he been the man on her property? She thought so. And it wasn't a comforting thought.

"That actually sounds good," Willow replied. "I'm a Southern girl at heart, and we do like our iced tea." Willow chatted with Grayson about new updates to the FBI facial recognition system as Laney grabbed the pitcher of tea from the fridge and tried to pour it into a tall glass. Her hands were shaking so hard, the tea sloshed over the sides of the glass, spilling onto the counter.

"Let me help with that," Grayson said, reaching around her, his chest nearly touching her back as he steadied her hand. The tea poured into the glass without a drop spilling, and Laney handed it to Willow, her cheeks warm, her heart racing.

Not because of the sketch. Because of Grayson.

The man was messing with her composure, and she didn't like it.

"Thanks," Willow said, not a trace of Southern accent in her voice. She took gulp of the tea, tilting her head back just enough for Laney to catch a glimpse of a thin scar extending from the bottom of her jaw horizontally across her neck. Even to Laney's untrained eye, it would have been a significant injury. Life-threatening, even. And definitely intentional.

She turned away, not wanting Willow to know she'd been staring.

Whatever had happened, it had been a long time ago. The scar was faded and old.

"Here." Grayson thrust a glass of tea into Laney's hand. "I think you need this. You look a little done-in."

"Gee, thanks," she responded, sipping the tea as she dropped back into her chair.

Willow and Grayson were still on their feet, both of them tall and fit. They looked good together, seemed comfortable with one another. For all Laney knew, they were dating. Good for them. Laney had better things to do with her life than devote it to a man. Her mother had done that. She'd spent her entire adult life trying to please a man who couldn't be pleased. Laney's dad had been a good-looking charmer.

When he wasn't drunk.

Most of the time he was. Behind closed doors, he was a mentally and physically abusive husband and father. Laney had watched her mother lose herself to depression, and she'd vowed never to be in the position where being with someone meant losing herself.

"Okay." Willow's voice jogged Laney out of her thoughts. "I'm ready if you are."

Within an hour, Willow had completed the second sketch. It was eerie how much the charcoal drawing resembled the man. Somehow Willow had even managed to capture his menacing stare.

In the family room, Grayson had set up his portable scanner and laptop.

Jax, Brody and Murphy were lying by the coffee table, watching him work, when Willow and Laney brought him the second sketch.

"This looks great," he said. "I'll get it scanned and entered into the system."

"How long will it take to get the results?" Laney asked.

"That depends. There are thousands of mug shots in the national database. If we don't get a hit there, the system will ping other participating statewide databases according to a query I've set up. This search will run against the California, Boston and Maryland databases first, then hit the rest of the states until all databases are exhausted." He carefully laid the second image down on the scanner. "I'll queue up the next query to run when the first is complete."

The dogs barked, announcing a visitor.

"Place," Laney commanded, going to the door. An overweight, balding man dressed in a blue uniform that read Carlston Construction stood on the threshold. With barely a glance at Laney, he began his practiced spiel. "Good afternoon. I'm here to replace a pane of glass in a window…" he said, flipping through a clipboard of invoices, oblivious to Grayson, who had followed Laney to the door.

"Looks like…back window. Double-paned glass." He looked up, finally seemed to notice Grayson and took a step back. "I do have the right house, don't I?" he asked, looking down at his invoice again.

"We've got a broken window in the back, but I didn't call in an order to have it fixed."

"It was called in by Rose Cantor."

Rose hadn't returned from the kennel. Laney suspected she was camped out in a lawn chair, reading one of her romance novels while Bria tended to the dogs.

A police officer approached the door. "Want me to show him around back, Agent DeMarco?" he asked, and Grayson nodded.

"Yes. Don't let him leave without a guarantee that window will be fixed tonight. It poses a security threat."

"Yes, sir."

The look on the contractor's face had Laney thinking he'd replace the entire window, not just the broken pane of glass, to keep Grayson happy. Of course, she'd be glad to have the window fixed. They'd nailed a sheet of plywood across the window last night, but that brought with it other concerns in case of a fire—a real consideration in light of today's events.

Grayson's laptop dinged twice as they returned to the family room.

Willow looked over at them, a grin spreading across her face. "We have a hit—with a 94 percent accuracy rate, Grayson."

Laney rushed over. Two images—Willow's sketch and a photograph of a convict—were on the screen.

"That's definitely him." She couldn't contain her smile. They had identified one of the kidnappers. That meant they were a step closer to finding the missing children and closing down the child trafficking ring.

"You were the perfect witness, Laney," Grayson said. "I knew you'd be the key to identifying the kidnappers."

"Willow was the key. If she hadn't been able to sketch what I saw—"

"Let's give credit where credit's due," Willow countered. "You managed to really see this guy and commit his face to memory. That's hard to do, even under the best of circumstances. I consider myself fortunate to get a 75 percent likelihood of a match."

"And that's a high average." Grayson added, saving the image to his laptop.

"What do we do now?" Laney asked.

"We put out an APB on David Rallings Jr. Tonight."

The sun was low in the sky, the air crisp. Grayson sat on the porch swing, rocking with one foot. The three dogs had followed him out, and after a brief romp around the yard, they had each found a place on the porch to relax in silence. The windows were open, the aroma of chicken and freshly baked Pillsbury rolls wafting through the screen, mixed with the scent of honeysuckle and pine, nearly masking the now faint smell of smoke. Light chatter and low bouts of laughter came from the kitchen where Laney and Willow were helping Rose prepare dinner.

In any other circumstances, this would have been an idyllic fall afternoon, the evening quiet and relaxing.

He was tense, though, anxious to hear from the local PD. The APB on David Rallings had been issued, and Grayson was hopeful they'd be able to bring the guy in for questioning soon. They had a name, a last known address. And a lengthy criminal record with multiple charges for assault, robbery and domestic violence. He'd served jail time five years ago, but had been clean—or just avoided being caught—ever since. Kent had sent officers to Rallings's house, and they were procuring a search warrant.

Things were coming together.

Unfortunately, there had been no match on the second suspect. They might have an ID soon, though. If Rallings wasn't at his house, if he couldn't be located, both sketches would be released to the media on the ten o'clock news.

The dogs came alert to the sound of tires on gravel, lifting their heads simultaneously, eyes focused on the driveway.

A candy-apple-red 1965 Camaro rounded a curve in the drive.

Arden. Finally.

He loved his sister, but her fear of flying made it difficult for her to move from location to location quickly. But he'd choose her any day over a more accessible computer expert.

She'd driven ten hours, from a contract job in Georgia, to make it to Maryland this morning, heading directly to the precinct to examine their system. He wondered what she'd found, but was certain if something was there, she'd know it. She was a genius, graduating from high school at fourteen and from college with a master's degree by the time she was eighteen. Focused and independent, she marched to her own drum. That was one of his favorite things about her. Unfortunately, along with the genius IQ came some quirks that didn't necessarily endear her to everyone.

She came up the walk, a backpack slung over her shoulder. With her black shoulder-length hair, fair skin and blue eyes, she looked much like their mom.

"Hi, Gray. Mom said to tell you you'll be in hot water if she doesn't hear from you before the week is out." She grinned, stepping into his embrace.

"Is that the way you greet the brother you haven't seen in six months—with threats from Mom?"

"Hey, don't shoot the messenger." She brushed a hand over her hair, sweeping thick, straight bangs from her eyes. It was a new look. One that had probably taken her a year to decide on.

"You look great, kid."

"Flattery won't get you anywhere. You owe me big time, and you know I'm keeping track."

Grayson laughed. "I'm sure you are."

"What's with the dogs?" she asked, bending down to scratch each behind the ears.

"Two of them belong to my witness, Laney. The other is a dog she's training for the MDP."

"Laney, huh? Chief Andrews told me about her this morning. He thinks highly of her."

"I do, too."

"Hmmm…guess I need to meet her, then." With that, she walked into the house without ringing the doorbell or knocking. That was pure Arden. No qualms about walking into other people's space, barely any acknowledgment of the boundaries most people lived inside. It wasn't that she didn't understand the rules. She just tended to ignore them unless it was absolutely necessary to do otherwise.

He followed her into the house and wasn't surprised when she made a beeline for the kitchen. Arden loved cars, computers and food.

Laney and Willow were slathering butter on slices of bread. Rose was tossing a salad. Hopefully she'd had nothing more to do with the cooking. If her burnt cinnamon rolls and mud-like cookies were any indication, the woman should be kept far away from meal preparations.

Inhaling deeply, Arden dropped her backpack on the floor.

"Something smells good. Do you have room for one more?" she asked, taking a seat at the kitchen table before she was invited to do so.

Grayson shook his head.

"Of course there's room," Rose said, setting a plate in front of her. "But get yourself out of that chair and help first. If you want to eat, you've got to work. Get the tea from the fridge and some glasses from the cupboard to the right of the sink."

Laney looked horrified at Rose's barked instructions, and Willow tried hard to squelch her snicker.

Arden laughed outright.

That was another thing Grayson loved about his sister. She knew how to laugh at herself. "Laney. Rose." Grayson gestured toward Arden as she got up to do as she'd been told. "This is my sister, Arden. She's the computer-forensics specialist I told you about."

Laney and Rose smiled in greeting. "Nice to meet you," Laney said. "Make yourself at home here."

"And you remember Willow..." Grayson began.

"Hey, Willow," Arden interrupted. "It's been a while. How's the facial-recognition system working out?"

"Perfectly. Which you know. So stop fishing for compliments," Willow responded with a smile, setting a platter of roasted chicken in the middle of the table.

"Not fishing. Making sure the program I designed works," Arden responded, reaching for a piece of bread and getting her hand slapped away by Rose. "Got paid a lot of money to do it, and I want to be sure the FBI is happy with the return on their investment. I've been toying with some upgrades to speed the processing, mostly by giving it the ability to read multiple file formats without conversion."

"I didn't know upgrades were in the budget." Grayson cut in, trying to steer away from the more technical discussion that was sure to ensue once Arden got on a roll.

"They aren't. I just feel it's not the best product I could have delivered. The first set of upgrades will be on me." Arden tried to snag a cookie from the jar on the counter, and Rose sighed.

"Young lady, we haven't even said our grace yet."

"Oh. Right. Let's do that, then." Arden sat, and everyone else followed suit.

"Grayson," Rose asked as she took a seat opposite him, "would you be willing to do the honors? And if it comes to mind, pray for my niece and her safety. She's too stubborn to listen at times, and we—"

"Rose!" Laney nearly shouted. "Enough!"

"Enough what, dear?" Rose asked with an innocent smile.

"Let's pray," Laney responded, and Grayson was pretty sure she mumbled *before I kill someone* under her breath as everyone bowed their heads.

When he finished praying, he leaned close to her ear and caught a whiff of freshly baked rolls and something flowery and sweet.

"Murder is a capital offense," he whispered, and she choked on her sip of tea.

He patted her back until she stopped coughing and thought about leaving his hand right where it was— resting between her shoulder blades, his fingers just touching the edges of her ponytail.

"So, Laney," Arden said suddenly, her voice a little too loud in the quiet room. "My brother tells me you're a dog trainer."

"That she is," Rose interjected. "Probably the best in the country."

"Let's not exaggerate, Aunt Rose." Laney shook her head.

"No," Arden argued. "Your aunt is right. I thought

you might be the Laney Kensington from Colorado, and you are, right?"

"Yes," Laney said, her voice tight, her expression unreadable.

"I've read all about you," Arden said through a mouthful of buttered bread.

"I'm sure there wasn't all that much to read."

"Sure there was. Up until the past couple of years, you were in the news all the time."

Uh-oh. Here she goes, Grayson thought. Arden had a photographic memory…and no filter. "I saw a picture of you, Brody and a family you and your team pulled off the mountain—they ran an article about you being the youngest dog handler on the Colorado Wilderness Search and Rescue Team."

Laney couldn't hide her surprise. "I thought that article only ran locally. Were you a Colorado resident?"

"Oh, no. I liked reading good news stories when I was a kid, so I developed an app that collects and downloads good news from more than three hundred online publications worldwide."

Grayson knew the real reason Arden had developed that application. At thirteen, she'd worried too much about the state of the world—the news stories would keep her up all night. In typical Arden fashion, she'd decided the best way to stop worrying about the bad news was to read only the good. She'd never told anyone but Grayson that, and he'd kept her secret. For her to even admit to the app…she was up to something.

"That must be a lot of reading each day," Willow interjected.

"Surprisingly, no. People would rather read about calamity, so that's what news reporters cover," Arden countered. "Anyway, when I saw that article, I put you and your team into my search engine so I could follow your adventures—they were pretty cool. Volunteers risking their lives to save others. I have tremendous respect for people like you."

"Um, thanks. But I gave that up a couple years ago." Laney's face had gone ashen, but of course Arden wouldn't stop.

"It's a shame. I read that you and Brody had the highest success rate for live finds of any dog-and-handler team in the nation."

"Those stats were probably inflated," Laney responded. "Besides, I retired Brody when he was six—bad hips."

"Do you think he misses the work?" Arden asked.

"At times."

"Do you?"

"No. I lost the passion for it, so it was better I walk away. You have to be on point for wilderness search and rescue. People's lives depend on your ability to stay focused and do your job."

It was a practiced answer, and Grayson wondered what the real reason was.

"What about Jax?" Arden pressed.

"What do you mean?"

"I read he was even better than Brody. Do you think he misses it?"

"Lay off with the twenty questions, Arden. Laney's had a rough couple of days." Grayson figured the direct approach would be the only chance of making his sister realize she was treading on thin ice.

"Sure. No problem." Arden grabbed another piece of bread. "I miss reading those stories, though. They were some of the best. It's a shame that avalanche killed your teammates. Must have been hard on you, huh?"

"I think," Laney said, pushing away from the table, "I'm done." She headed to the foyer.

Grayson got up to follow her.

Chapter Twelve

She needed some air, because she felt like she was suffocating. She unlocked the front door and yanked it open.

"Not the best idea, Laney," Grayson said quietly.

She turned to face him. "I have to check on the dogs."

"You have to stay safe," he responded, opening the coat closet and taking out her jacket. He dropped it over her shoulders, lifting her hair out from under the collar. "So if you need to check on the dogs, I'll go with you."

"You have your sketches and an ID. I'm not necessary to the case any longer, so maybe it's time for me to keep *myself* safe."

"Still grumpy?" he asked.

"No."

"Then I'll just assume my sister's comments upset you."

"They didn't." Not really. It was the memories that upset her. The guilt.

"Arden has no boundaries, but she doesn't mean any harm."

"I know." Laney walked outside.

The sun was just falling below the horizon, golden

rays resting on leaves tinged with gold and red. A hint of smoke still hung in the air, mixing with the crisp fresh scent of early fall. That she was there to enjoy the beauty of it was a matter of chance or circumstance. That's what she had always believed, because it had been too hard to believe that the God who had allowed her mother to be beaten and mistreated actually cared about the world or the people He'd created.

Her grandfather had disagreed. Rose disagreed, her years as a missionary in Africa sealing her belief in God's grace and mercy, His direction and guidance.

"You're sad," Grayson said, pressing a hand to her lower back and guiding her down the porch stairs.

"Not really. I just wish…"

"What?"

"That I had the kind of faith you have. The faith Rose has. The kind that says everything is going to be okay. No matter how bad things seem."

"Is that what you think my faith tells me?" he asked, his hand slipping from her back to her waist as they walked side by side. She could almost imagine that they were more than an FBI agent and his only witness. She could almost imagine that he was worth pinning hopes and dreams on, worthy of putting her trust in.

"Isn't it?"

"No." He stopped, urging her around so they were face-to-face. "It doesn't tell me that everything will be okay. It just tells me that no matter what happens, *I'll* be okay. Life is tough, Laney. No matter how strong my faith, no matter how much I believe, that doesn't change the fact that I'm living in a sinful and fallen world. Bad stuff happens." He frowned, touching the very edge of her head wound. "People are hurt. People are kidnapped. People die. I can't stop that from happening, but I can do everything in my power to make sure the people responsible pay for their crimes."

"Your purpose, huh?"

"Exactly." He smiled and started walking toward the kennels again.

It took two hours to check on the dogs, give them playtime and attention and settle them for the night. It was her normal routine, one she'd carved out of the ashes of her old life. She loved it, but on nights like tonight—with the early fall air touching her cheeks and the crisp hint of winter in the air—she longed to be out on the trail again, working with a team, searching for the missing. Grayson moved beside her as she fed the last dog, locked the last kennel.

"Done?" he asked.

"Yes. It takes a while. I'm sorry if I pulled you from your job."

"Right now, you're my job."

"Your job is to find Olivia and the other children."

"I'm working on that, too."

"Do you think it's really possible they'll be found?"

"I am going to do everything in my power to make it happen."

"If I'd been able to keep them from getting Olivia—"

"Don't," he cut in.

"What?"

"Don't play that 'if only' game with yourself. Regrets don't do anything for anyone. As a matter of fact, they usually just keep us from doing what we could and should and *would* accomplish if we weren't so caught up in the past."

"Did Rose pay you to say that?" she asked, because she'd heard the same thing from her aunt more than once.

"No." He laughed. "Why? Have you heard it one too many times?"

"Maybe."

"Because of what happened with your team?"

She stopped short at his words, her heart slamming so hard against her ribs, she thought it might burst. "That's something I don't talk about."

"Maybe you should," he countered.

"Maybe. But not tonight."

"Okay," he said simply. He didn't say any more. Didn't press her to tell him what had happened. If he asked Arden, he'd get the truth, but Laney doubted he'd ask. She had the feeling that he'd wait until she was ready to tell him.

She liked that about him, the patience, the willingness to allow her to reveal what she wanted when she wanted. She liked *him*.

Moonlight painted the grass gold. Crickets chirped a constant melody. And Laney? She felt oddly at peace. Just for a moment, she allowed herself really to believe that Grayson was right. That everything happened according to God's plan. Her childhood, career choices, and search-and-rescue successes and failures all converging to make her into the person God needed her to be.

And that maybe, just maybe, Olivia was in her path last night for a reason.

And maybe that reason was to bring Olivia and the others home. With hope in her heart, she silently prayed for the strength to see it through.

Laney looked beautiful in the moonlight.

The thought was one that Grayson couldn't allow himself to entertain. Eventually, the kidnapping case would be closed. Laney would no longer be part of his investigation.

And then what?

He knew what he should do. Walk away. Let Laney go her way while he went his.

But there was something about Laney, something that he couldn't ignore. Something he wasn't sure he wanted to ignore.

It had been ten years since Andrea had died. Murdered by a stray bullet that deep down Grayson knew had been meant for him. Her death, a month before their wedding, had been a wake-up call for Grayson. He'd doubted his purpose, second-guessed his career choice. He'd finally come to terms with the reality that his future, his calling, this life he had chosen, did not come without sacrifice. A wife and family of his own were not in his future. He'd been selfish to try to have that with Andrea—a selfishness that had led to her death. He didn't have the time to devote to a family. His job required that he miss birthdays, anniversaries, holidays. That wasn't fair. Not to anyone.

He wouldn't ask another woman to understand the demands of his work, his drive to be successful, not even someone like Laney.

She might understand his single-minded dedication to his work, but she had her own guilt, her own memories, her own reasons for doing the work she did. She didn't need anything else laid on her.

He led her to the sliding glass door, opened it and ushered her inside.

"Gray, is that you?" Arden called from the family room.

"Yes."

"Well, what took so long? I've been done for like... an hour!"

"Have you found anything?" he asked as he and Laney joined her.

Rose was on the recliner, a colorful quilt covering her equally colorful pajamas, nose buried in her devotional. Willow sat on the couch beside Arden, a glazed look on her face. She'd probably spent the past two hours listening to every excruciating detail of Arden's next project.

"Malware," Arden said, her gaze on Gray's laptop. "None of the data you've sent or received via email can be trusted. The malware is very sophisticated."

"Can you disable it?"

"Is there anything I can't do on computers?"

"Way to be vain, sis."

"Vanity is about beauty. I'm confident. But I'll admit, this is going to take some time. Simply put, someone set up a duplicate email account to intercept all your messages before you received them."

"Can you tell if anything was modified or removed?"

"Unfortunately, no. Because the full files were never saved to your hard drive, not even to your temp files, there is just no way to run a recovery program."

This was bad news. This was Grayson's official FBI email account; he trusted it and the data he received from it.

"Is there any way to tell how long this has been going on?

"I knew you'd ask that." Arden smiled. "It appears the duplicate account was set up about in January."

"So my email has been compromised for nearly a year?" Just about the time he was assigned to the case. Grayson didn't like the coincidence.

"Is there any way to trace who's been accessing the account?" he asked.

"I think so, given time. But until I do, any data you send over this account is in jeopardy. Anything you receive is suspect. You'll have to decide what's more important—to have a secure email account, or to track the hacker on the other end. We can close this account down now, but that means whoever is on the other end will know you're onto him."

"I need to know who's accessing my account." Pacing the length of the family room, Grayson outlined his plan. "I'll call the IT team tomorrow and request a new email account, but will keep this one open. Until I get the new account, I'll do everything the old-fashioned way." He glanced at his watch. "It's too late tonight, but tomorrow I'll call the local PD in California and Boston to request faxes of their case files. I can compare them with versions that were emailed to me."

"You think those files were tampered with?" Willow asked.

"I think there's got to be a reason someone hacked into this account."

He looked up at Laney. "Do you have a fax-machine number I can use, or should I have everything sent to Chief Andrews?

"I have a fax at the reception desk in the kennels. The fire didn't reach there, so it should be fine. Aunt Rose gave you one of my business cards. The number's on it."

"Be careful, Grayson," Arden added. "Make sure you contact someone you trust—otherwise the hard copies may be modified, as well."

"Got it covered."

"There is also the slim possibility that the duplicate account was set up by an FBI system administrator.

If that's the case, I won't have much time to complete my forensic investigation—I'd expect him to disable the mirror account, leaving no trace. I'll do what I can tonight, but there is no guarantee I'll be able to track this back."

"Well, Arden," Willow interjected. "it's been great seeing you again, but it sounds like you're planning to work most of the night on this thing and I've got a flight out tomorrow at ten. I think I need to find a hotel room and crash. I caught the redeye last night so I could get here as early as possible, and I'm beat."

Rose looked up from her reading then, glasses perched on her nose, "What's this I hear about hotel rooms when I have a perfectly good cottage just down the drive?"

"I wouldn't want to impose, Rose." Willow said.

"No imposition. I'm staying up here with Laney. My place is a bit smaller, one bedroom. But there's a pullout couch and clean sheets in the linen closet." She stood, folding the quilt neatly over the recliner. "I'll walk you down now. Arden can join you later."

"I'm sure I can find it on my own…"

"I'm sure you can, too," Rose cut her off. "But I need the stretch. I've been cooped up all day and some fresh air will do me good."

Laney frowned. "Aunt Rose, it's too dangerous for you to be walking outside alone right now. Maybe Grayson should—"

Rose sighed. "You young people ought not argue with your elders. Haven't you learned it's futile?"

Arden snickered at Rose's statement.

"Besides, who says I'm gonna be alone?" She started toward the kitchen. "I have two fresh chicken sandwiches and some raspberry tea prepared for the officers out front. I'm sure one of them will escort me down the drive and back in payment for a nice dinner." She emerged from the kitchen, lightweight blue jacket zipped over flowered pajamas, white Keds on her feet and a small picnic basket in her arms. "I threw in some cookies for good measure."

Grayson grimaced. Maybe he should warn the guys before they bit into one of them.

"Of course," Rose continued, "if I had my mace, I wouldn't have to go through the trouble of bribing a police officer with food. Come on, Willow. Let's get out of here."

She was out the door before Willow could make a move to follow.

"Well," Arden said.

"Well, what?" Grayson responded, his gaze on the open front door and on the officers who were being handed chicken sandwiches.

"I like that old lady. She's pretty cool."

"Get back to work, sis." He sighed as Willow walked outside and closed the door.

Chapter Thirteen

Laney toyed with the idea of sleeping in her very comfortable, yet extremely ugly, fuzzy frog pj's—a Christmas gift from Aunt Rose that, surprisingly, Laney actually used. But she did not want to be seen in public wearing them. Given the last twenty-four hours, she could not even begin to wonder what might interrupt her sleep.

Instead of the fuzzy pj's, she threw on a clean pair of yoga pants and a soft Under Armour T-shirt. Glancing in the mirror, she sighed at her reflection. With her hair pulled back into a loose braid, the staples at her hairline were not quite hidden and still inflamed. Her fair skin, made all the more pale from lack of sleep and worry, only served to accentuate further the unattractive yellowish-green bruise that shadowed her jaw.

It could be worse, she thought wryly, dropping onto the bed. She could be dead.

In the corner of her room, Murphy made himself comfortable between Jax and Brody. No doubt happy that he was not relegated to his usual kennel for the night, the younger dog lay upside down, belly showing, legs in the air, snoring. Head resting on Brody's back and a foot splayed over Jax's, he wiggled in his sleep. Brody let out a huff, but both dogs, friendly to a fault, accepted Murphy—at least for the night.

Good. Laney wanted a peaceful night's sleep. She needed one, because she was starting to think things she shouldn't. Things about Grayson, about her future, about maybe reconnecting with her old purpose, her old mission.

She frowned, touching the old family Bible again.

She wanted what her grandfather and aunt had, what Grayson had.

"Please, just show me what you want me to do," she whispered.

Brody opened one eye, gave a quiet little yip.

She smiled, turning off the light and lying down. She didn't think she'd be able to fall asleep with the events of the past twenty-four hours swirling in her head, but she must have. The next thing she knew, someone was pounding on the door. Loudly.

"Laney? You awake?"

Grayson. She knew the voice, could hear the urgency in it as she tumbled out of bed and across the room, nearly killing herself as she tried to rush to the door. She flung it open. "What's going on? Is it Rose?"

"No. Nothing like that."

"Then what?"

"I just got a call from Kent. We finally got the search warrant and entered David Rallings's house."

"Did they find anything?"

"They're still processing the scene, but a car registered to David Rallings Jr. was found on the premises. Inside, the television was blaring, and there was a half-eaten dinner on the table. The front door was open, screen door unlocked. No sign of Rallings or of foul play. Andrews figures that he was tipped off and knew they were coming for him."

"Okay." She wasn't sure why Grayson had thought it necessary to wake her to tell her that.

"There's more, Laney," he said, his expression grim. "Prince George's County Police are reporting a John Doe floating in the Patuxent River. Possible robbery victim. No wallet or ID on him."

Laney knew where this was going, and it wasn't good. "Rallings?"

"He fits the description, but the police haven't been able to find any family to identify him. They'll take prints at the morgue, but it will likely be tomorrow before they can search the databank and get a positive ID. I don't want to wait until tomorrow, Laney. If Rallings is dead, someone is afraid we're getting too close. If that's the case, there's every possibility the kids will be moved sooner rather than later."

"You want me to identify him, don't you?"

"I want you to do what feels comfortable and right. Identifying a body that's been in the water isn't pleasant, and I—"

"I've found drowning victims, Grayson. I've pulled them from rivers and ponds. Older people. Toddlers." They'd been the worst. They were the ones she hadn't been able to forget. "I think I can handle this."

He nodded, glancing at his watch. "I'll meet you in the family room. I need to call Andrews and tell him we'll be at the morgue before midnight."

Laney grabbed her oversize Colorado Search and Rescue sweatshirt from the closet, pulled it over her T-shirt, slipped into her shoes and followed him into the family room. He stood near the window, speaking quietly into his phone.

Arden was still on the couch, Grayson's laptop balanced on her thighs, several devices spread out on the coffee table. She had earbuds in and was bobbing her head to some song only she could hear. She didn't look up as Laney approached.

"Arden?" Laney touched Arden's shoulder, and Arden nearly jumped out of her skin.

"Wow! Man!" She tore the earbud from her left ear. "You scared me."

"Sorry, I just wanted to let you know I'm leaving with Grayson."

"Yeah. He told me," Arden responded, her gaze sliding back to the computer screen.

"I don't want to wake Rose to tell her. If she comes looking for me, can you let her know where I've gone?"

"Sure." Arden replaced the earbud and went back to work.

"Ready?" Grayson asked, shoving his phone into his pocket and taking Laney's elbow. "Andrews said he'll meet us at the morgue in twenty."

"What else did he say?"

"That the security guard who was at the hospital the night of the power outage may have skipped town. His girlfriend called the police to report that he never made it home from work last night. She's suspected him of cheating, so she went straight to the bank to clean their account out. Unfortunately, he'd already been there. Took every bit of the six hundred dollars they had and deposited it into a personal account." He paused as he opened the door and ushered her out onto the porch. "He also transferred ten thousand dollars that she had no idea was there. She was very willing and very able to give us a bank statement. The money was deposited by wire transfer. Half of it twenty minutes before the power outage. The rest after."

"Can Kent trace the transfer?"

"He did. It came from an overseas account. No way to find out who the account holder is. Andrews put out an APB on the security guard. Hopefully we can stop him before he goes too far underground."

"Or before he ends up in the Patuxent?"

"That, too."

The temperature had dropped, and dark rain clouds shadowed the moon. Laney could feel the moisture in the air. There'd be a storm soon. She hoped that wherever Olivia and the other kids were, they were warm and dry. More than that, she hoped that they'd be home soon. She *prayed* that they would, because she had nothing left but that. No power to change anything, no hope that identifying the body would bring them any closer to stopping the kidnappers. All she had was the feeling that maybe she'd spent her life putting her hope in the wrong things, that maybe she'd spent too much time believing in her own strength and power and not enough time relying on God's.

"Better get in," Grayson said as he opened the passenger door and helped her into his car. "The storm is almost on us."

He closed the door as the first raindrop fell.

The pelting rain made it difficult to drive as fast as Grayson would have liked. Even with the wipers swishing back and forth at full speed, visibility was still impaired. Laney was quiet in the seat next to him, her hands fisted in her lap.

"What are you thinking?" he asked, breaking the silence.

"That Olivia and the other two kids might be out in this mess."

"I doubt the kidnappers would risk the health of their sales product."

"Is that really all those kids are to them?"

"If it weren't, they'd never have taken them in the first place."

"That's sad."

"Lots of things in life are, but there's good stuff too. Like your dogs."

"And your sister."

"And food that Rose doesn't cook," he said, hoping to lighten her mood.

She laughed. "Poor Rose. She has an overinflated opinion of her cooking."

"She's a good lady, though."

"She is. I didn't see much of her while I was growing up. She and her husband were missionaries. She came home on furlough, but it wasn't enough for her to make a difference."

"Make a difference in what?" he asked, turning onto the main highway. They should be only ten minutes from the morgue, but it would take a little longer with the rain. Grayson hoped the medical examiner would stick around.

"My life," Laney said so softly that Grayson almost couldn't hear her. "She's always felt guilty about that. I think it's why she lives in the cottage instead of a retirement home with all her friends. She says she'd be bored there, but I know she'd be happy. Dozens of people around her all the time, plenty of things to do."

"You don't feel guilty about that, too, do you?"

She didn't respond, and he took her silence for assent. "Rose would tell you to get a grip. You know that, right?"

"Rose tells me lots of things. If I listened to all of them, I'd have blond hair and sixteen pairs of bright pink jeggings."

"And twenty of those fuzzy sweaters?"

"Exactly." She shifted in her seat, and he knew she was studying his profile. "Do you think they'll find anything at Rallings's house? Assuming he's dead, there's no hope of questioning him."

"Everyone leaves something behind." How valuable it would be remained to be seen, but Grayson was certain they would find something.

"They killed him because I identified him."

"Guilt again, Laney? Because it's totally misplaced. They killed him because he put their operation at risk."

In the center console, Grayson's phone vibrated, the name Ethan Conrad flashing on the dashboard media system. Grayson accepted the call. "Grayson here."

"Gray, it's Ethan. I got your message but was poring over the files you sent."

"I called to tell you to hold off, Ethan. The integrity of the files has come into question. My system's been hacked."

"Are you sure? Only a skilled hacker could get into the FBI system."

"Arden confirmed it."

"I guess you're sure, then. These guys may be more powerful than either of us imagined."

"I agree."

"It sounds like you're getting close. Be careful." Grayson could hear the concern in Ethan's voice.

"Don't worry, Ethan. I learned from the best. I can take care of myself."

"I know you can, but I think I'll take a trip out that way tomorrow and take a look at the police files on all the cases if you can set it up with the chief. Maybe I could talk to a few people, shake up a few leads."

"I think you'd be wasting your time, Ethan."

"Its possible, but I'd feel better doing something."

"Okay, I'll talk to the chief about it and call you in the morning."

"Sounds good." Ethan paused. "You're like a son to me, and I can't lose another one. Be safe." The connection ended before Grayson could respond.

"He sounds like he cares a lot about you," Laney commented.

"We go way back. He was my best friend's stepfather. Married Rick's mom when Rick was only seven. His own dad walked out on them when Rick was a toddler. Rick idolized Ethan, joined the bureau because of him."

"What happened to Rick?"

"Murdered. It was our first major case. We were both twenty-five. He called me and told me he'd had a breakthrough, but that it wasn't safe to talk over the phone."

Grayson remembered that night like it was yesterday, the loss of Rick and Andrea on the same day had been a blow he almost hadn't recovered from. He hadn't shared the story with many, but he had the sudden urge to tell Laney. He needed her to know. Understand how dangerous his life really was, not to him, but to those he loved.

"That night I'd picked up my fiancée from the elementary school where she worked. We'd been out for dinner and a movie, celebrating that the wedding planning was done and the date was in less than a month. I was on my way to drop her off at her parents' house when Rick called. He said it was important, sounded frantic. Andrea insisted we go, saying she'd wait in the car and grade some papers while Rick and I talked."

He glanced at Laney. Shadows of rain from the windshield ran over her face, and she looked soft and lovely, but strong in a way Andrea had never been. "When we got there, Rick was nowhere to be seen. I heard the first shot before it hit Andrea. It smashed through the passenger-side window. She fell into my lap, unconscious. Her blood..." He stopped himself. He could still smell the coppery scent of it. "It was an ambush. The second shot broke the windshield, narrowly missing me. The glass shards flew into my face."

"The scar over your eye?" she whispered.

"Yes."

"I drove to the hospital, only two blocks away. Andrea was still breathing, but the damage to her brain was irreversible. Telling her parents was the hardest thing I've ever had to do." They hadn't blamed him. Just cried for their daughter. "Her parents pulled her from life support that evening, after our families had said their goodbyes. She was twenty-three."

Later that night, after she was gone, her father had pulled him aside. *Find who did this to our girl, Gray. Find him and make him pay.*

"I'm so sorry, Grayson."

"I learned later that Rick was dead before we even arrived at the warehouse."

"Did you ever find out who did it?"

"Yes, no thanks to me. I was a basket case, but Ethan stepped in. He examined Rick's case files, traced his cell calls—he solved the case." And he'd made the guilty party pay.

"No wonder this case has him worried," she said.

"It has me worried, too, Laney, but for different reasons."

They fell silent then to the rhythmic cadence of the rain and windshield wipers, each lost in thought.

He glanced in the rearview mirror. In the distance, lights from another vehicle were approaching from behind.

Fast.

Grayson's grip on the steering wheel tightened as he stepped on the accelerator. These weren't ideal conditions for evasive driving, but he'd work with what he had. The old Bowie Race Track was a half mile ahead. Used now as a practice track only, it would be locked up for the night, but he could pull in the drive to let the car pass. If he made it that far.

If not, there was a ditch on one side of the road and the Patuxent River on the other. Neither a good option.

He glanced in his rearview mirror again. The car was approaching at a dangerous speed. They weren't going to make it to the racetrack.

He eased up on the accelerator. One of three things was about to happen. The guy would swerve around them and speed on, he'd slam into the back of the sedan or he'd pull up beside them and fire off some shots.

Better for Grayson to keep his speed down and retain control of the car than for him to try to outrun the vehicle in these conditions.

"Grab my phone, Laney. I want you to call 911."

Chapter Fourteen

Laney fumbled for Grayson's cell phone, making the call as he navigated the dark, winding road. She glanced out the back window as she spoke to the 911 operator, doing everything she could to keep her voice calm, her thoughts clear.

There was definitely a car behind them. It was definitely gaining fast.

"Don't look back, Laney. Keep your eyes and head forward. Hold on to the armrest."

Controlling her panic, she did what he asked.

"Shouldn't you speed up? He's gaining."

"I will. I'm waiting for the right moment."

Trusting Grayson, she watched the road ahead, the phone falling from her hand as she clutched the armrest and center console.

Grayson's gaze rapidly switched from the road ahead to the rearview mirror and back again. "Here he comes!"

Grayson hit the accelerator and the car lurched forward as the other vehicle slammed into the bumper. The sedan fishtailed, but Grayson maintained control. They were in the center of the two lanes, a curve fast approaching. If another vehicle was coming around the bend, they'd be in serious trouble.

Grayson slowed, getting back in the right lane. "He's coming again."

The impact was stronger this time, the other driver catching on to Grayson's evasive tactics. The sedan accelerated around the corner, Grayson struggling to maintain control. The tires couldn't find traction on the wet pavement. The car spun out, coming to a stop sideways in the middle of the road. The other driver was coming right for them.

Grayson would take the brunt of the impact. "Look out!" Laney screamed.

Grayson stomped on the accelerator, angling the car back into the street and speeding forward just before impact. The other car slammed into the back fender of the much larger sedan.

Pop, pop, pop.

A bullet pierced the rear windshield, exiting through the rear passenger's side window.

Laney heard a fourth gunshot even as Grayson pushed her head to her knees.

"Keep down!" he shouted as he accelerated into the next curve. Two quick shots and the car fishtailed out of control.

"He's taken out the rear tire!"

Laney braced for impact as the sedan careened off the road and into thick foliage.

Grayson struggled to steer the car between two big trees, missing each by mere inches. Laney could only grip the armrest in horror, flinching as branches and leaves smacked the car and windshield. The car jostled down the embankment, sideswiping a large tree and mowing down saplings before skidding sideways, the passenger's side slamming into a fallen tree, air bags exploding.

Grayson looked over his shoulder; Laney followed his stare. The other car's headlights were above them, at the road's edge.

"You have the cell phone?" Grayson asked, his voice calm.

"I dropped it!" She sounded nearly hysterical. She took a deep breath, tried to calm her frantic breathing.

"Check the floor. See if you can find it."

She did what he asked, reaching through pebble-like pieces of broken glass. There! She felt the smooth surface and rectangular shape of the phone.

"Found it!" Laney thrust it into his hands.

As he zipped it into his jacket pocket, Laney shoved at her door with everything she had. "It's wedged against a tree. Does yours open?"

He tried it. "No, it's jammed." He grabbed her hand, squeezed gently. "We'll go out through the window. Hurry."

Cold rain pelted her face and hands as she exited the vehicle and nearly fell headfirst into the roots of the fallen tree. Grayson squeezed out the window after her.

"Where—" she started to ask, but he pressed his fingers over her lips.

"Listen." He breathed the word near her ear, the sound more air than anything.

She froze, tried to hear above the frantic pounding of her heart.

Branches cracked, leaves crackled.

Someone was coming.

Grayson's hand slid from her lips, slipped down her shoulder and her arm until their hands met, their fingers linked. He didn't speak, barely made a sound as he led her quickly away from the car. The pouring rain muffled any noise they made, and she thought that maybe they had a chance of escaping.

There was no light. Nothing to guide their steps. Her eyes tried to adjust to the darkness, but the shadowy trees hid roots and rocks and fallen branches that seemed determined to trip her.

More than once, Laney stumbled over the unforgiving terrain.

They headed downhill, away from their pursuer and toward the Patuxent River. Rushing water drowned any sound of their pursuer but served to mask Laney and Grayson's progress, as well. Somewhere in the distance, sirens screamed. The police must be on their way.

She wasn't sure they'd arrive in time.

As close as she and Grayson were to civilization, they were cut off from everything.

Grayson pulled out his cell phone, "No signal," he muttered, shoving it back into his pocket. He tugged her close, pressed his lips to her ear, his breath warm against her chilled skin. "When we reach the bend in the river, we'll head up. There's help on the road. I can hear the sirens."

She nodded, clutching his hand as he led her around a curve in the river. From there, they climbed through thick foliage, clutching branches and trees to boost themselves up the steep, rain-soaked ravine.

Leaves had begun to fall for the season, making the ground cover slippery. Laney's feet went out from under her, and Grayson tightened his grip, pulling her back up.

The sound of sirens grew louder, but Laney could barely hear them. She was panting too loudly, her lungs screaming, her head pounding.

She'd thought she'd recovered from her concussion,

but her climb up the hill was proving otherwise. What should have been easy was agonizingly difficult, her feet sticking to the ground with every step, her arms shaking as she tried to pull herself up.

Grayson stopped short, Laney bumping into him from behind.

"What—"

"Shh," he cautioned, pulling her around so that they were side by side.

And she saw the problem.

She couldn't miss it.

Eight feet high with six inches of barbed wire across the top, the chain link fence might as well have been Mount Everest.

"We have to go back," she hissed.

"We have to go over, the race track is on the other side of this fence," he responded, scaling the fence easily and tossing his jacket over the barbed wire. "Come on," he urged, reaching down for her hand.

If he'd been anyone else, she would have said no. If he'd been anyone else, she would have come up with her own plan and trusted it to get her out of the trouble they were in.

But her gut was telling her she could trust Grayson. If there was a way out, he would find it.

She was feeling weak. She wasn't sure she could make it, but she climbed the first few links of the fence and managed to grab his hand.

Behind her, something crashed loudly in the brush.

She panicked, trying to scramble up, her feet slipping from the fence, her body dangling as Grayson clutched her hand and kept her from tumbling down.

"Get your feet back on the fence," he barked, and she somehow managed to do it.

Seconds later, she was beside him, looking straight into his eyes.

"This is the hard part," he murmured, his gaze jumping to some point beyond her shoulder. "I'll go over first, and then I'll help you. If you don't move fast, that barbed wire is going to slice through the jacket and into your skin. Be careful!'

He was over the fence in a heartbeat, and then it was her turn. She grabbed the barbed wire, wincing as it dug into her hands.

"Move fast. The weight of your body is going to sink that barb in deeper if you don't," Grayson encouraged her from the other side of the fence.

She nodded, her brain finally kicking in, all the panic suddenly gone. She'd done similar acts before, scaling rock walls to find the missing, climbing fences to check ponds and quarries. Only this time, the safety ropes were nonexistent, and there was a gun-toting maniac behind her.

The movement in the brush was growing closer, and it was human.

Grayson could hear whoever it was stopping every now and again to listen for signs of its quarry. Laney was scaling the fence more slowly than he would have hoped, but he was mostly relieved she'd made it this far. Her breathing had been labored during their ascent to the fence. It was obvious she was tired. But she never complained. Not one word. She just attempted to stick with him as if her life depended on it.

And it probably did.

Laney precariously straddled the jacket-covered barbed wire.

"Easy…" he cautioned, putting a hand on her arm as she maneuvered her second leg over.

The sound of their pursuer grew louder with every passing moment. He wanted to hurry Laney along, drag her down the fence and onto the solid ground.

If she fell, though, she could break a leg, sprain an ankle, slowing them even further.

She finally got solid footing on the links on the other side of the fence, then reached for the jacket and tugged.

"Just leave it," he hissed. "They're coming!"

"Your phone…" She gave the jacket one more firm tug and it broke free, but the jerking motion sent Laney careening backward.

He grabbed her shoulder, nearly losing his grip on the fence as he caught her.

A branch cracked in the woods on the other side of the fence, and Grayson was sure he saw a sapling sway.

"Let's go!" He scrambled down the fence, then reached for Laney's waist. "I've got you. Drop!"

At once, she released her grasp, falling into his arms, just as a quick pop sent a bullet whizzing by his head.

"Go!" He pulled his own gun, firing off a shot as he shouted for Laney to run. She took off, and he followed, zigzagging through the thick stand of trees that bordered the fence and surrounded the racetrack on all sides. Emerging from the trees, they sprinted across tall grass, coming upon a three-and-a-half-foot wooden railing surrounding the dirt racetrack. Laney was already tumbling over to the other side of it as Grayson reached her.

Across from them, the starting gates and now-rickety spectator stands stood sentry, shadows of a once-popular winter racing venue.

"Hurry. We need to get across the track and find

cover. I hope the police heard the gunshots and are heading this way."

They made it to the center of the track, unkempt with overgrown grass and weeds. The footing was uneven in places, holes in the ground threatening to twist an ankle, but they didn't slow their pace until they'd crossed the muddy track again and reached the next wooden rail. By the time their pursuers had cleared the stand of trees, Laney and Grayson were out of range. Grayson could see them racing toward the railing, two dark figures against the gray night.

Ducking behind the empty spectator bleachers, Grayson took stock of the situation. There was really no good place to hide. Every structure surrounding the track allowed entry from too many directions, and with two men after them, that left too many opportunities for ambush.

Beside him, Laney tried to catch her breath.

"Can you make it to the covered horse bridge?" he asked, pointing to the shadowy structure at the top of the hill, behind the bleachers.

She nodded, pushing a strand of wet hair from her eyes. "I can make it."

"Okay. I'm going to distract them. On my signal, you head for the bridge. Wait for me there. If we can get to the stables on the other side of Race Track Road, we'll have a better shot of getting a jump on them rather than the other way around." Putting on his jacket, Grayson removed his phone. "Take my phone. When you reach the bridge, check for a signal. If you get one, call Andrews and tell him to let the local police know that we're at the racetrack. They're looking for us, but if they don't look in the right place…" He didn't finish. There was no need. Laney knew what was at stake.

The men had already reached the overgrown center of the oval track and were steadily gaining on them.

"Let's give them a reason to proceed with caution," Grayson muttered, taking aim at the lower leg of the closest man. He wanted them alive, because he wanted whatever information he could get from them.

He wanted to live more. He wanted Laney to live.

One shot in the leg, and the guy went down. The other guy dropped too.

"Go!" he commanded Laney, firing a shot at the ground near the second guy's head.

Laney ran, sure that she had a huge glow-in-the-dark target plastered to her back.

At any second she expected to feel a bullet sear through her flesh.

She heard the loud pop of another shot as she reached the wooden bridge. Built nearly thirty years ago, it served as safe passage for Thoroughbred horses and their trainers across busy Race Track Road. The bridge was separated down the middle by a tall fence. Signs marking the exit and entrance gave clear directions to those passing through.

Laney veered to the right, choosing the entrance sign. Since Thoroughbred horses tend to be skittish, there were no windows in the bridge. Completely protected from the elements on all sides with the exception of the entrance and exit, the structure was eerily dark inside. Her footsteps echoed across the dry wood, breaking the silence as she pulled out Grayson's phone, checking for signal. Three bars. Better than none.

Making her way to the other side of the bridge, she dialed Kent's number. A shot rang out, startling her; she could only hope it was Grayson doing the shooting. Heart racing, she peered around the corner of the bridge. Shadows of the now-empty stables loomed directly ahead and to her left, a parking lot to her right. She hit the call button, putting the phone to her ear. It rang once, twice, a third time.

"Please. Please pick up." Laney whispered to the darkness.

"Andrews here."

"Kent, it's Laney."

"Laney, where are you? We expected you twenty minutes ago."

"In the covered bridge on Race Track Road and headed for the stables. We were shot at and our car was driven off the road and into an embankment. We left the car and were followed to the racetrack. We heard sirens close by. I called 911, but I don't think they know exactly where we are."

"Is DeMarco with you?"

"He's trying to keep the gunmen from advancing on us." The words were rushed, frantic-sounding even to her own ears, but she wasn't certain how much time she'd have before she'd need to take off for the stables.

"How many gunmen?"

"Two." Laney lowered her voice. Footsteps pounding on the dirt indicated someone was approaching the bridge. Fast. Was it Grayson or someone else?

"I've got to go. Someone's coming."

She disconnected the call.

Holding her breath and pressing herself into a dark corner of the bridge, she waited, watching the entrance, praying Grayson was the one who'd appear.

Finally, a shadow appeared, tall, broad, moving with a confidence she recognized immediately.

"Thank You, God!" she whispered, rushing to Grayson, throwing herself into his arms.

She wasn't sure who was more surprised. Her or Grayson.

His hands settled on her back, his fingers sliding across her spine.

"You okay?" he asked, his breath ruffling the air near her ear.

"Yes. And I got the call out to Kent."

"Good, but we're not out of danger. One of the guys is wounded, but he and his buddy are still on the move," Grayson whispered, pulling her in the direction of the stables. "If the police know our location, we just have to hold the perps off until help arrives."

Water pooled in small divots and dips in the ground as they left the bridge behind, the saturated ground sucking at Laney's soaked running shoes, leaving an easily traceable impression in the earth.

"We're leaving footprints," she whispered, following Grayson into the first of the two stables in the far corner of the training facility. Smelling of wood and hay, the interior was mostly dry, its windows having been shuttered against the elements.

"I know. I'm hoping they'll follow our tracks into this stable and waste time searching for us in here—we're headed out the back and will hide in the next stable over."

Huddling in one corner of the hayloft, arms wrapped around her legs, knees drawn to her chin, Laney strained to hear signs of their pursuers. Grayson's jacket, resting over her shoulders where he left it before taking his place in a stall below, offered necessary warmth, but she still shivered slightly with fear. A few minutes ago, the men had burst into the first stable. She had clearly heard doors slamming and wood banging, then nothing.

The hayloft, now mostly empty, spanned the middle of the stable, allowing hay to be thrown down from both sides into the walkway below. Grayson had placed a loose piece of plywood in front of her, leaning it against the wall, near other boards, tools and buckets. From her hiding place, she was just able to turn her head left and right, having a clear view of both rear and front of the stable. Below her, Grayson was hidden in shadows.

The front door creaked open. A man ducked in, pressing himself to the darkened corner of the wall. Remaining still, Laney controlled her breathing and waited. Grayson had explained that he wanted to catch one or both men alive. This was potentially a chance for them to get another lead in the case.

Laney trained her gaze on the man's position. Unmoving, he stood as if waiting. Hair prickled on the back of Laney's neck, and she turned just in time to see the second man drop soundlessly through an unshuttered window toward the back of the stable.

An ambush. Did Grayson know?

There was no way to warn him without giving her position away. Laney looked around for something, anything to arm herself with. Settling on a heavy rubberended mallet, she crept from her hiding place to the edge of the loft, Grayson's jacket sliding soundlessly from her shoulders. Peering down, she kept the second man in sight. A scuffling commotion behind her was met with a gunshot. Then another.

The second man rushed forward, gun drawn. It was probably an eight-foot drop, but Laney didn't hesitate. Pulling herself to a crouching position, hammer in hand, she leapt for him. He caught sight of her at the last minute, trying to duck while pointing his gun at her, but Laney's momentum carried her forward too fast, her knees slamming into his chest. They fell to the ground, his gun clattering against the stable wall, his body cushioning Laney's fall.

She scampered off him, trying to elude him. His calloused hand grasped her wrist, pulling her back toward him. Hammer in hand, she turned, intending to bring it down on his head. Raising his forearm, he blocked the blow, yelling in pain as the hammer smashed against bone.

Behind her, a gun exploded, its echo merging with the sound of screaming sirens. Outside the stable, car doors slammed and a dog barked.

Help had finally arrived.

Grayson rushed forward, yanked Laney back, and pointed his firearm at the attacker. "Don't move!"

In that moment, both the front and back doors of the stable burst open.

"Police. Drop your weapons!"

Laney froze, dropping her mallet.

"FBI!" Grayson shouted, throwing one hand in the air and slowly placing his gun on the ground. "Don't shoot!"

Kent Andrews and five officers converged on the scene, guns drawn.

"You two okay?" Kent asked, his gun trained on the man who lay on the floor.

"Barely," Grayson muttered, lifting his gun from the ground.

That's when the gunman moved, his hand snaking out as he reached for his weapon.

"He's going for his gun!" Laney cried.

The guy rolled to his side, the gun clutched tightly in his hand, his eyes gleaming.

Grayson shouted Laney's name, tackling her to the ground as the first bullet flew.

A quick succession of returned fire from the officers ended before Laney and Grayson had even hit the ground.

Chapter Fifteen

The rain had subsided, leaving in its place a cold chill that permeated the thick evening air. Grayson felt it to his bones as he led Laney out of the Prince George's County Morgue.

Despite the jacket he'd thrown over her shoulders, she was shivering violently, her teeth chattering as they walked into the parking lot.

He'd managed to keep her from being shot. Barely.

Grayson was worried. With three dead suspects, a probable arsonist on the run, a stolen car and one jailbird refusing to sing, Grayson was pinning his hopes on the idea that the search of David Rallings Jr.'s residence would yield some new clue. "You doing okay?" he asked, and Laney nodded.

"Aside from being half frozen to death, I'm fine."

"I may be able to help you with that," he responded, and she eyed him dubiously.

"If you're talking about a repeat of that hug—"

Her comment was so surprising, he laughed. "I wasn't, but now that you mentioned it, I don't think I'd mind a repeat performance."

"Grayson—"

"Tell you what," he said, reaching Andrews's police cruiser and popping the trunk. "How about we just worry about getting you warm?" The chief had given him the keys and told him that he and Laney could wait in the car. It had been as obvious to him as it had been to Grayson that Laney was at the end of what she could handle. She'd identified the deceased, answered a couple of dozen questions. Now she needed to be bundled up in a blanket and left alone.

Grayson grabbed a blanket from the emergency kit in the back of Andrews's car and wrapped it around her shoulders.

She didn't speak as he opened the passenger door and eased her into the front seat.

"Laney?" He touched her hand. It was ice-cold, her complexion so pallid he was surprised she was still conscious.

"I told you, I'm fine." But her voice broke, and she turned away, a single tear sliding down her cheek.

He closed the door, then walked around the car, slipping into the driver's seat.

Grayson started the car and got the heat going, then turned toward Laney.

"It's okay to cry after you see something like that."

"I'm not crying." She swiped another tear from her cheek.

"Your eyes are just leaking all over your face?"

"Something like that," she responded with a trembling smile.

"Do you want to tell me why?" he asked.

"I like you, Grayson. You know that?"

"You sound surprised."

"Maybe I am. I guess I didn't expect to..." She shrugged.

"What?"

"Ever meet someone who was as passionate about what he does as I am about what I do. You were great tonight. Calm and smart."

"Not smart enough. Both our perps are dead. I wanted to bring them in alive."

"I'd rather have you alive. And me." She shivered and tugged the blanket closer around her shoulders.

"You didn't answer my question," he prodded.

"About why I'm crying? I guess it's because three men are dead. They weren't good men, but they were human beings. And I guess it's also because I'm worried that their deaths mean we'll never find Olivia and the other children."

"It's not your job to find them," he reminded her gently, taking her hands, holding them between both of his, trying to warm them.

"Maybe it is, Grayson. If I had a location, I could take Jax and we could—"

"Laney, you don't have to be the responsible one all the time."

"I don't know how to be any other way," she replied softly.

"How about, just for now, you close your eyes and trust me to take care of the situation? I won't let you down." Even as the words rolled off his tongue, he knew he shouldn't have said them. He couldn't make any promises or guarantees. Not even for a night.

But deep down, he felt the need to say them. He wanted her to feel safe. More than that, he wanted to protect her. The alternative was unthinkable.

Chief Andrews rapped on the glass near Grayson's head, and he opened the door and got out. "Everything taken care of?"

"The medical examiner is getting prints from the deceased. Neither was carrying identification." Andrews looked tired, his eyes deeply shadowed. "I'll get you two back to Laney's place. She needs her rest. I'm afraid you'll have to ride in the back."

"No problem." Grayson slid into the back of the cruiser.

"You have any idea who knew you were coming out here tonight?" Andrews asked as he pulled out of the parking lot.

"Could have been someone at your office. Could have been someone with the FBI. Which means we're right back where we started."

"I just don't get it. The shooter is dead. The accomplice can't be identified through the facial recognition system. And even if we find a match later, the damage is done. Laney's already given us all the information she knows. Why continue to try to harm her?"

"I don't think it's just about Laney anymore. I believe we're getting close to the guy who's calling the shots. He's trying to buy time whatever way possible."

"You could be right," Andrews agreed. "If they can take out the lead investigator and the only material witness to the crime at the same time, the investigation could be set back a day or two."

"Just enough time to get the required number of children needed for the next delivery and stick with the prearranged shipping plans," Grayson said.

"It's also possible there's something significant in Rallings's place. We've got someone looking through his computer files now."

"I'm really hoping you're right, Andrews. But either way, I have a feeling we're on the verge of breaking this case wide open."

* * *

The ride home was short and, thankfully, uneventful. The house was dark as they pulled up to it. A patrol car guarded in the driveway. A black sedan was also in the driveway, its occupants concealed behind tinted windows. The FBI protection detail had arrived.

Laney didn't wait until Grayson and Kent got out of the car. She opened her door and hurried up the front steps. The door opened before she reached it. Arden stood silhouetted in the opening.

"Looks like you lived," she said without preamble.

"Yes. I guess we did." Laney sidled past her, the dogs wagging their tails happily as she entered the house.

"I heard all about it on the news. Crazy stuff. Bullets flying and two people dead. Called the chief to see if you and Grayson were involved. Glad it wasn't you or my brother in those body bags." She retreated to the couch and the laptop, shoving earbuds back in her ears.

Laney left her there. She wasn't in the mood for conversation. She was tired and cold. Thankfully, Rose was in bed, her door closed. Laney crept past the guest room and walked into her own.

Jax followed her, dropping down on the floor near the foot of her bed. She knelt down, putting her arms around his furry neck. He whined softly, and she knew he sensed her mood, felt the same need for action that she did.

"For someone who's nearly frozen, you move fast," Grayson said from the doorway.

"The car ride warmed me up."

"And what didn't get warm from the ride, Jax is taking care of?" He sat down next to her on the floor, his body close enough that she could share his warmth too. "He's a good-looking dog."

"I think so. The pick of the litter, and a gift from a team member." Remembering eight-week-old Jax brought a smile to her face. "Jeremy's mom bred Aussies. Jax's play drive was so good, even at eight weeks old, that Jeremy convinced his mom to let me have him."

"That was a generous thing to do."

"Yes. It was. She still sends me Christmas cards every year, and I send her pictures of Jax on his birthday."

"No pictures for Jeremy?"

"Jeremy died two years ago." She was quiet for a minute after that, thankful that Grayson didn't interrupt the silence, that he let her have the time to pull her thoughts together. It gave her the strength to continue. "We were best friends all through college, and he joined me in search-and-rescue training because he was jealous of the time I spent there. He was the flanker on my team. One of the best I ever had. Later he qualified with his own dog."

"Sounds like a good guy."

"He was."

"And after he died, you didn't want to work search and rescue anymore."

"I didn't, but not just because of him." She hesitated. This wasn't something she spoke about. Ever. But Jax's warm weight rested against her left side and Grayson's warm presence was to her right, and the words just spilled out. "I lost two other team members that day. It shouldn't have happened. We were on a routine search—three hikers had been reported lost on the peak. The conditions were good for a find that day. The temperatures were relatively mild."

It had started like any other search. Working with

local law enforcement, she'd mapped the search sectors based on the victims' supposed area of travel. "Tanya and Lee were Jeremy's flankers that day. Ironically, when I mapped the sectors, I took the steeper, more treacherous sector because Tanya was three months pregnant and tired a little more easily. I was working the east perimeter of my sector, which bordered Jeremy's sector, when I heard the first rumbling echoes of the avalanche. I called a warning to the team and base," Laney's voice broke. "But it happened so fast, not everyone was able to clear the area."

His arm slid around her shoulders, and he pulled her closer to his side. "You can't blame yourself for that."

"I try not to, but there's no one else to blame," she responded, her hand lying on Jax's soft head, her head resting against Grayson's shoulder.

"There is no one to blame. Nature is a hard taskmaster. There isn't a search-and-rescue professional alive who doesn't know it."

He was right. Her head knew it, but her heart was a different story.

Taking a breath, she fought to control her emotions, still raw after all this time. "It's easy to say when it isn't your team. I've heard it from everyone, and I still can't forget that I was the one who put them in that position and that I lived while they died."

"I don't think they would want things to be different," Grayson said, smoothing hair from her cheek, his fingers warm against her skin. "As a matter of fact, if they were standing in your shoes, if they were the ones who'd lived and you'd died, they'd be mourning your loss, wishing they could have taken your place."

"But they aren't here, Grayson," she said, and the tears she'd been holding back spilled out. "I am, and I can still remember every minute of the search, every second that ticked by in my head. I can remember digging them out and trying so desperately to breathe life back into them." Laney wiped the tears from her eyes, but the vivid memory of that day stayed with her, a picture in her mind, unblurred by her tears and not lessened by time.

Grabbing Laney's shoulders, Grayson turned her to face him, pulling her into a silent embrace. The soft scent of rain and pine trees mingled with a hint of aftershave. Relaxing into him, her tears fell freely. Tears for Jeremy, Tanya and Lee. Tears for herself. For the first time, she let someone else share the enormous weight of their deaths. Not just anyone, but Grayson. A stranger to her a mere day ago, yet her life was now inexplicably tied to his.

"Do you think I don't understand?" he asked gently. "After Andrea died, everyone told me it wasn't my fault. That everything would be okay. But the truth is, I knew it wasn't my fault. And yet I couldn't help feeling her safety and well-being were my responsibility. I had promised her forever when I gave her that ring, and we never got a chance to start our lives together— to raise the children she always wanted. It wasn't okay. Her death will never be okay. There will always be a place in my heart for her, and I'll always carry regrets. But I've learned to give them to God. Not to dwell on them. Not to lie in bed at night, reliving that day, playing the 'what if?' game. I've grown stronger through her life and death—Andrea wouldn't have wanted it any other way."

He pulled back and looked into her eyes, gently brushing tears from her cheeks.

"You honor your friends every day by your strength,

your kindness and your life. Let God bear the burden of their deaths while you rejoice in what you shared together. The good times. Not the bad ones."

Looking into his ocean-blue eyes, Laney could almost believe that was possible.

Chapter Sixteen

Morning came quickly. The antique grandfather clock in the corner chimed 6:00 a.m., but a soft clatter from the kitchen and the scent of coffee brewing told Grayson he wasn't the first to wake. Yawning, he rose from the couch and stretched. Some coffee would do him good. He'd had a restless sleep, haunted by nightmares and memories, and by the nagging feeling that he was missing something.

He'd spent a couple of hours looking through his files again, familiarizing himself with every word, making a list of every cataloged clue, every person who'd worked on each case, every interview, hoping that when the originals were faxed to him, it would be easier to pick out deleted information. He'd start making phone calls to Boston and California this morning, both local PD and the original FBI case agents. Hopefully he'd have the files in his hands this afternoon.

In the kitchen, Rose looked up from her task of pouring herself a cup of coffee.

"Here." She held the cup out. "It looks like you need this worse than I do. I'll pour myself another."

"Do I look that rough?"

She laughed, green eyes twinkling. "Well, let's just say you look as if a good, strong cup of coffee and a shower wouldn't hurt."

"Well, what a coincidence, because I was just thinking about both."

"Were you thinking about a slice of coffee cake? I've got some right here."

He hesitated, and she laughed again. "No worries, Gray. It's not homemade."

"I wasn't—"

"Of course you were." She cut a slice of coffee cake and put it on a plate. "Everyone who knows me knows I can't cook. I'm not one to give up, so I keep trying. Plus—" she looked around and lowered her voice "—I love to see the expressions on people's faces when they bite into something I bake. And watching them try to dispose of the food while I'm not looking? Priceless!"

"You're incorrigible, Rose," he said, sipping the coffee and letting the hot, bitter brew wipe away some of his fatigue.

"I am," she responded. "But I like you. So I won't make you eat any more of my homemade treats."

"Do I smell coffee?" Laney came around the corner into the kitchen, dressed in her work gear, hair pulled back in a high ponytail. Jax, Brody and Murphy were at her heels.

"Good morning, love," Rose said cheerfully. "I just made a pot, and I've got coffee cake to go with it. Fresh from Safeway. That sweet little Willow took my car and bought some groceries last night. There are a lot of mouths to feed in this house."

"You're up early, considering you didn't get to bed until after one this morning," Grayson commented as Laney sat at the table.

"You're one to talk," she countered. "You were still clicking away on your computer when I finally dozed off."

He nodded to concede the point. "What are your plans for today?"

"Bria is coming by this morning to help with the dogs. I need to run the board-and-trains through their paces today. I really don't like skipping a training day. I told Riley to take a few days off." Adding a generous portion of cream and sugar to her coffee, she took a sip. "You?"

"Well, after last night's incident, I don't have a car. The FBI is supposed to send me another one when the protection detail shift change occurs. But you're stuck with me until then."

The back door slid open and Arden entered, carting a backpack full of equipment and her laptop. Dropping her bags on the ground by the table, she barely remembered to say hello before starting in. "Is there any coffee cake left, Rose? I tried a piece last night, and it was delicious. Since my brother is a pig when it comes to things like cake, I thought I'd better hurry over before he finished it."

"I'm surprised *you* didn't finish it off last night, Arden," Grayson said as Rose placed a piece of coffee cake on a plate in front of her.

"I would have," Arden said, "but Willow told me she'd cut off both my hands if I touched it again before morning."

"You left for Rose's cottage before Laney and I were done talking, so I didn't get a chance to ask you what you found."

"Well, I haven't identified the hacker yet, but I'm pretty sure he's a hacker for hire."

"How do you know?" Grayson was almost afraid to ask since it was early, and Arden's technical speak could be quite off-putting at times.

"Well, he used some very sophisticated binary obfuscation techniques to prohibit reverse engineering that could identify the original malware commands and potentially lead to his identity. Fortunately for you, I'm familiar with all of the techniques used. Even more fortunately for you, one of the techniques can be traced to only four people in the world."

"How could you possibly know that?"

"Because I created it, and I limited distribution with a signed nondisclosure agreement."

Grayson was starting to get excited—he didn't know much about binary obfuscation or reverse engineering techniques, but he understood that the pool of potential hackers just got a whole lot smaller. "So, are you telling me that we can narrow the hacker down to three people?"

"I'm telling you we can narrow the release of the technique to three people. One could be the hacker, but it is just as feasible that one of them could have sold the technique illegally, in violation of the ten-year nondisclosure agreement."

"Well, that still seems promising."

"It is. I need to analyze my findings this morning, and I should have a name for you early this afternoon."

Getting up from his chair, he hugged Arden, then kissed her on the cheek. "Way to go, kid. I knew you would come through for me." His sister blushed under his public display of affection.

"Don't blow it out of proportion, Gray. You know Mom would kill me if I left you hanging—and Dad might help."

"I love you, too, sis." he countered, winking.

Winking back, she polished off the last bit of her slice of coffee cake. "All that late-night work sure did build up my appetite, Rose. I don't suppose you'd mind giving me another piece of that cake?"

Rose snorted, cutting another slice and placing it on Arden's plate. "Are you ever not hungry, child?"

"No. I don't think so."

Grayson laughed, stretching. "The apple definitely didn't fall far from the tree. Everyone in our family likes to eat. I'm going to hit the shower."

He turned to Laney, leaning down so that he could speak close to her ear. "Wait for me before you head to the kennels. I'll only be a minute."

Grayson's "minute" turned into thirty. Good thing Bria wasn't scheduled to arrive until seven.

Laney sipped her second cup of coffee, picking at the coffee cake that Rose had set in front of her. She wasn't hungry, but she knew she needed to eat. She had a lot to do, and doing it without nourishment would be foolish.

"My brother thinks highly of you," Arden said through a mouthful of toast. "What do you think of him?"

"Not very tactful, are you?" Smiling, Rose sipped her coffee. Then she turned to Laney. "But, since I'm curious, too, I won't chastise you for it."

A blush crept into Laney's cheeks. The answer should be simple, really. She hardly knew Grayson. He was obviously a good agent. A man of strong faith. A solid, dependable person willing to put his life on the line for her. She should feel respect for him—and nothing more.

"Umm… I think he's great?" It came out as a question. Stuffing her mouth with a bite of the coffee cake, Laney hoped to avoid another uncomfortable question.

"Good." Arden smiled with a conspiring glance at Rose.

Laney didn't like the direction she thought this conversation was about to take. It was hard enough to get the upper hand with Aunt Rose, but Laney suspected Arden would give her aunt a run for her money. She was thankful when a knock at the door set the dogs off. She excused herself to answer it.

"Good morning, Laney. Is Grayson up?" Kent asked, stepping into the house.

"He's in the shower."

"Not anymore." Grayson rounded the corner of the hallway, towel-drying his hair and carrying his dirty clothes. "What's up, Andrews?"

"There's been a development. I'm on my way to the scene of a possible kidnapping. The MO is different, but I'm not taking any chances. Deputy Wallace is en route, and I've got units dispatched. We've called in the Greater Maryland Region Search and Rescue Team. Since you're not due to get your replacement vehicle until later this morning, I thought I'd check to see if you want to ride along."

"I'm not sure I'm comfortable leaving Laney here."

"You need to go," Laney cut in. There was no way she wanted him babysitting her when he should be out in the field rescuing an abducted child. "I'll be fine. There are two FBI agents and two officers outside."

Grayson hesitated, then nodded. "Okay. Tell me what the situation is, Andrews."

"A group of fifth graders was on an overnight field trip at Arlington Echo last night. Four kids woke up before their chaperone and snuck out to find some poison ivy to shove in another kid's shoe."

"Nice," Laney said.

"Yeah. Not. One of the kids, ten-year-old Carson Proctor, got separated from his buddies. They were calling to him, trying to help him find the way back, when he started yelling for help. The other kids saw him being carted off into the woods."

"Arlington Echo is more than two hundred acres of forest," Laney said. "The kidnapper was on foot. He could still be out there with the boy. How many resources is the search and rescue team bringing?"

"Unfortunately, they have only two deployable dogs in the state right now. Seems the rest of the team is in New Jersey at the National Search and Rescue Conference. My guys are going to act as flankers since there's no telling if the guy is armed," Kent responded.

"Two dogs are not enough dogs to cover all that ground."

"We're calling other teams in the area, Laney. It's just going to take time to get them here."

"We don't have time," she responded, her heart thudding painfully.

Laney knew what she had to do, but she was almost too scared to say it.

She took a deep breath, thinking about what Grayson had told her. She couldn't keep mourning her team members' deaths. She had to start celebrating their lives. The best way to do it was to carry on with the work they'd been doing when they'd died. "I'm bringing Jax out of retirement."

"Since when?" Grayson asked, his gaze sharp.

"Since right this minute." She opened the hall closet, pulling out an orange Coaxsher search and rescue pack.

"I've got my ready pack here. I just need to fill the water bladder and I'll be set to go." She did it quickly, ignoring her aunt's questioning look and Arden's incessant chatter. Ignoring Grayson's worried look and Kent's excited one.

"Tell Bria I was called away, Aunt Rose. Tell her to feed the dogs. I'll be back when I can."

Laney grabbed a red lead off a hook in the closet.

The situation was critical. They needed to find the child, and the kidnapper, and they needed to do it quickly. Laney was pretty sure that if they missed this opportunity, it might be too late for Olivia and the rest of the children as well.

But she was scared out of her mind, terrified that she'd make a wrong decision, cause someone to be injured or killed.

She had to trust herself.

No. She had to trust God. He'd see her through this.

She wanted to believe that.

She would believe it.

"Jax, come."

Jax darted to her and sat at her feet, immediately giving her all his attention. Fastening the lead on his collar, she looked at Murphy and Brody.

"Sorry, boys, not today." Then she followed Grayson and Kent out to the patrol car.

The patrol-car sirens and lights were blasting as the cruiser sped down Route 2 toward Arlington Echo. The FBI detail was ill-equipped for a search, so they stayed behind to watch for signs of trouble at the house. Laney was quietly looking out the window as the scenery whizzed by. Jax, his head resting on her lap, was sprawled across the backseat. Laney absently petted his silky ears.

Grayson wondered what Laney must be feeling, headed to a search for the first time since the avalanche. From the tension in her face, he guessed whatever she felt, it wasn't good.

They reached Arlington Echo in under ten minutes and pulled into the lot where a table had been set up as a base. To Grayson, the scene looked a little disorganized, perhaps even chaotic. There were children, camp counselors and adult chaperones standing around the perimeter of the woods behind a line of bright orange flagging tape. Men and women in uniform stood near the table and milled around the parking lot.

They were waiting for direction, and apparently Laney planned to be the one to give it.

She jumped out of the car and hurried to the table. She had a compass hanging from her belt, along with a map pouch and a bottle of what looked like baby powder.

It took her about ten seconds to get people organized.

Two other dog handlers were suddenly at the table, photocopied pictures of the missing boy in their hands, listening as Laney explained how they'd sector off the area.

Grayson watched with interest as the dog handlers studied their maps, jotting notes on pads small enough to stuff in the pockets of tactical pants.

Andrews approached the group, giving clear-cut rules for engagement. They weren't just dealing with a missing child. They were dealing with a kidnapper.

The chief gave out the assignments. "Sector one is for team one, composed of Kensington, DeMarco and Reese. Sector two is team two with Collins, Gentry and

Pinkerton. And sector three is team three with Henderson, Graft, Wilfred and Davis. Any questions?"

"Which comms channel will you broadcast from?" The question was asked by a member of the volunteer search and rescue team.

"Set your radios to channel two. Maintain radio silence as much as possible. The suspect doesn't want to be found. If he hears you, he will go into hiding—or worse, he'll go for an attack. You need to be clue-aware, look for fresh tracks, articles of clothing, anything that could belong to our suspect or victim. Okay, unless there are any questions, I need you to get started," Andrews said, dismissing the group.

Grayson made his way over to Laney. She'd spread out her map on the car hood and was marking a point on it. Glancing over her shoulder, he could see she had drawn a circle for base. "Looks like I'm with you," he said.

"Can you find our other team member? I think his name is Reese. I want to go over our search strategy and get started quickly."

"I'm right here." An armed parks and recreation officer approached, a small pack on his back. He introduced himself, "I'm David Reese.

Laney stepped forward, extending her hand. "Pleased to meet you. I'm Laney Kensington. This is Grayson DeMarco. Have you had any prior search experience with dog handlers?'

"No, ma'am, but I've been on wilderness searches before without dogs."

"Good. There are three things to remember. First, don't pet or feed the dog when he's got his vest on. Second, keep up. And third, never get between the dog and the handler. Understand?"

Grayson and Reese nodded.

"Cool." She smiled, and Grayson could see that she was in her element, completely comfortable with what she was doing. "Take a look at this map. This is our sector. We'll check the wind when we get closer, but at first glance I'm inclined to follow this stream, because the terrain is relatively flat compared with the surrounding areas. With a seventy-pound kid in tow, the kidnapper will likely be looking for the path of least resistance." Laney folded the map and put it in her plastic map case, then used her compass to orient her map. "There's bottled water at the base. Both of you grab some. We'll be traveling fast, and you'll become dehydrated quickly. I'll vest up Jax, and we'll get moving."

Chapter Seventeen

It felt like coming home.

Every detail of the preparation, every whiff of pine needles and outdoors, every sound of dogs barking and people calling to one another felt as comfortable as a well-worn cardigan.

Laney led the way through a small clearing, moving into the tree line and the edge of their sector. She knew where they were heading, but she paused there to orient her map once more.

Beside her, Jax was visibly excited. He knew this wasn't just training. He always knew. She'd never been sure if it was because he was so in touch with her moods, but Jax's entire demeanor was different on a real search than during a training exercise.

She bent over, scratching him between the ears. "We're about to start, buddy. Just need to do one thing first."

Shrugging the pack from her back, she dug into the front pocket, pulling out a Leatherman.

"What are you doing?" Grayson asked, leaning over her as she opened the knife.

"I need to cut the bells off Jax's vest. They'll give

him away if the kidnapper is in our sector. Jax works fast and he ranges, so he'll be out of our sight sometimes. I use the bells to help me keep track of the direction he's traveling and the area he's covered. This time, we'll work without them." She sliced off the bells and stuffed them deep into her pack. Finally they were ready.

Her pulse raced, her heart tripping all over itself.

This might be like coming home, but that didn't mean she wasn't nervous about it. She took a deep breath, removed Jax's lead and placed that in her pack as well.

"Are you ready, Jax?"

He snuffed his agreement, tail wagging his excitement.

"Go find!"

At the search command, Jax was off, into the woods and out of sight.

Laney took off after him, Grayson and Reese two steps behind.

The trees offered plenty of shade from the early October sun, but the Maryland humidity was heavy, and it was tough navigating through the dense, thorny underbrush. They'd walked less than three minutes before coming upon the stream that served as a natural border for their sector. Jax was relentless in his work, making large circles around handler and flankers, nose to the air as they moved quickly forward, Laney leading them on with quiet confidence. Grayson was amazed at the speed at which they were covering ground.

But he was still worried that they weren't moving fast enough.

The kidnapper was on the run. It had been nearly forty minutes; if he was not already out of the woods, he was nearing the road, slowed only by what must feel like the growing weight of a child. After all, seventy pounds of dead weight would be challenging for anyone to cart through brush and over uneven ground as the heat and humidity of the day settled in the woods. Surely he would have to stop and rest.

Of course, if he had a weapon, he'd likely be forcing the child to walk through the woods himself, but then they'd have to go at the pace of a frightened ten-year-old.

Laney put her hand up. "Wait."

Grayson and Reese stopped dead in their tracks.

Laney's complete focus was on Jax.

"What is it?" Grayson asked

"He's caught scent. It's faint—I can tell he can't pinpoint the origin." Laney pulled her GPS from the large pocket of her cargo pants, "I'm marking the spot where Jax first showed interest." She released white powder from her puff bottle into the air. "The wind is pushing the scent across the creek. It's hitting the side of this hill and circling up. Scent forms a cone of sorts, stronger near the person and weakening as it gets further away, but sometimes the air movement can push it into a barrier where it gets trapped, leaving a heavy scent pool with no subject. This is when the handler has to read the dog and use whatever scent theory they know, and try to work out where the subject might actually be."

"What are you thinking?" Grayson asked. Could the kidnapper be somewhere close by, hiding until they passed?

"I think he's either picked up the kidnapper and victim, or he's picked up the scent of another dog team working the other side of the stream." Reaching for her radio, she called base.

"Go ahead, team one."

"Permission to go direct with team two."

"Team one, you have the frequency."

"Team two from team one."

"Go ahead, team one."

"Jax is picking up scent on the border of my sector. It's faint. Judging by the air current, my best guess is it's coming from across the stream in your sector. Are you working the vicinity?"

"Negative, team one. We're at the west end of our sector, near the lake."

"Copy. To be sure he's not picking up our victim or the perp, I'm going to cross the stream to see if the scent pool is stronger. I'll probably go about fifty meters in. If he picks up scent, I'll follow. If not, I'll return to my sector. I'll let you know when I've left the area."

"Copy, team one."

Holstering her radio, she backtracked about fifteen paces, checking the wind, then headed to the stream.

"Jax, this way." Looking over her shoulder, she gestured to Grayson and Reese. "Guys, stay close. Keep your eyes and ears open. My gut is telling me someone is across the stream, just upwind of us. Could be a random hiker, but one thing is certain. It's not a member of the search team."

Grayson and Reese followed single file behind Laney and Jax as they crossed the ankle-deep stream. The water, somewhat cloudy after the rain, moved swiftly over slippery rocks and a muddy stream bed.

Jax paused, lapping up some of the cool water. Bending down, Laney splashed the water under his belly. "Okay, this way Jax, go find!"

Jax paused, his head popped up in interest, nose to the wind, and he was off. Laney went after him, keeping up a fast jog over uneven ground, dodging tree branches and ripping away from thorny brush that reached out to grab her as she passed. Unencumbered by a pack, Grayson stayed on her heels. Reese fell back slightly, Laney's pace combined with the weight of his pack proving too much for him.

For a moment they lost sight of Jax. Laney stopped abruptly, motioning for them to do the same. The distant sound of the dog jumping quickly through the brush was met with another sound.

Something large was moving in the same general direction.

All at once, the second movement stopped, and the distinct sound of the dog running toward them grew closer.

Standing stock-still, Laney waited. Seconds later, Jax bounded into view, tongue lolling, ears back, at a full sprint. Launching himself in the air, straight at Laney, his front paws hit her in the torso before he landed in front of her, tail wagging.

"Show me!" Laney commanded, and Jax quickly started off again.

All three raced after Jax, crashing through the vegetation, jumping over downed branches. But there was no way they could keep up with the agile little Australian shepherd. It seemed to Grayson that Jax was well aware of this. He constantly circled back, ensuring Laney was right behind him.

Bursting through thick underbrush into a clearing, Jax stopped, then began circling the area—nose to the wind, taking in short quick snuffs of air.

"Grayson." Laney's voice was hushed. "The subject was here, but has moved. He's likely hiding. Jax is trained for this scenario—we sometimes see it with lost children and Alzheimer's patients. They are found by the dog and then move before we can get to them."

Fascinated, Grayson watched Jax work. The dog sniffed the ground, the trees, the air, looking for the scent. Even untrained, Grayson could tell when he found it. His head popped up again and his tail fanned out. In a flash, he was off. They followed him through a particularly thick stand of trees and brush and watched as he approached a large downed tree, its exposed roots jutting out, nearly four feet high in places.

A perfect hiding place.

Scampering up the downed trees limbs, Jax was quickly up and over the obstacle. Laney seemed poised to follow, but Grayson grabbed her arm, jerking her back toward him. He was about to have her call Jax back when a shot rang out.

Was Jax shot? Was he hurt, confused? Looking for her?

She had to get to him. Laney tried to shrug free of Grayson's grip, but he held tight as he ordered Reese to drop his pack.

Movement in the brush to their left had Grayson pushing Laney to the side, drawing his weapon. Bursting through the brush, Jax rushed forward, intent on indicating the re-find.

She hated to do it, but for his own safety, she gave the emergency stop command using the hand signal and whispering, "Halt."

His stop was immediate. He dropped to the ground in a down position.

Tapping her chest twice, her silent recall signal, she motioned Jax to her.

Once Jax was by her side, the reality of the situation

hit her hard. There was someone on the other side of the log, and he was armed.

Reese had dropped his pack and unholstered his weapon. Grayson drew them in a close circle, whispering, "Laney, mark our coordinates on your GPS, then take Jax back through the stand of trees. Move quickly and make noise as you go. When you reach the stream, take cover and call base for backup. Reese, you circle around the fallen tree as quietly as you can from the left. I'll take the right. Don't be seen. Try to get in a position where you can see the shooter—when Laney is out of earshot, he may make a run for it. Be ready."

Reese nodded.

Laney turned to go, but Grayson grabbed her arm and pulled her close. "Don't come back until I call you."

She nodded her understanding, but he didn't let her go. His gaze was dark, his ocean-blue eyes filled with concern.

He cupped her cheek, his fingers rough and a little cool. "Be careful, okay?"

She swallowed down words that she knew she shouldn't say, words about friendship, about connection, about wanting to know that this wouldn't be the last time she'd ever see him.

"You, too," she whispered to his back as he quietly headed for the downed tree.

She headed in the opposite direction, crashing through the underbrush.

"Jax, come!" she yelled, and the dog followed.

She reached the other side of the trees, took cover behind a giant oak and called for backup, providing the coordinates to base. Her voice shaking, she made sure the other dog teams understood they should stand down and stay away from the sector.

"Laney?" Kent's voice came over the radio.

"Go ahead, Kent."

"We have four officers stationed on the road in your vicinity—we're sending them in now. Stay where you are until they get to you."

They arrived quickly, slipping through the woods almost silently. Only Jax's soft huff of anxiety warned her before they appeared.

"Where's the perp?" a tall, dark-eyed man asked. She was sure she'd seen him before, had probably worked with him at some point.

"Follow me, and be as quiet as possible." Laney led the officers around the thickest part of the brush in an attempt to keep down the noise. They followed her one by one, in silence. She stopped, the fallen tree fifty feet in front of their location, roots snaking out four feet in every direction, ensnared with thick underbrush. Turning to them, she whispered, "The suspect is holed up behind that downed tree." She pointed. "Agent DeMarco went to the right, Officer Reese to the left. They intended to get a visual of the suspect and wait for backup."

"Okay. We've got it from here. I want you to take cover behind that stand of trees, then radio base that we are here and in position."

Laney nodded. Then the officer in charge turned to his guys. "Radio silence from this point on." Several of the officers turned their handheld radios off.

Laney crept to the stand of trees, finding a hiding place under a particularly thick bush. Then she called base, confirming the team's position. Motioning Jax to sit by her, she absently petted his head while she waited for something to happen. Anything.

Suddenly a voice broke the silence. Grayson's voice.

"This is the FBI. You're surrounded. Throw out your weapon and release the child."

"I'll kill the kid if you come any closer."

"Not before we kill you, so how about you make it easy on yourself? Send the boy out!" Grayson's last statement was met by a warning shot from the suspect.

It was then that Laney noticed the brush moving near the bottom of the fallen tree, where thick weeds and saplings were growing up around it. Could there be another way for the suspect to get out? If so, Grayson and the other officers were not in a position to see the suspect escape. Seconds later, a blond head popped out.

A child's tear-streaked face appeared as the boy pushed through the thick brush. Giving Jax the signal to stay, she grabbed her Leatherman out of her pack and opened it. She eased across the space that separated her from the tree and saw the boy's eyes widening with surprise as he spotted her. Holding a finger to her lips, she signaled him to stay quiet as he came out of the opening under the tree and stood. An adult's tanned hand was visible through the brush, grasping the boy's ankle. Laney readied herself, watching the brush move, the leaves rustle.

Was she the only one who noticed the movement?

Suddenly, the kidnapper's head and other hand pushed through the opening. That hand grasped a gun. He never released his hold in the boy's ankle as he snaked through the brush. The child stood still, blue eyes wide with fright, trained on her. Laney didn't intend to let the kidnapper make it out from under the tree. She took two steps closer and stomped with all her might on his hand.

He cursed, the gun dropping from his slack hand.

She kicked it away and grabbed the boy's arm, yanking him from the kidnapper.

"Run!" she screamed.

Chapter Eighteen

Hoisting himself quickly to the top of the downed tree, Grayson could scarcely believe what he was seeing. Hadn't he told her to stay by the creek? To wait in safety until he called her? She hadn't, and she was about to be taken down by a guy who looked like he'd gladly drag the knife from her hand and use it to slit her throat.

Grayson scrambled over the tree and tackled the guy as he lunged for Laney and the boy.

They all went down in a heap, tangled in weeds and thorny brush.

The guy was big. Maybe six-foot-four, muscular.

And angry.

He pushed himself to his knees and threw a punch; Grayson dodged it, the man's knuckles barely grazing his jaw. Grayson managed to land a well-placed blow to the man's cheek. The guy fell backward, knocking into Laney as she scrambled to her feet, grabbing the boy under the arm to drag him from the fray.

She stumbled. Falling to her knees, she shoved the boy out of reach. The kidnapper's arm shot out and grabbed Laney's calf. She tried unsuccessfully to kick him off while Grayson punched the guy in the back.

The man cursed but didn't relinquish his hold on Laney. He yanked her toward him across the brush like a rag doll. Grayson heard Laney gasp. Her chest hit the ground first, knocking the wind out of her.

Grayson landed a quick blow to the perp's head, and then another. Other than a faint grunt, there was no acknowledgment that the hits had any effect on the guy. Behind Grayson, the other officers were crashing through the brush to help.

The man relentlessly dragged Laney toward him, ignoring the kicks from her free leg.

Grabbing the guy in a choke hold, Grayson yanked him backward. Still he refused to release Laney.

Laney looked up, meeting Grayson's gaze over the perp's shoulders. He recognized the anger and determination he saw there. Without warning, she sliced her pocketknife across the guy's hand. With a howl, he let go of her leg.

She scrambled away and rushed to the boy, who stood watching wide-eyed by a tree. Grayson tightened his grip around the guy's neck. Reese nudged in beside Grayson, taking cuffs from his belt. He snapped them onto the suspect's wrists and pulled him to his feet.

"Hey! That crazy chick cut my hand! I need a medic!" the perp howled.

"You'll get one." *Eventually*, Grayson thought, but he didn't say it.

He was too busy striding to Laney's side, taking the knife from her hand. "Are you nuts?" he nearly shouted. "You could have gotten yourself killed!"

"What was I supposed to do?" she asked, touching the hair of the little boy who was clinging to her waist, his head buried against her abdomen. "Let the guy escape with Carson?"

"What you were supposed to do was stay away," he reminded her. "Until I told you differently."

"If she had," the boy said, shooting Grayson a dark look, "she couldn't have rescued me."

"I didn't rescue you. Jax did," Laney said. "Want to meet him?"

"Who's Jax?" Carson asked.

"I'll show you. Jax, come," Laney called, and the dog bounded out from the underbrush.

"He's so cool!" Carson dropped to his knees to pet Jax, his face suddenly animated. "When we saw the dog the first time, that guy made me hide under that tree with him so the dog wouldn't know where we went. He said I had to stay quiet or he'd kill me."

Grayson kneeled on the ground next to Carson. "So you did what he said, right?"

Nodding, Carson hugged Jax. "I was afraid of him. He was mean. He tried to shoot the dog, but I hit his arm so he would miss."

Laney went to her knees too, enveloping the boy and dog in a big bear hug. "Thank you for saving Jax."

"I knew Jax was good. We learned about search dogs in Boy Scouts. I knew he would bring me help, and he did."

"Yep, he did his job well. Now he gets his reward. Do you want to help me give it to him?" Laney asked.

"Sure, what is it?"

She pulled out two orange balls, squeaking them.

Jax turned toward the sound, ready to run.

"He gets playtime with his favorite toy for a job well done."

She chucked the ball as far as she could, and they both laughed as Jax rushed forward, jumping up and snatching it out of the air before it hit the ground.

Squeaking it in his mouth, the dog returned, dropping the ball at her feet as she launched the next one in the air.

"Grab that ball, Carson, and throw it as soon as he brings the other back—let's see who gets tired first, him or us!"

Grayson was betting on the two of them, since the ball of energy that was Jax showed no sign of stopping anytime soon.

Watching the woman who would likely never fail to surprise him, laughing and playing with the dog and the boy in the midst of what should have been a very traumatic day for all, Grayson realized Laney's affinity for dogs translated to children as well. Her fearless confidence and her empathy for the helpless attracted both to her. And right now, with this boy, she was managing to single-handedly end his bad day on a good note.

Although there were many people who had worked together to find and rescue Carson, Laney and her hero dog Jax would stay with the boy always. As he grew older and recounted this story, Laney would always be in it. His own fearless protector.

Funny. Grayson's story about the day would be the same.

Empty of the million little details that had made the rescue successful, and filled with hundreds of images of a woman he knew he would never forget.

Noon, and Laney was exhausted.

She should probably get up from the porch rocker and go inside, but she was too tired to move. Grayson and Kent were a few feet away, talking to the two FBI agents assigned to her protection detail for the next few days. The sun had grown warmer, but dark clouds rolled in on a humid breeze, threatening rain.

Tonight would mark forty-eight hours missing for Olivia.

Two days of tracking one clue after another, but never seeming to get closer to the answers they needed to bring Olivia home. Laney was frustrated, irritated, antsy to see progress made on the case.

She had sensed some frustration in Grayson, as well. He hadn't been happy that the kidnapper's interrogation had been put on hold to treat his hand. Laney was sorry that the interrogation would have to wait, but she couldn't say she completely regretted the bone-crushing stomp to his hand that had apparently broken two fingers. She didn't regret cutting him, either. He'd deserved it, and worse, as far as she was concerned. She only hoped that Grayson and Kent would be able to uncover some link between this kidnapping and the others.

One thing was certain. Today's kidnapper was not the same man who took Olivia.

Kent and Grayson came up the porch stairs, the two FBI agents right behind them. "Laney, if it's okay with you, we'd like to use your house to have the FBI agents work with Arden and me on reviewing some of the case files that were faxed over this afternoon...the more eyes the better," Kent said.

"Make yourselves at home," she responded, gesturing to the front door.

The three other men walked inside.

Grayson stayed put, his gaze on Laney.

"You don't really think I'm going to leave you out here alone, do you?" he asked.

"I was hoping."

"Tired of all the people in your house?" He reached for her hand, tugging her to her feet.

"Tired, period." She would have stepped away, but he pulled her closer, looked straight into her eyes.

"From the search?"

"From everything."

"Was it hard?" He traced a line from her ear to the corner of her jaw, his hand sliding down and resting on her nape. He kneaded the tense muscles there.

"Stopping the kidnapper?" she asked, her mind more on his touch than on his questions.

"Going back to search and rescue."

"It was as easy as taking my next breath," she admitted, and he smiled.

"I thought it would be."

He opened the door and let her walk inside ahead of him. They followed the sound of voices into the dining room.

Arden was there, Kent and the two FBI agents a few feet away, watching as she systematically stacked documents on the table.

Arden placed the last piece of paper in the pile and finally looked up.

"There. I've organized these records by date and placed the original records we received today via fax in front of the records Grayson downloaded from his system. This is how I propose we tackle the review." She was interrupted by Grayson's phone.

He glanced at his caller ID and frowned. "Excuse me, everyone. I need to take this call."

Laney watched him walk away and fought the urge to follow. It still bothered her that she was relying on him so completely, but not as much as it might have a couple of days ago. She realized now it was okay to accept help when needed. And deep down, she knew she would be all right when he was gone. Even though a small part of her would be sad to see him go, she would always be grateful for what he'd done. Not just protecting her, but helping her get back to the person she wanted to be.

She'd taken the first step in moving on. She'd brought herself and Jax out of retirement. Maybe it was time to take the next step and join another search and rescue team here in Maryland. When this was over, she'd have to thank Grayson for helping her remember that some things were worth fighting for.

"DeMarco," Grayson said, pressing the phone to his ear. If it had been anyone else, he wouldn't have taken the call, but it was Ethan, and Grayson would do anything for his friend.

"Gray, its Ethan. How are things going?"

"We might have something to go on. We stopped a kidnapping today. The perp will be brought in for questioning after he's released from the hospital."

"Do you have evidence that he's connected to the other kidnappings?"

"No."

"Could be coincidental."

"You know how rare stranger abductions are, Ethan."

"I do, but rare doesn't mean they don't happen," Ethan responded, a sharp edge to his voice. That surprised Grayson. In the years he'd known Ethan, he'd never known the man to be short-tempered or impatient.

"Either way, I have to look at every possibility."

"Right." Ethan laughed it off, any hint of impatience suddenly gone. "I actually didn't call to argue. I wanted to let you know it will likely be another day before I can get to the Maryland precinct—Judith's brother's in town, and she needs me to hang around and play host. If you can send me records, I can start to go through them for you."

"We've got a group of people comparing the hard copies with the electronic files I've been working with for months—I can have someone scan them in and send them to you if you think you'll have a chance to look at them."

"I'll make the time, Gray. Send them my way when you can."

"Thanks, Ethan, I'll talk to you soon." Grayson disconnected, less satisfied with the conversation than he usually was when he spoke to Ethan for some reason he couldn't quite define.

He shook off the unease, walking back into the dining room and taking a seat next to Laney.

"Great. You're here," Arden said. "Ready to work?" She handed him a stack of files. "This is our West Coast file."

Grayson started skimming the reports. Everything matched up until he reached the fifth page. There he found a name he hadn't seen before.

Ethan Conrad. Called in for consultation.

That's what the file said.

Why had Ethan failed to mention the consulting services to Grayson? Could there be a simple explanation? Maybe. But it didn't seem possible that he'd just forgotten. Even if he had, why was the information in one file and not the other? "Who has the original Boston files, months one and two?" he asked.

"I've got them," Kent said.

"Was any consulting company listed in the reports?"

"Not a company, but a man was mentioned. It was an FBI profiler, I think…here it is, Ethan Conrad."

Grayson skimmed the page, comparing this entry to the California entry.

Arden looked up at the mention of Ethan's name, catching Grayson's eye. "Ethan consulted on both those cases?"

"Yes. And that information was deleted from the doctored files."

"What about here in Maryland?"

Grayson grabbed the Maryland files, skimming them for Ethan's name, relieved when he didn't find it. Perhaps there was a legitimate reason for Ethan's involvement. "Nothing in Maryland."

But then, Grayson thought, there was no need to consult here in Maryland. Grayson had discussed the case at length with Ethan after taking over for the agents in Boston at Ethan's recommendation.

They talked almost daily, about everything. Ethan was a sounding board. A trusted advisor.

Could he also be a callous criminal?

Grayson's mind raced. He'd known Ethan for years, trusted him like family. There had to be another explanation.

Kent Andrews's phone rang.

He answered, his gaze focused on Grayson.

He was going to have to share his suspicions with Andrews. He had no choice. He had to run this lead down. If Ethan was innocent, he'd understand.

Andrews's phone conversation took less than a minute. When it was over, he smiled. "Good news, Grayson. We finally have a jailbird that's ready to sing."

"The suspect is talking?"

"Not just talking, singing like a jaybird! He said he was paid five grand to snatch a kid."

"Who paid him?" Grayson asked.

"A guy he met while incarcerated—David Rallings Jr."

"So our floater paid him to snatch a kid…"

"Yep, and deliver the kid to an access road near Camp Cone."

"Camp Cone is up there near Glenn Arm, isn't it?" Laney asked.

Grayson didn't answer.

He was too busy thinking, reaching a horrible and inevitable conclusion.

He'd spent a lot of summers at Camp Cone. He knew it well. The property was a little wild, a little rugged. He'd hunted squirrel there, hunted turkey, done all the things young boys liked to do.

And he'd done them all with Rick, because the property they spent their summers on, the little cabin where they used to stay, it belonged to Rick's parents. It belonged to Ethan.

He stood, pushing away from the table with so much force, his chair toppled over.

"Grayson?" Laney stood, touched his arm. "Are you okay?"

"It's pretty difficult to be okay when you've just realized that you've been betrayed by one of your most trusted friends."

"What do you mean?" Kent asked.

"Ethan Conrad owns property near Camp Cone."

Kent frowned, glancing at the report he still held. "The former FBI profiler? The same one who's listed as a consultant in these files?"

"He's not just listed there." Grayson set his paper down and pointed to the name. "He's listed here, too. But his name was taken out of the reports when they were tampered with. The hacker didn't want us to know that he was involved."

"Anyone else find his name in a report?" Kent asked.

"It's here," Laney said quietly.

He didn't have time to feel sorry for himself. Didn't have time to sit around moping. Ethan was one of the most intelligent men he knew, but even intelligent men made mistakes. "There's a cabin on Ethan's property, and an outbuilding used for hunting—either of those would be the perfect place to keep a bunch of kids," he said. "Arden, can you print me out a few topographical maps of the Glen Arm/Camp Cone area? And Kent, we'll need a search warrant to go on private property."

"I'll make some calls."

"How long do you think it will take?"

"A few hours? Maybe a day, tops—if we can convince them it's necessary."

"That's a long time if you're one of the kids he's kidnapped."

"I'll try to put a rush on it," Kent assured him.

"Good." Grayson glanced at the name, felt fury clogging his throat. "Because I suspect we found our leak, and the sooner we plug it, the happier I'll be."

Chapter Nineteen

Later that evening, after poring through files with Arden and the FBI agents, Laney retreated to her room, claiming exhaustion.

Earlier, Kent had gone to the precinct to see if he could call in some favors and help expedite a warrant on Ethan's property. Grayson was trying a different tactic. He'd driven away over an hour ago, determined to convince a reluctant judge to issue a search warrant.

He'd left Laney behind.

Grayson had thought it would be safer.

It would have been. If she'd actually intended to stay there.

Low voices and murmurs of activity carried down the hall to her room. Rose was clanging in the kitchen while the others worked in the dining room. Laney carefully removed the screen from her bedroom window. When she was done, she retrieved her small search-and-rescue day pack from the floor beside her bed, shoved a pilfered topographical map of Camp Cone in it, then turned off the light, dropping the pack out the window to the ground. Grabbing her work cell phone from the charger on the dresser, she shoved it into her cargo pants pocket. The sun had just set below the horizon. The grass was damp from the late afternoon showers.

Laney's heart raced. Climbing onto the windowsill, she dropped to the grass. The night was quiet. So far, so good.

Laney knew Grayson would not approve of her intent to give her FBI and MPD babysitters the slip.

She also knew that the chance of Grayson getting a warrant on a respected, retired FBI agent based on the circumstantial evidence they'd collected was slim. She'd heard the agents talking about it being a pipe dream that a warrant would be provided in time to rescue the kids.

But Laney understood law enforcement and probable cause. If she and Jax happened to be hiking in the area and came upon something that could point to the children, Grayson would have all the probable cause he needed for an official search.

She was determined to make sure that happened.

Olivia's life was at stake.

Shrugging the pack onto her back, she whistled twice. She heard the soft pad of Jax's feet in the yard behind the house before he raced around the corner and sat attentively in front of her. "Good boy," she whispered. Patting her thigh twice, the signal for heel, she started off at a quick jog. Jax kept pace by her side. Laney ran through the trees, sticking close to the edges of the woods.

She needed to get to Aunt Rose's house and borrow her car.

Rose kept the keys to her 1974 Hornet hatchback on a peg in the garage. So as long as the keys were there, borrowing the car would be easy. Laney just hoped the Hornet would make the hour-long drive to Camp Cone. As far as she knew, Willow was the first person to drive the car in months, and she'd taken a five-minute drive to the grocery store.

Of course, it was a bit premature to worry about the car breaking down when she first needed to get into the garage. Laney was counting on finding the spare house key in its usual spot—buried in the topsoil under the decorated stone turtle in the back flower bed. Hurrying across the well-manicured back yard, she found the turtle right where she'd expected it to be. Beside her, Jax's ears perked up, standing at alert. His eyes watched the corner of the house. Someone was coming.

She jumped back into the shadows. There was no time to get the key. The soft sound of footsteps on the grass grew closer. "Laney?" As usual, Aunt Rose's whisper was scarcely a decibel under a yell.

"Shh!" Laney responded quickly. "Aunt Rose, what are you doing out here?" she hissed.

"Looking for you, of course." Reaching in her pocket, she pulled out a car key on a small fuzzy dice keychain. "I thought you might need this."

"How'd you know I was here—and why on earth are you carrying around a key to a car you can't legally drive?"

Aunt Rose planted her hands on her hips. "First of all, after the last break-in, I didn't want to leave the key where it could be so easily found—James is a classic, you know?" James, of course, referred to Rose's car. As Rose told the story, she'd purchased it the summer after her husband Peter died, because they'd watched James Bond together and he'd been fascinated by the aerial flip the car performed in the movie. Thankfully Rose had not yet attempted to duplicate that flip.

"Secondly," Rose continued, "I heard Gray and Kent talking to those agents, too. I'm not deaf, you know. As soon as I heard that they probably didn't have enough evidence to get a warrant, I knew exactly what you were going to do."

Lifting the stone turtle, Rose buried her fingers in the dirt below, coming up with the spare key to the garage. She absently wiped the dirt off on her pants. "Here you go."

"Does this mean you approve of the plan?" Laney asked, unlocking the garage and opening it.

Rose shook her head and sighed. "I'm not saying it's the smartest thing to do, mind you, but I know I won't be able to talk you out of it. You have too much of the Travis blood in you. Much more than your mama ever did, God rest her soul."

Taking the keys, Laney embraced her aunt. "Thanks, Aunt Rose."

"Honey, I know you've always worried that you might end up like your mother, but even as a girl, your mama was never strong. Not like you."

Shaking her head vehemently, Laney argued, "I'm not strong, I just try to do what needs to be done."

"Because you have an inner strength, girl. The grit and moxie your mom never had—that comes from here and here." She pointed to her head then her heart.

"Mom did her best."

"No doubt, but she married the wrong man."

"I know, and the sad thing is, I can see how it happened. My father could be a real charmer at times—you just never know what lies underneath."

"Laney, I think deep down you know that's not true. Some men are exactly as they seem. For instance, your grandfather—my brother—and my own husband."

"I'm sorry I never got a chance to meet Uncle Peter."

"Me, too, but I won't romanticize him—he was far

from perfect. God knows none of us are perfect. But he tried to live God's plan for his life. That one simple act of faith made him perfect for me. Maybe you'll find the same to be true with Grayson."

"Aunt Rose, Grayson and I are just…" What were they? Working together? Friends? At times it seemed she'd known him forever. But really, did she know him at all?

"You can protest all you want, but you can't deny the attraction. But don't you think on it now. God's plan will unfold in its own time." She gave Laney a quick hug. "Give me two minutes before you start the car. I'll distract them with my new batch of grandma's whoopie pies."

"I love you, Aunt Rose."

"I know, and I love you, too."

Opening the car door, Laney motioned Jax inside. "Jax, place." Tail wagging, he hopped into the car.

Pausing at the entrance of the garage, Aunt Rose looked back over her shoulder. "Be careful, Laney. And leave the lights off until you get to the end of our drive. That's what I always do." Grinning, she was gone.

Grayson wasn't happy. He'd just left the judge's house—*without* a search warrant for Ethan's property. Despite the case Grayson had presented, the judge reasoned that Ethan appeared to have been a legitimate paid consultant on the cases, and that those records could have been doctored by anyone to cast the blame on Ethan. Furthermore, Camp Cone was a public park, backing up to several private properties, and since there was no evidence directly linking Ethan to any of the victims or suspects, the probable cause was not there.

The judge sympathized but told Grayson he needed to make a stronger case for a warrant to be issued.

Grayson had a decision to make. He could follow the rules and keep searching for more substantial evidence to link Ethan to the crimes, or he could search the property himself, perhaps finding the kids, but knowing that anything he found couldn't be used in a court of law.

For the first time in his life, Grayson was thinking about breaking the law.

There had to be a way around this. There must be a way to rescue the kids and still bring Ethan to justice.

Ethan, who'd recommended Grayson for the case in the first place, then used his relationship with Grayson to monitor the progress the bureau was making and plan his next move. Grayson tamped down his fury. Rage wasn't going to help him figure things out. It wasn't going to make things easier. He needed to stay calm and cool-headed if he was going to beat Ethan at his own game.

And that must be what this was to his mentor—a money-making game that he had been playing and winning for far too long.

What was worse, logic dictated that this wasn't Ethan's first venture into organized crime. Grayson wondered when Ethan had turned. Had Rick's death sent him over the edge? Or worse, could he have had something to do with Rick's death? And Andrea's?

The thought turned his blood cold. Grayson had always wondered how Ethan had wrapped up the case of Rick's murder so quickly, so cleanly. The perpetrators had died trying to keep from being taken into custody, and there'd been no one to interrogate. There was no telling how deep Ethan's betrayal ran, but Grayson wanted the chance to ask him.

His cell phone vibrated. Kent's name and number scrolled across the dashboard display. He grabbed the phone, his hand shaking with the force of his anger. "DeMarco here."

"Laney's gone. She took one of the topo maps and Jax with her."

"What? How? There are four armed law enforcement officers at the house, and her Jeep is still in the impound lot!"

"She snuck out through her bedroom window while the FBI agents were in the kitchen with your sister and Rose. They were going through the case files, and she said she needed to lie down—"

"That should have been their first clue that she was up to something!" he snapped.

"Don't shoot the messenger, DeMarco," Andrews bit out. They were both tense, both disappointed with the judge's decision regarding the search warrant.

"The good news is," Grayson said, trying to calm himself down, "she couldn't have gone far without a vehicle."

"You're assuming she doesn't have one."

"Where would she get…" Grayson paused, realizing just how easy he and everyone else had made Laney's escape. "Rose."

"Rose admits to handing over the keys to her '74 Hornet hatchback, then distracting my officers with a plate full of whoopie pies and milk. Both of my guys are now complaining of stomach pains. I swear she's a menace with the baked goods."

Grayson's grip tightened on the steering wheel. "I'm not sure I care about your officers' stomach problems. How long ago did Laney leave?"

"She's been gone about ninety minutes."

"She's had more than enough time to get to the Camp Cone area, then. Has anyone heard from her since?"

"No. I tried to call her work cell. No answer."

Grayson banged the steering wheel, his frustration making him reckless. "What was she thinking?"

"According to Rose, Laney went to get us our probable cause."

That wasn't what Grayson wanted to hear. It wasn't what he wanted to think about. Laney and Jax searching Ethan's property couldn't lead to anything good.

"I just left the judge's house," he growled. "I can be at Ethan's property in less than fifteen minutes. I'm turning around now."

"I'm on my way with two patrol cars. We'll be there in thirty minutes, tops."

Disconnecting the call, Grayson tried Laney's work phone. Straight to voice mail.

He drove faster than he should have, faster than was prudent, speeding toward Camp Cone. Dozens of memories flashed through his head. All the times Ethan had seemed interested, concerned, helpful, he'd been playing Grayson for a fool.

He managed to make it to Camp Cone Road in thirteen minutes. It wove through an older, established neighborhood and dead-ended at the park entrance, where visitors could gain free public access during park hours. Grayson was betting that Laney would pick that as her entry point.

The access gate would have been locked at sunset, but Laney could easily have parked in the small lot and walked in. From there, she'd have to navigate about twenty acres of heavily wooded parkland to get to the boundary of Ethan's property.

Remembering how quickly and easily Laney and

Jax had navigated the trees and brush during the morning's search, he was confident that she was well within Ethan's property line already. He was equally confident that he was ill-equipped to trail her through the woods.

No, he'd need to take the direct approach. He'd enter the property through Ethan's driveway and have a look around. At this point, he had no other choice.

The conditions were perfect. Temperature mild. A light, consistent breeze. Jax was definitely in scent. According to the compass and topographic map, they were less than fifty meters north of a man-made structure, possibly the hunting cabin that Grayson had mentioned. According to the map, it bordered the southern corner of Ethan Conrad's property. Laney decided that direction was as good as any to start. After all, if Ethan was hiding three children on the property, he'd need a secure place to keep them—a building away from the main house would be the best bet.

Laney didn't use a flashlight and did not turn on the lights on Jax's vest. Luckily, the night sky was clear, the almost full moon illuminating the woods. Jax's head popped up, and he stopped, nose to the wind. Over the light wind rustling through the trees, Laney thought she heard voices.

"Jax, come," she whispered. For a second Laney thought he wouldn't listen; she could see the reluctance as he looked at her, as if to say, "But the human is right there! Just a few more steps."

Laney touched her open hand to her chest, reinforcing her voice command with the hand recall command. This time Jax came.

"Heel," she said softly. They made their way slowly through the trees in the direction of the voices. The edge of the tree line was heavy with thick brush that made silence difficult. Jax moved through it easily, but Laney's clothing and hair caught on branches that snapped as she pulled away. Hidden within the tree line, she could just make out the outline of a very small, old outbuilding. Perhaps a one-room hunting cabin or large shed. If there were windows, she couldn't see them on the wall that faced her. No door, either, so she had to be looking at the back or side of the structure.

She crouched at the very edge of the trees, Jax beside her, his body tense with excitement. She scanned the clearing beyond the trees and spotted the source of the noise. Two men stood to the right of the structure, talking quietly. From her vantage point she could make out that the shorter of the two had a bald head. The other, bigger man was partially concealed by the building.

Headlights splashed light across a gravel drive choked with weeds. An uncomfortably familiar-looking dark panel van rolled toward the building, the driver guiding it into a position about a foot from the structure. He hopped out, then hurried to join the other men. Were they about to move the children? She would need to get closer if she hoped to learn anything. Both men disappeared around the corner of the structure.

She reached down and hoisted Jax into her arms, then took one slow, deliberate step at a time toward the edge of the tree line. She made it to a spot that was catercorner to the sliding panel door of the van. Setting Jax back on the grass, she gave him the hand motions for "down-stay" and crept toward the front of the structure.

She smelled cigarette smoke before she saw the third man. Seated in a folding camp chair, his back to her, he held the cigarette, its butt glowing orange in the darkness. Behind him, an open door revealed the black interior of the structure. Was someone in there?

"Hey!" the man called out, and she jumped, sure she'd been seen. "Hurry it up with those kids! We don't got all night to move them."

"They're not cooperating, so how about you get yourself in here and do something to help?" a muffled voice called from inside the structure. One of the three men she'd already seen? Or a fourth person?

"Do I gotta to do everything?" the man with the cigarette called back. He took a deep drag on the cigarette, tossed it onto the ground and crushed it under his foot. "You tell those brats I'm coming in. One more complaint from them and I'll set this whole place on fire with them in it."

"You don't do squat!" A man appeared in the doorway, and she recognized him immediately. The man who'd grabbed Olivia.

Silently pressing herself to the shadows of the building, she held her breath, praying that she wouldn't be seen.

"I do plenty. But if I got to help you load the brats, I'll help. Ship departs Baltimore at 6:00 a.m. We don't got a lot of time," the man said.

At that moment, the third man came out of the outbuilding, spouting a string of obscenities. He was bald, older than the other two, and smaller, but somehow more threatening.

"How about you two stop chatting and get back to work? In two hours, you can take your money and go your separate ways. For now, you'd better stick to the plan. Get in there and search the hold room for any evidence they may have left behind. We leave in ten. Either of you girls wants to slack off now, I can arrange for you not to leave at all."

The three entered the structure. The door slammed shut behind them.

Rushing to the tree line where Jax patiently waited, Laney pulled her cell phone out and powered it up. She had less than ten minutes to figure out how to stall the men. If they left, she'd have no way to follow them. She'd parked Aunt Rose's car a good twenty-minute trek back through the woods.

She could call 911 or she could call Grayson. She made the decision quickly, dialing the number and waiting as the phone rang twice.

"Laney! Where are you?" Grayson voice boomed through the phone.

"I'm at Ethan Conrad's property, and the kids are here."

"You've seen them?"

"No, but I saw Olivia's kidnapper and the van with the dented front end. The kidnappers are moving the kids to the Port of Baltimore. They'll be shipped out from there."

"When?"

"All I heard is that the ship leaves at six. I'm not sure what time they'll be loading the kids, but they're planning to leave here in ten minutes."

"I'm on my way. So is Andrews. I need you to get back to the woods and stay out of sight."

"Grayson, if I do that, the kids will be gone before you get here."

"And we'll have people at the Port of Baltimore waiting for them."

"The Port of Baltimore is huge. You'll never find them."

"Don't argue, Laney!" he growled. "You've given me the probable cause I need. Now step aside and let us handle things."

"I'll…stay safe," she said. "I've got to go. They'll be out with the kids any minute."

Laney disconnected and turned off the phone before shrugging out of her day pack.

Reaching into the front pocket, she pulled out a plastic Ziploc bag containing her NASAR-required first-aid kit. It included three extra-large safety pins. Fishing them out, she returned the rest of kit to her day pack. If she could wedge a safety pin or two firmly into a tire's valve stem, the air would be released slowly, possibly causing a flat tire before the men reached the port. She knew she had only minutes to make this work.

Ducking behind the front passenger tire, she quickly unscrewed the tire's valve cover. Then, using the tip of the safety pin to push down the valve core, she wedged in the pin to keep it from popping up. It held, but felt loose, so she shoved in the second pin. Better, but it would likely not hold when the tire began rotating at sixty-five miles an hour. Grabbing her last safety pin from her pocket, she opened it and forced it between the first two pins.

Solid. Holding her finger over the air valve, she could feel the slight but steady rush of air pushing out. The question was, if it held, how long would it take before the van was inoperable?

The door to the building was flung open. "I'll be at the van. Get those kids ready to move," someone called out.

Laney was out in plain sight with no choice but to run.

She darted away from the van, aiming for the tree line and Jax.

She didn't make it.

He was on her in an instant, tackling her to the ground so hard, every bit of air was knocked from her lungs.

He grabbed a fistful of her hair and yanked her head up so he could look at her face. "You!" he spat.

"What's going on?" The bald man stepped outside, two children beside him.

"Nothing I can't handle." The kidnapper pulled out a gun, pressed it to her head.

"Are you nuts? Put that thing away. We kill her here and there will be blood evidence everywhere. That happens and Conrad will put a mark on each of us. We'll be dead by sunrise."

The kidnapper cursed but hauled Laney to her feet. "I guess you've got a better plan?"

"Sure do. We sell her. Just like we're doing with the kids. We needed five live bodies. Now we've at least got four."

"Right. Fine. Whatever." The kidnapper shoved her toward the van with enough force to knock her off her feet.

She went down hard, her palms skidding along gravel, bits of dirt digging into her flesh.

A fast-approaching vehicle barreled down the access road, high beams blinding. Laney could only pray it was the cavalry.

Chapter Twenty

Grayson assessed the situation as his car barreled toward the old hunting cabin, high beams on in an attempt to blind the suspects.

Two men were loading kids into a van.

Laney was on the ground. He could see her clearly, and for a moment, he thought the worst.

Then she popped up and tried to run toward the trees.

A man grabbed her around the waist and hauled her toward the van. Another man jumped into the driver's seat.

Hitting the brakes, Grayson flung open the driver's door, pulled his service revolver and trained it on the guy who was manhandling Laney. "FBI. Throw your weapons down and put your hands in the air."

A third man ran out of the building and fired a shot at Grayson.

Laney screamed. Out of the corner of his eye, Grayson saw a brown-and-white ball of fur in a bright orange vest running in. Jax took hold of the kidnapper's pants leg while he struggled to push Laney into the van.

"Do something about this mutt!"

The bald guy turned, taking aim at Jax.

"No!" Laney yelled. "Jax off. Away!"

Jax immediately let go, backing away, the bullet missing him by mere inches as Laney was shoved in the van. The door closed behind her.

The man in the doorway of the building fired another shot. Grayson aimed and pulled the trigger.

The man went down, and the van took off, leaving the fallen kidnapper where he lay.

Grayson couldn't shoot at the van and risk a stray bullet hitting Laney or one of the children.

The perpetrators weren't as worried about that.

One of them leaned out the passenger side window and fired another shot at Grayson as the van barreled past. Grayson dove for cover, but the bullet dug into his shoulder, before he hit the ground. Pulling himself to his feet, he called in his location and the direction the perps were heading.

Blood oozed from the wound, but he didn't feel any pain. Couldn't feel anything but rage and fear.

"Jax, come!" he called.

The dog rushed to his side, looking up at him.

Grayson scooped him into his arms and deposited him on the passenger seat of his car.

His cell phone rang as he sped after the van. He took the call.

"DeMarco. Go ahead."

"It's Kent. I've got dozens of men heading to Conrad's place. Do you have Laney?"

"They've taken her and the kids to the Port of Baltimore," Grayson answered. "I'm headed there now."

"All right. I'll divert my guys there," Andrews acknowledged. "Do you still need resources at Ethan's property?"

"Send a patrol car and an ambulance. We've got one

perp down." He didn't mention his own wound. It didn't matter. All that mattered was closing in on the van and getting Laney and the kids out of it safely.

"Will do."

"Can you also send someone out to Conrad's full-time residence? He's in Silver Spring." Grayson rattled off the address. It was as familiar as his own.

"Consider it done," Kent confirmed. "Do you have a visual on the van?"

"Not yet, but I'm moving fast."

"Where do you want us to meet you?"

"The Maryland Port Administration offices on Pratt Street. Someone's going to tell me which ships are leaving Baltimore at 6:00 a.m., and from which docks."

Grayson had been driving at a fast pace for about twenty minutes without seeing the van. That worried him. Had Ethan changed the plans? Had he caught wind of what was going on and decided to move the kids somewhere else? Taking Charles Street, Grayson exited to Pratt Street, where he would meet Andrews.

And there it was.

Abandoned on a side street, the panel van had one pancake-flat tire.

Pulling up behind it, he got out and touched the hood of the vehicle. Still warm.

He crouched near the tire. Safety pins had been jammed in the stem.

Laney. She'd put herself in jeopardy to sabotage the van. A smart move, too, since the Port of Baltimore was one of the largest ports in North America. There was no way the perps could parade around the docks with four hostages in the middle of the night and not draw attention to themselves. They would need another vehicle to get the kids and Laney to the loading dock undetected.

Another vehicle didn't just happen. They'd have to find one.

Which meant that they'd stash the kids and Laney somewhere close by.

He tried the van door and found it unlocked. Laney's cell phone lay on the floor. He left it there and put in another call to Andrews.

He gave the location of the van, his communication quick and to the point.

They didn't have time to waste.

When he finished, he walked back to his vehicle. Jax, still in his bright orange vest, waited there, the equivalent of a homing beacon. "You want to work?" he asked the dog.

He was rewarded by an enthusiastic thump of the tail.

"Good. Me, too." He lifted the dog out of the vehicle, ignoring the stabbing pain in his shoulder as he set him on the ground, then issued the command as he'd seen Laney do. He pointed to the van. "Jax, place!"

Jax leapt inside and immediately seemed to pick up on Laney's scent, going right to her cell phone with a little whine, then pressing his nose in all the rear seats of the vehicle.

Finally, when it was apparent Laney was not in the van, Jax sat down beside her phone, looking sadly at Grayson.

"Where's Laney?" Grayson asked.

At the sound of her name, Jax cocked his head. His ears perked up.

"Laney?" he repeated. He knew Jax was an air scent dog, not a tracking dog. He could only hope Jax understood what Grayson was asking him to do.

Jax barked and stood, tail wagging, tongue lolling. Grabbing Laney's phone, Grayson put it up to Jax's nose. When he was done sniffing, Grayson dropped the phone in his pocket. "Jax, go find Laney!"

Grayson didn't have to tell him twice. Jax leapt from the van, put his nose to the ground, then to the wind, then back to the ground, and started across the street, heading straight toward a warehouse. Grayson could see the door had recent damage, as if someone had taken a crowbar and pried it open. Testing it, he found it unlocked. He drew his service revolver and stepped into the dark interior.

It was almost pitch black and a little cool in the storage room where Laney and the kids were waiting.

Laney pressed her ear to the door, trying to hear into the warehouse beyond their prison. She was pretty sure at least one of the bad guys was in the vicinity. The other had gone to find a new vehicle. He hadn't been happy when the tire went flat.

Laney had the bruise on her cheek to prove it.

She couldn't feel the pain of it. All she could feel was the panicked need to escape the room, to get the kids to safety, to make sure that Grayson was okay. She tried the door handle again. Locked. Still.

There had to be a way out. Had to be.

She turned back to the kids, felt something slap against her thigh, felt a moment of hope so pure and real that she nearly shouted with the excitement of it.

Her emergency penlight. She always carried it on searches. She yanked it from her cargo pocket and flashed it across the three huddled kids.

"Don't worry," she said. "I'm going to find a way out of this."

She hoped.

She shone the light on the floor and pointed it into the dark corners. Boxes lined the walls and took up most of the floor space. Trails of rat droppings and dust dotted the old tiles. There was only the one door, but maybe there was a vent she could shimmy through, some other way of escaping. She flashed the light onto the ceiling. Old 1970s panels threatened to fall out of the drop ceiling.

Perfect!

Laney knew that if she could get to the top of the wall and push up a tile, all that would separate her from whatever was next door would be more tiles. She thought about dropping straight into the warehouse, but she didn't know where the kidnappers were. Four lives depended on her escaping without notice—including her own. She could climb over the support beam and drop into the next room. Ideally find an unlocked door there and move into the warehouse, where she'd find a way to smuggle the kids out.

She turned the light back in the direction of the kids.

They looked terrified, their faces streaked with grime, tears and, in some cases, a few bruises. Olivia was hugging a girl who looked much smaller and younger than she was. Laney recognized her from the Amber alerts and news stories surrounding her abduction. Eight-year-old Marissa James. The dark haired, slim boy standing beside them was eleven-year-old Adam Presley.

"I need you guys to help me move some of those boxes to the corner," Laney whispered. "We need to stack them so I can climb up."

She flashed the light so they could all see the area.

The kids moved quickly and more quietly than Laney expected.

Fear was a powerful motivator.

It didn't take long to create a sturdy platform. "I'm going to climb through," she whispered. "Once I make it to the other side, I'll unlock the door."

"Why can't we all climb through?" Adam asked. "If you go and don't come back—"

"I'll come back."

"But if you don't," Olivia whispered, "we're stuck."

"I will either open this door and get you out or come back through the ceiling. Either way, I'm not leaving anyone behind." She meant it. And she hoped she could follow through.

If something happened, and she was killed...

It was a thought she couldn't dwell on. God was in control. He saw. He knew. She had to believe that He'd act.

Laney said a quick prayer as she hoisted herself to the top of the storage room wall. She removed the drop ceiling tile, carefully handing it down to Adam. Using her penlight, she peered over the wall into an office space. It was empty. Pocketing her light, she started to formulate the best plan for lowering herself down to the next room.

The telltale sound of clicking of paws moving rapidly across the concrete floor grabbed her attention.

Could it be?

Had Grayson and Jax somehow found the warehouse?

And where was the kidnapper with the gun?

Her question was answered when the guy lumbered into the office, closing and locking the door behind him, then quietly peering through the blinds of a window that opened into the warehouse.

Jax was out there. Laney knew it, and she thought Grayson was with him. She hoped he was. She'd overheard one of the kidnappers say he'd shot him. If he was in the warehouse, he'd survived, but he was also a sitting duck. There were windows in the interior office wall that looked out into the warehouse. If Jax and Grayson walked by where the kidnapper could see them… Her blood grew cold at the thought.

She scrambled back down into the storage room.

"New plan," she whispered to the kids. "The kidnapper is in the room next door. I'm heading into the warehouse. I'll open the door when I get to the other side. When I do, everyone needs to leave single file and quietly. Hug the wall to the right, hold hands and stay together."

Removing her boots so her drop to the floor would not be heard, she climbed through the open ceiling tile and sat on the top of the wall. It was a good eight-foot drop. She lowered herself until she was hanging by her hands, her socked feet dangling about three feet from the floor. Holding her breath, she prepared to let go.

Keeping to the edges of the open warehouse, Grayson followed Jax toward a row of offices. Jax looked up.

Grayson followed his gaze and saw a pair of legs dangling from an open panel in the ceiling.

Laney!

He rushed forward, touched her ankle.

She let out a bloodcurdling scream, and the silent warehouse suddenly turned to chaos. Kids screamed from the other side of a closed door. Distant footsteps pounded on old tile.

Grayson yanked hard enough to pull Laney down, catching her as she tumbled into his arms.

"Grayson!" she cried, throwing her arms around his neck. "I thought you were dead."

"Not yet, but we both might be if we don't get moving."

"The children!" She broke away and unlocked and opened a door.

Three kids emerged, all of them in various states of hysteria.

An office door opened. The kidnapper rushed toward them, gun in hand.

"Everyone down!" Grayson hollered.

Laney, the children and even Jax hit the floor, leaving the gunman an easy target. Grayson got off his shot first. The man went down. But there had been two men in the van earlier. Where was his accomplice?

Thundering footsteps were getting closer, and Jax growled, sensing danger before any of them could see it.

Grayson scooped up the smallest child in his left arm, wincing as she latched onto his wounded shoulder. There was cover of sorts near the edges of the warehouse, where the shadows were deepest and machinery crowded the floor.

"Come on!" he urged.

Laney grabbed the hands of the other two children and followed Grayson closely.

Somewhere in the distance, a door opened and closed. Feet tapped on concrete. Not one set of footsteps. Several. Grayson was maintaining radio silence, but he'd called the warehouse location in, and he knew the cavalry had arrived. He just had to keep the kids and Laney safe until Andrew's men could take Conrad's remaining thug down.

Hugging the shadows, he led them down a shelf-lined corridor, toward the emergency exit.

Behind them, a commotion ensued—shouts and gunshots as the remaining kidnapper met the cavalry.

Kicking open the emergency exit door, Grayson led them to the alley, where the flashing red and blue lights of the first responders were a welcoming sight.

They were met by police and paramedics, who took the children from their arms and ushered them to the safety of an ambulance.

Laney turned to Grayson, her eyes drawn to the blood dripping down his arm from his wounded shoulder.

"You're hurt!" She motioned to a paramedic, who grabbed her bag and headed toward them.

"It's not serious."

But Laney insisted he push up his sleeve and allow the paramedic to take a look.

"You've got a nasty gash," she said, removing a sterile pad and some gauze from her medical kit. "You need to have this properly cleaned and sutured. Looks like you've lost a considerable amount of blood, so I can't clear you to drive yourself."

Just then, Kent and two officers came out through the warehouse door, ushering the handcuffed kidnapper out into the alley and the waiting patrol car.

Kent jogged over to him as the paramedic finished field-dressing the wound and called for a gurney to be brought over. "Well, DeMarco, it looks like you're a little worse for wear."

"It's just a flesh wound. I'll be fine." Especially now that he knew Laney and the children were safe.

A second paramedic wheeled over a gurney. "It's time to go, sir."

Grayson sighed. "It looks like we're in for an ER visit," he said, reaching his hand out to Laney.

"We?"

"If you think I'm leaving you here on your own, you can forget it." He rubbed her palm with his thumb. "With your track record, that's much too risky—I need a vacation before I allow you to pull me into the next case."

Laney smiled, shaking her head. "I guess I had that coming." Her green eyes filled with laughter as she followed along for the ride.

Chapter Twenty-One

Almost two weeks later, thanks in part to the computer forensic work Arden had performed on both the FBI networks and Ethan Conrad's personal computers and cell phone, there was enough physical and forensic evidence to get an indictment against Ethan and seventeen other accomplices. Charges spanned from murder to child trafficking. The previous night, Ethan, who had been stopped after crossing the border into Mexico and extradited to Maryland, had been charged with three counts of child abduction in Maryland, plus the thirteen others in Boston and California.

That was great news. Laney was glad Ethan was behind bars where he'd be unable to tear another family apart.

She smiled as she brushed her hair into a high ponytail and fingered the purple scar near her hairline. The staples had been removed, but it would be a while before the scar looked less raw and angry.

She didn't care.

All that mattered was that Olivia and the other kids were safe, and that there was hope of more children being recovered.

That Grayson...

She smiled again, because thinking about him always made her do that.

He'd recovered from his gunshot wound.

It might take a little while longer for him to get over Ethan's betrayal. Ethan's computer logs had revealed that he'd also been part of a money-laundering scheme his stepson had discovered. When Rick had confronted him, Ethan had killed him. Fearing that Rick had revealed information to Grayson, Ethan made an attempt on Grayson's life, too. His bullet had missed its mark and killed Andrea instead. Pinning the murders on two high-level gang members, he closed up the case while Grayson mourned his fiancée and friend, then continued, without missing a step, with his mentorship of Grayson.

It was a sad story that had come out in bits and pieces of forensic information—bank account records, phone records, the testimonies of some of Ethan's coconspirators.

Since the children had been recovered, there had been a whirlwind of activity—interviews with the press, law enforcement, judges and a prosecutor. Between that and work, Laney barely had time to think, but when she did, she found herself thinking about Grayson. Obviously he'd spent some time thinking about her, too. He called or visited almost every day. He'd even made it to the ceremony that morning.

Laney glanced at Jax, smiling at the little medal attached to his collar. The FBI had honored Jax, Arden and Laney for their part in recovering the children.

"But you're the only one who got a medal, Jax," Laney said, walking out onto the porch and taking a seat on the swing. Jax padded along beside her and found a comfortable spot in the sunlight. They'd trained hard the day before, and they were both tired. It was worth it, though. Being out of retirement made Laney feel more alive than she'd felt in years.

A car drove toward the house, and Laney recognized it immediately. Grayson had said he'd stop by when he finished work for the day.

One thing she was learning about him—he always kept his word.

Jax stood as the car parked, excited to see his new friend.

Grayson jumped out, his black hair gleaming in the sunlight, his face soft with his feelings for her.

He walked up the steps and took both her hands in his. "I've been waiting to do this all day," he said, pressing a sweet kiss to her lips.

She would have begged for more, but Jax nosed in between them, looking up with dark eyes and a silly grin.

"He looks great in his medal," Grayson said with a grin.

"Yes." She laughed. "He's been strutting around shamelessly since they put it on him."

"You, on the other hand," he said, "don't need a medal to look great. You're beautiful in fuzzy dog sweaters and weird leggings, with staples in your head and bruises on your face. You're beautiful out in the field with sunlight dappling your hair. And you're beautiful here, with your hair up and your face scrubbed clean."

"Grayson, I…"

"Don't make me stop, Laney. I might chicken out. There's something I want to tell you. I need to tell you. When I lost Andrea, I decided that was God's way of showing me that my plans for a family had to take second place to my career. For the past ten years, I've dedicated myself to this purpose God had for me." He touched her cheek, his fingers trailing down to her collar bone and resting there. "But something happened two weeks ago. It took a punch in the jaw from a pretty girl to bring me to my senses."

Laney laughed. "Yeah, sorry about that, but in my defense, I was concussed."

He smiled. "I had decided that because Andrea was taken from me, I wasn't meant to have a wife and family—to make promises to a woman that I might not be able to keep. I convinced myself it was God's plan for me to focus solely on my career, but the truth is, I was protecting myself from the possibility of finding someone and possibly losing them. I didn't want to hurt again the way I'd hurt when I lost Andrea. Her death left a hole in my heart."

"I'm so sorry, Grayson."

"I don't want you to be. I want you to know that you woke me up to the possibility that God might intend more for me. Everything happens according to plan, Laney, and meeting you, working together on this case, was all part of His plan.

"I can't promise you happily-ever-after, because the future isn't written in stone. But what I can promise you, Laney Kensington, is that if you take a chance on me, I will put your needs before my own, and I will protect you, and cherish you for the wondrously special and unique person that you are, for as long as I live."

Looking into his ocean-blue eyes, she saw the sincerity in them. His faith and strength of character were a constant, steadfast testament to who Grayson De-Marco was. And she knew that she believed him and trusted him with all her heart. Something that she never thought possible. She felt a tear fall before she realized she was crying.

He gently whisked the tear away with the pad of his thumb. "Why are you crying? Have I said something, done something…"

She shook her head and smiled. "I've never believed in happily-ever-after, Grayson, and I wouldn't believe anyone who offered it to me. But then again, I never used to believe in tears of joy, either, but you just wiped one off my cheek."

He kissed her then, gently, pulling her into his arms, then resting his chin on her hair. "Who knows, Laney? Maybe one day we'll both believe that happily-ever-after really is possible."

"Truthfully," she answered, "I think I already do."

* * * * *

Becky Avella grew up in Washington State with her nose in a book and her imagination in the clouds. These days she spends her time dreaming up heart-pounding fiction full of romance and faith. Becky married a real-life hero and follows him around begging him to give her material she can use in her stories. Together with their children, they make their home in the beautiful Northwest.

Books by Becky Avella

Love Inspired Suspense

Targeted
Crash Landing

TARGETED

Becky Avella

A man's heart deviseth his way:
but the Lord directeth his steps.
—*Proverbs* 16:9

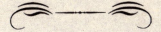

To Pat, my hero and my happily-ever-after.
We both know this book wouldn't exist without you.

Chapter One

Saturday

"**S**eattle Police, K-9 Unit. Announce yourself." Officer Rick Powell's voice boomed through the open door. "If you do not announce yourself, we will send in the dog. If you surrender now, you will not be harmed!"

Rick kept the leash taut and his hand steady on his K-9 partner's back. The dog's training held him still, but Rick knew the Belgian Malinois wanted to go, his muscles quivering to be set free to work again. Only absolute devotion to Rick held the dog back.

Kneeling beside him, Rick crooned the German command for *stay* and stroked the fur along Axle's back. *I understand, buddy. I'm ready to work, too.*

The city block surrounding the early-twentieth-century brick town house had been cordoned off. SWAT team members were poised for action, waiting for the signal that would allow them to penetrate the building, too eager to capture the killer inside to mind the pouring rain running down their stoic faces. Intel indicated the suspect was home and hiding. If their information was correct, then he would soon be calling prison home. Rick believed it was more than he deserved, and it was about time.

"Ready?" Sergeant Terrell Watkins asked Rick.

"Very," Rick answered.

Terrell was Rick's supervisor, but the two had been friends for a long time. It was Rick's first day back on regular duty after an extensive medical leave, and Terrell knew better than any of the others around him how important it was to Rick to be back in the field.

Rick nodded his head in the direction of a wiry man pacing the sidewalk behind the two of them. "But maybe not quite as ready as Shelton is to get this guy."

Terrell's gaze followed where Rick pointed and chuckled. "No kidding."

Detective Gary Shelton deserved the credit for cracking this case. Three unsolved and particularly gruesome murders had terrified the city of Seattle for over a year. It was Shelton who had finally identified Julian Hale as the man responsible for the deaths of those women. And it was Julian Hale whom they believed was hiding inside this town house now.

Investigating the killings had consumed the detective's life, and bringing Hale to justice had become Shelton's personal mission. They were so close to making that happen. Rick leaned forward, anxious to serve this warrant. He hoped that capturing Hale would allow Shelton some much-earned peace.

Rick called his warning into the house once again, his voice even louder and deeper. "You are surrounded. Announce yourself *now*."

Axle squirmed, his tail thumping on the doorjamb. The dog knew it was go time.

Stroking Axle's fur, Rick's fingers brushed across the healed scar running along the dog's side. Rick had similar scars across his own abdomen. A quick flood of panic raced through his body. Were they both ready to face what was about to go down? *Don't go there. This is a new start, no wallowing in the past.*

"This is your last chance to surrender." Rick's warning echoed into the house, answered only by silence. He unclasped Axle's leash, but kept his hand firm on the dog's back, containing him. Axle's tail thumped harder and faster. No answer came. No one exited the building.

No more chances.

Axle's muscles quivered in anticipation. Rick might have doubts, but Axle didn't. The dog whined as if to say, "Let me go!"

Pride for Axle pushed away the panic. After a confrontation with human traffickers had left both Axle and Rick near death, the dog had defied all the odds and all of the claims that he would never recover. It was only their first day back, but Rick knew that Axle was stronger than ever and more than capable of doing what was needed. He drew strength from Axle and raised his hand, shouting the command to search. *"Reveire!"*

That one word ignited the built-up energy within Axle's body, propelling the dog forward off his haunches. He disappeared into the house as the men outside waited for barking to alert them to the hidden suspect's location. After several moments of silence, they couldn't wait any longer. The SWAT commander's signal sent Rick and the rest of the Metro team crashing into the house with weapons raised.

The baritone shouts of "Police!" and the urgent calls of "Go, go, go!" harmonized with the high crystal notes of shattering glass, all of it fueling Rick's adrenaline. He caught sight of Axle and trailed after the dog through the chaos, tuning his ears for the sound of barks. *Come on, Axle, show me where the bad guy is hiding.*

Between the men and the dog, the systematic search of the small town house didn't last long. Shout after shout of "Clear!" filled Rick with more disappointment. His sense of justice cried to see this man in handcuffs. Julian Hale had to be in here somewhere.

Rick followed Axle up the stairs to a landing, where he spotted a pull-down attic entrance in the ceiling. He lowered the trapdoor, revealing a wooden staircase. Could Hale be hiding in the attic? Rick trained his gun on the stairs and called out his standard warning one more time. He gave Hale no longer than a heartbeat to comply, then shouted the command to go ahead: "Axle, *geh voraus*!"

Rick envied the dog's unwavering bravery. Without a second of hesitation, Axle shot up the stairs, eager for a new area to search as if he couldn't remember the stabbing they had both lived through. Rick remembered clearly the streetlights flickering off the slashing blade, the sight of Axle airborne, latching his teeth into the man wielding the knife, the feel of pain so searing Rick hadn't been able to believe it was his own. It would all be forever embedded in his memory.

But Axle was right. Those memories had nothing to do with the job at hand. There was a serial killer loose. Getting Julian Hale behind bars before he hurt someone again was the only thing Rick should be thinking about. Axle was relying on his training, and appeared as unwilling to admit defeat as his human coworkers. Taking the dog's lead, Rick shook away the bad memories clouding his mind and focused.

He crouched low, taking the stairs much slower than Axle had done. Although he was convinced by this point that Hale probably wasn't up there, he wasn't taking any chances. He bent and entered the attic space gun first, his eyes fighting to adjust in the dim light coming from a window in the sloped ceiling. The gray drizzle outside made it even darker, but soon his eyes were able to make out the layout of the room.

The attic had been remodeled from its original intended storage space. Two overstuffed chairs and a small love seat were arranged into a conversational sitting space in the center of the room, and a small home office area with bookshelves lined the far wall.

Instead of evoking the cozy feeling it looked as though it should, the room triggered Rick's internal radar. After seven years of law enforcement, he had encountered enough evil to be able to sense when something just wasn't right. Axle's whine confirmed that feeling sending goose bumps popping up along Rick's arm.

Inching his way around the room, Rick searched every nook or possible hiding place. His jaw clenched. The room was clear. How had Hale gotten away?

He joined Axle by the desk. Rick fumbled with the lamp until he found the switch, illuminating the desk and the wall behind it. Dread settled into his stomach as heavy as if he had swallowed cement.

Two bulletin boards hung on the wall. On the left board there were six photographs stapled in a three-by-two grid. In the second row, Rick recognized the photographs of the three women he already knew Hale had killed. But the upper three photographs were of unfamiliar faces. Were they also victims? Was it possible detectives had missed Hale's connection to other murders? Somehow he knew all of these women were dead. His breathing slowed as he stared at the six pictures.

Thinking about the young lives represented in them made the air around him almost too heavy to breathe.

His gaze moved to the second board. White three-by-five cards, small photographs and highlighted spreadsheets were stapled across the outside edges of the board, creating a homemade flowchart, but it was the eight-by-ten photograph in the center that concerned him the most.

Rick studied the girl-next-door beauty smiling back at him from the picture. He noted her heart-shaped face and her long strawberry-blond curls. It was a simple photograph, exactly the type of blue-background portrait that schoolkids brought home each year, or the type that schoolteachers had taken for their staff photo. The innocence of it screamed at him. This picture did not belong in the house of a killer.

He spoke into his radio. "Attic's clear, and Sarge?" He swallowed, hating to be the bearer of such bad news, but if anyone could help this woman right now, it was Terrell Watkins. "Sarge, you need to get up here and see this."

His eyes traveled back to the photo. She must be Hale's next victim. Rick groaned. She was out there somewhere in the city, unprotected and unaware that she was standing in the crosshairs of a psychopath.

But that wasn't the worst of it. The worst part was, Rick knew her.

A car in the distance backfired, causing Stephanie O'Brien to drop her keys. She scooped them up and stomped the rest of the way past the playground's graffiti-decorated retaining wall to the front doors of Lincoln Elementary School.

Stephanie rolled her eyes. It wasn't like her to be so

jumpy, but about halfway through her trek to the school she had begun to feel as if someone were following her. But every time she peered over her shoulder, she didn't see anyone behind her other than a few bustling people who seemed a lot more concerned with getting out of the freezing rain than with causing her any trouble.

You traveled alone to Africa and back three times before your twenty-fifth birthday, and now you're afraid of walking a few blocks to school? She had hoped that common sense would drive away the uneasiness, but it hadn't. Stephanie pulled her arms in tight to her body and tried to talk herself out of the anxiety creeping up her spine and into her imagination.

To get to the elementary school where she taught fifth grade, Stephanie walked through familiar neighborhoods full of run-down houses that begged for fresh paint and small apartment buildings with rusted metal swing sets in their play areas. Properties and cars were locked behind six-foot-tall chain-link fences, and overgrown, neglected rhododendron bushes commandeered the sidewalk, forcing Stephanie to step into the street if she wanted to pass. Garbage blown out of Dumpsters lay damp along the edges of the buildings and the fences.

The area was a bit rough around the edges, but until today, it had never felt dangerous to her. In fact, these neighborhoods bordered the neighborhood where she lived. Stephanie didn't own a car, so it was routine to trudge back and forth between home and work through this area. It was also common for her to be working in her classroom over the weekend to prepare for the school week ahead. She looked over her shoulder again. This wasn't different from any other trip to school, so why did it *feel* so different?

Tiny droplets from the hood of her raincoat dripped onto her cold nose, reminding her she needed to shake off this silliness and get inside before she drowned. Real Seattleites might be too cool for umbrellas, but at the moment Stephanie would gladly look like a tourist if it meant being dry. It was May for goodness' sake; shouldn't it be warmer?

She glanced over her shoulder one final time before she let herself into the dark building and typed in the security code. The door shut with a *bang* and a *click* as it locked behind her. Other than the squeak of her wet tennis shoes on the waxed tile floor, the hallway stretched into silent darkness.

She flipped on the light in her classroom and locked the door behind her. She threw her keys on her desk and shimmied out of her wet coat. She cranked up her stereo extra loud. The music and the light drove away the eeriness as Stephanie sat down and grabbed the stack of work waiting for her.

Settling into her chair, Stephanie spread open her lesson plan book and lifted the photo she kept paper-clipped to the inside cover. In the picture she held Moses, the sweet, chubby toddler who had stolen her heart the last time she had visited her younger sister, Emily, in Liberia. Moses's round black face looked straight into the camera, his smile wide, while the photograph captured Stephanie's profile as she stared adoringly at the little boy on her hip. Stephanie's heart lurched with longing as she relived the moment in her mind now.

After her third trip to visit her sister and brother-in-law in West Africa, Stephanie had physically boarded the plane for home, but she had left her heart behind in the red African dirt. Her life now revolved around figuring out how to get back there as a full-time missionary, but the process wasn't going well at all. She didn't have the money to sustain herself without being a burden to Emily and Ty, and with their first baby on the way, they didn't need to take care of her as well on the meager salary they received from an international missions board.

Stephanie swiped her finger across the picture of Moses's face. *I miss you, baby boy. I wonder how big you've gotten this year.* She needed to ask Emily for a more recent picture. She clipped the photo to the book where it belonged, sighed and settled in to do the work in front of her.

An hour passed before the sound of jingling keys in the hallway jerked her attention away from the stack of essays she was reading. The doorknob to her classroom turned. Was a janitor working today? They didn't usually work this late on weekends, but who else would have a master key? Maybe Jim Mendoza, the principal?

Stephanie bit the inside of her cheek. Who was it? Reaching behind her, she fished her cell phone out of the pocket of her wet coat hanging on the back of her desk chair. She glanced at the phone and then tossed it on the stack of papers in front of her. She had forgotten to charge the battery again. Her stomach knotted as she waited for whoever it was behind the door to enter.

"Who's there?" she called.

The door swung open, and a pallid face peeked around it. His washed-out blue eyes widened. "It's just me."

She released all the air she'd been holding as she realized it was the IT guy who had been helping her install all of the new technology she had received from a grant she had won for her classroom. He dropped in unannounced all the time, but this was the first time he had come on a weekend.

Stephanie lowered the stapler in her hand. She must have grabbed it without realizing it before the door opened. Her cheeks burned. She hoped he hadn't noticed the threatening way she had held it. What good would a stapler have done her if it truly had been an emergency?

Her laugh sounded forced and flat in her own ears. "You scared me."

The blond man stood on the classroom door's threshold, his tool bag in hand. He stood perfectly erect, unblinking.

"I didn't mean to startle you," he said. "I didn't expect anyone to be here."

"Did you need anything?"

He pointed at a stack of shipping boxes she hadn't noticed sitting near the front whiteboard. "I thought I would get a head start setting those up for you so you can use them on Monday," he said.

After she won the grant, boxes like these had slowly trickled into her classroom. It felt like Christmas every time a new one arrived. She eyed a large flat box and hoped that the smart board she was looking forward to using was inside it.

Stephanie nibbled on her lower lip, not liking being alone with a man she didn't know well, but she was unsure of what to say or do that wouldn't come across as rude. "Um, sure, I'll just get out of your way, then."

"Thank you, Stephanie."

It was probably nothing more than the overactive imagination she had been combating all day, but something about the way he pronounced her name sent a shiver scampering up her spine. She gathered up her lesson plan book and the stack of essays and moved to the opposite corner from where he stood in the doorway.

"You're welcome, Julian. Let me know if you need anything."

She walked to the round worktable, but before she sat, movement outside startled her.

"Rick?" She cocked her head, confused.

Why was Terrell's friend Rick Powell out there? She gasped. Rick wasn't just standing at the window; his gun was pointing directly at her through the glass.

Chapter Two

Rick's spirits had lifted when he rounded the corner of the school building and saw the glow of artificial light coming from the fourth classroom down the wall. He had hoped he would simply have to knock on Stephanie's classroom window and all of this would be behind them. But once he peeked into her classroom, he knew it wouldn't be that simple.

Even through the window's dirty glass, Rick had recognized Stephanie immediately, but it was the man standing in the doorway behind her, fitting the exact description of Julian Hale, that had caused him to pop back and draw his weapon.

"Freeze!" Rick shouted through the window. He doubted they could hear him clearly, if at all, but he hoped the raised gun made enough of a statement. The glass wouldn't stop him if he had to shoot.

Rick's gaze locked on Hale, trying to anticipate his next move. What was Hale going to do? Run? Try to take out Stephanie? Hale was caught, and Rick expected to read surprise or even fear displayed in the other man's body language. Instead, Hale appeared unfazed by the gun and strangely poised.

Rick needed to get Stephanie out of here and deliver her safely to Terrell Watkins. When they had split up to look for her, Rick had promised Terrell that he would get to her before Hale did. Rick's gut twisted. He had failed to keep that promise.

Terrell and his wife, Val, viewed Stephanie O'Brien as a member of their family. The three of them had known one another for years, and Rick had run into Stephanie so often at their house, he had finally asked Terrell if she was living with them. To which Terrell had laughed and answered, "Practically."

But Terrell wasn't laughing now. Back in the attic, Terrell's broad shoulders had slumped and deep lines of worry had furrowed his forehead as he tried to reach Stephanie on her cell phone.

"My calls are going straight to voice mail," Terrell had said, skimming his tightly cropped black hair with his large hand. "That girl never keeps her cell phone charged, and Val hasn't seen her at all today."

Rick had hated seeing Terrell so upset. The team counted on their sergeant's lighthearted personality to ease the tense situations. His jokes had gotten Rick through a lot of heavy spots, but with the roles reversed, Rick hadn't known what to say. Finding the photograph of one of your closest friends in the attic of a wanted killer wasn't a light thing.

And now here she was right in front of him. How was he going to get her away from Hale?

Without lowering his gun, Rick reached up and grabbed his mic. "Code 3 assist. I've got a visual on the suspect."

Stephanie wasn't sure which of the two men to look to for answers. She turned back and forth between Rick at the window and Julian in the doorway until it dawned on her. Rick's gun wasn't aimed at her; his target was Julian, and Stephanie was in the way.

She dropped to her stomach, scattering the papers she held in her arms, and scooted toward the window on her belly. Was that the right thing to do? She wished she could read Rick's mind. Right or wrong, she had to put distance between her and the doorway where Julian still stood.

"Stop moving, Stephanie," Julian's icy voice instructed her.

She froze midcrawl. "Why are the police here, Julian? What have you done?"

Although he spoke to her, his eyes stayed on the window and Rick's gun. "I suspect the officer is here not only because of what I've already done, but because he knows what I'm planning to do next."

From her vantage point on the ground, Stephanie looked up and studied Julian's face. A slow, small smile spread, then flickered out, leaving the flat, emotionless affect he always wore. She had noticed his oddities before—his formal speech, erect posture and unwavering calm. She had written them off as nothing more than a social awkwardness from a man who spent all of his time working with computers instead of people. Now she found the same mannerisms cold and calculating.

What are you planning to do?

Fear amplified the flow of blood behind her ears as it raced adrenaline through her body. Her heartbeat paralleled the ticking of the old clock in the front of the classroom. The minute hand kept bouncing into place, marking how long Stephanie lay on the ground waiting for something to happen.

Julian didn't say any more; his eyes remained locked

on Rick. She waited for Rick's gun to shatter the glass, but that didn't happen, either. She remained motionless on her stomach, stuck in the middle of a standoff with no idea what she should do next.

The distant sound of approaching sirens hit her ears. From the sound of it, a lot of law enforcement was about to descend on this place, yet Julian seemed unperturbed by it all. Maybe she could stall him until they arrived.

"What are you planning to do, Julian?" she asked him.

His soulless eyes turned her direction, making her shiver from the coldness she saw in them. "You will have to wait and see, Stephanie. I promise you will know soon enough." Then he bolted from the doorway and disappeared down the dark hallway.

Hammering hit the window above her. Stephanie peered through her lifted arm and watched the old window splinter from the force of Rick's nightstick. Stephanie moved to stand up as Rick raked out the remaining glass, but she fell back down flat again when a large dog flew through the broken window. Stephanie screamed and covered her head.

Rick climbed in the window. "The dog won't hurt you," he reassured her. "Axle, *sitz*!" he commanded, and the dog froze and sat at attention.

"Did you see which way Hale ran?" Rick asked her.

"I don't know. Right, I think?"

Rick spoke into his radio. "Suspect is running toward the front of the school. I won't be able to intercept. Have incoming units set up a perimeter."

Rick squatted beside her. "Are you okay, Stephanie?"

She wanted to yell, *Scared to death, how do you think I'm feeling?* But the concern in his eyes stopped her. "Fine," she told him.

Rick offered Stephanie a hand up, steadying her as she wobbled to her feet. She had been around Rick many times at Val and Terrell's house, but she had never been this close to him. She blushed. The skip in her heartbeat could not be blamed on fear.

"Hale may be hiding in the building. We need to get you to a safer location." Rick let go of her arms and walked to the window. "Can you crawl out with me?"

Stephanie followed him through the window and accepted his outstretched hand on the other side. He guided her to the ground, and the dog leaped through behind them.

"Keep low and stay close behind me. We're going to move along the building to minimize visibility. Understand?"

"Visibility?" she asked him. "Does Julian have a gun?"

Was Julian really that dangerous? She shuddered, thinking of all of the times she had been alone with him in her classroom. What was he capable of doing?

"He's more worried about avoiding capture than he is with hurting you now, but I don't gamble. Stay low."

Rick's long legs covered ground much faster than Stephanie's shorter legs could manage. She jogged behind him trying to keep up. When they rounded the building, Rick called to her over his shoulder, "The cavalry has arrived."

Patrol car after patrol car surrounded them, filling the parking lot. The flashing lights and number of arriving vehicles mesmerized her. People in a variety of uniforms and suits piled out of their cars, sprinting in different directions.

All of this for Julian? A typical criminal would not invite this intense of a response, would he? She spotted uniforms from Seattle Police Department and King County Sheriff's Office and read "SWAT" on the back of several officers advancing on the building. She swallowed as her eyes landed on the FBI label on the side of a parked SUV.

Rick placed a warm hand on the small of Stephanie's back and guided her to the passenger door of a blue patrol car with "K-9" painted on the side.

"Watch your head," he said.

She backed down onto the passenger seat facing out. Rick kept his hand on the door and knelt in front of her. His nearness and direct gaze made her squirm. "Did Hale hurt you at all?"

She blushed and shook her head. "No. Julian had just arrived. He hadn't even stepped out of the doorway before you came."

"Did he say anything to you?" Rick eyes roved across her face, looking as if he thought he would be able to read what he wanted to know written there. But she didn't have any answers. She didn't know what he needed her to tell him.

"I don't know. He said that you knew what he was planning to do next, or that you knew what he had already done, or something like that." She closed her eyes trying to remember more, anything that would be useful.

"Did he say where he was going? What his plans were specifically?"

"No. I told you, Rick. I don't know anything. He wasn't making any sense. When I asked him what he was talking about, all he said was that I would know soon enough, and then he ran down the hall."

"That's it? You're sure you can't remember anything else? This is important, Stephanie."

It felt as though he was interrogating her. "I told you everything I can remember. There wasn't time for anything else." She looked down into Rick's upturned face. His expression was hard, his mouth a straight line. She knew he wanted her to give him some clue, but she wanted some answers of her own. "Rick, you need to tell me what is going on."

He stood up and leaned in close so she could hear his words above the racket. "I need to talk to these guys and then we'll get out of here, okay?"

"Okay," she said, turning forward so her feet were in the car. Then the door slammed shut, leaving her alone in the silence to try to sort through all of the activity happening around her. He hadn't answered her question.

She scanned the bustling crowd outside the car and found Rick's tall form. He stood side by side with two other Seattle PD officers, each with their arms crossed over their chest, deep in serious conversation. Set in this scene, Rick's natural presence and rugged good looks made it easy to pretend he was the star of some crime show on prime time. But this was real life, and somehow she was involved in it. How had her quiet afternoon of lesson planning morphed into a TV drama?

Rick's dog waited at his side. His alert ears and long black snout reminded Stephanie of a German shepherd, but his coloring was a light brown and he seemed too small for a shepherd. Whatever breed he was, Stephanie could read the mutual devotion dog and handler had for each other. This dog didn't fit the image she had of intimidating and snarling K-9 dogs. This one looked more like an overgrown puppy with his tail in constant wag mode.

For the briefest moment, Rick's gaze held hers through the windshield. Her stomach tightened, and she held her breath. Time stretched, feeling longer than four heartbeats. What was he thinking? Had they caught Julian?

Rick's eyes remained fixed on where she sat watching him inside the car. He finished his conversation and walked away from the other officers, his dog jogging along beside him. *Finally, he'll be able to tell me what is going on.*

Rick opened the rear door, allowing the dog to jump into the kennel in the back of the car. "Stephanie, meet Axle. Axle, meet Stephanie."

Stephanie smiled over her shoulder. "Hey, Axle. Nice to meet you."

Rick climbed into the front seat next to her. Stephanie turned her smile to him. "I'm not sure what all of this is about, but somehow I think I need to thank you for coming to my rescue."

"My pleasure, Miss O'Brien," he said in a bad impression of John Wayne. Rick's smile was wide and genuine, revealing a dimple in his left cheek she hadn't noticed before.

"Did you catch Julian?" *Are you going to tell me who he really is? What you want him for?*

Rick's smile faded. "No, he got away from us for the second time today." He maneuvered the car out of the parking lot. "Our job's not done yet. He's still loose, and he's still a threat."

A stab of guilt hit Stephanie. Maybe Rick could have caught Julian if he hadn't stopped to take care of her first. "I'm sorry I kept you from going after him."

"No. Don't be sorry." He averted his eyes and quietly added, "You have no idea how happy I was to find you safe, and not…"

Stephanie waited for him to fill in that blank, but he let it drop. "Not what?" she probed.

Instead of a direct answer, he started the car's ignition and said, "I'm under strict orders to deliver you to Terrell. He'll fill you in on everything when we get to his house."

Then he winked at her, and his dimple made its second appearance. "Right after he finishes yelling at you for not charging your cell phone."

Chapter Three

Rick maneuvered around the tricycle blocking the walkway leading up to the Watkinses' modest blue bungalow. He gestured for Stephanie to climb the steps to the front door ahead of him. Savory aromas wafted out to them like a welcoming committee. Rick's stomach contracted, begging him to feed it. It had been a long day with no food, and his shift didn't end for another two hours, and that was only if he didn't get held for overtime. Rick couldn't help but hope Val would feed him before he rejoined the search for Hale. Nothing he could make for himself or grab at a drive-through window would compare to her cooking.

Valencia Watkins came from a long line of Latina women famous for their skill in the kitchen. She did not believe a single bachelor could cook well enough to keep himself alive. All six feet five inches of her well-fed African-American husband revealed how Val loved people. She fed them, and one bite of her cooking had forever convinced Rick he would never turn down an offer to eat at her table.

"Mmm. I can smell Val's cooking all the way out here," Stephanie said. She gave him a crooked half smile. The urge to do or say something to make that smile reach her eyes, to light up her face as it usually did, hit him hard.

It relieved Rick to deliver Stephanie here. With Hale loose, she wasn't completely safe, but he couldn't imagine her being in much danger in this place. This little blue house full of good smells and toys underfoot always felt like a haven to him.

The Watkinses' six-year-old son, Joash, answered the doorbell. His dark eyes lit up when he saw Rick and Stephanie standing on his front porch. The boy hugged Stephanie, then he turned to Rick and lifted the baseball mitt on his left hand. "It isn't raining as hard now. Wanna come out and play catch with me?"

"Sorry, Joe. Can't today, I'm working." As he ruffled the boy's black hair, the gesture left him hollow. Although he often ruffled the fur on top of Axle's head, this time the motion reminded him of someone else.

Allie.

Rick hadn't allowed himself a conscious thought about his former fiancée in a long time. It was always safer to block memories after she called off their engagement, but every once in a while a stray one like this floated to the surface before he could stop it.

Allie had always been so proud of her glossy dark hair. She would spend hours fixing it with a pile of products and styling tools Rick couldn't imagine counting. Sometimes he would be a pest and mess up her hair on purpose, but other times it was simply an unconscious show of affection. Regardless of what his intentions might have been, Allie's response had always been the same: ducking, slapping away his hand and moaning, "Knock it off, Rick, I just fixed my hair." He figured the rich, ambulance-chasing attorney that Allie had married this past summer never messed up her hair like that. Rick shoved his memories down deep where they belonged and commanded them to stay put, turning his attention back to his friends in the present.

Terrell stood in the doorway and waved them inside while Joash ran through the house announcing their arrival, "Mama! Stephanie and Officer Powell are here!"

Val appeared with her three-year-old daughter, Hadassah, trailing behind her. When Val saw Stephanie, she said, "Stephanie. Thank God you are all right."

"Hi, Haddie," Rick said to the little girl. She hid behind her mom, but peeked out around her to grin at him.

Val wrapped Stephanie up into her arms. "I have been so worried about you."

"Thanks, Val," Stephanie told her friend. She glanced from Val to Rick to Terrell. "I'm fine. Still a little confused about what's going on, though."

Rick winced. He should have told her something during the car ride from the school to the Watkinses' house. Even if it were glossed over, some information would have helped to put her mind at ease, but no matter how he rehearsed it in his head, the explanation kept sounding something a little like, *Hey, Stephanie, you know that serial killer the news has been talking about for the past year. Guess what? That's Julian Hale. And by the way, I sure like your last staff photo. Hale must have liked it, too, because he has it pinned to his "People to Kill Next" bulletin board.*

He had never been known for his eloquence, especially with women. Eventually she had stopped asking, making the rest of the car ride quiet and awkward. He had convinced himself that not answering her was the right thing to do. Terrell and Stephanie had a long history together. He would know best how to tell her.

They all stepped into the living room. Terrell's raised eyebrows asked Rick behind Stephanie's back, *you didn't tell her?*

Rick shook his head negative.

"Come eat," Val said. "You, too, Rick," she instructed. "Everything will seem better on a full stomach."

Rick's grinned, "Well, if you *insist.*"

"I insist," Val informed him as she ushered Stephanie out of the living room and into the kitchen to help her put the meal on.

"You didn't tell her anything about Hale yet?" Terrell asked him as soon as Stephanie was out of earshot. When Rick shrugged his shoulders, Terrell rolled his eyes and shook his head, "Didn't know you were a coward, Powell."

"Ha!" Rick pointed a finger at Terrell. "You just wish I had gotten it over with so you wouldn't have to break it to her yourself."

"Guilty as charged. Hopefully Val is telling her now." Terrell clapped a large hand on Rick's shoulder. "Well, you heard the lady. Check out for your lunch break, and let's get in there and eat." Then he added, his signature goofy grin back in place, "Like I always say, don't try to catch a serial killer on an empty stomach."

"That's what you always say, huh?" Rick chuckled and then checked out on his radio. He would have thirty minutes to eat before he had to get back to work. He hoped an urgent call wouldn't come over the radio before he got to taste what he could smell. Lunch break or not, he had to run when certain calls came over the air, even if it meant leaving Val's amazing cooking behind.

Joash ran into the room and tugged on his arm. "Can I say hi to Axle?"

"If there's time, I'll get him out for a bit after we eat, but Axle and I and your dad have some important work to do today."

Joash beamed and smacked an imaginary ball into the baseball mitt he still wore. "Officer Powell, can I sit next to you at dinner?"

"Sure, bud." Joash was such a cute kid, with his missing front teeth. Rick had tried to get Joash and Haddie to call him by his first name long ago, but Terrell had put the kibosh on it, insisting the kids remain respectful and use his title. Rick wondered how Stephanie had managed to get them to call her by her first name.

Haddie reached her little arms up to her dad. Terrell swung her up to his shoulder one-handed. Haddie squealed, delighted.

The domestic bliss of this house hit Rick the way it always did: with envy. It was the future he had dreamed of having with Allie, although now that he had moved past the initial pain of their breakup, he could admit there was nothing about this scene that Allie would have wanted. While he had been dreaming of backyard barbecues, T-ball games and ballet recitals, Allie had been dreaming of foreign cars, exotic vacations and a sprawling home in Medina where she could host cocktail parties.

But even if she had wanted this kind of life, the scars on Rick's stomach reminded him of the danger and demands of his job. Could he blame Allie for walking away? Some guys learned how to be a cop and maintain relationships, but the statistics proved that not many did it well. Terrell Watkins had it figured out, it seemed, but Rick didn't know the secret.

"Duck your head, baby girl," Terrell said before he led them through the arched doorway.

Entering the kitchen, Rick's eyes found Stephanie's pale face. Her lips were tight, as if she were afraid to breathe. He looked at her hand gripping the countertop, and he knew that she knew.

Val had wanted to eat before talking, but Stephanie wouldn't have it. There was no way she was going to sit patiently through a meal pretending that there wasn't a weighted secret hovering above everyone's heads. As soon as they were alone in the kitchen, she'd grabbed Val's arm and demanded to be told the truth.

"All three of you know something you aren't telling me," she had insisted. "I'm a big girl, Val. What is going on?"

So Val had held her hand and told her everything she knew about Julian Hale. Now Stephanie wished she could take it back. Maybe she wasn't such a big girl, after all, because she didn't want *this* truth. Stephanie held on to the edge of the counter to steady herself. The solid surface squeezed between her fingers and thumb gave her something real to grasp when everything around her felt dreamlike. *Julian Hale is a murderer. I've been alone with him many times. He has killed before, and he wants to kill me.*

Another question nagged at her subconscious, begging to be answered. *Why hasn't he tried to kill me already? He's had so many opportunities.* Somehow she knew that today had been the day he planned to do it.

Her gut ached as she watched Terrell lifting Haddie off his shoulders. Yes, she wanted to return to Africa and to mission work, but she also dreamed of being married someday. She dreamed of having a family of her own like this one, with kids like Haddie and Joash, and a husband who loved her the way that Terrell loved

Val. If Rick Powell hadn't shown up exactly when he had, Julian could have killed her today. He could have blotted out her future completely.

Then she remembered the worst of it. *He is still out there. They haven't caught him yet.* Fear swam through her, blurring her vision.

Val ushered the two kids to the sink to wash their hands for dinner. Stephanie glanced at them, making sure they were out of earshot. "Thank you, Rick," she squeaked out. "Thank you for finding me in time." The words were inadequate, but she didn't know what else to say.

Rick sucked his lips inward and breathed through his nose deeply. His hand curled as if he were fighting the urge to punch something. "You're welcome, Stephanie. I wish we had caught him so you wouldn't have to be afraid."

As their eyes met, Stephanie tried to send her gratitude across the space between them. An unexpected urge to walk right into his arms overcame her. She longed to be held by someone stronger than she was, to have muscular arms wrap around her, making her feel safe again. It was a silly thought, though, and if she acted on it she would look like a fool. Rick was nothing more than an acquaintance. After he ate this meal, he would leave. He would return to his own life and his own problems.

Her throat thickened as loneliness joined her fear. She needed family to turn to, but she didn't have anyone close enough to help her. She had Val and Terrell, but they had a real family of their own to worry about. Her sister was in Africa, and the last time Stephanie had spoken to her immature and unreliable mother, she was living in Eastern Oregon working at some casino.

Stephanie sneered at the thought of calling her. Somehow her mother would find a way to spin Stephanie's problems into being all about her, anyway. And her father wasn't an option, either. He had walked out on their family when Stephanie was the same age as Haddie. She couldn't even remember what he looked like. There was nobody. There never had been.

Stephanie had always taken care of herself and everyone else, as well. Her mom had fallen apart after her dad deserted them, leaving Stephanie to raise her little sister. Stephanie had paid her own way through school and Emily's Bible college bills, too. She had never expected anyone to take care of her, but nothing she had faced up to this point had felt so big and so completely beyond her own ability to handle.

All of her energy was gone, her arms suddenly too heavy to lift. "I don't know what to do," Stephanie admitted. Tears pooled, threatening to fall.

Val's arm circled her waist. "We'll figure it out together, honey." She guided Stephanie into a chair at the table. "And in the meantime, we eat."

Chairs scraped across the hardwood floor as everyone took a seat, crowding around the small round oak table. Val and Terrell nestled close together, and Haddie and Joash sat beside each of them. Rick scooted his squeaky chair in next to Stephanie, so close she could feel the heat radiating from his leg. The realization of his nearness made heat move through her own body to her cheeks.

She couldn't count how many times she had been in this house feeling like a third or fifth wheel. That is, unless someone had been playing matchmaker, then of course she would be sitting next to some awkward blind date. But this felt different, comfortable even. If the reason they were here together wasn't so heavy, she would choose to stay in this moment for a long time.

You are grasping for security, Stephanie O'Brien. You are scared, and Rick saved you today. That's all this is. Don't read any more into it than that.

Stephanie wiggled in her chair. Thank goodness no one could read her mind and see her silly fantasy. Rick Powell wasn't even her type. He couldn't be. He had a career in Seattle and a purpose to fulfill here. She wasn't his type, either. If she could stay alive long enough to do it, she was moving to Liberia full-time. Stephanie wanted a life like the one her sister had found when she married Ty and started their mission work together. The right man for her would want that, too.

She caught Rick's profile in her peripheral vision. His espresso-colored hair was cropped short on the sides, but he kept it a bit longer and messier on top. She liked how his strong square jaw saved him from looking too cute. She had never been a fan of men who looked like catalog models. The skin around his hazel eyes crinkled kindly as he smiled at a story Joash was telling him.

Stephanie sighed. As good as it felt to forget about Julian Hale for a minute and pretend she was here with this attractive man in a uniform, it could never be more than a fun diversion. They were two people on different life tracks.

"Hadassah Grace, it's your turn to say the blessing," Terrell told his daughter.

Haddie stuck her fingers in her mouth and shook her head with vigor. "Huh-uh. You pray, Daddy." She hid her face in her mom's arm. Stephanie had never seen the spunky girl so bashful. Rick Powell's presence must be affecting both of them. *No one can blame us, Haddie. He is cute.*

Terrell grasped Val's hand on his right and Joash's hand on his left. Stephanie jumped as Rick's large hand wrapped around her smaller one. She had forgotten about the Watkins family tradition of holding hands when they prayed. Stephanie relaxed and wrapped her fingers around Rick's palm, feeling his calluses and his strength. Tears pricked her eyes again as Haddie's little fingers grasped her other hand. Stephanie was so grateful to be a part of this circle.

"Father, we thank You for the blessing of this food," Terrell prayed. "We praise You that Stephanie is safe with us, and we pray that You would continue to watch over her and protect her. Grant her peace and the ability to trust You. Equip Rick and me in our work and help us to bring Julian Hale to justice soon."

Amens circled the table, but Rick did not drop Stephanie's hand after the last one. Instead, he squeezed it. She met his gaze. His eyes were amazing. If she had to define the color, she would probably call them hazel, but they had a metallic, reflective quality that gave them a silvery glow. She forgot to blink.

"We'll find him, Stephanie. I won't stop until we do."

"Thank you, Rick," she whispered. Once again she hoped he knew how much that meant to her.

During the rest of the dinner they all tried valiantly to keep the tone light. The kids finished earlier than the adults and were excused to watch a cartoon and eat their dessert in the living room. Joash skated around the kitchen in his socks, while Haddie bobbed with excitement. Val didn't let them eat outside the kitchen often.

Stephanie had hardly tasted her food. It was difficult to swallow anything with her stomach in so many anxious knots. She tried to decline dessert, but Val set the pie and mug of hot coffee in front of her despite her protests.

"You are an evil temptress," Stephanie accused her. Val returned a smug smile.

"Hey, you can tempt me all you want," Terrell informed his wife, patting the empty spot at the table in front of him. "Where's my pie?"

"I'll eat yours for you, Stephanie," Rick teased. He leaned back in his chair and winked. "It's a dirty job, but…" He shrugged.

Stephanie pulled her pie close and encircled it with her arms. "Back off, Powell. Now that it's in front of me, it's all mine."

The laughter swirled around her, lifting the weight off her chest. *Could we all just stay right here, happy and safe like this?* But she knew they couldn't. It was too soon before Terrell and Rick pushed back from the table, their half-hour lunch break long past.

Terrell pulled Val into his arms and kissed her forehead. A pang of jealousy hit Stephanie as it always did when the Watkinses were affectionate in front of her. Terrell and Val fit together; they had always been a perfect match. What would it feel like to be loved like that?

Terrell walked to Stephanie's chair and squeezed her shoulder. "Until Hale is captured, I think it is a good idea for you to stay here with us," he told her. "I can drive you over to your place after work to pick up whatever you need."

"I don't want to put you guys in danger," Stephanie protested. "You said Julian has been following me and had a detailed list of all of my activities. I'm sure your address showed up on that chart a few times."

"It's a risk we are willing to take," Val said, her

hands on her hips. "You can't go back to your house alone."

Stephanie didn't like the idea, but where else could she go? Should she try to leave town? What about teaching in the morning? Should she show up at her school or take a leave of absence?

Question after question marched across her mind demanding answers, making her head pound. There were so many details to figure out. She would impose on Terrell and Val only as long as it took for her to figure out an alternative plan.

Haddie waddled into the kitchen rubbing her eyes. Stephanie didn't know a more adorable little girl. Haddie's creamy brown skin and melted-chocolate eyes came from Val, but the black hair that her parents left all natural came from her daddy. She always wore bows or headbands, but her beautiful hair made a statement all by itself. Haddie was a walking, talking reminder of Stephanie's dreams for the future. She reminded Stephanie of all of the girls waiting for her in the Liberian orphanages. Stephanie wanted to fill up those hungry little girls until they radiated as much life, love and health as this sweet girl did.

"Mommy," Haddie said to Val. She crinkled her button nose. "I no like smoke."

Val scooped her into her lap. "What, baby? Are you sleepy?"

"No, I not sleepy!" Haddie pounded her fists on her thighs. She tried to get her point across again, "I said, I no like..." but if she finished the sentence, it was impossible to hear her tiny voice over the screaming smoke detector.

Chapter Four

The demanding wails of the fire alarm assaulted Rick's ears as fingers of smoke slithered into the kitchen along the ceiling. The acrid scent and quickly filling air left no doubt that they were dealing with real fire. One of the chairs crashed backward, but no one bothered to set it back up in their haste to escape.

Haddie plugged her ears, her wails competing in volume with the alarm. "Turn it off, Daddy. Turn it off!"

Rick yelled for help into his radio, hoping dispatch could make sense of his words on their end because he was struggling to hear their responses back to him.

"Go to the alley!" Terrell shouted as he pushed the women and Haddie out the kitchen door into the backyard.

The encroaching smoke drove Rick and Terrell to their knees in search of fresher air. Rick began crawling on all fours toward the living room, but Terrell grabbed his shoulder and hollered, "I'll get Joash," Terrell pointed at the back door. "The girls shouldn't be out there alone."

Did Hale do this? Rick crawled fast for the back door, wondering if the women were in more danger outside all alone than if they had stayed together. Emerging from the house, he drank in the rain-washed air in greedy gulps, thankful to be free of the choking smoke. His eyes still burned as he ran toward the women and Haddie. Although they looked unharmed, their faces were slack with shock, and the orange glow flickering in their eyes made Rick dread turning around to look for himself.

The little blue house, the sweet haven Rick loved, was reducing to a glowing skeleton before his eyes. Giant tongues of fire licked the roofline, then converged into pillars of flame and black smoke billowing into the late-afternoon sky. Burning bits and pieces of the house floated on the air before landing on wet grass and smoldering out. The fire had already consumed the front half of the house, and the glow from the back windows said the kitchen would be next.

Rick imagined the family photos hanging on the walls. He pictured the kids' bedrooms and their toys. He saw all of the little things that made Val and Terrell's house a home. He couldn't stand the thought of it all burning. This was not right, and if this was Hale's doing, he would pay for it. Rick would make sure of it.

Rick leaned toward the house, eager to go back for Terrell, but the women beside him needed him, too. He was torn about who needed him the most. *Hurry up, Terrell. Get out of there.*

The insistent syllables of approaching sirens confirmed the chattering radio in his ear. Responders were almost there. Rick placed a hand on Val's shoulder and tried to comfort her, "Can you hear that, Val? They're on their way to help. It's going to be okay."

Both Stephanie and Val turned worried eyes to him. Val shifted Haddie to her opposite hip and asked, "But where are Terrell and JoJo? Why aren't they out here yet?"

"They're coming," Rick assured them, hoping he spoke the truth. Stephanie gave him a look behind Val's back. Her expression and raised eyebrow seemed to silently ask him, *are they?*

Stephanie took Haddie from Val's arms. "Sweetie," she asked the girl, "where was Joash in the house?"

"Him's sleeping," Haddie answered and pointed to the house. "On the couch in the libbing room."

Rick tensed. It was only late afternoon. Being asleep this early in the day did not seem right for the active little boy. Had Joash already succumbed to smoke inhalation? His eyes scanned the house, searching for signs of Terrell and his son. Would he need to go in after them?

Another flame leaped high into the sky, directly above where Haddie last saw Joash. Still Terrell did not appear, but they couldn't wait in the alleyway any longer. If it was Hale who had set the fire, he could still be nearby, and if he was, the isolated alleyway wasn't the best place to protect everyone. Setting a fire in broad daylight showed just how bold Hale was willing to be. They had to move even if it meant temporarily abandoning Terrell and Joash.

"We need to get out front," he told the women. Hopefully the growing crowd of emergency vehicles and curious neighbors would spook Hale enough to keep him far away for the time being. Rick was also concerned about Axle. Rick couldn't imagine how freaked out the dog must be stuck inside the backseat kennel with all this commotion going on around him.

He ran a few paces down the alley before realizing that Val and Stephanie weren't following him. "Come on." But Val stood her ground. She seemed unable to turn from the burning inferno that held her husband and her son.

Stephanie balanced Haddie on her hip, then grabbed Val's hand and tugged. "Come on, Val. Maybe Terrell and Joash went out the front door. We need to follow Rick."

Finally, Val relented. They all jogged down the alley to a place where they could safely cut through a neighbor's backyard, stepping onto the front sidewalk at the same moment that the first of the fire engines arrived. An ambulance parked behind the engine, and then behind that, Terrell ran from the same neighbor's yard with Joash in his arms. Rick's shoulders slumped in relief.

"*¡Gracias a Dios!*" Val cried out, thanking God out loud with every step as she ran to her husband and son. Haddie wiggled out of Stephanie's arms and joined her family, leaving Rick and Stephanie alone by his patrol car, where they could hear the muffled sounds of Axle's anxious barks coming through the windows.

Rick opened the kennel in the back, and an agitated Axle flew out onto the sidewalk, running circles around Rick's legs, unsure of which direction he wanted to go. Rick squatted and pulled Axle in close. He massaged big fistfuls of fur along Axle's neck, trying to calm the dog with his voice and touch. "You're okay, buddy. Everything's okay." It took extra effort, but once Axle was reassured, Rick was able to turn his focus back to Stephanie. She stared at the burning house, hardly blinking. Creases formed between her eyes. He stood back up, not liking the look on her face.

"Are you okay, Stephanie?"

She didn't answer him, just hugged her bare arms around her slim waist and shivered. He grabbed a blanket from the trunk and wrapped it around her shoulders. "Didn't your mama ever tell you not to go out in the rain without a coat?"

She humored him with a small smile and a quick, absentminded "thanks" for the blanket and returned her attention to the fire.

Given the circumstances, it wasn't the most relevant or professional thing to be focusing on, but Rick couldn't help noticing how pretty Stephanie looked. Even after all that she had endured today—crawling through windows, running away from a psychopath, escaping a burning building—Stephanie was still stunning.

It wasn't the first time Rick had noticed her beauty. He had always thought of her as an attractive girl, but watching her now he was struck by how naturally that beauty came to her. It was effortless. Without a bit of makeup, standing in drizzling rain, she was beautiful. He thought of the photo of her hanging on Hale's attic wall. He saw again the joy in her eyes and her easy smile. He did not like seeing anxiety dimming that joy.

Without turning her head from the scene in front of her, Stephanie said to him, "This is because of me, isn't it." She didn't say it like a question. She was declaring what she had already decided to be true.

He turned her by the shoulders to face him before he said, "This is not your fault, Stephanie. That is an old house with outdated wiring, and a chimney that probably hasn't been cleaned in a while. It could have been any number of things that started that fire." She tried to turn away, but he held her shoulders and made her look him in the eyes. "I mean it. This is not your fault."

"But look what I've brought on my friends," she said, gesturing toward the house. "They do not deserve this."

The anxiety he had seen on her face hardened into determination. Stephanie looked him in the eyes and said, "I know they will still want me to stay with them. But I can't. I will not put them in any more danger. Wherever I go, I know that Julian will follow."

Rick looked down into her determined face, respecting the strength of character he saw there. But he also felt her fine-boned shoulders under his hands, and an urge to protect her surprised him. Years of training and experience told him not to get involved. He had to do whatever he could to keep his professional distance. If he let things get personal, the job would consume him.

Yet here he was, holding a pretty girl by the shoulders, searching her anxious eyes for something he could do or say that would do any good, discovering that as foolish as it may be, he did not want to keep his distance.

He wanted to give her more than a pep talk, but it was all he had at the moment. "Look, you've been through a terrible day. Don't worry about anything until we know more. One thing at a time, okay?"

He left one hand on her shoulder and looked toward the ambulance. Joash wore an oxygen mask and was being loaded into the back of the truck. Terrell sat on the back edge with his own oxygen mask while Val and Haddie climbed inside with Joash.

Watching them, Rick remembered the long hours Terrell had sat by him in the hospital when he was recovering from the stabbing. He remembered how Val had stocked his freezer with ready-to-eat meals, and how they had cared for Axle until Rick was on his feet again. The Watkinses were the best kind of people, the best kind of friends. Now they were facing their own crisis. It was his turn to step up and help them. And he suddenly knew the best thing he could do to help.

"Stay right here," he told Stephanie. "I need to talk with Terrell."

Julian Hale.

Until this afternoon, Stephanie hadn't known Julian's last name. In her mind, he had simply been Julian, the IT guy. She had never talked to him much, because he seemed like the kind of guy who was happiest when you got out of his way and left him alone to work. Any small talk she had attempted only seemed to make him uncomfortable, so whenever he was in her classroom, she would leave. She would walk down the hallway to the office to make copies or check her always-overflowing mailbox, anything she could find to burn the time. On the days she had chosen to stay in her classroom, she had purposefully kept the chitchat to a minimum for his sake. She had thought that was what he wanted her to do.

For as little as she knew of him, he apparently knew all about her, though. Every. Detail. Rick and Terrell had told her about the bulletin board in his attic. She shivered at the thought of her school picture stapled up there. Julian probably knew her middle name and her social security number. What other trivial details of her life had he uncovered? Did he know the name of her kindergarten teacher? Or what kind of cereal she liked to eat in the morning?

Stephanie pulled the blanket Rick had given her tighter around her shoulders. What she really wanted to ask was *why me?* What was it about her that had convinced Julian she deserved to die? She thought she had been kind to him. What had made him hate her so much that he wanted to kill her?

Another patrol car pulled in behind the ambulance where Rick stood talking with Terrell. Terrell had slipped off his own oxygen mask, and the two men kept glancing her way. Stephanie cringed. *They are trying to figure out what to do with me.*

She hated being a burden. She preferred the caretaker role. It had always been important to her to be strong and independent, not needy and self-centered like her broken mother. This whole situation had slipped out of her control. Somehow she needed to take it back, to take care of herself instead of standing here waiting for Val and Terrell to make everything better for her, or for Rick Powell to feel he had some kind of obligation to become her knight in shining armor.

It looked as though the firefighters were gaining the advantage over the fire. Would the house ever be what it once was? She closed her eyes. *Thank you, Lord, that everyone got out okay.*

She knew this was her fault. She might not have lit the match, but she did not believe this was an accident. How else would her friends suffer if they continued trying to protect her? What would Julian try next time that could hurt them? Stephanie slipped the blanket off her shoulders, folded it and placed it on the hood of Rick's car. She wasn't going to let there be a next time.

By the ambulance, Rick nodded at something Terrell said, and then he turned his body with his back toward her blocking Terrell from her view. Rick leaned in closer, absorbed in their conversation. This was her cue to exit. She could slip away now while Val was preoccupied with the kids and paramedics and Terrell was talking to Rick. She had to do this her own way, but Val and Terrell would stop her if they knew what she planned to do.

Stephanie stopped a passing paramedic. He didn't look too busy, or in too much of a hurry to get somewhere else, but it still embarrassed her to interrupt him from his work. She couldn't just disappear, though. Taking off with no explanation would send them all looking for her again. "Excuse me," she asked him, her voice too squeaky. She cleared her throat and tried again. "Do you happen to have a piece of paper and a pen I could borrow?"

"Yeah, sure." He pulled a small notepad and pen from the breast pocket on his uniform. Ripping off a sheet of paper, he handed both to her. "Just keep the pen."

The paramedic walked a few paces away, then turned. "Hey, weren't you inside the house? Has anyone checked you out yet?"

Stephanie hated lying to him, but she hadn't been near the fire long enough to inhale any smoke. The longer she stood around chatting, the more her window for slipping away undetected was shrinking.

"Yeah. I'm good. Thanks for the pen." She flashed him what she hoped was a confident "I'm just fine" smile. He nodded and left her to fend for herself.

Using Rick's patrol car hood as a hard surface, Stephanie wrote a quick message:

T and Val—I know you want to help me, but you have enough to deal with right now. Don't worry about me.

I promise I'll be smart. Praying for you guys. I'll check in soon. Love, Stephanie.

And Rick—Thanks again for all your help. I'm

pretty sure you literally saved my life today. I'm grateful.

She anchored the paper with Rick's windshield wiper. When she turned, she saw Axle standing on the sidewalk watching her. He cocked his head, looking curious.

"Take care of them for me, okay, Axle?" The dog wagged his tail.

She didn't have a plan yet, not even a clue where she should go first. She did know, however, that she could not stick around and allow Julian Hale to harm little Haddie or Joash or their parents any more than he already had done.

It was cold, and it was wet. She had no coat, no money and no cell phone. She had no idea what came next, but Stephanie put one foot in front of the other, determined to lead Julian Hale away from the people she loved.

Chapter Five

"Are you sure?" Terrell sat on the back edge of the ambulance. His eyes blinked rapidly as he gaped at Rick. "I mean, I'm thankful for your help, but you've worked so hard to get back out in the field. It's been such a long road to recovery. I would never dream of asking you to put that on hold, especially not on your first day back on duty."

Rick kicked a pebble away with the toe of his boot. He rammed his hands deep into his pockets and fiddled with a challenge coin he always carried. Was he sure? The decision was made—he was going to protect Stephanie and help Terrell and Val. It wasn't about what he did or did not *want* to do. This was about the meaning of friendship.

He swallowed down what he wanted. He wanted to be a member of his team again and to be back at work with Axle. Law enforcement was his calling. It ran in his blood. His grandfather, his dad and his uncle were all retired cops. Rick had not been one of those kids who followed in his family's footsteps because he thought it was what he was supposed to do. Rick had become a cop because it was what he loved to do. The whole first year of work at SPD, he had marveled at the thought, *I'm getting paid to do this?* Eventually over the years, he had settled into it being demanding work with a lot of sacrifice involved. His failed relationship was proof of that, but through it all there had been a sense that he was doing what he was meant to do. Being injured for so long and cut off from that world had made him feel lost.

Rick cleared his throat. If he thought about this for too long, he might wimp out and take back his offer. "Getting back to work can wait," he told Terrell. "It shouldn't take you that long to get your family squared away. Besides, after all that you and Val did for me and Axle, it's the least I can do."

It wasn't the least he could do. It was a huge sacrifice, and Rick knew that Terrell was fully aware of how much it was costing Rick. Terrell stood up from the ambulance and held out his hand to shake. Pulling their grasped hands across his heart, Terrell reeled Rick in for a manly hug, slapping him on the back twice.

"Thank you," Terrell said before he set Rick free from his solid embrace. "I should only need a week. If you can keep her safe for me until then, I should be able to take over from there."

Rick nodded. "Not a problem," he assured Terrell.

Terrell chuckled. "But now you've got to tackle the hard part."

"What's that?" Rick asked.

"Convincing Stephanie to *let* you help her." Terrell shook his head. "I love that girl like my own sister, but she is stubborn and she won't enjoy being needy. She has been the rock of her family for a long time, and no one has ever looked out for her. Don't take it personally if she isn't too keen on the idea of having a bodyguard."

Val walked over and joined the men, balancing Haddie on her hip. "Hey." Her eyebrows pinched together as she made eye contact with Rick. "Have you guys seen Stephanie?" she asked. "I can't find her."

"Yeah, she's waiting by my…" Rick pointed at his car, but she wasn't there. Axle sat on the sidewalk in front of it, but Stephanie was gone. The hairs on the back of his neck raised.

"Axle, *hier*," Rick called Axle to come to him. The dog trotted to his side obediently. Rick patted Axle's saddle area. Axle had been sitting by the car and Stephanie the whole time. If something malicious had happened to Stephanie, he would have alerted Rick. Where was she?

Rick started toward his car with Terrell, Val and Axle following him, but the paramedic called out to Terrell. "Sir, you really need to keep that mask on, and I think we're ready to transport your son to the hospital."

Terrell and Val froze. Their dark complexions paled with worry. Both of their gazes flitted between the ambulance and Rick's patrol car.

Rick put a hand on Terrell's shoulder. "Go!" he commanded. "This is part of what I just volunteered to do. You take care of your family. I'll take care of Stephanie."

It had taken him two hours to find her, and he was not happy. He wanted to chew her out for being so stupid, but finding her on her knees in the front of the church sanctuary dissolved his anger. Well, it dissolved it a little bit. Seeing her alone and praying tugged at his compassion. He was relieved that she was alive and well and not floating upside down near the Ballard docks as Hale's other victims had been. But he was still plenty angry with her. What had she been thinking, taking off like that with nothing more than a note to explain? Didn't her friends deserve better than that?

And why did he care so much? The smart thing would be to leave her right where she was to fend for herself. He had already gone above and beyond what duty dictated. Where had his objectivity gone? Victims had a right to refuse help. But this victim mattered a lot to Val and Terrell, and they mattered too much to Rick to let them down. Like it or not, he was involved for their sake.

Rick crossed his arms and called out down the church aisle, "So are you planning to make me chase you all over this city today, or what?"

Stephanie scrambled up from the front altar and spun to face him. Her body was set to run or fight, and her face was so pale he almost felt guilty for startling her like that. *Almost.*

He raised his hands and stepped closer so she could see him. "Hey. Calm down. It's just me."

Stephanie closed her eyes and relaxed, letting out an audible sigh. Her eyebrows crinkled together. "How'd you find me?"

"The question should be why I had to go looking for you again in the first place. Wasn't saving you once today enough?"

She squared her shoulders. "Terrell would have insisted that I stay with them." She crossed her own arms, mirroring Rick's stance, holding her ground. "They don't need to babysit me, Rick, and sticking around gave Julian opportunity to hurt them more than he already had. Making everyone mad at me was a small price to pay to keep them all safe."

He admired her selflessness, but her actions were still foolish. The minute she'd walked away from the crowd, she had allowed herself to be an easy target. He took a step closer to her. "You could have asked me for help. Terrell and I were setting up a plan for your protection."

"As a favor to Terrell, right?" Her jaw tightened. "I am not your responsibility, Rick. I've always taken care of myself. I'm trying to figure out how to keep doing that."

He had made a promise to Terrell. Now he needed to convince Stephanie to let him fulfill it. "Lone ranger tactics get people killed, Stephanie. Even the toughest cops call for backup."

As soon as he said it, memories flashed, and in his mind he was instantly back on the sidewalk by the warehouse in the Industrial District on the night that he and Axle had been stabbed. He was once again in the dark, rain falling on his face while he waited for either rescue or death, unable to move, unable to do anything but wait for backup to save him.

Most of all he remembered the blood. *Blood on the man's chest where Rick's bullets had entered. Axle's blood. Rick's blood.* And he remembered the sounds. *Sirens. Pounding feet of his backup finally arriving, running to help. Shouts of "Officer down. Officer down."*

Rick shook his head to clear it, returning to the present. "I understand not wanting to be in need of help, believe me, I get that better than you know. But can't you see that taking off on your own and refusing their help has made you more of a burden for Val and Terrell? You should see how worried they are about you right now."

Her face was turned up toward his, and he noticed how close they had moved to each other as they talked. Even in the dim lighting of the sanctuary, he was near enough to see her eyes change to a different shade of blue as they filled with tears. Her head dropped, and she slid her hands up into her hairline and grabbed at her roots. "Ugh. That was not what I was trying to do."

He reached out and pulled her hands down to her sides. "I know it wasn't what you wanted to do, but Stephanie, it took me only two hours to find you in the city. It could have been Hale who found you instead of me. What was your plan?"

She plopped down onto the nearest seat. She rested her head on the back of the chair and stared up at the ceiling. "I didn't have a plan," she admitted, but added, "Yet. I was going to figure it out, maybe find a women's shelter or something that would help me. But once I started walking, I didn't know where to go. I thought about going back to the school to get the stuff I had left there, or going home and making some phone calls. But I was too scared to go to any of the places Julian knew about so I ended up here. Our pastor is meeting with the worship team upstairs, and he said I could hang out here for a while and pray."

She rolled her head to the side in order to look in his direction. "So how did you find me?"

Rick shrugged, then sat down on the chair next to her. "Not sure. Just knew you would want to feel safe and thought your church might be a place you'd go in search of help."

"Yeah, I thought someone would be here and that maybe the office would have a flier or a phone number for a shelter or something." She laughed. "But as silly as it is to say out loud, I also kind of hoped maybe a killer wouldn't want to come into God's house, like church was home base or something."

She sat up and turned toward Rick. She curled one leg under her on the seat and shifted to face him. "I'm really sorry, Rick. About making you hunt me down again. I figured you would be done trying to save me if I didn't want to be saved."

"It's tempting," he told her, even though his anger had fizzled out. He understood her thinking. "But I owe Terrell more than I will ever be able to pay back in this lifetime, so if being your personal bodyguard for a little bit frees him up and eases his mind, that's what I'm going to do."

During the long months of fighting off infection and suffering through rehab, throughout all of the boring hours of being a desk jockey on light duty, all he had cared about was getting back to doing real police work. And now after only one day back at it, he was volunteering to walk away from it again. This girl better be worth it. Apparently she was to Val and Terrell, and they were definitely worth it to him. He couldn't think of any of his other friends who would be able to call in a favor like this.

Stephanie bumped her shoulder against his. "That is if I *let* you be my bodyguard." She was teasing now. Was she giving in?

"Terrell asked for one week to get organized. After that you guys can make whatever other plans you want to make." Rick waited for an answer. "So, think you can put up with me for a week, or do I have to keep hunting you down all night? It's been a long day and I wouldn't mind clocking out and getting something to eat."

She bit her bottom lip. He could tell it was hard for her to admit she didn't have any other options. Then she smiled a real smile like the one in the photograph. She held her hands up in surrender. "Okay. You win. What's the plan?"

Chapter Six

Stephanie inserted the key and unlocked the dead bolt. Her front door was dingy and in need of a clean coat of paint. It routinely stuck, requiring her to slam her shoulder against it to get it loose. The groaning sound the door always made as it slowly swung open sounded to Stephanie as if it were whining in a proper English accent, *Really? Again? Is this* quite *necessary?* Typically, she would tell it to stop being lazy and to quit whining, but she doubted Rick Powell had the scope of imagination necessary to understand her having a conversation with her front door.

When she had left the house earlier that afternoon, she hadn't expected to be bringing home company. Especially not company that made her as nervous as Rick did. What condition had she left everything? Was there anything embarrassing left out that she wouldn't want him to see? She lived what most would consider a minimalist lifestyle in preparation for Liberia, so it shouldn't be too messy. Still, she couldn't help but wonder what her little duplex would look like through Rick's eyes.

Before she stepped over the threshold, Rick pulled her back. She jumped at the sight of his drawn gun. "Let me go ahead of you. I want to clear it first." He gave Axle a command sending him in the door before them.

He was going to search her whole house? Now she had more than just breakfast dishes left out to worry about. "Um, I was hoping to clear it first myself," she said. She gave him a crooked smile. "Don't look too closely, okay?"

Rick's dimple flashed and he winked. "No promises."

Stephanie trailed behind him, her heart racing. Rick's vigilance reminded her that nowhere was safe anymore, not even her own home. Although small, old and quirky, it was cheap, and she loved it. It always felt good to be home, but now tainted by her fear, it felt different and foreign.

"All clear." Rick returned to the kitchen with Axle at his heels and holstered his weapon.

With the threat of a bogeyman jumping out at her gone, Stephanie scanned the house. There were a few dirty dishes on the counter, a basket of laundry to fold on the couch and a mess of papers surrounding her open laptop on her kitchen table. Nothing too embarrassing, but now what was she supposed to do with him?

"Can I get you something? Tea? Coffee?"

"No, thanks. I can entertain myself while you pack." Rick sat down on the couch and the basket of laundry tipped against him.

Stephanie rushed to rescue it before it spilled into his lap. "I am so sorry."

Axle lay down at Rick's feet but cocked his head at her as if he were trying to figure her out. Stephanie had grown up in a house of women. What was she going to do for a whole week with a man and his dog? If she didn't get over her nervousness around them, it was going to be a long, awkward week.

"Well, make yourselves at home. I'm sorry I don't have a TV." She set the laundry basket down behind the couch. "I'll try not to be too long. What am I packing for exactly?"

Rick's gear squeaked as he shifted on the couch to look back at her. He looked so uncomfortable sitting in his uniform with its bulky gun belt. "There's a safe house the US marshals keep near Lake Union. One of our detectives worked out a deal for us to use it for the week. It's a two-bedroom hotel suite that's kind of like a mini-apartment. Just pack whatever clothes and personal items you want, and maybe a few books or movies or something to keep from getting too bored."

A knock on the front door interrupted them. Rick and Axle both sprang up, alert. "You expecting anyone?" Rick asked, drawing his gun again.

Stephanie shook her head.

"Get down behind the couch while I answer it." She shoved the laundry basket aside and squatted down, not liking that she couldn't see what was happening. She strained to hear, then peeked out around the bottom of the couch to watch.

Rick looked through the peephole, then inched open the door. "Can I help you?"

A voice Stephanie didn't recognize answered. "Delivery for, uh…" The voice stalled, probably looking at an address. "Stephanie O'Brien. She live here?" It sounded like a man in his late teens, maybe early twenties, and his nervous tone also sounded like he wasn't expecting a cop to answer the door. She wanted to get a look at him but she didn't dare move out that far from behind the couch.

"Who's it from?" Rick asked him.

"I'm just the delivery boy for the courier company. I don't know anything about the packages or where they come from."

"You're delivering on a Saturday?"

"Twenty-four/seven. Keeps our company competitive with the big guys." The poor kid sounded so nervous, Stephanie felt sorry for him.

Rick grilled him a little bit more, asking for his name and the courier company's name and address, until he finally let the poor guy off the hook.

"What is it?" Stephanie asked, standing up as he closed the door.

In his hand, Rick held a large manila envelope. He placed it down on her kitchen table just as his cell phone rang. "Hey, Gary. What's up?"

Stephanie fingered the envelope. What was it? Dread mixed with curiosity. Was it from Julian?

She turned the envelope around in her hand, examining it. She found no return address, of course, only her name and her own address chicken-scratched out on the front in blue ink. The envelope looked harmless enough. She peeked at Rick. His back was turned toward her as he spoke to someone on his cell.

Curiosity won out, and because she knew Rick would probably stop her from doing it, she sliced the top open and dumped the contents into her hand before he got off the phone and stopped her. She had to know what was inside.

Rick ended his phone call. "Does the word *anthrax* mean nothing to you?"

But Stephanie wasn't listening to his words; she was too captivated by the stack of photos that had fallen out of the envelope. There were pictures of several of her students leaving school for the day; there was a picture of Joash wearing his backpack running into his school, another of Val and Haddie out shopping, and others of Terrell at work. There were shots of her church, of her pastor and of Stephanie standing outside talking with some of the women from her Bible study. There were photos taken from her sister's Liberia blog showing Emily and Ty, and many of the kids from the orphanage that Stephanie loved. There was even a photo of her mother in front of the casino. Had he gone to Oregon to find her? Picture after picture revealed a location she frequented or a person connected to her.

She reached the final photo. It was a shot taken outside of the Watkinses' house fire earlier that day. In the picture, Rick was draping the blanket over her shoulders and the camera lens had zoomed in on the look of tender concern he had on his face. Scrawled across the corner of the picture in black permanent marker were the words, "Awww, how sweet."

Rick reached out his hand. "Let me see."

Stephanie handed him the stack. "Rick, if I care about someone, their picture is in there. He didn't leave anyone out." She could hear her own panic.

Then she handed him the note that came with the photos in the envelope. In the same chicken-scratch handwriting, the sender had written: *You can run, but can* they *hide?*

It had to be Julian Hale.

Rick flipped the last photo over, examining the back. "These pictures came from the one-hour at Walmart. We can look into their security cameras, but we already know who they're from. Let's not touch them anymore, and I'll send them to the lab to be fingerprinted. But for now, we've got another more pressing problem."

Chapter Seven

Stephanie wondered what could possibly be bigger than this threat, but she asked, anyway, "What problem?"

"That was Gary Shelton on the phone. He's the head detective on this case, and he's been going through all of the stuff we found at Hale's house today." Rick paused, turning in circles, searching for something. "Gary called to warn us that he can see us."

"What did he mean, he can see us?"

"He meant what he said. Gary is on Hale's personal computer right now, and…" Rick reached across the kitchen table and slammed her laptop closed. "We better hope Hale doesn't have one of those with him with the same software as his home computer, because Gary was looking *through* this and seeing *us*."

She shook her head, refusing to believe it. "No way." She backed away from the table. "No way." She would not accept that Julian Hale had been spying on her in her own home. For how long? What had he seen?

"How?"

Rick pointed at her closed laptop. "Do you have a webcam on that?"

"Yes. I video chat with my sister on it." Nausea rolled. The violation she felt was indescribable. "I think I'm going to be sick."

"I know this is hard, but we don't have time to deal with it. If he was monitoring your house remotely, he knows we are here. We need to move and somehow avoid being followed."

He's been watching me. Where else? At school, too? He's threatened everyone. Everyone. There had been too many blows today. She looked at her couch situated in front of the little gas fireplace. She wanted to quit, to wrap up in a quilt with a cup of tea on her couch and process all that had hit her in such a short time. But Rick was right. She needed to act, not think. Once they were in the safe house, there would be plenty of time to think.

"Okay."

"There's no way to know what other technology he has messed with. Don't pack anything that he could trace. Leave your phone here. Don't bring your laptop or a tablet."

"I can't leave my phone." She held up the stack of photos. "I need my contact list to call these people to warn them."

"Just leave it. We're going to the police department. I can help you contact your friends from there."

Axle circled Rick's feet, most likely assuming Rick's agitation meant it was work time. It fascinated her how quickly Axle transformed from a playful puppy to an intense animal who seemed human in his desire to work with his partner. She was beginning to love that dog.

"Stephanie?" Rick was pacing, and rubbing his palms together. She looked up from Axle to Rick, expecting more instructions. Instead, he waved a hand toward her bedroom door. "Hurry."

Five minutes later, Stephanie handed him a duffel bag.

"That's it?" Rick asked, sounding shocked.

"I've got enough clothes and a toiletry bag. What else do I need?"

"No complaints here," he assured her. "My experience with women made me expect three rolling suitcases and a gigantic bathroom bag."

"I travel light," she told him. *His experience with women?* A stab of jealousy hit her. She began to imagine his past girlfriends, wondering what they looked like and why he hadn't ever been married. He must have a reason for still being single. *Stop it, Stephanie. More important things to focus on at the moment.*

Rick's hand found her back and guided her toward the front door. Before he opened it, he said, "Go for the car as quickly as possible."

They rushed down her front stoop to Rick's waiting car. Stephanie ducked in while Rick kenneled Axle and tossed her bag into the back. The whole process from front door to pulling away from the curb had taken less than two minutes.

Rick's headlights reflected off the wet streets. Stephanie noted that the night sky had finally caught up with her sense of the length of this day. It felt so much later than only eight o'clock. Was constantly running her new reality? Would she forever be dodging the balls Julian threw at her, or was there hope of being free of him? *Lord, please let them catch him. I don't want to live like this forever.*

"Where are we going?" she asked Rick.

"To the department to meet with Gary Shelton," he said, looking into the rearview mirror. "I don't want to risk Hale following us to the hotel. Gary wants to talk with you, and I need to go home to change and pack. Gary will transport you to the safe house, and I'll meet you there."

Stephanie blinked. Rick was leaving her alone at the police department? She picked at a hangnail while he explained his plan. It made sense—the last thing she needed was Julian knowing where she was hiding— but the idea of separating from Rick made her nervous.

Rick entered a security code, and a gate clicked open, allowing them to enter the department parking lot. Stephanie breathed easy for the first time since leaving her house. She had never seen so many police cars in one place. A fleet of vehicles backed into their parking spaces looked like an army ready to go when called. Julian couldn't get in here. Where could she be safer than locked behind fences surrounded by cops? Maybe she should move in here to hide from Julian. She could find some unused storage room out of the way and hole up until he was arrested.

That helps you, but what about your friends? She would love to forget, even if for only five minutes, how much was really at stake.

Inside, Rick led her through a maze of cubicles until they came to a messy desk where an older man sat. He rose to greet them. "Aw, here's our girl," he said.

His dark eyes and full brows contrasted dramatically with his receding salt-and-pepper hair. He appeared to be in his fifties, but he exuded an energy Stephanie didn't usually see even in men much younger than him. The marathon race number and medal he had framed and hanging on his cubicle wall explained why.

He extended his hand to Stephanie. "Gary Shelton. You have no idea how glad I am to see you safe, young lady." The lines surrounding his sad eyes made her believe he had seen his share of *unsafe* young ladies. Goose bumps ran up her arms at the thought.

"Thank you," Stephanie said. She glanced at Rick and added, "I'm glad to *be* safe."

"Detective Shelton is leading our investigation on this case," Rick explained to Stephanie and then asked the other man, "Anything new?"

The detective handed Rick a folder. "This is the updated FBI profile report."

Rick's eyebrows furrowed as he scanned the report he held in his hands. Stephanie hoped he would hand it to her next. She wanted to know everything she could about Julian, to understand why he had targeted her like this, but giving her access to an FBI report probably wasn't going to happen.

Rick looked up from the file and asked Shelton, "What about those other three photographs I saw in his attic?"

"They were out-of-state victims that we didn't know about," Shelton told him. "I've been on the phone all day with other departments connecting the dots."

The detective pointed to a map he had pinned to his cubicle wall. "Lora Johnson, 35, Saint Paul, Minnesota." Then he moved his finger to a different location and said, "Kelly Halloway, 32, and Naomi Folsom, 25, both from Milwaukee, Wisconsin." He dropped his arm to his side as if it were suddenly too heavy. "Hale grew up in a suburb of Saint Paul and went to school with Johnson. Before moving to Seattle, he worked for a tech company in Milwaukee. There will be a solid case against him once we bring him in."

"Same MO?" Rick asked.

Stephanie caught the questioning look the detective

shot Rick. "It's okay," she assured him. "Don't water it down for me. I need to know the truth."

Shelton gave a curt nod before he responded, "Final cause of death for all six was strangulation and..." His gaze flitted back to Stephanie before he added, "All six victims were educators of some form."

Stephanie stepped back, shocked. "Julian is killing teachers?"

"Yes. Lora Johnson was a high school computer applications teacher in Saint Paul, and the other two taught together at a school in Milwaukee. The Seattle victims were a preschool teacher, another high school teacher and a tutor at a learning center."

Rick read out loud from the profile report in his hands, "The suspect is likely a white male in his late thirties, early forties. He is likely motivated by a need for power and dominance stemming from early childhood feelings of helplessness after suffering abuse at the hands of a male authority figure. The victimization of educators is most likely the result of a perceived failed romantic relationship or personal rejection from a member of that demographic."

He stopped reading and asked Shelton, "That first victim, Lora Johnson?"

"It looks like she paid the ultimate price for spurning his love, and all the rest were guilty of reminding him of her," Shelton said.

"Why me?" Stephanie asked the detective. "I mean besides being a teacher like the other women, why did he choose me? I thought I was always kind to him. I can't think of anything I did or said to make him hate me like this."

"It isn't anything you did to him that motivates him, it is simply who you are." Shelton nodded toward the file Rick held. "You fit his profile. You are young, and although you have friends, you are basically alone in the city with no immediate family connections in the area. He saw you as an easy target. Julian Hale is a systematic and patient killer. He targets people he thinks will be easy to capture, but then he takes his time getting to know them, knowing their routines and their friends. He becomes obsessed."

"Let me show you something." The detective beckoned Stephanie and Rick over to a computer on his desk. "This is the computer we took from Hale's property today." He tapped the screen and asked Stephanie, "Recognize this place?"

Both Rick and Stephanie leaned toward the screen, eager to get a look. Stephanie leaned in even farther, squinting at the grainy images, looking for clues that would tell her what was on the screen. She felt warmth radiating from Rick as he leaned across her back, straining to get a look at the computer over the top of her head.

Stephanie grimaced. She knew exactly what place the camera was recording. "My classroom," she spat out.

She turned her back to the computer. She was done looking at it. First her home, now her classroom—how dare Julian desecrate her safe places? She rubbed her arms, trying to wipe away the thought of Julian's eyes spying on her.

The detective turned his chair to face her and then sat down. He leaned on his knees, looking at his feet instead of making eye contact with her. "Hale doesn't strike until he is sure of his success," Shelton said. "He hasn't left room for error in the past."

He sat back up. "But you have one advantage the others don't have."

"What's that?" Stephanie asked him.

"You are alive."

He reached up and touched her arm. "You are the one that got away. We know who he is now, and we got to you before he did."

Stephanie sat down in a chair by the cubicle wall. "But he's threatened everyone I care about. I'm alive, but are the people I love safe?" She felt Rick's reassuring hand on her shoulder and appreciated his strong grip.

Detective Shelton crossed his arms and leaned back in his chair again. "I know you are worried about your friends, but for now I'm pretty sure you are Hale's primary target. I've been studying this case for over a year, and my guess is he has fixated on you, not your friends. The threats today are just a way to scare you and prove to you once again that he is in control. For now, your safety has to be your top priority. And ours."

"My priority is seeing him caught. I want to be free, and I want the people I love safe. I'm not going to be content sitting around in hiding for long." Stephanie leaned back in her chair and crossed her own arms, trying to appear bigger than her five-foot-three frame. Somehow she needed to get them to stop seeing her as a fragile thing about to break, and convince them to focus on the bigger picture. "I don't know a lot about Julian, but I know some. I've got to be able to help somehow. Can't you use me as bait or something?"

Gary Shelton smiled up at Rick. "I like this girl." Then he patted Stephanie's arm before rolling his chair away from her. "For now we focus on getting you two into hiding without Hale knowing your location. Rick will go home in a different car than he came in. We'll put you in a disguise and take you out of here in a separate car. Once we're sure there's no tail, we'll meet Rick at the marshals' hotel suite."

"Thanks, Gary," Rick said, shaking the detective's hand. To Stephanie he said, "See you soon."

When Rick was out of earshot, the detective turned back to Stephanie. "Get a good night's sleep. Lie low for a few days and let the dust settle." He put a hand on her shoulder. "Then I just might take you up on that offer."

Later that night, Rick tossed in the grip of a nightmare. Against the backdrop of a dark Seattle industrial complex, Stephanie begged him to help her as Julian Hale backed her into a corner, swinging a gigantic knife. Rain ran into Rick's eyes, his mouth, choking him and drenching his clothing. He was frozen. He couldn't move to help Stephanie. He could only stand and listen to her screams, watching as helplessness enveloped him.

The clicking of the hotel heater turning on woke him up. He was soaked with sweat and his heart raced. *It's just the dream again.* Different versions of the same nightmare had played out for over a year now. The dream's setting never changed. It was always the same dark, rainy exterior of the warehouse where he and Axle had been attacked and stabbed, but somehow the old dream had adapted to his new reality by including Stephanie and Julian Hale. He breathed deeply, trying to slow his heart and orient himself with the unfamiliar room he had woken up in.

He remembered he was in the hotel safe house, but beyond that there was something that was still off, something that didn't feel right. What was it? The bed was so cold and empty. He patted around the sheets. Where was Axle?

After the stabbing, Axle had assigned himself as Rick's personal bodyguard. Apparently Axle's guard duty included protecting Rick while he slept, as well. Training him to do otherwise had been an exercise in futility. Rick often thought, *Good thing I'm not married.* Instead of a wife, he always awoke to Axle snoring next to him with his left paw covering his chest protectively. The dog was the most loyal partner ever. But where was he now?

Rick slipped out of the covers and grabbed his pistol out of the nightstand. He searched the living room and kitchenette space of the suite. Axle was nowhere to be found. Stephanie's bedroom door was cracked open slightly. Should he check on her, or was that invading her privacy too much?

Saturday had been such a long day for her, and they hadn't gotten settled into the suite until after midnight. He hoped she was fast asleep, forgetting all the fear of the day before. The microwave in the kitchenette said it was only five in the morning. He didn't want to disturb her, but with Axle MIA, he needed to make sure she was okay. Rick pushed on the door and peeked inside.

Stephanie was sound asleep on her back under the covers, her strawberry blond curls splayed out around her like a halo. She looked so peaceful. Next to her was a sleeping Axle, his left paw draped over her protectively. Axle lifted one eyelid, then promptly closed it again as if to say, *Go away, you're interrupting my beauty sleep.*

"Traitor," Rick whispered.

Stephanie sat straight up in bed and gasped. Rick

jumped back behind the door. *Wow. Light sleeper.* Maybe her sleep wasn't as peaceful as he thought.

Rick peeked around the door, feeling guilty. "Sorry. Don't wake up. I just couldn't find Axle. Looks like he thought you needed his company more than I did."

Stephanie squinted her eyes, looking so cute in her confusion. She glanced from Rick in the doorway to Axle on the bed and then smiled. She patted Axle and then said in a hoarse voice, "Thanks for looking out for me, pal." Axle yawned his noisy response.

"Want me to get him off?" Rick asked her.

Stephanie lay back down on her pillow. "Not unless you miss him too much."

"Go back to sleep," Rick whispered, and closed her door.

Back in his own bed, Rick couldn't sleep. He would never admit it to anyone, but he did miss Axle's company. And if he was continuing with the honesty, he also wished he had someone special in his life. But the scar across his belly, the nightmares and the memories of Allie walking away all reminded him why that was a life he couldn't have. The sooner he accepted that he wasn't Terrell Watkins, the better off he would be. It was good to manage his expectations.

He tossed and turned until he finally threw off the comforter and swung his legs over the edge of the bed. *I give up.* After taking a quick shower and dressing, Rick wandered into the kitchenette and found the coffeepot. He could hear Stephanie's shower running. The coffee aroma was just beginning to hit his nose when she emerged from her room.

"I'm sorry I woke you up," he told her.

She shook her head and started scrunching her damp

curls between her hands. "It wasn't you. I never can sleep well in a hotel. It's too noisy."

On cue, the sounds of rolling suitcases passed by their front door. Above their heads, water ran through the pipes. Someone upstairs must be showering, too. Rick had to agree with her, it was noisy.

"Breakfast?" he asked. He shuffled through the groceries he had brought with him last night, but nothing looked too appetizing. Stephanie opened the blinds to a predawn view of houseboats and yachts floating on Lake Union. Sunrise peeked a bit from behind a distant hill. The scene looked peaceful and hopeful, not like a city hiding a murderer.

"I've got to give Axle a bathroom break. When we get back up, should we make this feel like a real vacation and order room service?"

She flashed him the grin he was beginning to anticipate. "I'm a sucker for breakfast," she said. "It's my favorite meal."

"Then it's a deal." He liked making her happy, especially when she rewarded him with that gorgeous smile.

"Can I go outside with you guys?" she asked him, a hopeful look on her face. "I'd love to get some fresh air."

Frowning, he said, "Better not."

How quickly they had moved from his being able to make her smile to having to tell her no. "Until we are sure we weren't followed last night, I'm afraid you're stuck in here," he explained.

Disappointment flashed on her face, but she replaced it quickly with a look of resolve and said, "I understand."

Rick hated that she had to be a virtual prisoner in this hotel room, but he couldn't risk taking her out in the open. "Shelton has a security detail set up in the hotel. They've got an officer on his way to stay with you until Axle and I get back up here."

Having a strange cop standing guard in the room would make her feel even more like a prisoner, but it couldn't be helped, and Axle was pacing by the door.

He gave her what he hoped was an apologetic smile. "We'll be quick, and then we'll get that breakfast I promised you."

Outside, Rick kept catching himself glancing up at the fifth floor of the hotel. He was feeling so antsy. Someone else was doing his job. Having a security detail to monitor the hotel and spell him as he needed made sense, of course, but being apart from Stephanie unsettled him. Axle wanted to play, but Rick cut it short. He couldn't get back to the room fast enough, and when he dismissed the other officer, he saw a look of relief cross Stephanie's face, too. It felt good to know she was getting comfortable with him, or that at least he made her feel safe.

He called down their breakfast order right away, but it felt like an eternity passed before they finally heard a knock at the door.

"Room service."

Stephanie's stomach growled so loud, Rick heard it. "Ah, I can smell it," she said, giggling.

Rick opened the door and found the covered tray waiting on the floor. She was right, it did smell incredible. Axle squeezed past Rick into the hallway, barking loudly at the tray in Rick's hands.

"Axle, *pfui*!" *Stop that!* Rick nudged Axle back into the room with his knee, but the dog wouldn't shut up. "*Pfui!* Are you trying to get us kicked out of the hotel, dog? Be quiet."

The dog didn't like it, but he obeyed, replacing the barking with a much quieter whine as he paced.

Stephanie wriggled forward on the red microfiber couch as Rick placed the tray on the coffee table in front of her. "Madam, as you requested," he said.

Stephanie shut her eyes and inhaled. "Yum. Val's dinner was so long ago, I'm starving." She turned a sympathetic face toward the dog. "Sorry to eat in front of you, Axle. I'll share," she promised him.

Rick's stomach growled, too. "He's fine. He knows better than to beg like that."

Axle barked sharply. He was picking up bad manners.

Stephanie reached over and lifted the cover off two steaming plates of golden pancakes. The pats of butter had melted to perfection. Rick stared at the tray, precious seconds ticking away as *something is wrong* needled his brain. It took about three seconds to register what his eyes were seeing.

An antique-style alarm clock sat between the two plates. Rick saw the blast cap, the wires and the large bundle of dynamite.

He grabbed Stephanie's wrist and yanked her off the couch, shoving her forward.

"Run!" He pushed her out the door, praying every footstep would take them far enough away.

Chapter Eight

It took Stephanie several seconds for her mind to catch up to her running feet. There had been a bomb on the breakfast tray. She had seen it with her own eyes. *A bomb.*

The hotel was laid out in a crescent shape with several floors of open balconies overlooking a central patio-style courtyard. Unsuspecting guests filled the courtyard below where they ate breakfast, read their newspapers and drank coffee, oblivious to the bomb about to explode in the fifth-floor suite above their heads. The same bomb that could detonate behind Stephanie's back at any moment. Her leg muscles twitched. She needed to run away.

Rick hung over the balcony. "There's a bomb," he bellowed. A few people stared up at him in shock, a few pointed up at him, probably wondering what that crazy person was yelling about up there.

"Evacuate the building!" Rick screamed once more and then gave up. Stephanie and Axle followed him. They couldn't waste time waiting to see if anyone acted on Rick's warning or not. *Please let people hear him; let them get out before it goes off.*

Dialing his cell as he ran, Rick breathlessly relayed the news to Shelton and then screamed yet another warning to two businessmen in suits waiting by the elevator ahead of them. When they heard Rick's words, they dropped their bags and ran.

Sweat trickled down Stephanie's neck under her hair. Would Rick's warning reach anyone else in time? Who would get hurt when the bomb detonated?

A door opened into the hallway, and a woman holding a baby carrier stepped in front of them. The woman's other hand clasped the hand of a toddler. The little boy's eyes widened at the sight of the crazy people and the dog running toward his little family.

Stephanie slowed her running and shuddered. *Lord, no! Not babies.* Her lungs burned. Gasping to regain her breath, she managed to yell at the woman, "There's a bomb! Get them out of here! Run!"

The woman froze with a deer-in-the-headlights gaze. Stephanie estimated at least three minutes had passed. When would the explosion hit them? They were wasting precious seconds.

"Run!" Stephanie screamed at her again. "Get your kids away from here."

The woman snapped awake and ran a few slow steps with the cumbersome baby carrier, dragging the toddler behind her before she stopped and sobbed, "But my husband's in the shower. We were just getting breakfast."

Stephanie scooped up the little boy, while Rick said, "Keep running, I'll get your husband."

"Rick, no," Stephanie protested. *Save yourself. I need you with me.*

"Go. Get those kids as far away as you can." Rick pounded his flat palm against the door where the family had emerged. "Police! Open the door!" He was still pounding and yelling as Stephanie and the woman continued down the hall.

Every fiber in her being fought against abandoning Rick, but Stephanie couldn't listen to her instincts. Silent tears streamed down her cheeks as she left him. They had to get these babies to safety. It was probably already too late.

As they reached the stairwell, the wailing screams and flashing strobe lights of the hotel's alarm system kicked in. Shelton must have warned the front desk. Stephanie was grateful for the blaring warning. The more time that passed before the bomb went off meant more people would hear it and get out safely, and the fewer injuries or deaths she would have on her conscience.

Doors slammed as people abandoned their rooms, shoving past the two slower-moving women and children on the stairs. Stephanie winced at every noise or touch, but if the bomb hadn't detonated already, would it at all? So much time had gone by already, maybe the bomb was a dud, just Julian's idea of a joke.

Axle whizzed by her legs, running down the stairs several floors, and then circling back. He barked at her and repeated the same cycle over and over, urging the two women to hurry. The toddler screamed in Stephanie's ear, squirming and reaching for his mother. Stephanie's arms were sweaty and slippery. She was afraid she might drop the boy if he kept moving like that.

"Sit still, sweetie. I'll give you to your mom when we're outside, okay?" His poor mother stumbled behind Stephanie several times. Running down steep stairs while juggling a heavy baby carrier at the same time didn't look like an easy task.

"You're okay, Max," the woman yelled to her son. "Be a good boy."

Other people rushed past them on the stairs, slowing their progress even further. It felt like the entire hotel full of people was attempting an escape down this one tight stairwell.

They were almost to the ground floor when the woman stopped, red-faced and heaving for air. She knelt and started unlatching the straps securing her baby. "I'm going to take her out of the carrier. Keep going."

Not wanting to leave her, Stephanie stopped and said, "Hurry."

Then she heard more running footsteps above them, and a male voice called out, "Marla, I'm coming."

A man in boxers and a damp T-shirt ran barefoot around the corner, grabbing the baby from his wife. Marla turned to Stephanie and reached for her son.

Stephanie handed the boy to his mother. Stretching up on tiptoes, she peered around the couple and up the stairs behind them. "Where's Rick?" she asked Marla's husband. "Why isn't he with you?"

But Stephanie never got her answer. An explosive shock wave hit her first, knocking her to her knees, erasing all doubt of the bomb's authenticity. The lights flickered for a second and then a heavy *boom* sound echoed down the stairwell, sending vibrations right through Stephanie's bones. Marla and her husband flung themselves over their children. Stephanie covered her ears and huddled against the wall. Warm fur blanketed her as Axle positioned himself close around her body, ever her vigilant protector.

"Rick," she screamed. "Rick!" She squeezed her eyes shut and pulled into a fetal position.

Then a strong arm wrapped around her shoulders,

pulling her in, and she heard Rick's voice speaking in her ear. "I'm right here."

A sense of déjà vu settled on Stephanie as she and Rick watched the commotion from the edge of the crowd gathered in the hotel parking lot. It was her third experience in two days of watching a bunch of emergency responders cleaning up a mess that Julian Hale had made.

Axle was thirsty and hungry, so when another K-9 officer offered to get him some food and water and to kennel the dog in his patrol car, Rick thanked him and handed him the leash. Then he began pointing out the different agencies and command staff to Stephanie, helping her to understand what she was seeing. Police officers, SWAT, FBI, ATF, paramedics and firefighters swarmed around them. He pointed to a tall man in a tailored suit with silver hair and a trimmed gray goatee. "There's the mayor."

"Looks like a good time to rob a bank," she said, her eyes wide in awe of the response. "Is *everyone* here?"

"We don't take a bomb going off in our city lightly."

They had been told that a hotel employee—the same one who had left the kitchen with their room service order—had been found unconscious in a utility closet. That meant Julian had delivered the bomb himself. Was he still close by? Stephanie imagined him hiding somewhere in the bushes watching the scene, thrilled by the chaos and mess he had created. She wondered if the huge scale of descending law enforcement and media attention delighted him. Did this enormous response, along with the heightened human emotion, feed his sickness? Would it fuel him on to bigger and better things than chasing after an unimportant schoolteacher?

The entire block had been cordoned off, and all area buildings had been evacuated. Police were escorting curious pedestrians outside of the crime-scene tape, and refusing to comment to all of the members of the media who were leaning across the barricades crying out for information.

Clumps of people stood by the barricades and answered the reporters' questions, eager for their fifteen minutes of fame. How soon until the reporters figured out Stephanie and Rick's connection with the explosion? She spotted an attractive blonde woman wearing a blue parka with a Channel 4 News patch on its sleeve. It was Kristine Scott, the news anchor Stephanie watched every night before bed, and she was interviewing one of the men Stephanie and Rick had warned outside the elevator. Stephanie averted her eyes and stepped behind a large pillar to hide from his view before he recognized her and pointed her out to the newswoman.

Rick draped his arm around her shoulder and put his lips to her ear so no one else could hear. "Play it cool and try to blend in, but stay alert. Hale could be nearby. Shelton is on his way with a car to get us out of here, but in the meantime, I don't want a camera or microphone shoved in our faces. The less attention we draw, the better."

Stephanie agreed. She did not want her students' parents turning on the eleven o'clock news and seeing their child's teacher on the screen. Rick guided her behind an ambulance and then farther down a sidewalk. On any other morning this street would be busy with traffic. Today it was empty of cars and eerily silent.

Stephanie had to remind herself to breathe. They had distanced themselves from the crowd and the watchful eyes of the media, but if Julian was out there somewhere paying attention, the new spot also made them more vulnerable to another attack. Maybe they should go back to the parking lot to wait. Without thinking about it, she stepped closer to Rick's side for comfort.

"Shelton will be here any minute," he reassured her. "We need to be ready to jump in when he pulls up. Then we can go get Axle."

The Space Needle stood tall in the skyline on Stephanie's left, the iconic landmark reminding her of how far downtown they were. Over four million people lived in the Seattle area, yet somehow Julian Hale kept zeroing in on their location. He was doing the impossible.

"How is he doing it?" she asked Rick, sensing the same frustration eating at him. "It shouldn't be this hard to hide in a city the size of Seattle." Maybe she and Rick should forget about waiting for Shelton and find their own hiding place. But remembering how well taking off on her own had worked out for her yesterday convinced her that was not a feasible option.

"I don't know," Rick answered her. "We've got to figure it out or it's useless to even try to hide. He's got to be doing more than just following us, but I can't figure out how he's tracking us."

Stephanie stared at the shops across the street that bumped up to Lake Union. There was a chowder restaurant, and a marina selling yachts. On another day, she would have had fun crossing the street and exploring the shops and luxury boats for sale. But in reality, on a normal Sunday morning like this one, she wouldn't be downtown at all. She would be at church, sitting next to Val. She would probably have Haddie cuddled up on her lap and Joash snuggled next to her side. She wanted to be in that place of safety and contentment instead of standing outside a crime scene investigation knowing that she was the reason for all of this uproar.

Her mind wandered to her school. She imagined the kids climbing off their school buses tomorrow morning, dragging backpacks behind them, and then finding a substitute teacher when they walked in the door. A pang of something like homesickness hit her. She missed her normal routine. She surveyed the chaos surrounding her and pressed her fingers to her lips. *Thank You that all of this happened on a weekend and not while I was at school. Please don't let Julian hurt my kids.*

As soon as she and Rick got to somewhere safe, she needed to call her principal. She had already talked to him, and Detective Shelton had promised to contact him, too, but she needed to reinforce with Jim again just how much danger they could be in at the school. She wouldn't be able to live with one of her kids getting hurt because of her.

Stephanie scanned the crowd behind her trying to assess the damage. Their hotel suite had been completely destroyed in the blast, taking out much of the surrounding rooms, including those above and below theirs. She could see a paramedic working on a woman's hand, and a few people had bleeding cuts on their faces. They must have been hit by flying debris, but so far it didn't look to her that people had been hurt too seriously. Julian had given them all enough time to get out. Why was that?

She turned to Rick and said, "Another thing I don't understand is why it took so long for the bomb to go off." She didn't mean to sound ungrateful for the extra time that had saved so many lives.

"Not that I'm complaining," she corrected herself, "But when we were running, I kept expecting the explosion to happen at any moment. It seemed like it took forever."

"No. I thought the same thing." Rick shuffled his feet and crossed his arms, his biceps stretching the sleeves of his T-shirt. He looked so strong, yet Julian had him perplexed, too. It made the ground beneath Stephanie feel unsteady, as if she were standing on one of the swaying boats moored at the docks across the street.

"I think he was giving us time to get out," Rick said.

"What?" Nothing Julian was doing made any sense to her. There had been so many opportunities for him to kill her already if that was his intent; why did he keep letting her live? "Why bother sending the bomb at all if he wasn't trying to kill us?"

"Remember what Gary Shelton told you? You are the fish that got away. Hale needs to feel in control, to believe he holds all the power. The bomb was just a message. He's telling us that when he is ready to do it, he's going to do it his way."

"By *it*, you mean kill me," Stephanie said.

"That's not going to happen, Stephanie." Rick reached out for her hand and she took it, comforted by the gesture. It was just palm to palm, not as meaningful as if their fingers interlaced, but it wasn't something that two strangers would do. Rick was beginning to feel less like an acquaintance and more like a friend.

"I'm sick of Julian having the upper hand," she said.

"Me, too," Rick agreed. "But you can't let him get inside your head. Otherwise he accomplished exactly what he set out to do. We've had some setbacks, but it is past time for the tide to turn in our favor."

It was strangely peaceful holding Rick's hand and watching the floating boats bobbing in the water across the street. She wished they could get in one of those yachts and sail far, far away from the threat of Julian Hale and all of the fear and guilt he had brought into her life. Getting back to Africa had never sounded better to her. How far would Julian be willing to go before he gave up on her?

Something in the parking lot kitty-corner to where they stood pulled her attention. She squinted to clear her vision. A man stood at the far side of the lot, too far away from her to see him clearly. Hadn't the police already evacuated all of those buildings? He was probably just some looky-lou checking out all the excitement. But the more she stared at him, the more intrigued she became. Instead of looking at the spectacle around the hotel, he seemed to be staring at her instead. He stood abnormally still, with a perfect, erect posture she knew too well. He raised a hand in a wave and Stephanie's insides turned to ice.

"Rick, there he is." Stephanie gasped out the words, scarcely believing he was really standing there and not a figment of her imagination. She dropped Rick's hand and pointed at the man's retreating figure. "Julian Hale is right there across the street."

"Wait here for Shelton," Rick shouted back to Stephanie.

Pistol in hand, he sprinted across the street and hurdled over low shrubbery into the parking lot on the other side. He wobbled some on his landing, but continued running. He struggled to keep his eye on Hale's head as he weaved between cars. Rick pushed his legs and pumped his arms harder, needing to increase his speed and decrease Hale's significant head start. Rick didn't know how he could ever catch up on foot.

"Stop! Police!" Rick yelled after Hale's retreating

form. It was useless. Even if Hale could hear the command, he probably wouldn't obey it.

He needed backup, but he would have lost Hale if he hadn't immediately taken off after him. Rick kept running and grabbed at his cell phone on his belt. In the movies it always looked so easy for the hero to dial a phone, carry on a conversation and continue to pursue the bad guy. It wasn't easy. At all.

Desperate for air, he tried to spit out words to communicate the situation and his location to Shelton without losing sight of Hale. *Where'd he go?*

"You've got to get me some backup," Rick panted. "He had too big of a head start. I've lost sight of him. We've got to stop him before he disappears into the downtown crowd."

Two seconds later, Rick heard the screams of pursuing patrol cars and the shouts of men on foot coming to his aid far behind him. They had to flush Hale out of hiding. Rick didn't think he could stand it if Hale escaped again.

When the parking lot ended, Rick came to a crossroads. He had to decide if Hale would turn into the city or go for the docks. Heading toward the lake was a dead end, but his backup was already searching the streets and no one was searching the boats yet. Rick's instinct sent him sprinting for the docks.

His lungs were on fire. He hadn't run this hard in a long time. All of the rehab he had done during the past year had left him stronger than ever, but his endurance still needed work. If only he hadn't let Randy Mitchell take Axle to his car. He needed his partner with him. Axle would have found Hale by now. Rick imagined the dog sprinting ahead of him, tackling Hale to the ground and ending this whole deal.

Adrenaline surged, pumping strength into his limbs. Visualizing himself capturing Hale and setting Stephanie free of this life of hiding drove Rick forward. He covered ground faster than he thought possible. He spotted a brief flash of movement. Rick's instinct had been right; Hale had gone toward the water instead of downtown. But why? It was a dead end unless he planned on swimming away.

Rick slowed and ducked behind a nearby sign. He raised his gun, his pounding heart contrasting with the serenity of his surroundings. Seagulls circled lazily overhead, chattering to one another as they searched for food. Water lapped a steady rhythm against the gently rocking boats. Then, *crack.*

The gunshot rang out, splintering the peace and sending the gulls squawking. Hale had a gun!

Rick ran down the dock, firing his own gun in response. The pungent scent of seawater and fish filled his nostrils. Images of the night he and Axle were stabbed assaulted his memory. The warehouse where it had happened was only three miles away from these docks, and the same salty smell had been in his nose that night as well. History could not repeat itself here. Rick had fought too hard. He would not allow Julian Hale to take him down again.

Hale dived onto the deck of the nearest yacht, glass shattering from the cabin door where Rick's bullet hit directly above him. Hale popped up and fired back at Rick, but he was an inexperienced shot, unable to hit a moving target.

Rick jumped onboard the boat nearest him and ripped his cell phone from his belt once again. He rolled to his back and dialed Gary Shelton. "Hale's firing at me, Gary. Where's that backup you promised me?"

"Where are you?"

"Last set of docks before the park. Do you have Stephanie?"

"Yes. Almost to you," Gary shouted into the phone. "Don't lose him."

"Not planning on it." Rick hung up and called down the dock. "Give it up, Hale. You're trapped."

But Hale didn't answer. The silence unsettled Rick as he rolled over and popped up to look again over the edge of the boat. He scanned the dock. Where was Hale hiding now? "My backup will be here any second," Rick shouted. "This is a dead end. Turn yourself in before you make it worse."

But his words flew out to sea, useless. No one was listening.

In his peripheral vision, Rick saw movement. He spun in time to watch Hale sprinting down an adjoining dock. He must have hopped across to a different boat when Rick dropped down on this other yacht. Rick leaped off the boat and ran, jumping from boat to boat until he clambered onto the same dock as the fleeing man. Rick could hear the distant squeal of Gary Shelton's tires as his car turned into the parking lot behind him, and the screaming sirens of the patrol cars he brought with him. He heard slamming doors, shouting men and stomping boots. He'd have help soon. Would it be soon enough?

Hale reached the end of the dock. "Dead end, Hale," Rick yelled. They both raised their guns and fired at each other simultaneously. As the bullet left his gun, Rick wasn't sure where it struck, but he was certain he had hit Hale somewhere.

He tried to raise his gun to fire again, but his hadn't been the only bullet to find its target. One of Hale's bullets had sliced across Rick's shoulder. Searing white pain erupted across his brain. Rick heard the splash of Hale's body hitting the water. Had he killed him?

With his right arm hanging limp at his side, Rick launched himself forward, willing back the black edges of pain threatening to take him under. It wasn't until he was going down himself that Rick realized he had tripped on a knotted piece of rope. His injured arm refused to rise in his defense, and it was the smack of his forehead striking a metal tie-down on the dock that eventually broke his fall.

Chapter Nine

Detective Shelton's last words to Stephanie before he rushed after Rick and Julian had been, "Stay in the car."

At first she obeyed his command, but that had been before she saw Julian's bullet rip into Rick's shoulder, before she watched Rick stagger from the impact, and before the *pop, pop, pop* sounds confirmed what her eyes were telling her brain.

Any instructions the detective had given her disappeared the moment she knew Rick was hurt. Her hands flung open the door handle and she was already running when Julian's body toppled into the water. She watched Rick trip and fall, his forehead bouncing off something on the dock, and then he rolled over and remained completely still.

She found a trail of blood beginning where Rick had first taken the bullet and leading to where he had eventually fallen. Stephanie backpedaled a few steps. What would she see when she got to him? Was she prepared for the worst? Detective Shelton and another dark-haired officer were kneeling next to Rick. The rest of the officers had spread out, continuing the search.

Rick still wasn't moving. Stephanie forced herself

back into a run. She needed to see with her own eyes that Rick was only injured. He couldn't be dead. She skidded to a stop next to Rick's motionless body, skinning her knees in the process.

"Is he okay?" she asked, her voice shrill.

"He's alive," the detective said. "I've got to go after Hale. You two stay with him. Paramedics are on their way."

Stephanie wanted to beg the detective not to leave them, but he had already run off the docks yelling into his cell phone. Rick would want Detective Shelton to go after Hale, but Stephanie was scared.

Laying trembling fingers on Rick's neck, she checked his pulse and leaned her cheek down to his mouth to see if he was still breathing. The thump of his pulse was strong under her fingers, and his breath warmed her cheek. Her head flopped back and she breathed a prayer of gratitude.

"He's breathing," she told the young cop on the other side of Rick.

"Yes, but we need to stop the bleeding," he said.

Her eyes took in all of the blood coming from Rick's shoulder and forehead. The smell of it made her stomach roll in waves that crested at the top of her throat. She fought against the wooziness. She couldn't pass out. Rick needed her. But she had never had much of a stomach for seeing other people's blood, and this was the most blood she had seen in her whole life.

Stephanie breathed in through her nose, counting to three with each inhale, then exhaling through her mouth, calming the nausea the best that she could. They had to stop the bleeding, but which wound was the most important to treat first? The forehead was bleeding the heaviest, but didn't all head wounds bleed profusely, even if they were minor? She had had some first-aid training in preparation for her mission trips, but gunshot wounds were way outside of her league.

Detective Shelton said the paramedics were coming; she could hear the sirens, but she didn't think Rick could wait that long for them to get to him.

The officer ripped a section off the bottom of Rick's T-shirt, revealing Rick's muscular stomach, as well as multiple jagged scars covering his abdomen and chest.

Stephanie sucked in a deep breath, stunned at the sight of all of those scars. She didn't want to imagine the pain they represented. She remembered feeling similar scars on Axle when she had petted him in the hotel. Intense admiration and compassion filled her for the unconscious man on the ground in front of her.

What kind of battle were you two in to get those?

"Here, use this and put gentle pressure on his forehead," the officer said, handing her part of Rick's shirt. "I'll take a look at his shoulder."

She gently applied the cloth to Rick's bleeding head. She watched as the officer examined Rick's shoulder. She could see where the bullet had entered and exited his shoulder. Not having the bullet still in there had to be a good thing, wasn't it?

At the sound of the paramedics' running steps, Stephanie rolled back onto her heels, relieved. The closer they got, the more the dock swayed under her. She popped up and got out of the way, allowing the professionals to take over.

"How is he?" a deep voice asked from behind her. She spun and found that Detective Shelton had returned.

"I don't know," she answered in a voice barely above a whisper. "Did you catch Julian?"

"No sign of him. Every officer in the city is looking.

We have helicopters in the air and a dive team prepping. I'm hoping Rick got him and we will find him on the bottom of the lake."

Please let them catch him. Let this nightmare end.

It probably wasn't any of her business, but her curiosity couldn't be contained. "Do you know where Rick got those scars on his stomach?" she asked the detective.

"Ah, those. Those came from being in the wrong place at the wrong time and running into a nut job with a knife. You'll have to ask Rick about that story when he wakes up."

Rick moaned, startling Stephanie. Was he waking up?

"Come on," Shelton said. "We'll meet the ambulance at the hospital." The detective sighed deeply and hung his head. "And I can guarantee that Rick is not going to be happy when he wakes up. He's already done enough time in that place."

"Officer Powell. Wake up, please."

Rick opened his eyes to a woman hovering over him. She was far too old for the hot-pink streak in her hair, and her raspy smoker's voice was far too chipper for 4:00 a.m. He was sick of her interrupting his sleep.

He squinted at the far wall. Under "Your Nurse's Name Is:" she had printed "Yvonne" in big slanted letters with a green dry-erase marker.

"And how are we feeling?" Yvonne asked as she checked his vitals. It was the same question she had just asked him an hour ago.

"Peachy," he mumbled. The whiteboard said Yvonne's shift ended at 7:00 a.m. Not soon enough for his liking. *I'd be better if you people would quit waking me up.*

Because of the concussion, the nurses had been waking him every hour to make sure he was still alive. It was annoying. The pain meds dripping through his IV made him want to sleep, but every time he closed his eyes, Yvonne's singsong voice dragged him back awake again.

The gown they had him wearing felt like a dress. His mind was groggy and his head and shoulder throbbed. It was probably time to ask Yvonne for more pain meds, but Rick preferred to feel the pain over the fog and fatigue brought on by the narcotics. He was done being weak and needy.

He hated everything about this place. The familiar muted sounds and smells of a hospital floor in the middle of the night seeped in from the hallway like a bad dream. He heard the squeak of a nurse's shoe and the swishing sounds and beeps of the multitude of medical equipment. He smelled the lingering odor of antibacterial soap Yvonne put on before examining him.

After they released him last year, he had promised himself that he would never return to this place. Yet here he was lying in the same hospital. No matter how hard he fought to make it line up with his desires, life kept going its own way, forging its own path. It made him want to push harder.

Light from the hallway broke through the semidarkness of the room, spotlighting the recliner next to his bed where Stephanie had curled up and fallen asleep. It looked uncomfortable, but at least the nurses had given her a blanket and a pillow.

His memory of what had happened since Hale's bullet hit him was fuzzy, but of what he could remember, Stephanie had been present the whole time.

Allie didn't stay. Allie didn't even make it through one

night with me. Apparently the last time he had been in the hospital, three hours of bedside vigil had been his former fiancée's limit.

The last real conversation he'd had with Allie had been in a hospital room like this one. It was even possible that this was the actual room where that conversation had taken place. This could be the same bed he had been lying in when Allie started weeping and told him, "I can't do this anymore, Rick. I love you, but we both know I am not cut out to be a cop's wife."

The strain his job placed on their relationship had been building for a long time. There had been one too many night shifts, and one too many plans ruined when he was held over for mandatory overtime. Seeing him near death in a hospital bed had been her breaking point.

He saw again Allie's tearful face, heard again her apologies as she slipped off the engagement ring. She had left the ring beside his water cup before she walked out the door, leaving a gaping wound no doctor could stitch back up for him.

"Rick?" Stephanie's sleepy voice asked from the recliner. "Are you awake?"

Rick worked to bring his mind out of the past. Stephanie kicked off her blanket and padded in her socks to his bedside. "Do you need anything?"

He stared at the ceiling. "Nah, I'm fine. Just ready to get out of this place. You didn't have to stay."

"Where was I supposed to go?" Stephanie sat on the edge of his bed. "You're my bodyguard, remember?"

He released bitter air between his lips. "Some bodyguard."

"I'm still alive, aren't I?"

"No thanks to me." He turned his head on the pillow to look at her. "Thanks for sticking around, though."

She waved her hand out in front of her. "Look at these luxury accommodations. There's even an officer standing guard out there in the hallway. Where could I be that's any better than this?"

He gave her a thin smile. "I'm thankful for the company, but I wish you didn't have to be so uncomfortable. Hospitals are no fun."

"What do you mean? Yvonne isn't enough fun for you?"

Rick snorted in response. "Oh, yeah. She is loads of fun."

Stephanie placed a soft hand on top of his. He soaked up the comfort from it. Everything about her seemed soft in the dim light. Soft curls, soft pink lips. And although he couldn't see it, he knew her heart was soft, too. He couldn't help noticing again how very different she was from Allie.

Even in high school, Allie was sophisticated and high-maintenance. Moving into her twenties, she had become more and more polished, with a coolness that was alluring. But sitting next to him on the edge of his hospital bed in the middle of the night, Stephanie was all lightness and ease. The warmth radiating from the inside out was so comfortable and inviting.

He really did appreciate her company, although *appreciate* felt like the wrong word. It was more than that; he felt it much deeper. He turned his hand over and squeezed hers, thankful that she hadn't pulled it away.

She continued, "Seriously, don't worry about me being uncomfortable. I really don't mind." Her voice light and teasing, she said, "I'm not the one with a bullet wound and a busted-open forehead."

"What? This?" he asked, lifting the bandaged arm. "It's merely a flesh wound."

He almost wished the bullet wound was more serious so he could blame it for being stuck in the hospital again. The bullet had entered and exited his shoulder without too much damage. They probably would have released him already if that was all that ailed him. It was the stupid bump on the head that had made the doctor insist that he stay overnight for observation. Taking a bullet was so much more heroic than tripping over his own feet.

Stephanie squirmed a little. "Can I ask you a question? It's kind of personal."

He winced. "You saw the scars?"

"Yeah"

"Pretty ugly, huh?"

"More like badges of honor. I was pretty impressed, actually."

She glanced down at their hands clasped together, and said in a quieter voice, "I felt the scars on Axle's belly, too, and I have been wondering about it, but you don't have to talk about it if you don't want to." She tried to pull her hand away, but he grasped it tighter, unwilling to break the connection so soon.

Until now, he had not wanted to discuss that night. He had been too busy trying to recover, and he'd resented everyone wanting him to relive the nightmare. It had been important to put it all behind him and move on. But talking to Stephanie felt natural. He wanted her to know him.

"I was working a night shift, and I got an alarm call from the Industrial District. A security guard thought he saw suspicious activity going on at the warehouse across the street from his building." Rick's mind took him back. "I wasn't too concerned. We had been slammed with a string of false alarms at businesses all year long.

While I waited for my backup, Axle and I searched the perimeter. I had no idea that we had actually stumbled onto a holding site for a human trafficking ring. Several women and girls were being held prisoner inside that building until they could be moved to some other location along the I-5 corridor. We must have spooked their guards when we showed up. One of them jumped us with a knife."

Stephanie's fingers squeezed his hand gently, encouraging him to keep going with the story. That night, Rick had been maybe fifteen feet back from rounding the building when a man flew around the corner at him wielding a knife. He had been trained to understand how fast and lethal a knife could be. He knew how within seconds fingers could be sliced off or tendons severed, or how within the span of those same seconds, a person could be lying on the ground with a knife sticking out of a vital organ. But no amount of training scenarios could have prepared him for the speed and intensity of the real thing.

Looking back, he was able to recall the man's face. In his dreams he still saw how those eyes were filled with both rage and fear simultaneously. But in the moments of the attack, Rick had had no time to observe. There had only been time to act. The scene replayed across his memory again now. He saw the flashes of movement in sync with his heartbeat, the glint of streetlight off the blade, slashing, slashing and then stabbing. He saw his gun rising, heard the bullets, as round after round fired from his gun. He saw his assailant crumple to the ground, dead. Rick had killed a man.

Rick closed his eyes, but kept talking. "I was finally able to fire my gun, but not before his knife had done a lot of damage to both me and Axle."

"Wow." Stephanie was quiet for a while. Then she said, "Those women owe you their freedom, Rick. It sounds like a story from a third-world country, but not here, not in America."

"It's more common here than anyone wants to admit."

"You're a hero," she said.

Rick shook his head, making him dizzy. "I'm no hero. I just stumbled onto that situation and barely made it back out alive."

She didn't say anything more, and Rick didn't feel the need to talk more, either. He had avoided talking about that night for so long, it surprised him how easily it had spilled out of him and how good it felt to tell her.

Rick wasn't sure how much time passed before he remembered that he was holding Stephanie's hand again. He did not want to let go of her, but the very room they were sitting in reminded him of the way he had failed Allie. He couldn't want this. Yes, Stephanie was a very different woman from Allie, but she was still a woman who deserved better than what he would be able to offer her. What she needed from him was to help her stay safe, not to be confused by his developing feelings for her. He let go, hating how empty his hand felt after he did.

She cleared her throat and stood up. "You better go back to sleep while you can," she said, a teasing tone returning to her voice. "It won't be long before you get another visit from your friend Yvonne."

"Okay," he said, fatigue pulling him under fast. "But be ready to go early. If you aren't firing me as your bodyguard, I've got a new plan."

Chapter Ten

Monday

Detective Shelton leaned against the doorjamb of Rick's hospital room. He sighed and made an announcement: "No sign of Hale, in or out of the water."

Stephanie's head dropped. She had heard the news from another officer in the ER waiting room, but she hadn't had the courage to tell Rick last night. She had been holding out hope for Julian's being caught overnight. Her eyes flew to Rick to see his reaction. He struggled to sit up in his bed, worrying her that he would reopen his stitches. She ran to his side to help him, but he waved her off. His anger was palpable.

"How could that happen?" Rick demanded. "We had him in the water."

The detective's shoulders slumped. "We searched all day and through the night. They brought the dogs. Divers looked for his body in the water. We had helicopters in the air. All manpower not tied up in the bombing investigation at the hotel scoured the area. Somehow he pulled another disappearing act on us. I'm thinking he must have slipped out of the water and into the downtown crowd while we were still on the dock. With all that construction happening, I'm guessing he was gone before we even got the search truly off the ground."

Rick punched the bed with his good hand. Even though it was Stephanie's life being threatened, Julian's capture was just as important to these two men as it was to her. Having these driven men on her side made her feel somehow safer, even if Julian Hale was still out there somewhere. These two would not stop until she was safe again. Actually they wouldn't stop until all of Seattle was safe from him again.

"There was some good news from yesterday, though," Detective Shelton said.

"Really? I'm definitely ready for some good news," Stephanie told him.

"Hale is taking risks he hasn't taken in the past. He is so desperate to prove that he is in control and holding the power, his pride is going to be his downfall. At some point he is going to trip up, and we are going to be there to get him when he does."

"I hope you're right," Rick said. "But if Hale is still loose, then Stephanie and I need to get out of here, the sooner the better." He swung his legs over the edge of the bed. All the color drained from his face and he dropped his head into his hand.

"Dizzy?" Stephanie asked, but this time she held herself back, not wanting to annoy him again by being too helpful.

"I'm fine," Rick said, but he kept his head on his hand. "Or at least I will be," he conceded.

The doctor had ordered a twenty-four-hour watch on his concussion. It was 7:00 a.m., six hours short of the twenty-four-hour mark. Stephanie tried to reason with Rick. "But why the hurry? We're safe here, aren't we?"

Rick lifted his head off his hand and squinted at her as if she had a third eye. "Safe? Like we were in the hotel?" He put his head back in his hand. "Do you want to wait around for Hale to deliver another present for you? Maybe I'll call down and order breakfast and see what he has next on the menu."

"All right, I get it." He didn't have to be such a jerk about it. Where had the softness she had seen in him the night before gone? He was being so cold to her this morning. "I'm just worried about you. You don't seem ready to go anywhere."

"If you want to worry about something, worry about the kind of damage Julian Hale could do here if we stay," Rick told her.

Imagining another bomb going off, this time in the hospital full of fragile people, was enough to make Stephanie swallow her other retorts. They might be safer in here, but the other patients wouldn't be safe if they stayed. She and Rick were like Jonah on the ship during the storm when he fled from Nineveh—throw them out and the hospital would be a safe haven again. If Rick was physically capable of leaving, they really did need to get far away.

"Where do we go from here?" she asked. "Last night you said you had a new plan."

"As soon as I can break out of here," Rick said, looking anxious to make that happen soon, "I am taking you camping."

"Camping?" she asked, but he wouldn't elaborate.

Stephanie signaled and then double-checked over her shoulder before changing lanes. She wiped her sweaty palms on her jeans one at a time. It had been a long time since she had driven any vehicle in the city traffic, let alone one as big as Rick's pickup. Even with a dog in the backseat, it smelled masculine and clean and *new*.

Rick's head rested against the passenger seat with his eyes closed. She was glad he couldn't critique her driving, but she still worried she would mess up and do something to damage his truck. *Watch me crash a police officer's $30,000 truck.*

She looked over at Rick, hating how pale he looked. During the hospital discharge process, they had handed him painkillers and a prescription for more as needed, but so far he had refused to take any of them, claiming he wanted to stay sharp. From her perspective, he didn't look alert; he only looked miserable. She wished she knew how to help, but he'd probably be too stubborn to accept her help, anyway, even if she did know what to do.

He still hadn't explained the new plan to her, but she didn't want to bother him to ask about it. Before they left the hospital, Detective Shelton had brought Rick a change of clothes, given him his gun and cell phone, and dropped off Axle along with Rick's truck. Nobody had told Stephanie anything except to drive the truck around to the entrance. She had pulled through the circular driveway and found Rick with a police escort and a volunteer who had wheeled him out in a wheelchair. He hadn't opened his eyes since he had climbed into the cab of the truck. All he had said to her was, "Start driving north."

She had fought the urge to salute him with a "Yes, sir." Why wouldn't he just tell her where they were going?

She glanced sideways again. She didn't think he was actually sleeping. *He's probably awake and just doesn't want to see it happen when I total his truck.*

A red Mazda Miata chose that moment to zip in front of her without signaling, forcing her to stomp on the brake. "Nice blinker, dude," she hollered after him. The driver waved his apology as he whipped ahead of her and off the next exit.

"Relax," Rick said without opening his eyes, his face pinched with pain. That sudden stop couldn't have felt good.

"That's easy for you to say. I don't even know where I'm going."

Rick slowly sat up and moved the car seat back into an upright position. "We are going to my grandparents' cabin on the Skagit River. It's in the mountains off the North Cascades Highway about two hundred miles from here. It's the most remote place I know to go. I'm hoping it's remote enough to finally shake Hale off our trail."

"You never know with Julian, though, do you?" she said. "But why didn't you tell me where we were going? Why all this secrecy?"

"Maybe I'm getting paranoid, but I'm sick of Hale popping up like a Whac-a-Mole everywhere we go. I figured the fewer people who knew our plans, the better."

"Including me?" She probably sounded snarky, but the lack of sleep was making her feel grumpy, and she didn't like being kept in the dark.

"Of course not. When could I have explained things to you without being overheard?"

"You should have found a way. I deserve to know what's going on." She blew a curl out of her eyes and stared ahead.

"Fair enough," he mumbled.

She signaled and changed lanes again, looking for

the nearest exit for I-5 North. "Do you think he has someone telling him where we are?" she asked Rick.

"I don't know. I can't imagine anyone in the department feeding Hale information, but I still can't figure out how he's tracking us. Until I know how he's doing it, we have to be careful who we trust. That's why Shelton and I decided to decrease our security detail and to keep our plans quiet. I have two buddies from the department—Russ Miller and Jason King—who will meet us up at the cabin, but other than that there are only a select few in the loop."

Stephanie searched the traffic behind her in the rear-view mirror. All the cars and drivers looked like innocent, bored commuters to her. "How will I know if he's following us?"

"You won't be able to tell in the city. We'll stop in Marysville for food and supplies. The traffic will thin out after that and we'll be able to tell more." He leaned his head back and closed his eyes again. "Hopefully we'll catch a break for once."

Stephanie agreed. *And hopefully the nice Rick from last night will come back.*

After the stop for supplies and a run through the McDonald's drive-through window, Rick noticed that Stephanie's death grip on the wheel began to loosen. The farther north they drove, the more they both seemed to relax. He kept an eye on the traffic around and behind them, but he didn't see anything suspicious. It didn't mean Hale hadn't followed them again, but if he had, Rick couldn't see him.

He wasn't used to being a passenger, but the dizziness was still too strong for him to drive safely. The over-the-counter painkiller he had swallowed with his soda at lunch had taken the edge off his pain, though, and eventually he began enjoying the drive. As they started the slow climb up into the Cascade Mountains, the scenery became less urban and more rustic and nostalgic by the minute. It was the background of so many of his childhood memories.

"The highway reopened only a few weeks ago, so the road might be a little rough," he told Stephanie. "They always close it for the winter."

Stately evergreens lined the highway, and giant mountains still wearing their winter white loomed all around them. "Ever been across this pass before?" he asked Stephanie.

"No," Stephanie answered. "It's gorgeous."

Rick agreed. "They call these the American Alps."

She leaned forward and peered through the windshield. "I grew up in Eastern Washington, but we always took Stevens or Snoqualmie Pass to get to Seattle. Those passes have pretty views, but this…this is…wow."

Rick smiled. It was fun seeing it all anew through Stephanie's eyes. She was having a hard time keeping her eye on the road as she gawked at the passing vistas.

"Wow," she said again.

"I spent a lot of time up here as a kid fishing with my grandpa Powell," Rick said, gazing at the Skagit River running along the highway. The river surged strong and high, bloated with spring melt. It would be another month before they opened the season for chinook. Rick longed to have a fly rod in his hands.

"I wish it was good fishing right now," he told her. "Actually, fall is my favorite time of year to fish up here, though. You should see how beautiful it is when the trees are on fire with color."

Rick almost added, *I'll have to bring you up here*

again then and teach you how to fish, but he remembered that his protection duty would be over long before the leaves turned. Stephanie wouldn't be a part of his life by then. Besides, who knew if she would even be interested in fishing?

"I grew up in a house full of girls. I've never even touched a fishing pole," she admitted. "It sounds fun."

"It is fun," Rick said. "But it's more than that for me. More like an art, or an obsession. Some people paint, I guess I fish."

"I thought fishing was a summer sport," she said.

"No." Rick chuckled. "If I try hard enough, I can find somewhere to fish year round. Coho run in the fall, and on odd years, we get a good humpy run then, too."

Rick sighed, soaking up the scenery. It had been too long since he'd gotten away from the city. He used to fish every chance he got, but he had been too preoccupied with recovery and rehab to make the drive up here. Prior to his injury, he had wanted to come, but Allie hated leaving civilization behind. How long *had* it been since he'd had a fishing pole in his hands?

Axle whimpered from the backseat. The dog stared longingly out the back windows, probably imagining a romp through the woods. "Not much longer now, buddy, and you can get out and run," Rick assured him.

About an hour later, Rick directed Stephanie to turn off the main highway, and they began weaving along the opposite banks of the meandering Skagit River until they arrived at the old wooden Powell Family sign. His nana had hand-painted it herself to mark the top of their private lane.

Stephanie giggled as the truck bumped along the rutted path. "Just try to find us all the way out here, Julian Hale."

Rick sat up straight and leaned forward, eager to spot the cabin site. As the trees thinned and the A-frame cabin with its wraparound porch and sloped green metal roof greeted his hungry eyes, he felt all of the weariness and heartache he had been carrying around with him throughout the past year begin to evaporate. He flopped back against the car seat, his lips curling up at the corners.

He was home.

Chapter Eleven

Tuesday Night

Rick's eyelashes fluttered as he fought to clear his vision and to wake up his mind. Moonlight slipped through the slats of the venetian blinds, projecting white stripes across his nana's patchwork quilt. He remembered arriving at the cabin and helping Stephanie unload the supplies. Then his coworkers Russ Miller and Jason King had shown up to help with security. Rick had known he could trust them to take over, so he'd crawled into this bed and crashed. He had no idea how much time had passed since then. He smacked his dry tongue against the roof of his mouth. He needed water. His stomach rumbled. And food.

Rick squinted at the red block numbers of the alarm clock. It read 9:00 p.m. His hand slapped around on the nightstand until his fingers found his cell phone. He held it above his head, grimacing away from the bright glare in the dark room.

He sat straight up. The time on the alarm clock was correct, but the date on the phone said he had slept longer than a few hours. He had slept all of the night before and through the following day. He hopped out of bed and jogged down the hallway to the living room in search of Stephanie and Axle.

He found Stephanie wrapped in a quilt, fast asleep, with Axle cuddled up next to her on the couch. A warm glow from the fireplace enhanced the cozy scene. Rick sighed, his concern melting away. It didn't look as if they had missed him too much. He may have failed as a bodyguard, but they both appeared to have survived just fine without him.

In the kitchen, he found Miller and apologized for sleeping through his guard duty shifts. Miller assured him that he and King had been fine.

"It's been uneventful," he said, stifling a yawn. Rick still felt the guilt of shirking his duty. King had driven up a fifth wheel trailer for the two men to stay in, but he doubted they had gotten much downtime yet with Rick sleeping through his turn standing watch. From the look of boredom and fatigue on Miller's face, Rick could see the man was ready to be off duty.

"I need a quick shower and then I can take over," Rick said. "I've had enough sleep to carry me through the night shift and then some."

After showering and grabbing the two-way radio from Miller, Rick meandered back into the living room feeling refreshed. His sense of time was still disoriented, but the dizziness and pain from the concussion and the wound on his shoulder had lifted considerably. It felt good to be up and out of bed.

He sat, balancing on the back edge of the couch, and peered down at Stephanie. Her long blond eyelashes rested on her cheeks in peaceful sleep. She seemed to fit here in this simpler environment more than she did in the busy city. There was a rare sweetness to her that he liked. A desire to protect her beat inside him stronger than ever. Miller and King were good guys and great cops. He had left her in capable hands, but he didn't want her to be anyone else's responsibility.

When had keeping her safe shifted from being a favor for Terrell to being something he wanted to do for himself? Maybe it had happened when he heard her yelling for him in the hotel stairway after the bomb, or maybe it was when she held his hand and stayed with him in the hospital. All he knew was he had to do a better job of watching out for her now that he was awake and somewhat recovered.

He tucked a few stray curls behind one of her ears to get a clearer view of her face. She had such a fresh beauty. Her sun-kissed skin was flawless but for the few freckles that crossed her nose. At his touch, Stephanie turned her face into his hand. He cupped her cheek while his thumb gently ran across her eyebrow. He hadn't noticed before that her right eyebrow arched a bit higher than her left one, giving her a look of constant curiosity. Why would anyone want to hurt her?

"Wake up, sleeping beauty," he whispered.

He absentmindedly played with the piping along the edge of the couch as he fought his desire to kiss her. He leaned down, his lips hovering above her face. He gently kissed the tip of her nose and popped back up to standing. What was he doing? Being in the cabin, a place of so many warm and secure memories, was messing with his brain and making him too relaxed.

There were several days left in the week he had promised Terrell. He didn't want to spend those days constantly fighting the temptation to kiss Stephanie. If he was going to succeed in keeping her safe, he needed to be able to focus. He walked to the fireplace, pretending to warm his hands. Anything to distract him from her lips.

Stephanie stretched and said in a sleepy voice, "You're awake." She kicked off the quilt and joined him in front of the fire. Putting her hand on his elbow, she asked, "Feeling better?"

He jumped a little at her touch. Her face had a look of such sincere concern, he had to fight himself even more. "Much better, but I didn't mean to abandon you like that."

She shrugged her right shoulder. "It wasn't a big deal. Your friends kept us safe. I was glad Julian left us alone long enough for you to get the rest you needed. Maybe we've finally found a good hiding place."

Axle slid off the couch into a full body stretch on the floor, followed by a noisy yawn, and then weaseled his way between the two of them. "Axle and I have been fine, haven't we?" Stephanie said as she petted the top of Axle's head. When she stopped, Axle bumped her hand with his head, insisting that she keep up the petting. Stephanie obliged him, and asked Rick, "What breed is Axle?"

"He's a Belgian Malinois." Talking about Axle always made him proud. "Malies are quick and smart. They make great police dogs." He reached down to pet Axle, and as he did his fingers brushed against Stephanie's hand on Axle's back. Only their pinkies touched, but Rick could feel the contact down into his core. For a few beats, neither of them moved their hand away. The corners of Stephanie's mouth tipped up into a small, demure smile.

Rick was the first to move. He shoved his hands into his pockets, thankful that Axle acted as a barrier between him and Stephanie. Rocking back on his heels,

Rick said. "I hope His Royal Highness hasn't been too demanding of you while I was out of it. He's looking a little spoiled to me."

Stephanie continued massaging Axle's withers. "Nah. He's been a good boy. We've had fun. I called my school and checked in with my principal, and then I found the bookshelf." She lifted up the half-read novel she held in her other hand. "I feel like I'm on a vacation."

Warmth spread throughout him. He loved this place. It felt good to have someone else to share it with, someone who appreciated it and wasn't itching to get back to the city. He pointed at the crackling fire. "Did you do that?"

She looked sheepish. "It got chilly, and I found the firewood." Her right eyebrow arched even higher. "Was that okay?"

Rick turned his back to the fire's warmth. "It's great. I'm impressed."

She rewarded his compliment with a full smile that reached her eyes and made them dance in the firelight. The dim glow from the fireplace softened her already-beautiful features, the orange hues reflecting in her blue eyes and lighting up the red highlights in her hair. Rick stepped around Axle, and moved so close to her that only inches separated them. He breathed in her faint perfume. He was losing his resolve.

The same rebellious curls he had tucked behind her ear when she was sleeping had fallen forward again. He reached out for them, winding the silky strands around his finger. His breathing slowed, deepening further when Stephanie didn't pull away. She looked up at him, her mouth so close, all it would take was a decision and his lips would find hers.

He let go of her hair. "I think we better say good-night before I forget my job," he whispered and then cleared his throat.

Stephanie placed her open palm on his chest. "Rick, I…"

"Trust me, I want to kiss you," he interrupted her, backing away. "But it's complicated."

She dropped her hand and blinked, the moment broken for both of them as reality came rushing in like cold air. "Yeah, *complicated* is a good word for me, too."

She turned and walked toward the stairs that led up to the room she was using, leaving him alone by the fireplace. He planted his feet. He wanted to follow her, to pull her back into his arms and kiss her the way his brain was screaming for him to do, but it was Stephanie who returned to him. She stood so close, he could see himself reflected back in her eyes. Stephanie took both of his hands in hers. "Rick?"

He groaned inwardly. Her eyes were so blue.

"Yeah?" He ran his thumbs over the backs of her hands.

"Thank you. For everything. I don't know what I would have done."

"It's okay."

"No. I've been thinking about it all so much while you were sleeping. I don't know how I'm ever going to repay you for all of this. I am so grateful to be alive and safe and in this place. Thank you." The sheen of grateful tears over her eyes made them look like tiny tide pools.

He weaved his fingers into her hair and pulled her close enough to kiss her forehead. Then he turned her by the shoulders away from him. "Now go to bed. You're killing me. You have no idea how beautiful you look in this light."

She giggled. "Me? You should get a look at yourself."

She began climbing the stairs, but before she reached the top, Rick made a decision and stopped her. "Stephanie?"

"Yes?" Her now-familiar arched eyebrow rose higher like an endearing question mark.

"Make sure you get lots of rest." He grinned. "I think you've been cooped up long enough. Tomorrow you are going to learn how to shoot a gun."

Chapter Twelve

Wednesday

"Ready to make some stuff blow up?" Rick teased her.

No. Her insides wobbled like Jell-O. Stephanie had never touched a gun. Growing up on the rural eastern side of Washington State, she had gone to school with plenty of boys—and some girls, too—who drove trucks with gun racks. Many of them took two weeks off school every November to hunt elk. But living with just her sister and her mom, the only guns Stephanie had ever seen up close were on TV.

Rick unlocked his grandfather's oak gun cabinet and handed her a rifle. In her hands, it was lighter than it looked, but still cumbersome. She shifted it around, trying to figure out the right way to hold it.

"Whoa!" Rick ducked. Laughing, he said, "Give me that thing."

Her face flushed. This was a very bad idea. She had no clue what she was doing holding a gun. She couldn't hand it back to him fast enough.

"Rule number one," he said. "The gun is always loaded."

Her eyes widened. "Is it loaded right now?" She licked her lips, her mouth suddenly very dry. The way she had been swinging that gun around, she could have fired it in the cabin by accident.

"Whether it is or isn't loaded doesn't matter. You treat it as if the gun is always loaded, and you don't point it at anything, or *anyone*, that you don't intend to shoot." He tried to put it back in her hands, but she shook her head. He wouldn't take no for an answer, though, pushing it back into her grip. "The safety is on, and just to make you feel better, it is not loaded at the moment."

She scrambled for more excuses to postpone the shooting lesson. "But is it safe for me to be outside?"

"We are so remote up here and we haven't heard from Julian in two days—we'll be fine. We're well hidden, but to be on the safe side, Miller just did a sweep of the area where I'm taking you, and he and King are going to patrol the road. We're going to be just fine."

Axle pushed past them and out the cabin door. He flew off the porch in hot pursuit of a chipmunk. Rick and Stephanie followed him into the sunshine. A sharp bite in the air and the visible puffs of their breath showed that winter was still clinging on at this elevation, but on this bright morning, spring popped up everywhere. Patches of green peeked through the residual snow and although it was chilly, bright sunshine claimed the blue sky, proclaiming hope. They couldn't have asked for a prettier day to spend outside. It was the perfect cure for the cabin fever she had been feeling. Stephanie inhaled the crisp air through her nose, and exhaled a prayer. *Thank You that I'm alive to see this beauty.*

She jogged to catch up with Rick, careful to point

the gun she carried down and away as he had instructed her. Axle reveled in his freedom, bolting ahead of them, chasing more chipmunks and barking at birds. Rick carried a blanket, the ammunition they would need, two pistols and a picnic lunch they had packed.

If it weren't for the scary guns and bullets part, Stephanie might enjoy the romance of this whole excursion. Flashbacks of the night before and the almost-kiss in front of the fireplace made her blush. It was a good thing Rick had been thinking logically, because she sure hadn't been, and given another chance she wasn't sure she would have resisted.

The river's edge was covered with loose rock. It was peaceful and remote, but not quiet. They had to raise their voices to hear each other over the roar of the bulging river as it carried down snowmelt. The highway ran high above the opposite bank. It was pretty far away, but the sounds of semi trucks and cars rounding the corner echoed off the cliffs near them, making it feel closer. It was the same highway she and Rick had driven only two days ago to get to the cabin. It had been such a peaceful two days it had almost slipped her mind why they were there, forgetting for a bit that her life was still in danger and this was not a vacation.

"There's a cut bank up here that will be perfect for setting up the targets," Rick called back to her. The little-boy grin on his face made her happy. "It's the same place I learned to shoot a gun." There was a skip in Rick's step she hadn't seen before. How fun would it have been to grow up coming to a place like this? It was kid paradise.

They stepped high over a sun-bleached log before Rick stopped and set down the cooler. He spread out the blanket, then knelt down to line up the boxes of ammo and the two pistols. He reached up for her rifle. Stephanie handed it to him, trying to appear brave. Had she fooled him or could he read her thoughts of *scared, scared, scared*?

He squinted up at her. "Lunch or lessons first?"

Stephanie chewed her bottom lip. "Better do the lessons first." Her stomach ached from nerves, and her throat was so dry she couldn't swallow. She should have thought to grab a water bottle from the cabin before they left. *I don't want to do this.*

Rick lined the targets up against a sheer cliff the rushing water had worn away over the years. He talked while he worked. "So, when I was in your apartment, I noticed a lot of African decor. Have you been to Africa?" She knew he was trying small talk in order to ease her nerves. So she hadn't hidden her fear very well after all. His attempts to calm her were sweet.

"I've been to Liberia several times, actually." Stephanie was surprised by the emotion that hit her thinking about her love for the country. "My younger sister and her husband are missionaries there, and my plan is to join them as soon as I can afford it."

"Really?" He turned away from the targets and walked back to the blanket. He seemed genuinely taken aback; then again, how many girls could he possibly know who were planning to run off to West Africa? *Probably just one.*

"Will you teach there?" he asked.

She shrugged her shoulders. "I'm not sure. It's all so unsettled. My dream is to work with orphans, but I'm not exactly sure how to finance it all yet." Talking about Liberia reminded her that running from Julian wasn't the only part of her life in limbo. "To be honest, it's kind of driving me crazy," she admitted. "I keep waiting for the big neon sign, you know? The one that says God's Will Is This Way."

She hung her head. "I only know I need to do something more meaningful than what I'm doing now. I want to make God happy, but He isn't talking yet and all of the doors are still shut."

Rick was quiet for a moment. She wished she could read his thoughts. "I'm sure your students would say your job is pretty meaningful," he said. "My fifth-grade teacher got me through my parents' divorce." Then he dropped the subject and picked up one of the handguns off the blanket. "Well, Miss Future Missionary, are you ready to learn how to shoot this thing?"

"Ready," she lied.

"I know you aren't thrilled about this, but once you get familiar with shooting it won't seem so scary. After you hit a few targets, you might even start to have fun." He turned the gun over in his hand. "This .45 will be a good one to start with."

Stephanie eyeballed the gun in his hand as if it were another bomb about to explode. "Tell me again why I need to do this? Even if I know how to shoot it, that doesn't mean I could ever actually shoot someone."

"Even someone bent on killing you or threatening someone you love?"

"I don't know. It isn't a moral dilemma I've wrestled much with before now." She didn't like the way that question made her squirm.

"What if Julian was about to harm Joash or Haddie?"

She didn't answer so he went on. "I keep thinking about the other night at the Watkinses' place. I keep seeing the kids sliding around the kitchen in their socks and how excited they were about eating their dessert in the living room." Rick's forehead scrunched up with emotion. Stephanie replayed the scene in her own mind as he spoke, her stomach twisting.

Rick stared at the gun in his hands. "Julian Hale lit a house on fire that he knew had innocent women and kids inside…" Rick looked into her eyes and said, "This guy is serious, Stephanie." He held up the gun in his hand. "It makes me sick thinking that he might hurt you. I need to know you can defend yourself."

When she nodded, he began, "Okay, lesson number one review… The gun is always loaded…"

Her stomach was Jell-O again, and her hands felt unnaturally light. Rick taught her how to slap in the magazine and how to chamber the bullet, then the gun was all hers. His arms encircled her from behind, showing her how to hold the gun properly. "Remember." His mouth was so close she felt the air skim her ear as he spoke, but with the orange foam earplugs in, he had to shout for her to hear him. "Finger off the trigger until you are ready to shoot."

She held the pistol straight out in front of her. Rick's hands gripped her waist. "Relax. Bend your knees. Lean in to it." She tried to remember all of the instructions he had rattled off about the different stances, the breathing, squeezing versus pulling the trigger, not trying to anticipate the noise.

Rick pointed at the orange disks sitting in metal stands against the cut bank. They looked like the bottoms of flower pots. "Line up your sights on the target. Good." He leaned with her, talking her through the steps. "Okay. As soon as you're ready, go ahead." He let go of her and stepped away.

"Wait. I'm not ready."

"Once you blow up one of those targets you'll be

hooked." He crossed his arms and waited for her to squeeze the trigger. *Squeeze, not pull.* She remembered that much. *Or was it the other way around?*

"Any day now, Stephanie," Rick teased. "It's nothing more than target practice. Bend your knees. Don't try to anticipate the—"

Bang. Bang. Bang. Bang. Bang.

All five of the targets exploded, one after the other, orange fragments flying through the air.

"Whoa!" Rick was flabbergasted. His hands flew to the top of his head. He hopped around in excitement. "I can't believe it. You hit every one of them."

Stephanie still held her arms up, frozen in place. Then suddenly she fell prone in the dirt and screamed, "Rick, get down."

He knelt beside her and asked, "Did you faint? That can happen…"

"Rick, get down!" She popped up and tackled him to the ground. She looked down into his confused face. "I never pulled the trigger."

Bullets peppered the ground, preventing him from standing. Rick pushed Stephanie off him and grabbed the gun she still clutched in her hand. The shots came from somewhere behind them, on the other side of the river.

Rick rolled and fired, searching for cover. They were too exposed by the river, but the tree line was too far to run without getting shot. He spotted the log they had climbed over earlier. It was small, but some cover was better than none. "Follow me," he shouted to her. Grabbing her hand, they bolted for the log.

Only a few paces away, the ground in front of the log exploded with rapid bullets splaying rocks, knock-

ing them to the ground for the second time. Rick landed
on top of Stephanie, shielding her body from the raining lead. "You're okay, Steph. Hang on," he shouted
into her ear.

Lord, save us. Rick was praying for the first time in
too long. It was true, the old saying about remembering
God in foxholes. His prayer life had been nonexistent
lately. *I've been trying to fix this whole mess on my own,
trying to keep Stephanie and everyone else safe in my
own strength.* A bullet hit to his left, spraying gravel
into his eyes. Stephanie coughed underneath him.

*You could hit us if you wanted to. Where are you,
Hale?*

Cliffs and plateaus surrounded the river on both
sides, providing a number of perfect hiding spots for
a sniper. The highway traffic masked the noise, and
the shooter had the perfect vantage point to see their
defenseless position below. They were sitting ducks.
With the right scope and a regular hunting rifle, even
an average shot could pick them off from three to four
hundred yards away. It had to be Julian Hale. Wherever
he was hiding, it was far enough to remain unseen, but
close enough to completely destroy their targets with
perfect aim.

Stephanie whimpered at each *ping* of a bullet. Rick
winced, expecting pain.

Rick returned fire, shooting blind. His bullets
sprayed rocks less than one hundred yards away. He
couldn't risk hitting a car on the highway. As he continued firing and praying for their safety, the bullets hit
close but never struck them.

"He's playing games with us again," he yelled, hoping to somehow reassure Stephanie.

Then as quickly as they had begun falling, the bullets completely stopped. Rick counted ten seconds. Did he dare move? His body weight was surely crushing Stephanie underneath him.

Rick army-crawled to the blanket and grabbed the rifle, then crawled back to where Stephanie lay on the ground. He pulled the two-way radio off his belt and called for help.

Miller's voice crackled. "We're on the highway. We'll find him."

No more shots fired.

"Leave everything and run for the trees," Rick told Stephanie. "Stay low and get inside the cabin.

"I'm right behind you all the way, okay? I'll be firing the gun to cover us. You do not stop. No matter what you think is happening behind you, you do not stop until you are safe inside. Understand?"

Stephanie's pupils dominated her irises, but she scrambled up and began to run. Rick moved to follow after her, but in his peripheral vision he spotted movement. A blur of brown fur burst from the tree line farther down the river.

"Axle, *bleib*! *Bleib!*" Rick screamed the command for *stay* over and over and over again, but the dog either couldn't hear him or simply refused to obey.

Lord, help, Stephanie prayed. She couldn't find any other words to string together. That would have to be enough.

Was this what war felt like? Feeling the futility of the situation, knowing the enemy was stronger than you? Waiting to be shot, wondering if each breath was the last before a bullet sliced through you?

When I'm shot, what will it feel like?

Rick had shoved her forward, shouting instructions

at her, but her confused mind had jumbled them. *Run. To the cabin. Don't look back. Don't stop.*

"Go! Go! Go!"

The running felt surreal, as though she were moving through the landscape of a vaguely familiar nightmare. Stephanie didn't think, only ran. She remembered the foam earplugs were still in place. She popped them out and dropped them to the ground. She heard Rick's gun firing behind her, she heard him screaming something, but she did not stop.

Each step and heartbeat brought a question. Step. *Am I alive?* Beat. *Is Rick behind me?* Step. *How much farther?* Step. *Where is Axle?* She reached the tree line and the path toward the cabin. She stopped. *Wait, where is Axle?*

Stephanie spun around, searching before she even knew what she was looking to find. Her eyes locked on Rick crouched behind the log for cover. Why wasn't he following her? He promised he would be right behind her.

The desperation in the commands Rick screamed paralyzed her. A flash of brown drew her eye farther down the river's bank. Axle sprinted toward Rick, the dog's athleticism and heroic heart on display leaving her breathless. His determination to ignore Rick's commands and to protect his master sent her to her knees. She heard the shots firing again, hating how helpless she was to stop what was about to happen. Axle flew at Rick, knocking him to the ground. She covered her ears, unable to accept that Axle had been shot, unable to stand the raw agony she heard in the dog's wails of pain.

Chapter Thirteen

The bullets were silent again, leaving only Axle's cries to compete with the river's roar. Each of the dog's painful yelps entered Rick's heart like a knife.

"Oh, buddy. I'm so sorry." Rick's hands shook as they hovered over Axle's writhing body. He was afraid to touch, but he needed to search for the wound. He gently worked through the fur, looking for where the bullet entered. He found a small hole in the back of his upper right shoulder and a larger exit wound on his front shoulder. He must have taken the bullet as he dived through the air for Rick.

"Hang in there, partner. You're going to be okay." Rick continued to croon words of comfort as he worked, trying to keep Axle still.

"You have to be okay." Tears welled, threatening to fall. Not much could make Rick cry. When he was a kid, if his dad or his grandfathers ever caught him crying, they would insist he knock it off and act like a man. Grandpa Powell would smack Rick on the arm and tell him to cowboy up. The last time he had cried was during his parents' divorce, in private, sitting inside his bedroom closet where no one could witness it. He hadn't even allowed himself to cry over Allie's leaving him.

With Axle quivering in pain before him, he was finding it difficult to cowboy up this time, but Axle needed him to be strong and to think clearly without letting the emotion take over. Rick willed away the tears. He would not lose Axle. He wouldn't even allow himself to think it. They hadn't battled this hard to survive these past months to have it end like this.

"You coward!" Rick screamed across the river in the direction he thought Hale was hiding, but his accusation echoed back to his own ears. Hale probably couldn't hear him. Was he even still up there? The gutless cur had probably already run away.

Hale's rifle remained silent, tempting Rick to make a run for it himself. He needed to get Axle to the truck and go for help, but what if moving Axle hurt him more? It was a risk he was going to have to take. But before Rick could scoop the dog into his arms, Stephanie stepped out from the tree line and started running toward him.

She was supposed to be in the cabin and safe by now. "What are you doing? Go back," he hollered at her.

Ignoring him, she kept running, using a large flat piece of scrap metal as a shield.

He tried to wave her off, his voice hoarse from all of the yelling he had done. "Get back in the cabin. Are you insane?"

She slid to the ground next to them, spitting up pebbles as she landed. Fury at the ridiculous stunt she had just pulled pumped through his veins. "What were you thinking? Now I've got two of you to get out of here safely."

"No, Rick, you don't understand. It's okay. I've figured something out." She dropped the scrap metal on to the ground. "I found this by the cabin. We can use it to carry Axle, to keep him still in case he has any broken bones."

He shook his head. "I told you no matter what was happening behind you, you were to get inside that cabin."

"I know what you said," she shouted. "But Axle needs help, and he wouldn't be hurt at all if it weren't for me. Besides, I've figured something out. When I was watching from the trail it occurred to me." She looked at him as though her words should make perfect sense. Well, they didn't make any sense at all to him.

"What are you talking about?"

"Don't you see?" She reached for him and gripped his upper arms. "I am Axle's best shield."

Rick's jaw dropped at her absurd claim. Shield? Rick pulled from her grip and pointed to the other side of the river. "That man up there with the gun? Remember him, Stephanie? He is shooting at us in order to kill you. Have you forgotten that?"

"You don't understand." She crawled away from Rick across the gravel toward the blanket. Dragging it back, she covered the metal with it and made a bed for Axle.

There was no question. She had lost it, snapped somehow under the stress, but he didn't have time to figure her out. He scooped Axle gently onto the make-shift gurney and wrapped the blanket tightly around the dog. He hoped its warmth would prevent Axle from going into shock. He didn't like that Stephanie had put herself in so much danger to get it down here, but he had to admit he was thankful for the way to transport the sixty-five-pound dog without causing further injury.

"I'll pick up the rear, you lead," he told her.

"Rick, you aren't listening to me." She flung her hands in the air in frustration. "Keep me between you and Julian at all times."

"I am not letting you turn suicidal on me, Stephanie."

She grabbed his arm, looking desperate to make him understand her. "Trust me, Rick. Shooting me from a distance is not what Julian has in mind for me. I'm figuring out the way he operates. He won't hesitate to shoot you or Axle to prove his power or to get to me, but he won't shoot me."

She bit her lip, and then she added in a voice so quiet he almost couldn't hear it above the river, "I think he has other plans for me."

Her crazy theory had some merit. Sniper fire was not Hale's style. He strangled his victims, preferring a more up close and brutal method. Rick had seen files that Stephanie hadn't. The photographs of the women Hale had murdered played like a slideshow across his mind.

Rick remembered how long it had taken for the bomb to detonate at the hotel. Hale had protected Stephanie then, preserving her for his future plans. The FBI profile had said he was motivated by a need for power and dominance. Stephanie might be right. This could be another display of strength so she wouldn't forget who was in control. Even if he was willing to shoot Axle and Rick, Hale probably wouldn't be satisfied with killing Stephanie from afar.

Finally he conceded, "All right. But move quickly and stay low."

Rick's foot pressed on the accelerator, his truck tires squealing around the corners on the steep mountain highway. With every curve, inertia pressed him hard against the driver's side door. He was pushing the speed as far as he dared. He didn't want to hurt Axle further with all of the bumps and sharp turns. Any faster and the next bend might send them soaring off a cliff.

Stephanie attempted to hold Axle still in the backseat with one hand and search Rick's cell phone for the nearest vet office with her other hand. She read out loud the directions to the closest one she could find.

"It's in Sedro-Woolley. Can we make it in time?"

"We have to make it in time," he told her, or was he telling God how it was going to be?

Rick heard tears in Stephanie's songlike words as she comforted Axle. "Shhh. It's okay. It's okay. Hang in there, Axle. Not long now and we will get you all fixed up, boy."

"Axle's a fighter," Rick told Stephanie. The reassurance was for his own benefit as much as it was for hers. "He'll make it."

When Rick was still in the hospital after the stabbing, the city bigwigs had decided they couldn't justify the huge vet bills for the surgeries Axle required. They concluded Axle was too badly injured to ever recover and that the most humane thing was to put him down. Rick had protested, begging from his hospital bed that they do all that was necessary to save Axle's life and he would personally cover the bills. No matter what they all thought, he was Rick's partner, and even if Axle never walked or ran or even worked again, he was Rick's friend, and Rick had never regretted that decision. Axle had fought so hard and come back stronger than ever, proving everybody wrong.

Rick glanced over his shoulder to the backseat again. Axle was still, calmed by Stephanie's soothing voice, breathing deeply through the pain. "You're a fighter, buddy. Don't forget that," he commanded Axle. Rick knew in his gut that Axle would make it. He had to make it.

Rick thought back to the fancy ceremony he and Axle had attended after they'd recovered. They were both awarded the Medal of Valor. When the mayor handed Rick the box at the ceremony, he had felt like a hack accepting it. The intent of the award was to celebrate officers who go above and beyond the call of duty, showing great bravery or heroism without thought to their own safety in the face of extreme danger. Rick hadn't done anything exceptionally brave that night. He walked into a trap and almost got himself killed is what he had done. He had expected a reprimand or an internal affairs investigation, not a medal. He had felt ridiculous accepting the praise, and as soon as he got home that night he hid the box in his underwear drawer.

Not Axle. Rick had never seen Axle prouder. When the mayor slipped that medal over the dog's head, Axle's chest puffed out and he sat up as tall as he could possibly stretch himself. Later that evening when Rick tried to lift the ribbon off Axle's neck, Axle had growled at him and bared his teeth. It took two days before Rick could coax him into letting the medal go, and it was only after Rick showed him where the medal would be displayed.

You are a fighter, Axle. You're a hero, too. Axle had just saved Rick's life. The dog he loved had just taken a bullet to protect him. Rick's heart ached. He pushed the accelerator a smidge farther. He would risk flying off the highway. He had to get to that vet in time.

Stephanie flipped through a copy of *Horse&Rider* magazine she had picked up off the end table in the waiting room, but she wasn't reading or even seeing, only occupying her hands. Rick paced. He sat down. He jumped back up. He paced some more. It was an excruciating wait, and she wished she knew how to comfort him. Every time she opened her mouth to say something, the words she planned seemed so cliché that she clamped her mouth shut again.

The staff behind the reception counter looked a little shell-shocked by the sheer number of law enforcement officers coming in and out the door of their tiny clinic. Stephanie wanted to say, *Welcome to my life*.

Shelton and another detective had made an appearance, and the Skagit County sheriff had stopped by to interview them, leaving behind deputies to guard the clinic while others searched for Julian. They were the second local agency to show up. Stephanie appreciated their presence. If Julian could find them in the middle of a national forest, he could find them anywhere. She had learned her lesson. Never again would she let down her guard.

The rest of the cops who squeezed into the room were off-duty SPD officers, coworkers of Rick's who had driven north to support him when they heard about what had happened to Axle. Stephanie was beginning to understand what people meant when they talked about the law enforcement brotherhood. It was an amazing community.

She tossed the magazine down and replaced it with *Vets Life* instead. An adorable black-and-white pig smiled at her from the cover. She flipped, flipped, flipped the pages, not even reading a sentence, until she gave up and tossed the magazine on top of the other one.

Resting her head back against the wall, she closed her eyes. It was making her crazy that she couldn't *do* anything to help Rick or Axle other than sit here.

Stephanie knew nothing about dogs or gunshot wounds, but Axle had been in so much pain when she and Rick carried him in through these doors. She opened one eye and looked at Rick. The relationship he had with Axle was more than a typical pet and owner. As heartbreaking as it would be to lose a pet, for Rick, losing Axle was losing a comrade, a partner, someone who had faced death alongside him.

She stood up and stretched. For a moment she couldn't remember what day it was. Only Wednesday? How was that even possible?

She walked over to Rick, still unsure of what to say. He stopped pacing when she stood in front of him. She took one of his hands and squeezed it. "Rick. It's going to be okay."

His expression iced over, and he jerked his hand away from her. Then pacing started again. "There are no guarantees, Stephanie. Outside of your civilian fairy-tale world, life usually isn't okay."

She didn't want to feel the anger burning in her. She wanted to be understanding, but all she could think of was *don't take this out on me*. Her nostrils flared as she breathed for composure. "You don't think I've seen my fair share of life? I'll skip the sob story about my dad abandoning us when I was only three years old, and the one about my mom checking out, counting on me to be the parent. I've been to *Africa*, Rick. I've seen life."

He looked at her with bloodshot eyes and a forlorn expression that melted away her anger. She stepped forward and embraced his stiff body. She held on. *Come on, Rick. Let me help. Let me share it.*

"All I'm saying is that we got Axle in here. Surely the vet will be able to help him."

Rick patted her back as if he were hugging a great-aunt. "Thanks, Stephanie." He stepped away from her and rubbed his hands down his thighs a few times.

Stephanie tried not to let his dismissal hurt, tried to explain it away as his way of dealing with the anxiety. He was too tough a guy to want to lose it in front of these strangers and his coworkers, but the wall she sensed he had now constructed seemed insurmountable.

He's shutting me out.

The assistant spoke to Rick. "Dr. Bailey will be right out to talk with you as soon as he's finished up in there."

Rick's jaw clenched. "Thanks."

Stephanie wished Rick would look at her, not over her or around her, but actually at her. If she could make eye contact maybe she could read what he needed from her, but he stared ahead, watching the assistant plod away.

As they sat next to each other in silence, Stephanie had too much time to think about Julian Hale. Righteous anger burned inside her, but its companion was a slow vacuum of fear sucking her in. When it came to Julian, she was done asking "what" and "how"; now the most natural next question had to be "who." *Who is next?*

"Mr. Powell?"

Stephanie and Rick rose from their seats. A man looking to be in his fifties wearing a lab coat over his Wranglers stepped toward them. Stephanie noticed his eyes were kind, but behind the kindness she recognized something else that scared her. Pity. Goose bumps ran up her legs and through her heart. *Don't you dare give us any bad news.*

"Mr. Powell, I'm Leo Bailey." He extended his hand. Rick shook it. "I've finished examining Axle. Why don't we sit—"

Rick cut him off. "I don't want to sit. Tell me how he

is." Rick crossed his arms and took on his police stance. "I don't care what it costs. Whatever it takes to make Axle well again, I'll pay for it."

The vet nodded. "Well, Mr. Powell, when I first examined Axle, I was worried we would be having a much more difficult conversation. He's been hurt badly, but you've got a very tough and very determined dog in there."

It was as if Stephanie had sucked in all of their combined worry and then hadn't exhaled for hours. After hearing the vet's hope-filled words, Stephanie's whole body deflated in relief. Axle was going to be okay. She squeezed Rick's hand again, hoping that the good news would thaw the new coldness that had suddenly descended on him, but there was no squeeze back from him. She sensed the frozen wall between them growing taller and thicker by the minute. What had she done? Why was he treating her like this?

Dr. Bailey continued his prognosis. "Thankfully, the bullet missed some vital areas and then exited without too much internal damage. Axle's going to need antibiotics and time to rest and heal, but he'll pull through." The vet flipped through the chart he held. "It looks like Axle has already proved that he is not one to stay down for long."

The vet smiled and dropped the chart to his side. "I have a feeling you haven't seen the end of this dog's heroics yet."

Chapter Fourteen

How long until he finds us here?

Stephanie sat on the edge of the hotel bed, running her hands along the comforter, picking at the tiny matted balls on the old pilled material. Her eyes roamed her new surroundings, taking in the 1980s pastel decor. A slight antiseptic scent made the room seem uninviting, but at least it was clean and cheap. She was going to owe Rick so much money by the time this week ended. Most importantly, though, the single-level roadside hotel was close to Axle at the vet's office in case he needed them overnight.

Stephanie had always been an introvert, requiring more alone time than other people to recharge, but now she was restless, too keyed up to enjoy the quiet. She needed something to occupy her mind so she could stop wondering if Julian Hale knew exactly where they were.

Rick was next door in the adjoining room with only an interior door separating them. She knew that all she would have to do was cry out for him and he would come crashing in to her rescue. Jason King was in the room on her other side. She stood up and peeked around the curtain into the parking lot. At that moment a sheriff's department patrol car rolled by on the street, and parked in the space directly in front of her room was a truck with Russ Miller in the cab staring at her door. He waved at her. She gave a tiny, embarrassed wave back and dropped the curtain. She was definitely well guarded.

It was too early to sleep, and she had left the book she had started reading behind at the cabin. She paced the room and then stopped to listen. She couldn't hear anything coming from Rick's room. What was he doing? Probably wondering if there was any way he could get out of babysitting her sooner than he had promised Terrell.

Turning on the TV didn't help her restlessness. She flipped through every station, but it all annoyed her. How could the world go on like normal? She felt too jaded to laugh at corny sitcoms and too consumed with her own issues to care about the world's news. She turned it off. What she didn't want to admit was that she was lonely. After spending so much time with Rick and Axle for company, she missed them. She missed Val, too. Maybe Rick would let her use his phone to call her.

Stephanie's hand hovered inches away from the door that separated their adjoining rooms, trying to decide if she should knock or not. He had been acting so distant and aloof, she was sure he wanted to be left alone. But after all the adrenaline and worry over Axle, this letdown was making her feel stir-crazy. She needed to talk to another human being.

She rapped lightly on the door. "Rick? Are you awake?"

The door swung open with so much force, Stephanie popped back.

"What's wrong?" he asked. His brows were pinched

together, his eyes searching first her, and then the room behind her.

She put her hands up. "Nothing's wrong."

Why had she bothered him? Her question seemed so stupid now. She stumbled over her words. "I just wondered if I could borrow your phone."

He cocked his head, looking confused. A few seconds ticked by before her words convinced him she truly was okay, and his alert posture relaxed. He turned, leaving the door open behind him.

Returning with his phone, he tossed it to her. "Just keep it with you for now."

She caught the phone down low by her knees, grateful that she didn't drop it. Without saying anything more, he shut the door, leaving her alone again.

"Thanks," she said to the closed door. Then she kicked it, which she regretted when pain shot up from her stubbed toe. She fell backward onto the scratchy bed and dialed Val's cell number. She stared at the ceiling waiting for Val to answer.

"Hello?" The smooth, warm voice of her friend wirelessly crossed the miles and embraced Stephanie's heart.

"Val?" She swallowed, trying to control the flood of emotion.

"Steph? Are you safe?"

Stephanie winced. Her every attempt to talk with someone tonight made them worry something was wrong. "I'm okay."

"Then why do I hear tears?"

"I didn't call to talk about me," Stephanie insisted.

"But how you are is what I care about."

After several moments of silence, Val let out an exasperated sounding sigh. "Oh, all right." She started talking in rapid-fire sentences. "We're all fine. Living in a hotel with kids is about to send me over the edge. The house can be fixed, but it is going to take several months before it is livable again, so we're shopping for a rental. At least we have the swimming pool at the hotel because it is saving my sanity." Val's report ended abruptly. Stephanie heard the deep inhale she took before she declared, "There, you're all caught up on us. Now spill it, *chica*."

Val could be so bossy, but Stephanie loved her for it. She told her friend everything that had happened over the past few days, trying to downgrade the danger they had faced, but Val couldn't be fooled. She kept pressing for more details, peeling back the layers of facts until she got to how Stephanie was feeling about all of it.

"What about Rick?" Val asked. "How's he doing?"

"Rick's…" Stephanie stared at the closed door in the center of her wall. "Rick's fine, I guess. I wouldn't know for sure. He's too busy being a jerk and giving me the cold shoulder."

"I knew it," Val said excitedly. She sounded so happy, as if she had won the lottery or something. "Hee hee. I knew it, I knew it."

Stephanie scooted up against the headboard and hugged a pillow. "Valencia Watkins, what do you *know*?"

"You *like* him."

Stephanie slipped her head under the water line of the bathtub, her curls floating around her. The shampoo fizzed in her ear. *I am not interested in Rick Powell.*

She had denied it on the phone. "It's only been five days, Val. That's too fast to be accusing me of falling for the guy."

"Says who?" Val had said. "Besides, you have known

Rick for a lot longer than that. You both needed to be pushed a little to pay attention to each other, that's all."

Stephanie spit air at a bubble on her nose and lathered the hotel's old-fashioned-smelling soap between her hands. *I'm not falling in love with him, am I? Because that could mess everything up.* She could deal with a little crush. Anything deeper than that would be more complicated. Stephanie viciously scrubbed her arms as if she could rub off the doubts along with the dirt.

She had collected so much grime. Lying facedown along the river's rocky bank while a madman used her for target practice could do that to a girl, she supposed. The whole ordeal had left her scraped up and filthy. It felt good to soak it all away.

"I'm not falling for him, Val," she had said.

But Val had only asked her, "Are you trying to convince me or yourself?"

Stephanie had changed her strategy. "How I feel is irrelevant, anyway. Rick is hardly even talking to me anymore."

"Your feelings are not irrelevant. Rick has his guard up. Terrell did the same thing to me when we were dating. It's a sign that you're working your way into his heart. He's afraid of caring about you, especially after watching Axle get shot. It scares him to imagine something like that happening to you. I've got faith in Rick. He'll come around," Val had countered.

"Valencia Watkins, I love Liberia, not Rick Powell. Are you trying to confuse me?"

"And you don't think God has made your heart big enough for both?" Val had challenged her.

Stephanie unplugged the bathtub while Val's question battered around in her head. God had called her to Liberia, hadn't He? She had been so sure that she was supposed to be there, but she couldn't find any open door for her to walk through at the moment. She loved the country and the people too much to believe that God wasn't sending her there. She forced the silly ideas Val had put in her head to slide down the drain with the last bit of dirty bathwater.

As soon as Julian Hale was caught and behind bars, she and Rick would be able to go back to their normal lives and to their own plans for the future. She stepped from the bathtub, determined that Val's teasing would not distract her any further.

She dressed in the same dirty clothes she had worn before the bath, wishing she had some fresh ones. She grabbed Rick's phone and logged on to her email account. Scanning through all the junk mail, her eyes landed on a message from her sister.

Her heart skipped in anticipation. Stephanie skimmed the note, searching for names of the people she missed so much and for word about how Emily's pregnancy was going. Hungry for news, she picked out certain words and phrases, eating them up like an appetizer to take the edge off the hunger before she went back to the beginning and read every word slower. There were stories about Moses and how much he had grown, funny anecdotes about the Liberian people and a few new Liberian phrases Emily had picked up. Stephanie devoured every word her sister had written.

She remembered the threatening printouts from Emily's blog that Julian had sent to her. Julian's hands had reached everywhere. He had messed with every area of her life, threatened everyone she loved. His eyes had seen every move she and Rick had made. How? She stared at Rick's phone, pondering. Then, slowly, she began to see the common denominator. She knew how Julian was finding them.

She was holding it in her hands.

Rick put his ear to the door to Stephanie's room. Would he be able to hear her if she called for help? After the cold shoulder he'd given her, he doubted he would see her again tonight unless she was in danger. Grandpa Powell would skin him if he saw how he had been treating Stephanie today. He could hear his grandfather's voice saying, "Son, that is not how we raised you to treat a lady."

And Grandpa Powell would be right. Rick knew he was being a jerk, but keeping her at a distance was for the best. All it took was closing his eyes and he could see Stephanie in the cabin last night, her face lit up by the flickering firelight. It took effort not to walk through the door separating them and repeat that closeness. If he didn't keep his distance both physically and emotionally, he would be too tempted and distracted. He had already crossed the professional line and allowed this case to become far too personal. He had to rectify that if he was going to be able to do his job well, and if hurting her feelings a little was the cost of keeping her safe, so be it.

Are you trying to protect her or yourself?

Stephanie's theory had been that Hale wouldn't shoot her from a distance, but she could have been wrong. She could have been shot just as Axle had been. Rick could have lost both of them by that river today. Sure, he had wanted her to learn to defend herself, but he also had treated her shooting lesson more like a date than a true self-defense lesson. And obviously, he hadn't chosen a secure enough location. He had failed to protect her because he was distracted by his attraction to her. He'd been stupid, and he couldn't keep making that same mistake.

His memory replayed the sound the bullets had made as they pinged off the rocks around them. He imagined one of those bullets hitting Stephanie. Rick turned away from her door and paced the room, unwilling to allow his imagination to go any further with that scenario.

Pounding knocks from Stephanie's side of the door startled him. Her knocking was more insistent this time. He yanked the door open.

Stephanie rushed past him and tossed his cell phone away from her and onto his bed as if it were burning her hand. She pointed at it. "Julian knows we're here."

Her hair was soaking wet, leaving dark wet spots on the shoulders of her T-shirt. The protective instinct he felt for her flared. He put his hands on her shoulders and searched her for injury. Her pupils were dilated and her skin pale again, but she didn't look hurt.

"What's wrong?" he demanded.

"He knows we're here."

"How do you know?" Rick went to the window and flicked aside the drapes. The parking lot held the same cars he had seen the last time he had checked, and Russ Miller was still guarding her door. He couldn't find anything out of place. "Did you see Hale?"

Stephanie grabbed his upper arms and turned him away from the window, her grip tight. "Your phone, Rick." She pointed at the bed. "Who's the carrier?"

It was an odd question. "The city has a contract with VoiceOne for all the department's cell phones."

Stephanie covered her face with her hands, talking to him through her closed fingers. "Ahh. I don't know why I didn't think about it when you told me to leave behind all my electronic devices."

"They're the biggest carrier in the nation, Stephanie. Almost everyone I know uses VoiceOne for their cell coverage. What's the connection here?"

She removed her hands so she could look directly at him. "I won a technology grant from VoiceOne for my classroom."

"So?" *Who cares? Is Hale here or not?*

Her shoulders sagged and she collapsed onto the edge of his bed. "When I won that grant, they sent one of their IT guys to set up my new equipment." She looked up and asked, "Does that ring any bells?"

Rick could feel the snarl on his face as he spit out, "Hale worked for VoiceOne?"

Stephanie nodded. "It's possible to find someone's location through their cell phone, right?"

Rick growled his frustration and started pacing. "Yes. You can ping the cell towers and locate to within three miles of their location, a lot closer if that phone is GPS enabled, which mine is."

How could he have been so stupid? They already knew Hale was a technological genius. Rick remembered the photograph Hale had sent to Stephanie, the one where he put a blanket around her shoulders outside the fire. The image captured a look of tenderness on his own face that had surprised him. Hale must have known that Rick wouldn't stop looking out for her. Matching the police officer he saw protecting Stephanie to the department-issued phone would have been elementary for someone like Hale, especially if he had access to VoiceOne records. Rick reached for the phone to power it down, but Stephanie's slender fingers wrapped around his wrist to stop him. "Wait," she said. He jolted at her touch.

She had the same determined line to her mouth that he had seen on her face outside the Watkins house right before she took off on her own. She had made some kind of decision, and he guessed he wasn't going to like what she had on her mind.

The blue of Stephanie's eyes deepened to navy, the intensity of her gaze imploring him to listen to her. She dropped his wrist, and he immediately missed the warmth of her touch. "We can use this, Rick," she said softly.

"No." Trying to trap Hale wasn't worth the risk it would take to pull it off.

"Yes," she countered. She crossed her arms and lifted her chin in defiance. "You don't get to call all of the shots, Rick. This is my life, my problem."

"We need to power down the cell now and get Hale off our trail. Then we need to get out of here and warn the vet."

She shook her wet head. "No, Rick. What we need is to stop Julian. This phone is our way to do that."

Rick was tired of arguing. He leaned down to reach around her and grab the phone off the bed, but Stephanie blocked him. She placed her hands on his upper arms again, holding him back. Their faces were only inches apart. Rick's chest tightened at the nearness. He swallowed and then stepped back and let her talk.

"We've been in this hotel long enough for Julian to locate us again already. If he suddenly loses our trail he'll know that we've figured out how he's tracking us."

"So what if he knows that we're onto him? He'll have to come up with a new game plan. That will give us time to find a real safe house for once." Rick was ready to take back the upper hand. No more Julian Hale popping up unexpected sounded very appealing. He could take Stephanie far away and leave the work of taking down Hale to his colleagues.

She put her fingertips against her temples and squeezed her eyes shut. "You're not seeing the bigger picture, Rick. Don't you remember what Detective Shelton told us at the hospital? That Julian's pride would be his downfall? This is our chance to trip him up."

She kept her hand on the phone behind her back and out of his reach. "If we play dumb and let him follow us, we can lure him wherever we want him to go."

"I suppose you think I'm going to let you play some kind of bait in order to do that? Because I'm not." Rick widened his stance. He wasn't backing down on that part. He had promised Terrell that he would protect Stephanie as if she were a member of his own family. Terrell would never let her purposefully put herself in danger, and neither would Rick.

"Like you care." She mumbled so low it was almost too quiet for him to hear what she said. Her already-flushed face deepened to a horrified purple. Rick guessed she hadn't meant to say that out loud.

Rick's voice rose a little in volume. "What is that supposed to mean, Stephanie? I don't put my life on hold like this for people I don't care about. I've done nothing but try to protect you."

"And ignore me." Her gaze locked onto a hangnail she picked at on her thumb.

Her words were like a kick in the gut because they were true. He should clear the air right now and let her know it wasn't anything she had done, that he had only been trying to maintain a professional distance, that she shouldn't take it personally. He reached for her. "Stephanie, I…"

But before he could apologize, she popped up off the bed and put her own distance between them. "I shouldn't have said all of that. You're right, you have put your life on hold for me, and I appreciate it so much. I really only want for you to be able to go back to your normal life and not have to be responsible for me anymore." She squeezed her arms around herself. "This favor for Terrell has been too much to ask of anyone."

Tell her you're sorry. Tell her that you've enjoyed being with her and that you care about her safety, too, not just for Terrell's sake. But Rick bit back his apology. It was better this way.

Flustered, Stephanie changed the subject back to Hale. "Aren't you sick of Julian having all the power?"

"Yes, but putting you at risk on purpose is too high a price to pay in order to tip the scales. I'm not going to let it happen."

"Well, it might not be up to you." Stephanie hung her head. "Because I've already called Detective Shelton."

Chapter Fifteen

Thursday

Rick filled the doorway of Gary Shelton's cubicle. He flexed his fingers, trying to control his anger and annoyance at being called back to Seattle for a chat with the detective. He had to leave Axle all alone in that vet's office hours away in order to humor the man, but he refused to be bullied into using Stephanie as bait. "You do not outrank me, Gary."

Shelton shook his head. "You're right, I don't outrank you, Powell, but those who do are on my side on this one," he said. "And frankly, if your head was in the right place, you'd be on board, too. I'm not asking that much."

Rick's fists clenched tight. It would feel good to knock the smug look off Shelton's face. Gary Shelton was a friend, but not so good a friend that Rick would put Stephanie's life in danger in order to please him.

Am I making too big a deal of this? After all, Shelton was only asking him to stay in Seattle and to leave his cell phone turned on so Hale could track it. Rick wanted to destroy the stupid phone and drive Stephanie far, far away. Maybe that desire was more evidence that he had gotten too close to her and too emotionally invested to do his job well.

But his gut told him that somehow Hale would figure out how to twist this to his own advantage. His intuition also told him that Shelton would see any harm that might come to Stephanie as simply a sad but necessary price to pay for protecting the greater good. Shelton viewed Stephanie as nothing more than a pawn in the big picture.

Rick towered over the smaller man sitting at his desk, but Shelton wasn't backing down. The detective stood to his full height, his eyes turned to steel. "This is our chance to stop this maniac, Rick. It's time to put an end to this cat-and-mouse game you've been playing with him. We can't blow this opportunity just because you are sweet on her."

Rick slammed his fists onto the detective's desk sending papers flying. "Don't try to make this about me. You're the one who has let this get far too personal. You want to catch Hale so badly you can taste it. I'm not going to let you gamble with her life."

"This isn't your call anymore, Rick. It's gotten bigger than you, and if you can't maintain your professionalism, I'll make sure they take you off Stephanie's protection detail."

Neither man paid any attention to Stephanie sitting in her chair inside the cubicle, her face turning a deeper cherry red by the minute. She cleared her throat, drawing the men's attention to where she sat. "I'm sitting right here. Don't I have a say in this?"

The detective answered, "Of course you do" at the same time that Rick growled, "No, you don't."

Her blue eyes connected with Rick's. "Come on,

Rick. We've been over this. You know you are tired of playing Julian's game."

Rick glared at her. He *was* tired of Hale's cat-and-mouse game. He wanted Hale to know what it felt like to be the mouse for a change, but he didn't want Stephanie to be the cheese in order for that to happen. If they left the cell phone behind, they could disappear without being followed by Hale for once. That had to be the best course of action to keep Stephanie safe.

She stood up and went toe-to-toe with him. "Well, I'm tired of it. I want my life back."

The detective sat back down in his desk chair; the smug tip to the edges of his mouth had returned. "Go back and get your dog, Rick. Hole up in another hotel if you want to. It doesn't matter where you two go as long as we make it look like you are still running and trying to hide. In the meantime, we will set up a team to nab Hale whenever he shows up again."

Rick looked into Stephanie's imploring eyes, ignoring the detective. "It's not going to work," he told her. He couldn't care less what Gary Shelton wanted him to do at this moment. This was between him and Stephanie. "Julian Hale is too smart for this. He'll see right through it."

"Then nothing has changed," she said.

Stephanie and Rick breathed in and out in unison. It became a game of who would blink first.

"Fine," Rick said, throwing up his hands. "But we are doing nothing more than keeping the cell turned on. We are not sending Hale a formal invitation to join us, and you are not putting yourself in any unnecessary danger, got it?"

She smiled. "Got it."

Rick kneaded the back of his neck. "You are a real pain, you know that?"

"Yup." She scrunched up her nose. Then she gave him a goofy, crooked smile and held up her index finger. "But I'm cute."

Rick chuckled. "That you are."

The demanding cry of Rick's cell phone ringtone interrupted them, making all three people in the cubicle jump. He unclipped his phone from his belt and stared at it. "Call from," the robotic voice of his phone's operating system announced, "Allison Townsend."

Allie? He blinked at the caller ID on the screen, unbelieving. *Really?* He hadn't heard from her in a year. He had forgotten that he'd added her married name to his contacts. What could she want to talk to him about now all of a sudden?

"Rick, it's Allie." Her voice shook with emotion. "We need to talk. Is there somewhere we could meet?"

He listened to what she had to say. Something had really scared her, but she refused to talk about it over the phone. She insisted they had to meet in person.

"I'll call you back," he told her, and that was as much of a promise Allie was going to get from him now or ever.

After Rick explained Allie's request, Shelton rubbed his hands together.

"Well, look what we have here," he said. "The perfect scenario just dropped into our lap."

Rick could almost see steam coming from Shelton's ears as the gears inside his brain turned.

"You should go meet your fiancée for coffee and take Stephanie along with you. It's a perfect way to draw Julian out of hiding. You ignore Stephanie while you make goo-goo eyes with your long lost love. Stephanie acts all rejected and hurt and wanders off on her own. Meanwhile we watch and hope Hale will try to capitalize on the situation." Shelton looked as though he was enjoying the soap opera scene he was dreaming up, but the idea did not sit right in Rick's stomach.

This smelled of setup. It had to be more of Hale's games. Rick couldn't shake the feeling that they were walking into a trap.

"She is my *ex*-fiancée. And she happens to be married, by the way—let's not forget that important detail."

Gary Shelton wasn't known for his fidelity or for any long-lasting relationships. In his mind that would probably be an insignificant distinction, but Rick wanted Stephanie to know the difference.

Shelton waved off his words as if he were swatting away annoying flies. "Semantics. Just give the woman your full attention and keep your back turned to Stephanie while you're at it."

"It's the 'hopefully Hale will try to capitalize on the situation' that concerns me most," Rick grumbled.

"We'll have more guys than you can count who won't take their eyes off her for a second. You have to trust your team, Rick. Nothing's going to go wrong."

Famous last words, Shelton.

The silver BMW slipped effortlessly between two cars into an open parking spot across the street. *She even parks elegantly.*

The sporty car fit the image Stephanie had created in her mind of the type of women Rick would have dated in the past. Women who were completely unlike her. Allie Townsend's long legs swung out of the door before the beautiful brunette rose from the car and jogged toward the corner coffee shop where Rick and Stephanie stood waiting for her.

Allie swept past Stephanie, leaving a cloud of high-end floral fragrance lingering behind her. Stephanie inhaled the subtle rose and sandalwood tones. It was a lovely scent and a perfect match for the chic woman in front of her. Stephanie tugged at the hem of her dirty T-shirt, remembering she was still wearing the clothes Rick had bought her at the Marysville Walmart several days ago. What must she smell like? She had washed out the clothes in the hotel sink and let them air-dry, but the bar of soap had left them stiff and still dingy. Her other clothes had either blown up in the bomb, or had been left behind at the cabin in their haste to get Axle help. Stephanie shrank back as Allie embraced Rick.

With her immaculate tailored clothing and her flawless makeup, Allie appeared sophisticated and in charge, but her white-knuckle grip on Rick's arms and the way her eyebrows pinched together spoke volumes. *Julian has gotten to her, too.* Stephanie sighed as an almost motherly pity squeezed her heart.

Allie's head snapped to where Stephanie stood. All evidence of fear vanished as Allie's facial features smoothed into a nonchalant expression. A smidgen of curiosity peeked through, but otherwise Allie became a vision of total control. She stepped from the embrace and ran her hands down Rick's arms. "How are you, Rick?"

Sunlight glinted off the giant diamond on Allie's left ring finger, evaporating Stephanie's pity. She wanted to swat the married woman's French-manicured hands away from Rick's arms. *He's not yours to worry about any more,* Mrs. *Townsend.* But she restrained herself, remembering that Rick didn't belong to her any more than he belonged to Allie. With the history the two of them shared, Allie did have more right to Rick than Stephanie, even if she had let him get away. Stephanie remained silent, waiting for Rick to recall that she was standing there, waiting for him to care enough to introduce them.

He didn't.

Detective Shelton had told Rick to "ignore Stephanie while you make goo-goo eyes with your long lost love."

So the charade begins. Stephanie shifted her weight from foot to foot and wondered what she was supposed to do. Detective Shelton hadn't given her very clear directions other than to wander off and feign hurt. That wouldn't take much acting on her part. She had played the third wheel before; why was it bothering her so much today? Rick was playing his part perfectly, however. *Maybe he isn't acting.*

Cars and cyclists passed on the street, braking and honking at jaywalkers. Yuppie-looking pedestrians streamed by their spot on the sidewalk. Stephanie squinted into the bright sunshine, wondering about the people passing her. Which of them were police in disguise sent to protect her and nab Julian, and which were simply real Seattleites and tourists enjoying an unseasonably warm afternoon? More importantly, where was Julian Hale? Could he see her?

A sweet preschooler bumped against Stephanie's leg. The little girl held a red balloon animal and smiled up at her before her mother led her farther down the street. Stephanie watched a college-age boy lock his bike onto the rack next to her. The first real spring weather in many weeks had driven people tired of the drizzle out of doors en masse. The street was full of color and movement and innocent bystanders. What if Julian started shooting at them again in this crowd? Who would get hit in the cross fire?

Allie's gaze moved between Rick and Stephanie. "You two look like you've been through a war zone."

"Something like that," Rick answered her. Stephanie noticed his eyes doing their own scan of their surroundings. He pointed toward the door of the coffee shop. "Can we get inside now?"

Thankfully this gorgeous woman hadn't distracted him too much. Even if he had been giving Stephanie the cold shoulder lately, and was now too wrapped up in this reunion with his former fiancée to remember she was standing next to him, at least he was still the hypervigilant cop Stephanie had come to rely on for her protection.

Allie pouted and flipped her smooth dark hair over her shoulder. "Aren't you going to introduce us first, Rick?"

Before Rick could do the honors, Allie held out her slender hand to Stephanie, keeping her eyes on Rick. "He never was much for manners. I'm Allison Townsend."

Stephanie shook Allie's hand, feeling as though she wanted to fall into a hole. "I'm Stephanie. It's nice to meet you."

"So—" Allie elbowed Rick and winked "—does she know about us?" she asked him, her laugh brittle.

Bile burned Stephanie's throat. Val was right, and Stephanie was the fool. She couldn't deny her feelings for Rick any longer, but this woman from his past was so far out of her league. Stephanie's hand rose to smooth down her frizzy, disobedient hair. This tan, elegant woman with her Coach purse, her sculpted eyebrows and her perfect shampoo-commercial hair was Rick's type, not Stephanie in her frumpy Walmart couture. How had she let this happen? When had she stopped fighting against the attraction? She tried desperately to reel her heart back in, to reclaim it for herself, but it refused to obey.

Allie addressed her next question directly to Stephanie. "Did he mention how he broke my heart?"

Chapter Sixteen

Rick's blood pounded behind his ears. Allie's accusation left him so enraged, he was speechless. His eyes darted to Stephanie. What was she thinking? If he didn't have to worry about blowing Shelton's little soap opera charade, he would be in Allie's face and have it out with her right there on the sidewalk. *I broke your heart? Are you kidding me?*

His hands shook as he swung open the glass door for the two women to walk into the crowded coffee shop ahead of him. Before he stepped inside, his eyes settled on the shiny new BMW across the street. *Married life appears to be treating her well.*

He had been with Allie when she bought her old blue Honda Civic. It was right after she closed her first big real estate deal. He had never seen her prouder than she was using that commission as a down payment on the car. Apparently a five-year-old Honda was beneath her current social status.

A little bitter, aren't we? Well, why not? Wasn't he due a little bitterness? "I can't do this anymore" were the last words she had spoken to him when he was lying in a hospital bed, followed by zero contact until today's phone call dropped on him out of nowhere. The size of the engagement ring that she had left sitting by his hospital bed had been laughably small compared to the gaudy diamond she was flaunting now.

When she had introduced herself to Stephanie as Allison Townsend, he almost corrected her. She had always been Allie Driscoll to him. Allie Driscoll was the girl in the eighth grade who stole his heart and gave him his first kiss. She was the girl he had thought he wanted to marry. This angular, pretentious woman named Allison Townsend was foreign to him. Her hug out on the sidewalk had felt bony and cold compared to the softness and warmth he had felt holding Stephanie.

Stephanie. There was nothing cold about her. Her smile alone could raise the temperature in a room. It took all his willpower not to look over at her. *Shelton said to ignore her.* Even though he doubted that Hale could see into the coffee shop, Rick still needed to get into character, to play the part of the smitten ex-fiancé. He cleared his mind and let the hissing steam, the baristas' shouts of ready orders and the other patron's chipmunk-like chatter barrage his senses. He had been so tuned in to protecting Stephanie, it was difficult to give in to the noise and chaos and let it distract him.

But when Allie started rattling off her long-winded order for a one-pump, no whip, skinny, tall, vanilla, soy *thingamajig* drink, Rick couldn't help but meet Stephanie's gaze and roll his eyes. She giggled and put her hand over her mouth to stop it. Somehow he expected that Stephanie's order would be much less complicated.

He stepped close to Stephanie and said quietly in her ear, "That girl deserves a raise if she can remember all of that order."

"For sure," Stephanie agreed, her blue eyes dancing with delight.

Drinks in hand, the three of them searched but couldn't find a seat in the standing-room-only shop. Outside, one tiny bistro table with two chairs, not three, remained open. It was too small for the three of them to fit.

One table over from them, a North Face–clad customer sipped his drink as he read a tablet. There was nothing particularly noticeable about the guy—he looked like everyone else out today—but Rick recognized him. He had worked with the guy before. *Nowhere open for all three of us to sit together. Well played, Shelton.*

"I, uh, should, um, let you two catch up." Stephanie stammered.

Warning bells rang in Rick's head. *I don't like this, I don't like this.* Out loud he said, "Are you sure you don't mind?"

Stephanie's face paled. "Not at all."

She pointed down the sidewalk to a clothing boutique. "I'm sure it's been a while since the two of you have talked, and I wanted to check out the store next door, anyway."

Allie plopped down and scooted her chair up to the table. "That's sweet of you, Stephanie." Then she dismissed Stephanie with a blatant head-to-toe perusal of her clothing and said, "Have fun shopping." Rick gritted his teeth. Had Allie always been this snooty?

The empty chair across from Allie would leave his back turned to the direction Stephanie was about to walk. The seating situation would please Shelton, and would maybe tempt Hale out of hiding, but it was mutiny to Rick's training and instincts. As Stephanie moved past him, Rick reached out and stopped her. The bright sun made her eyes a brilliant sapphire, and the hurt feelings he could see in them tempted him to abandon the plan altogether. She had honest eyes that were easy to read. There was never any pretense in Stephanie. He had been such a jerk to her after Axle got hurt. He would need to make it up to her somehow.

"Be careful," he said, and dropped her arm. He willed himself to keep his eyes on Allie instead of turning to watch Stephanie walk away. He had to trust his team to take care of her.

To Allie he said, "Tell me what this is all about."

With his back turned, Rick couldn't see it, but he knew the moment Stephanie was out of earshot because Allie's calm and collected facade melted. She leaned forward and whispered, "Maybe you should tell *me* what's going on, Rick."

"You called me."

"I watch the news. I've seen the coverage of that killer on the loose and heard about that bomb going off at that hotel. I know you're involved. Don't deny it. You can't stay away from that kind of drama."

His chuckle was stiff. "Yeah, that's me, always on the lookout for drama." He drained his coffee cup with one long, exaggerated drink. "So you called to tell me you were worried about me?" He couldn't help the sarcasm.

"Of course I have been worried about you, Rick. Contrary to popular belief, I do not hate you." She sat back in her chair. "But that's not why I called."

Allie dug into her handbag and pulled out an envelope that looked similar to the one that had carried Stephanie's threatening photos from Hale. Rick poured the contents onto the table. Two items fell out: a black-and-white glossy photograph and a small square slip of paper with typed print on it. The photograph was of Rick and Axle walking into the hotel, the place that was supposed to be a "safe" house, on Sunday evening. A crude target had been drawn over top of his image with a red paint marker. The slip of paper had typed notes about Allie:

Allison Townsend (née Driscoll)
Owner of Puget Sound Realty Execs/SeaHome Property Management
Husband: Attorney, Timothy Townsend
Children: None

Along the bottom, Hale had written the phrase *unresolved heartbreak* in the same chicken-scratch handwriting he'd seen on Stephanie's envelope.

"He called our house, Rick." Allie's year-round tan paled around her mouth as she whispered the words. "It's him, isn't it? It's that killer on the news."

Rick inhaled and exhaled through his nose, trying to get professional control over his rage. "I'm sorry you were dragged into this, Al, I really am."

"That's not the worst of it." Tears pooled, threatening to run her mascara. "He said…" Allie choked down a sob. "He said that I had to tell you he would be willing to make a trade."

"A trade? What kind of trade?"

She quit trying to hold back the flow of tears, and let them streak black down her cheeks. "He said to tell you he didn't mind trading me for Stephanie if you wanted her to live instead." Allie's voice shook again as it had on the phone earlier. "He said to tell you he wasn't picky as long as he gets one of us."

Rick tried to cover one of her hands to comfort her,

but she swatted it away. "No. This is what I walked away from, Rick. I told you I wasn't cut out for this." She paused, and then added in a quieter voice, "I'm not brave like you."

"No one is going to die, Allie. Hale isn't getting either one of you. I won't let him."

"Well, he's not getting me. I'm leaving town tonight." She opened a compact and wiped away the mascara mess. She smoothed her hair. When she was composed she said, "Timothy has arranged a trip for us to Cancun." Allie dropped her compact back into her bag and dug out a business card with "Timothy Townsend, Attorney-at-Law" embossed along the top. "Here's Tim's number. Call us when it is safe to come home."

She stood up and slung her purse over her shoulder. She squeezed her arms tight around her waist. "Rick, I know you think I'm selfish…"

"Wanting to be safe isn't selfish, Allie…"

"I never meant to hurt you like I did. But it is what it is." Her brown eyes were full of regret. "And we both know you are better off without me. I only came here to warn you so you could keep her safe, but it looks like you are already doing that."

Rick cleared his throat. "Stephanie and I aren't seeing each other…"

"Well, you should be. She seems like a nice girl. Treat her right, okay?"

He heard the *better than you treated me* part that she really meant. Rick stood and gave Allie a sideways squeeze on her shoulders. "I will. Thank you, Al."

"I mean it. You deserve to be happy."

He watched her leave. He could see her dark hair bouncing as she jogged back to her car. "Goodbye,

Allie." In his mind it was a forever goodbye. *We are done. Go on with your life. I'm free.*

There had been a time when Allie's very presence in a room consumed him. He had loved her. She had broken him, but her power was gone. It was the one good thing in this bleak, stress-filled week, knowing that his heart belonged to himself again. Hale had been so wrong. *Heartbreak resolved.*

Hale had meant to play with Rick's emotions, but instead he had given Rick the gift of closure and clarity. He could see Allie for who she really was now. Comparing her character to the caliber of a woman like Stephanie made him question for the first time whether or not his failure at love had less to do with his career and a lot more to do with the type of woman he had chosen. *Thank you, God, for unanswered prayers.*

His cell phone rang, followed by the monotone voice announcement, "Call from... Gary Shelton."

Rick answered it, spinning in circles as he searched for Stephanie. "Shelton, you had better have good news for me."

Stephanie fingered the hem of a dress hanging on a sale rack outside the boutique. The silk fabric was smooth and the blue color would look good on her, but her mind was far from clothes. Her attention was locked on the cozy-looking couple sitting outside of the coffee shop down the street. *Stop stalking them, Stephanie.*

Her face flushed as she remembered all of the unknown eyes of the cops who were watching her at that very moment. To Rick's coworkers, she must look like a lovesick puppy. She dropped the hem and turned her back on Rick and Allie. *Rick and Allie.* She imagined their picture in their high school yearbook with the "Cutest Couple" caption underneath it.

She stepped around a seagull hopping on the sidewalk and walked uphill to the bookstore next door. She did not like this jealous monologue playing out in her mind. Shouldn't someone dedicated to serving God overseas as a missionary have her mind set on more noble things? She must have something to think about other than the cute boy and his former girlfriend on their little date. She needed to get a grip.

Scanning her surroundings for a possible threat was becoming second nature to her. *Which one of you is watching me?* It was so weird to know she was being monitored, but to still be unable to identify who was doing the watching. Whoever they were, they were good at making themselves invisible.

At first her eyes almost completely missed the man standing a block away on the other side of the street. Other than the bright red ball cap he wore, his drab clothing blended into the crowd. It was his stillness contrasted with the pedestrians streaming past him that finally caught her attention and caused her to squint into the distance to try to see his face.

Warm fear spread to her fingertips, making her feel weightless and outside her own body. He was here. Shelton's plan had worked. She couldn't see well enough to make a positive ID, but every cell in her body screamed that that was Julian Hale watching her.

Her heart hammered, demanding to be released from her chest. She averted her eyes and made herself walk forward. *Play it cool. Make him believe that you don't see him.*

She picked up a book off one of the clearance tables on the sidewalk and pretended to be engrossed in the story of one man's trek across the Sahara on his motorcycle. The words melded into a blurry string as she tried to swallow her panic. She couldn't stand it any longer; she looked up. Where was he now? She couldn't find the red hat. He had moved, but where?

Stephanie slammed the book closed and held it to her chest, clutching it like a life preserver. She searched for Julian, but couldn't find him. She frantically scanned the crowds, moving farther away from the bookstore.

"Hey lady, you going to buy that book, or what?" yelled the store clerk.

"Oh, no, sorry," she mumbled and tossed the book onto the nearest table. She had to locate Julian. Why had she looked down for so long? She should not have lost track of him. *Look natural. He'll bolt if he thinks you are onto him.*

At that moment, a heavy hand lit on her shoulder from behind her. The touch caused an unhindered scream of terror to burst from Stephanie's mouth. She spun around, fist raised, but instead of Julian Hale, she found a flinching Rick ducking away from her before she swung at him.

He pulled her fists down and wrapped his arms around her. "It's me," he crooned into her ear. "I'm sorry. It was stupid to sneak up on you like that."

Stephanie squirmed to get out of his embrace. "Rick, he's across the street. I just saw him." She frantically spun around and around in circles, searching everywhere for the red ball cap. It was gone. "He was there, I saw him!"

Rick shook his head and grinned. "No, you didn't. You might have thought you saw him, but it wasn't him." Rick's face was shining. "It's over, Stephanie."

She had never seen Rick looking this happy. "How

do you know it wasn't him? I saw him. I mean I thought it was him, but I wasn't close enough to see for sure." Rick's calm reaction was confusing her.

He lifted her off the ground and swung her in circles. When he placed her back down and let go, she giggled. "What is that all about? Are you sure you only had coffee to drink?"

"I just have really, really, *really* good news for you."

Stephanie rubbed at the crease between her eyebrows, trying to get her forehead to relax. *Really good news, huh?* So Rick was talking to her again? What had happened to the frozen Rick she had encountered at the vet's office? This guy was so hot and cold. She never knew what to expect from him. It was disorienting to have him change personalities so abruptly.

She urged him on. "And this good news is…"

"Gary Shelton called me." A gigantic grin took over Rick's entire face, making that gorgeous dimple reappear, deeper than she had seen it yet. *That's not fair, God. That dimple is an unfair advantage.*

"And?" Stephanie urged. *Would he just spit the news out already?*

"And, Shelton got a call from the Bellingham Police Department. They pulled over a drunk driver and they got an NCIC hit when they ran him."

She tugged on her earlobe, rolling it between her fingers. *Would you speak English?* "What is NCIC?"

"NCIC stands for the National Crime Information Center. It's a nationwide database for felony warrants. We can run a person's information anywhere in the country and see if they have a felony warrant from somewhere else. When Bellingham ran their driver, they got a hit." Rick paused for another huge grin. "It was Julian Hale, Stephanie. They *arrested* him an hour ago."

She blinked a few times. Her brain was having a hard time processing what Rick was saying. "You mean…"

Then Rick cupped his hand behind her neck, touching his forehead to hers, and said, "You, Stephanie O'Brien, are a free woman."

But she had been so sure it was Julian looking at her from across the street. Her nerves must have been playing tricks on her imagination. She hadn't seen the man's face. He could have been anyone and she would have seen Julian because that's what she had expected to see.

Rick pulled her into a hug. She wrapped her arms around his waist and leaned into his chest. She liked how she tucked easily underneath his chin. She didn't care that they were standing on a sidewalk surrounded by tons of people. And she didn't care that tomorrow Rick would probably go back to acting as if he didn't even know her. Right now, she needed to be held, to feel anchored down, before she could fully grasp the words Rick had told her.

"It's really over?" she whispered.

He pulled her in tighter. She felt his jaw moving on top of her head as he spoke, his voice deeper. "It's really over, Stephanie. Julian Hale is ninety miles away from here behind bars where he belongs. You're safe."

Chapter Seventeen

Monday Morning

Stephanie awoke to a kidney shot from a small brown foot. She wasn't sure at what hour Joash and Haddie had transitioned from their sleeping bags in the living room to sleeping with her, but her muscles were sore from being held in unnatural positions for too long.

The foot responsible for her aching kidney belonged to Joash on her left side. He stretched out horizontally, taking up over two-thirds of Stephanie's small full-size bed. Using Stephanie's right arm as her pillow, Haddie sucked her thumb and curled deeper into Stephanie's side.

All of the bed covers had been kicked off them and Stephanie was freezing. She needed to get up and get ready for work, but she didn't want to wake up the sleeping kids this early in the morning. She slid her arm out from under Haddie's head, cushioning the girls' dark curls with her other hand, lowering it slowly, slowly, hoping to escape without waking her. She moved her pillow up against Haddie's side to be her substitute. She scooted down and exited at the foot of the bed.

There hadn't been enough room for the three of them to sleep comfortably, but Stephanie was glad the kids had found her, anyway.

Waking up to the two tiny companions had comforted her in such a deep place. She stood at the foot of the bed watching them sleep. Her chest ached with longing. The peace on their faces was beautiful. In his sleep, Joash scooted closer to his sister for warmth. Stephanie spread the covers over both of them.

As much as she loved these two spooning kids, they did not belong to her. Would she ever stand in the dark watching her own babies sleep, or was that the cost of the meaningful life she wanted? She had always said she wanted to be different, to have a life that meant something, and to do something big for God. Maybe giving this up was her cross to bear. She shook her head to free it from the melancholy. She had allowed too much distraction over the past week in the form of Rick Powell. She needed to get her head back on the goal. Especially now that Julian had been arrested, and she was free to go on with her plans. That is if she could figure out what those plans were even suppose to be.

Stephanie rubbed at the kink in her neck as she tiptoed past Val's air mattress on the living room floor on her way to the kitchen. Val had sensed Stephanie's apprehension at being alone and had spent the past two nights with her. Knowing Julian was in jail in Bellingham made her feel safer, but it would take some time before she would be completely comfortable with being alone.

In the kitchen, she started a pot of coffee. Too impatient to wait until it was done, she poured herself a quick cup and then slid the pot back under to finish filling. She wrapped her hands around the steaming mug and gazed outside into the predawn dark.

"Up already?"

Stephanie jumped, spilling hot coffee on her hand. "Val. You're supposed to be sleeping in."

Val shrugged. "Want me to make you breakfast?"

"I'd love it, but there's no time." Stephanie set her mug in the sink and dried off her hand. "I've got to get to school."

Val rubbed her eyes and stretched her arms high above her head. "This early? But it's still dark out there."

"Yeah, but I've been gone all week. I need an early start." Stephanie dreaded the mess waiting for her after being away from her classroom. It was going to be a long day of retraining her kids in classroom expectations, and catching up on paperwork and planning. The sooner she got to school the smoother her day would be. "I'm going to shower and go. Don't worry about me for breakfast. I'll pick up a bagel on the way."

Val poured herself a mug of coffee. "So have you talked to Rick?"

Stephanie nodded. "He and Detective Shelton are driving to Bellingham this morning. The extradition hearing will be at eight o'clock, and then they can bring Julian back to Seattle."

Val took a long swig from her mug and then turned a teasing grin on Stephanie. "That will be nice, but what I meant was have you and Rick talked about *you and Rick.*"

Stephanie's heart squeezed. She hadn't seen much of Rick at all this weekend. He had come to the early service at church with the Watkinses, but Axle was home from the vet, and Rick had needed to hurry back to take care of him before his work shift started. Stephanie didn't want to admit to Val how disappointed she felt at how little she had seen of Rick or how lonely that lack of contact had made her feel.

"There is no *me and Rick*, Val."

Val blew on the top of her steaming cup and asked, "And why is that?"

Stephanie rolled her eyes. "Okay, matchmaker. I'm not his type. Have you ever met his ex-fiancée? She is so gorgeous. I have never felt like such a hick as I did standing next to her."

"You mean the woman who left him alone when he needed her the most? Allie abandoned him, Stephanie. You are the gorgeous one—inside and out—and Rick sees that, too. I saw the way he looked at you at church yesterday. No matter what you say, I believe that you two belong together. You can't deny that you have feelings for him."

Stephanie closed her eyes and sighed. "Yeah, I do." It was surprisingly freeing to admit it out loud. "But what good do feelings do me? I'm supposed to be a missionary, and isn't that the cost of following my calling? Giving up earthly pleasure, even love if need be, for the greater gain? Look at all the missionaries in history, like Amy Carmichael. She gave up everything to serve God on the mission field."

"Amy Carmichael was obedient to the calling God had on *her* life. You need to be sure of only what He is asking of *you*, Stephanie. And why can't you have both? Serve the Lord and love someone. It doesn't have to be mutually exclusive."

Val was quiet for a moment. Then she continued in a softer tone. "I know this is going to come out all wrong, but I'm going to say it, anyway. Sometimes I wonder if you are afraid of losing God's love, that He'll reject you like your dad did. I don't deny that you love Liberia, or even that God is calling you to serve the people there, but—" she hugged Stephanie around the waist "—you have to live your life, Stephanie. Not your sister's life, not your heroes' lives, only your own life. God's love for you is not dependent on how well you perform for Him. You know that you don't have to earn it, right? That it's a gift."

Stephanie frowned. Her mouth gaped. She opened and closed it several times as she groped for words to explain herself. When she couldn't find them, she shook her head and waved off Val's concern. "Of course I know that, Val. That's not it. You just don't understand. You haven't been there. You haven't seen what I've seen. I *love* Liberia."

"But you want to love Rick, too, don't you?"

Stephanie flinched from the sting of the words. She didn't have time for a heart-to-heart. "I've got to go, Val. Help yourself to whatever you want to make for yourself and the kids for breakfast."

Rick's knee bobbed. He drummed his fingers on the car's armrest, and then stopped to check the clock app on his phone for what must be the thirtieth time. Shelton was driving as fast as he could get away with, but for Rick, the two-hour drive had felt like five already.

He didn't have to come along. Now that Axle had been discharged, Rick could have chosen to stay at home with him and let someone else go with Shelton to pick up Hale. But Axle was in good hands with Cindy, his retired, dog-loving next-door neighbor, and Rick needed to see Julian Hale wearing handcuffs with his own eyes.

Finally Shelton's phone droned out the last of the GPS's turn-by-turn directions. "Your destination will be on the right," it intoned in its signature science fiction–like voice.

Rick released a breath of relief. *About time.*

Shelton pulled the department's transport van into the jail's sally port and put it into park. "I can't wait for Hale to face the justice he deserves," Shelton said. "I'm going to have a tough time not delivering it myself."

"Me, too," agreed Rick.

The detective reached behind the van's front seat and grabbed his briefcase. "So after this case is wrapped up, are you planning on making a move on the girl, or what?" Shelton asked Rick.

Rick snorted as he climbed out of the van. "Why? Are you interested in her, Gary?" He tapped the hood. "I can always see if Stephanie wants a date with you."

"Watch it, you young punk," Shelton said. Then he winked. "I will say that if I had a better track record with relationships, and I thought for a minute she'd be interested in an old man like me, you might have some competition on your hands."

An image of Stephanie's beautiful face projected on the screen of Rick's imagination, but he pushed the thought away. He might want to pursue it, but he couldn't think about romantic involvement with her. She had plans that didn't involve settling down with a cop. The best he could hope to give her was seeing Julian Hale put away for life, to give her the gift of never having to worry about a killer chasing her again. "Let's just go get our guy and forget about my love life for now, okay?"

"Fine," Shelton said. "But will you take some advice from an old man?"

"Depends on the old man," Rick joked.

"When you find the good one, you don't let her get away." A faraway, wistful expression crossed Shelton's face.

She is "the good one," but I can't ask her to give up her dreams for me. Rick tapped the hood again with his fist. "It's a little late for that. She's leaving for Africa," Rick said. He paused for effect. "She's going to be a missionary."

"A missionary?" Shelton spit out air in disbelief. "With all your good looks and charm, you can't change her mind about that?"

Rick gave him a wary smile. "Not sure that I could or should try to change those kinds of plans even if I was able."

Shelton answered with a small nod. "I suppose we can't get in the way of the Big Man upstairs." He averted his eyes from Rick and shifted his weight. He didn't seem comfortable with the deep turn the conversation had taken. "Whatever you do, though, don't end up an old man and all alone like me, okay, kid? The job isn't worth that kind of price."

A guard opened the jail door and asked, "Detective Shelton?"

"That's me." Shelton shook the man's hand and then introduced Rick. "This is Officer Powell."

The man smiled and offered Rick his hand next. "Adam Kerns. It's nice to meet you both."

Rick shook and returned the grin. "Can't tell you how happy we will be to see Julian Hale in handcuffs. So who do we get to thank for catching our bad guy for us?"

Deputy Kerns smiled. "That would be me. I wanted to be here to meet you guys. I guess I know how that trooper in Oklahoma must have felt when he pulled over Timothy McVeigh. Sometimes we stumble on the bad guys without even looking."

He grinned again. "I'll tell you what, that NCIC hit was quite a shock. Didn't see that coming."

"I'm sure it was." Rick could easily imagine the jolt of adrenaline seeing that warrant pop up on the computer screen would cause.

Kerns scanned the paperwork that Shelton had handed him. "This all looks good. Are you guys ready for him?"

"More than ready," Rick answered.

The deputy spoke into his radio. Rick's fingers were in constant, anxious motion, drumming the air at his side. He heard a buzzer and then the *click* of an automatic lock opening. He strained his neck to peer around the guard to see clearly as another deputy guided a prisoner through the door.

Rick's eyes narrowed as he studied the prisoner. He guessed the man to be in his early fifties, about the same age as Shelton. But instead of the fitness and vigor of the running-addicted detective, this man was slouched over as he shuffled into the room. His face was haggard and unshaven, and under the gray stubble, the man's puffy face and yellow skin tone were those of a heavy drinker. Rick frowned, confused.

Shelton cocked his head as he addressed the guard. "Who's this?"

The new deputy answered him. "This is Julian Hale. Aren't you guys here to pick him up?"

Shelton swore and slapped the clipboard he was holding against his thighs.

Sweat beaded on Rick's neck. *No, no, no, no. Hale couldn't have played us again.* He shook his head and said, "There must be a mistake. This man is most definitely not Julian Hale."

The prisoner's head popped up. The man's whole demeanor changed. He stood straight, color flowed into his cheeks, and his eyes sparkled with hope. "See! I've been telling you that all weekend," the man told the guards. "It's not me they want." He looked back and forth between Shelton and Rick, his eyes wide. "I tried to tell the judge but she wouldn't listen."

"Who are you?" Shelton demanded, his nostrils flaring.

"I *am* Julian Hale. But not the Julian Hale that you want. Maybe there are two of us. All I know is I'm no killer. I'll admit all day long that I drink too much, and how stupid it was for me to get behind the wheel drunk, but I ain't never killed nobody, never. You've got to believe me."

Shelton shoved the papers back at the deputies. "I appreciate your help," he said. "But we're not taking custody of this man. He's not our guy."

"But we found evidence in his car. His description was dead-on, and his Social Security number fit the NCIC hit," Kerns demanded.

"That's your problem," Shelton told the dumbstruck deputies standing next to the grinning prisoner.

Rick felt sick. Hale must have known about the other man who shared his name, a man with a bad habit for repeatedly drinking too much and then getting behind the wheel afterward. It was like Hale to have a contingency plan set up as decoy. How long had he been planning this? But the deputies had found incriminating evidence in the trunk of the wrong Julian's car. Hale would have had to plant that evidence in the trunk and then watch until the man started driving. After that it would only take a phone call complaining about a dangerous drunk driver on the road, and Hale would be able to play them once again.

Had Hale also hacked into the NCIC database? He would have had to change the Social Security number and physical description on the warrant. Julian Hale disgusted Rick, but he had to respect his brilliance. When would they stop underestimating this guy?

Rick and Shelton sprinted toward the van. Over his shoulder Shelton called back to them, "We've still got a killer on the loose and more importantly, we've got a woman who's about to become a victim if we don't get to her first."

Winter's fingers clung to the spring morning with damp, bone-chilling mist. Friday's beautiful sunshine had only been a tease. Spring in Seattle would arrive, but not anytime soon. It was running late this year. Stephanie ripped off a vicious bite of her bagel and trudged on through the cold morning. She loved being a teacher. Why was she so blue about going to school? Her heart wasn't in it this morning, but her crankiness probably had more to do with her conversation with Val than it had to do with not wanting to go to work. Stomping her feet to warm up her toes, she continued up the steep sidewalk to the school.

Only a week ago, she had been running from a bomb. She didn't know how to easily return to her mundane life as if none of it had happened. The adrenaline and adventure had made the days seem to fly by, but the closeness she had shared with Rick had made the single week feel ages long, as if Rick and Axle had always been a part of her life. She pulled off another chunk of bagel and shoved it into her mouth. She chewed aggressively, hating how much she missed them. Life had been so much easier when Rick Powell had been nothing more than a cute acquaintance.

Stephanie turned into the nearly empty staff parking lot. Only a few cars dotted the blacktop this early in the morning. She slipped off her backpack and dug through its contents in search of her keys. Not watching where she was walking, she collided with a man crossing the parking lot in the opposite direction.

The man helped her regain her footing. Tipping the brim of his ball cap down at her, he said in a hoarse voice, "I'm sorry about that. Didn't see you there."

"That was my fault. I walked right into you," Stephanie chuckled, smoothing her curls. She swung her backpack over her shoulder and looked directly at the stranger.

A pair of dull cornflower-blue eyes peered out from under the red hat brim, taking Stephanie's breath away. She stumbled back a step. "But…but you're…"

He grabbed her elbow and shoved the tip of a gun into the fleshy part of her stomach. Ice filled her veins. "Hello, Stephanie. Surprised to see me?"

He shoved her head into his chest. There was no one in the parking lot to hear her muffled screams.

Chapter Eighteen

Bumping around in the backseat, Stephanie forced herself to recall everything she had ever heard or read about self-protection. It was all bits and pieces, nothing concrete. The one thing she did remember was that whatever it took—biting, screaming, kicking, scratching— it was crucial that a victim never allow herself to be taken into an attacker's car.

That was great in theory, but there hadn't been time to fight back before Julian's gun was thrust into her abdomen. Her mind had been busy turning over her conversation with Val, and because she thought Julian was in jail, Stephanie's guard had been lowered. Before her fight instinct could think about kicking in, Julian had already held a cloth over her face until everything went black. She woke up in the backseat of this car, her hands and feet bound in zip ties and a blindfold tied tightly around her eyes.

Stephanie wiggled in the seat, trying to find a comfortable position. She tasted blood in her mouth from gnawing on her inside cheek so hard. *I've got to get out of here.* Dread weighed heavy on her mind, making it difficult to strategize. Stephanie worked to toss off the

feeling of doom. If she was going to survive this, she
had to stay positive. Although she could feel the vibrations of the moving car, she couldn't see behind the
blackness of the blindfold to determine what direction
they were traveling, and she couldn't get a feel for how
much time had passed. How long had she been passed
out? The driver was so silent, she wasn't even completely sure that it was still Julian behind the wheel.

Faces of everyone she loved loomed in her mind. She
could see them in such vivid detail, these people she had
to see again, people who made her want to live, but of
all the faces, it was Rick's that stood out the most. *I want
a chance to know him, to love him.* Why was that clear
to her now, when she couldn't act on it? It was too late.

She wondered what Julian planned to do with her.
Stephanie curled into a fetal position. She wasn't afraid
of being dead. She had hope. It was the process of dying,
and the pain Julian Hale had in store for her, that terrified her the most.

The hours it took to drive back to Seattle from Bellingham had been pure torture for both men. They tried
to reach her, but after it was clear Stephanie wasn't
answering their calls, Rick and Detective Shelton had
taken turns yelling at people through their cell phones.
Eventually there was nothing left to do but rely on their
friends in Seattle to find Stephanie until they could
get there to help. They had settled into a mutual stony
silence while Shelton obliterated every speeding law
along I-5.

Finally, Shelton had dropped Rick off at the department and the two separated to start the search in their
own way. Rick met Terrell at Stephanie's house.

"Anything?" he asked Terrell as he burst through

her door. Terrell shook his head. A lump rose in Rick's throat at the look of sadness in his friend's eyes. Rick nodded. "Okay, I'll start looking in the back."

Standing in the doorway of Stephanie's bedroom, Rick choked on a sob, forcing himself to swallow his grief. Her bedroom reminded him of her—feminine and cozy, but clutter-free. A chilly breeze tossed gauzy blue curtains around her open window. He pulled the curtains aside to see that the window had been left open a crack. Had Hale ever been inside her house? Rick knew he had spied on her through the webcam, but he wondered if Hale had ever come inside her home. Nausea rolled at the thought.

They were all fools. And he blamed himself the most. Until he had seen Hale behind bars with his own eyes, he should never have let Stephanie out of his sight. Hale had lulled them all into a false sense of security, and Rick had fallen for it right along with the rest of them. After all of the technology tricks that Hale had pulled off this week, why hadn't any of them thought that he might still be manipulating them? They had ignored the precedent, and Stephanie had disappeared because of their complacency.

Hale probably hadn't snatched Stephanie from her house. Val and the kids were the last to see her after she said goodbye to them and left for work, and they had still been here when the school called looking for her. It was more likely that he had picked her up somewhere along her walking route to the school. A girl at a bakery Stephanie had stopped at remembered selling her a bagel, but that was where her trail ended.

Rick leaned against the door frame. Maybe being here was nothing more than his need to feel close to her, but they had no clues yet to work from. They needed to start somewhere, and her room was as good a place to start as any. He stepped across the threshold feeling as if he were entering a sanctuary.

At her desk, Rick riffled through her papers and books, doubting he would find anything helpful, but doing a thorough job of it, anyway. He would never forgive himself if he missed something important. He spotted a scrapbook in the hutch above the desk. He pulled it down and sat down on her bed. Stephanie had hand-lettered the word *Liberia* across the entire page and then filled in the letters with bright colors and textures. He didn't know she was so artistic. He mourned for all of the things he didn't know about her yet. Was she even still alive?

He flipped through the pages, his eyes hungry to find her face. In every picture, the poverty of both the country and the people photographed was evident, but that wasn't what Rick noticed. Instead, he noticed the beauty and the joy, especially present in the photos that had Stephanie in them. In his favorite picture she smiled wide, dressed in a brightly patterned dress. Her hair was wrapped up in a head scarf, and she leaned against an African woman wearing a matching outfit. The two women were so different yet there was an evident sisterhood between them. Their huge smiles spoke of a love he knew nothing about, a love he wanted to know.

Stephanie! Where are you? How do I find you?

He gasped for air, his own powerlessness suffocating him. It was becoming an all-too-familiar emotion. The first time had been the night he was stabbed and left for dead. His own mortality and lack of control over his life had been so clear as he bled onto the pavement. He had felt the same way on Wednesday listening to

Axle's pain-filled howls by the river, hating how helpless he was to make it better for the dog he loved. And each time Julian Hale had been successful at threatening Stephanie's safety without being caught, Rick had been humbled. He might wear a gun and a badge, but he wasn't in charge. He couldn't control life no matter how much he might want to, and he had absolutely no idea how to save Stephanie now.

He closed the book and tossed it aside onto her bed. Sliding off the bed, he hit his knees. *Lord, help.*

"Home sweet home." Julian's voice chimed from the front seat. So it was still Julian with her. She heard the engine turn off.

Stephanie stiffened. This might be her only chance left to slip out of the zip ties and make a run for it. She wiggled and writhed, trying anything to loosen their grip, but nothing worked.

The back passenger door opened next to her head, and she felt the cool air on her face. "Where are you taking me?"

"Now what fun would it be if I told you everything? Let's see if you can guess." Amusement edged Julian's voice as he taunted her.

"I'm tired of your games," she told him.

"Well, that's too bad, because the games are only beginning. I'm not done having fun yet," he said.

His arms slipped under her armpits, yanking hard. Her eyes and arms were useless but she blindly whipped her bound legs around like a mermaid tail, trying to make it as difficult as possible to drag her. He had gotten her into a car, but now that she was outside it, she was fighting back with everything that she could throw at him.

Stephanie screamed, "Help me! Someone help…"

But Julian was prepared. Intense bursts of electricity coursed through her body, paralyzing her. She couldn't move or speak; she could only feel the pulsing pain.

"You like that?" Julian asked her, the energy level increasing in his voice that had been lacking only moments ago. "That was fifty-thousand volts of electricity. You took it pretty well, Stephanie. I'm impressed."

She wished for her eyesight so she could anticipate the next shock and prepare herself for the pain that could come again on his next whim. Behind the blindfold she wouldn't have any warning.

"What was that?" she asked him.

"That, my dear, was a Taser. I'm sure your boyfriend has one on his gun belt."

Stephanie flung her head in the direction of Julian's voice, tightening her body to prepare for more pain. "I'm going to leave these barbs attached to you. That means I can fire again anytime I need to. Now," Julian asked her, "would you like another round of electricity or are you done fighting me?"

"I'm done," she whimpered.

Julian dragged her tied-up body indoors, her legs bumping over gravel and grass and finally up concrete steps. She heard a door slam behind them before he dumped her onto a soft couch. She strained to hear anything. She inhaled deep breaths through her nose, searching for any scent that might clue her in to where Julian had taken her. Nothing struck her as familiar.

"I'm going to remove the blindfold now, and you will remain calm or I will shock you again, is that understood?"

The agony from the jolts still fresh, Stephanie nodded her agreement. Julian Hale would not take her out without a fight, but for now she didn't mind avoiding further pain in order to get her sight back. If she could see, she would have all of her senses to help her plan.

She felt Julian's fleshy fingers cold against her skin as he unwound the fabric. The blackness receded, but the pressure from the tight blindfold had blurred her vision, making it difficult to get her bearings even with it off. Lights were on, but she sensed it was still daylight, afternoon maybe? She twisted her head around looking for visual cues to where Julian had taken her.

"Where are we?" she asked him.

"You don't recognize where we are? Interesting..." He stretched the word out as if her ignorance genuinely fascinated him. Her vision was still a little blurry, but from the couch he had tossed her on, she could see a flat-screen TV and a bookshelf. The room was masculine and boring, some kind of bachelor pad. *This place needs a woman's touch.*

Julian sat on the ottoman in front of her. His thin ash-blond hair fell in straight bangs that looked like he used a ruler to cut them. She could see his bald scalp through his wide, precise part. Pale hair, washed-out eyes, pallid skin, and monochromatic clothing—Julian Hale's appearance was as lifeless as his eyes.

"Are you going to tell me where we are?" she asked him again.

"I answered that question outside. If I tell you where we are, what fun would that be?" Julian stood and slapped his thighs. "Well, why don't you settle in and search for some clues while you wait? I need to have a little chat with your boyfriend."

"He's not my boyfriend," she yelled at his retreating back.

* * *

Terrell tapped on the wall of Stephanie's bedroom. "Hate to interrupt a brother in prayer, but we've got something."

Rick scrambled to his feet. "What did you find?"

"I didn't *find* anything, but Julian Hale just called the department claiming responsibility for Stephanie's disappearance."

Rick froze. "Did he say where he's holding her?" If they knew where she was, they might be able to rescue her. Hope swirled in his stomach and chest, wanting him to grab hold.

"No. He didn't mention location." Terrell ran a hand across his hair. *Now what?* "How much experience do you have with hostage negotiation, Rick?"

"None," Rick answered. "Why?"

Terrell scratched his head. "Better learn quick, because Hale made it clear. He speaks with no one but you."

Chapter Nineteen

Terrell Watkins and Gary Shelton listened in on another line while Rick grabbed the blinking phone in front of him. "This is Powell."

"Hello, Rick."

Rick's lips stretched into a snarl at the sound of Julian Hale's arrogant voice. Of all the things Rick wanted to say, a pleasant greeting didn't appear anywhere on that list.

"Hale," he finally choked out. He wanted to reach through the phone line and strangle the man, but he had to stay calm and keep Hale talking.

"I assume that you have already searched Stephanie's house, as well as mine again." Hale said. "Find anything interesting?"

He's controlling the conversation.

Rick needed to flip this around, to tip the power back in his direction. He couldn't allow Hale to continue pulling the puppet strings.

"Let's skip the small talk and get to your demands," Rick told him.

"You need a little practice in negotiation, Officer

Powell. Aren't you supposed to be building trust, assuring me you have my best interests at heart?"

Rick huffed. "You and I have too much history between us to be anything but honest. We've exchanged bullets, Julian. I think we can skip the pretense of liking each other and move past the chitchat. What do you want?"

Hale chuckled. "This is true," he agreed. "So, I've been waiting patiently. Have you figured out our location yet?"

He's having fun with this. It is all a big game to him. Rick hated to answer that he didn't know where Hale and Stephanie were located. The SWAT team was pre-alerted, waiting to hear where to show up. They had been told, "We've got something going down but we don't know where to send you yet. Hang tight." Nothing in Stephanie's house had pointed them to her location, and all of their attempts to locate her cell phone had failed because her phone was powered down.

Using enhanced caller ID, dispatch advised that Hale's call had come in on a prepaid phone without GPS. They were working on figuring out which cell tower he was using.

Rick directed the conversation down a different path, hoping Hale would slip in a clue. "Is Stephanie okay?"

"Are you changing the subject? So, that would be a no, then, you don't know where we are?" Hale snickered. "I'm disappointed. I thought I made it so easy to find us. Maybe if I stay on the line a bit longer, you'll trace the call like they do in the movies."

The yellow pencil Rick had been twirling snapped in two.

Hale's taunting continued. "Or maybe you'll be smart

enough to find me on your own. I'll call back in fifteen minutes and see if you've made any progress."

Rick waited for Hale to hang up, but he started to speak again. "Oh, and Rick."

"Yes."

"You better hurry. Stephanie's time is running out."

Stephanie had heard Julian's threats to Rick. *How much time do I have left?* Her body began to shake, first in her legs, and then the trembling moved up her spine and then back down to her bound hands. She tried to control the shaking with deep breathing, but she was having a hard time calming the fear.

"Julian?" she whispered. "Why?"

He lunged at her, his pale skin blotchy and his empty eyes bulging. Stephanie flinched from his hot breath so close to her face. Sneering, Julian spoke to her between gritted teeth. "Don't talk unless spoken to first."

Anger sparked in his eyes, revealing a sign of life underneath his unnaturally placid exterior. His reaction startled her. It was so unlike Julian to be so passionate about anything. What was it about her question that had aroused his temper? Maybe he didn't like her using his name.

"I need to understand why this is happening." Her arms ached from being pinned behind her for so long. "Why me?" she squeaked out.

His face contorted, his fight against an internal storm playing out on his face. She winced. Would he shock her again?

"Why *not* you, Stephanie? I kill people. That's what I do. Are you so special you think someone else deserved to die in your place? Who should it be instead? Allison Townsend, perhaps?"

"Wasn't I kind to you?" Stephanie asked him. "What did I do to you that made you hate me?"

Julian's face relaxed back into its familiar void-of-emotion expression. "You annoyed me when you slipped away like you did, but if it is any comfort to you, Stephanie, I do not hate you." He turned his back to her and walked to the bookshelf. He picked up a framed photograph from a shelf. "In fact, in my own way, I highly value you," he said.

Value me? Enough to take my life away from me?

"You should consider yourself fortunate. The pain I inflict before you die will allow you to feel, to know for certain that you are alive." He turned his dead eyes back on to her. She recoiled from the sickness she saw in them.

Julian returned his gaze to the photo he held in his hands. He lowered his voice even further. "You won't believe me when I tell you this, but I will be doing you a favor."

She choked out a half chuckle, half sob. "I should thank you for killing me?"

"Yes. You should. You won't have leprosy of the soul like me."

Leprosy of the soul? What was that supposed to mean? Blood pounded between her ears, making her head ache. Julian's mind was too twisted for her to follow his train of thought.

He remained silent for several heartbeats. His voice was only a notch above a whisper when he added, "You will die in pain, but you will die loving and being loved."

Her eyes stung and blurred. She shivered. The desperation of this man chilled her. Her heart lurched with pity at the thought of his emptiness. *He's jealous of me?*

Of all the things to envy her for, Julian had chosen her ability to give and receive love. *Me, the abandoned and fatherless, the single woman with no relationship.* He had picked the one thing she thought she lacked the most.

The slideshow of faces started to march across her mind again. She saw Terrell and Val and remembered how lost and lonely she had been when she wandered into the junior high youth group they were leading. They had taken her under their wings back then, and all these years later they were still loving her. She saw the faces of Joash and Haddie, and those of the countless people she knew in Liberia. She felt again Axle's warmth when he guarded her in the hotel stairwell from the bomb. She felt again Rick's arms around her. All the people she loved and who loved her back. It had never occurred to her before this moment just how rich in love her life was, but a stranger had been able to see it and want it for himself.

"You are loved, too, Julian," she whispered.

"What do you mean?" His body snapped into a rigid, defensive stance. His eyes narrowed. Currents of hatred sparked off him like the electricity he had shot at her. Stephanie pulled back into the couch as far as she could. "Do you mean by your *God*, Stephanie? Are you trying to *save* me?"

Warmth started in her core and radiated through her. It was unexplainable. She sat facing a killer who planned to torture and kill her; she should be terrified, yet strangely she was basking in peace. Cleansing tears flowed unhindered down her cheeks. Julian had given her a gift, the chance to see the truth even if he wouldn't accept it for himself. A Bible verse Terrell had made her memorize all those years ago in youth group floated to the surface. "The LORD appeared to us in the past, saying: 'I have loved you with an everlasting love; I have drawn you with unfailing kindness.'" She was loved. And so was Julian.

"Yes, Julian. You are loved by God. If you want it, it's yours."

Julian slammed the photo back on the shelf. "You can keep your little missionary spiel to yourself." He laughed a manic cackle. "You don't need to practice your speeches. You won't be running off to Africa anymore. What are you going to do now that you can't earn those brownie points?"

Julian's words seared her heart. They were basically the same sentiment that Val had tried to tell her that morning. She had believed the lie that if she worked hard enough, did something grand enough, then maybe, just maybe, God wouldn't reject her as her father had done.

"God's love is a gift," she stammered. "I couldn't earn it even if I tried." Light filled her mind as more truth dawned. "And nothing will separate me from that love. Even if you kill me, Julian, I'll still have it."

Julian cocked an eyebrow. "Well, you will have a chance to test that theory soon enough."

Courage and peace she could not explain continued to buoy her, but her curiosity had one more question needing answered. "Why are you waiting, Julian? Why haven't you killed me already?"

His chuckle was low and soft this time. "Your time is coming soon enough, but I have big plans of my own, and I need you to stay alive long enough to bring me my audience. We wouldn't want your *boyfriend* to miss out on all the fun, would we?" He waved her off, dismissing their conversation. "If you'll excuse me, I need to make a phone call."

As he stepped away from the bookshelf, Stephanie looked at the photograph he had re-shelved. She saw a typical department store backdrop behind a smiling couple. The picture could have been taken at any mall and could be of anybody's grandparents. But these particular smiles, this particular couple, Stephanie recognized.

She sat straighter. It made perfect sense. Of course he would come here. It was a case of good old-fashioned revenge. She glanced again at the framed photograph of Rick's smiling grandparents. A larger version of the same photograph hung on their cabin wall.

The police had invaded his home. Now Julian had invaded one of theirs.

Stephanie surveyed her surroundings with a new appreciation. She was sitting inside Rick's house.

Rick tapped his fingers on Shelton's desk, waiting for Hale's next call. Other officers were out searching for Stephanie while he sat on his rear end. He wanted to be out there with them, doing something more productive than sitting here waiting for Julian's next chess move.

Shelton pointed at him. "Back on line one."

Rick punched the button and lifted the receiver. "Julian. What have you got for me?"

"Ha! What have I got for you?" Hale laughed at him. "I gave you homework. I'm getting bored sitting here waiting for you to come over and play. Trust me, you don't want me bored."

"We know where you are," Rick lied.

Shelton ripped off a sheet of paper from a notebook

and slid it in front of Rick. *Call is coming from some-where in or near Greenwood.*

Finally a clue. Rick grinned at the detective and then at Terrell. Julian hadn't taken Stephanie outside of the Seattle metro area, and he was hiding in an area of town they all knew well. Both Rick's and the Watkinses' houses were in Greenwood. Together they should be able to come up with ideas of where to search. It was just a matter of time. But how much time did they have?

"What happened to all of our history keeping us honest, Rick? If you knew where I was, you'd be here by now." Hale cackled again, but there was another sound Rick strained to hear behind the laugh.

At first he wondered if he was hearing things, but he heard it again. It was definitely Stephanie's voice screaming in the background. He jumped from his chair. "Rick, we're in your house. Rick! We are…inside…your house. I saw a picture of your nana and…"

The next sounds made his stomach drop. He closed his eyes as the easily recognizable *zzit, zzit, zzit, zzit, zzit, zzit, zzit,* sound of a Taser firing blended with Stephanie's screams of pain.

"Hale, stop!" Rick bellowed into the phone.

Shelton and Watkins had scrambled away already, alerting SWAT and sending cars.

"Well, I guess I won't be bored for long," Hale said. "But you need to understand something, Rick. I am in control here, not you, and not the hordes of police you've probably already sent this way. You better stop them if you want her to stay alive."

Silent beats followed, and Rick wondered how he should respond. But Hale wasn't finished talking. "If you think you're man enough to take me, come on over, but you better come alone."

Chapter Twenty

At the command post, Rick swung open the door of the mobile home that served as the SWAT team's Tactical Operations Center and stepped inside. All of this planning and talking was taking up precious time. Hale knew they were onto him. How much longer would he allow Stephanie to live? Rick's heart screamed *hurry up and get her out of there,* but his brain and training knew proper planning was critical to success. Despite how much he wanted them to, the SWAT team couldn't storm the house without cause. Unless the threat to Stephanie's life was imminent, they'd keep trying to negotiate. Rick took a deep breath to calm his panic and shook hands with the SWAT commander.

The commander swept a hand toward TV monitors. "We've got cameras up on the windows of your house. Tell me what we're seeing here."

The image was partially blocked by the wooden slats of his window blinds, but Rick recognized the room and the people in it. Hale stood with his back to the window, gesturing wildly as he made some kind of speech. Tears pricked behind Rick's eyes when he spotted Stephanie lying bound on the floor. He held his breath until he saw her foot move. She was still alive for now.

Rick handed the commander the sketch he had made of his home's floor plan and pointed out the location of the room they were viewing. "That's my den. You enter the living room from the front door. The den is here, behind that wall."

The commander nodded, studying Rick's drawing. "Be prepared to take your position soon. Since you are without your K-9, we'll make you point man on the front entry team." He patted Rick's shoulder with a heavy hand. "Don't worry. We'll have your friend out of there soon."

Rick stood next to Terrell, waiting for the order to take their positions. It felt strange to be working without Axle, but Rick was glad the dog had been with his neighbor getting the rest he needed to recuperate instead of at home when Hale showed up with Stephanie.

An officer walked past them and into the hostage negotiation trailer. Rick rubbed his hand across his mouth. Were they going about this the right way? The scurrying activity of the command post reminded Rick of Hale's demand that he come alone. They were a few blocks away and hidden from Hale's view for now, but soon the team would move and prepare to strike. What would Hale do to Stephanie when he discovered there was a small army camped outside?

Rick wiped the sweat off his forehead. How much longer would they have to wait? He gazed around his neighborhood, seeing the familiar landscape in a new light. He was so close to Stephanie, yet so far away.

Only slightly over a week had passed since he and Terrell had prepared just like this to serve Hale's warrant. He couldn't have known that morning how much would change in only a week's time, especially not how much his own heart would change.

He reached into his pocket and felt his fingers wrap around the coin he always kept there. Grandpa Powell had given it to him at his swearing-in ceremony for SPD. Rick didn't need to take it out of his pocket to know what was engraved on the coin. He had carried it for over seven years; the words were written on his memory. First Corinthians 16:13: "Be on your guard; stand firm in the faith; be men of courage; be strong."

Be men of courage. What if Stephanie did survive? Would he pursue a relationship with her?

He turned to Terrell. "Sarge, I…"

Terrell interrupted him. "We're going to win tonight, Powell. I can feel it. Don't lose hope."

Be on your guard. Rick looked up to the sky. "I shouldn't have left her alone. How could I have not seen that we were falling for another one of Hale's tricks? I should have driven up to Bellingham right away and confirmed Hale was in that jail cell with my own eyes." Guilt ate away at Rick's gut.

Be strong. "I don't know how you can do it."

"Do what?" Terrell asked him.

"You know…" Rick struggled for the words he wanted. *"Love."*

Instead of laughing at him as he expected, Terrell turned his wise eyes toward Rick with a look of compassion. "Love requires us to do the opposite of what we are trained to do. That's why it is so hard for cops to do it. We have to disarm and allow ourselves to be vulnerable."

"How did you do it?" Rick swallowed. "With Val, I mean." He shouldn't be bringing all of this up now, but he needed these answers. If Stephanie survived, he would have a choice to make.

"It wasn't easy, but I couldn't live without her. Val was worth the risk," Terrell said. "And I didn't want fear to rule my life."

"What about your kids? Don't you fear for their safety?"

Terrell looked away and nodded, thinking. "Outside of what God allows, there is no guarantee of safety in this life. I could be an accountant instead, and it wouldn't change a thing. Our lives are in His hands and we are safest inside His will. My kids' dad is a cop and that isn't a surprise to God. He can handle it. He's got them." Terrell paused. "He's got Stephanie, too, Rick."

Stand firm in the faith. Rick hung his head. "I want that kind of faith."

"Then ask for it." Terrell placed a hand on Rick's shoulder. "Look. You and I—we know the darker side of life. We have to face it every single day and don't have the luxury of pretending it isn't there. We put on our badge and our gun and we try our best to fulfill our calling to serve and protect, but at the end of the day when we strip it all off, we know we are still only men underneath. We fool ourselves if we don't. That's why the real battle has to be done on our knees. That's how I do it."

Rick's cell vibrated, letting him know a text was coming through. When he saw it was from his neighbor, Cindy, he scanned it quickly. He groaned. "Oh, no."

"What?" Terrell asked him.

"It's Axle. My neighbor took him with her when they evacuated. He freaked when they got to her friend's house and bolted. They've been looking for him, but can't find him. She thinks he might be heading this way."

Rick could just imagine how agitated the dog must have been during the evacuation process. But he couldn't go looking for him now. *Please watch out for him, Lord, until I can go find him. Thank You.* He was still so out of practice, the praying felt rusty. But he felt the loosening of his own grip as he took his first baby step toward more faith.

"He'll be okay. We'll find him after this," Terrell assured him.

One of the SWAT guys interrupted. "It's go time, gentlemen."

During the last electric shock, Stephanie had fallen off the couch to the floor. Julian had pulled the trigger three times after her attempt to alert Rick to their location. As he prepared to fire a fourth shot, she begged him, "Please. Not again."

She didn't regret trying to pass the information on to Rick, but she wasn't sure if she had even succeeded. Had he heard her? She was paying a painful price for her act of rebellion. If he did hear her, was he coming?

"Every time I pull the trigger it lasts for five seconds. Feels like longer, doesn't it?" Julian turned the weapon around in his hand, admiring it. "This was a good purchase. I like it."

He squatted down next to her and put it to her temple. She wanted to be tough, but she couldn't help but whimper at the thought of another round of shock. He grinned, apparently pleased at her reaction. "You and your big mouth ruined my agenda. Officer Powell wasn't supposed to show up for another few hours, after I finished with you."

Julian stood up. He put the stun gun down on an end table and pulled a pistol from his waistband. He turned it over, admiring it. "Guess I'll just have to be flexible and go with plan B." He squatted back down so she could see him. He placed the gun in her line of sight. "I'll give you a break for now. Think of it as a little intermission before the final act."

He waved the gun around a bit. "What's your weapon of choice, Stephanie? Gun or..." He walked back beside the couch and placed a large bundle on the floor where she could see it.

Stephanie cringed. More dynamite?

"Which do you prefer? Quick gunshot wound? That's not usually *my* preferred method, a bit too quick and cliché for my taste." He pointed to the dynamite. "Or do you and Rick go out together in a romantic blaze of glory?"

Stephanie rested her forehead against the carpet and prayed. She understood Julian's goals better now. She had been wondering why he was waiting to kill her, why he was giving the police time to get there. He was luring Rick here so he could kill them both. They had defied him and ruined his plans. Now they would pay together. She wished there were some way to warn Rick about the dynamite.

Bullet or bomb? She couldn't make that choice. Silence was her only response.

Stephanie was afraid, but as she prayed, her breathing slowed, the peace from earlier continuing to bathe her. Tears flowed silently as she lifted up all the people she loved in prayer. She prayed for her sister Emily's baby, the niece or nephew she would now never know. She prayed for Joash and Haddie and the future ahead of them. She prayed for Val and Terrell, and finally she prayed for Rick.

Lord, I want to live. I want Rick to live.

Julian's face perked up in attention. He must have heard something he didn't like. He moved away from her toward the window. She couldn't see him, but she could sense his agitation and pacing. He was back on his cell phone.

"I see your men out there. I gave Officer Powell the chance to be a hero. It wouldn't have ended like this if he had just done what I told him to do and came alone. You tell him her death is on him, because this ends now."

Stephanie jumped at the sound of Hale's cell phone crashing against the wall.

Julian walked back into her line of sight and pointed the pistol at her face. "It looks as if your boyfriend made the choice for you."

Stephanie screwed her eyes shut tight and started praying one last desperate cry for help. Her prayers ceased at the sound of shattering glass. Deafening explosions and blinding white light brought dust and chunks of plaster raining down from the ceiling. She had always wondered what dying would feel like. It sounded as though she was about to find out.

Rick lined up in his position with the front entry team, his heart pounding in his ears. He remembered Terrell's words: *The real battle has to be done on our knees. That's how I do it.* If that was Terrell's secret, then Rick would follow his lead. *Lord, make me firm in faith, stronger and braver than I am on my own. If You allow Stephanie to live, I promise I will let You teach me how to love her right, no matter what it costs me.*

I'll trust You. It was all he had time to think before the "Go, go, go, go" screamed into his ear.

It was a beautifully executed dynamic entry. The windows of his house shattered as the 40 mm wood batons blasted the windows, followed by the mesmerizing strobes of flashbang grenades detonating inside. One swing of the battering ram demolished his front door and they were inside. Rick sprinted, the first of the front entry team to penetrate the house. They had mere seconds to reach Hale before he recovered from the shock and disorientation and shot Stephanie.

Find her, find her, find her chanted through his mind, propelling him forward. One way or the other, it would all be over in a matter of minutes. Soon he would know if he would get the chance to tell Stephanie that he loved her. He searched through the chaos around him. He coughed out dust. *Be alive, be alive.*

Rick struggled to recognize the place as his own through the haze. He rounded the corner to the living room and saw Stephanie's body, bound and lying motionless on the floor. He ran toward her, but movement in his peripheral vision made him turn.

The tip of Hale's gun shook from the tremor in his unsteady hands, but it was pointed right at Rick's head.

Rick spun and fired, *pop, pop, pop, pop.* Hale dropped his gun, swaying like a tree about to topple. Rick knew he had fatally wounded Hale, but he couldn't let down his guard until he was sure it was over. Instead of dropping as Rick expected him to do, Hale raised and flicked to life a lighter. He staggered toward a large bundle on the floor.

Coldness spiraled through Rick's belly. *It's dynamite!* "No! Don't do it!" Time stretched as Rick lunged toward the man.

A deep, throaty snarl came from behind Rick and before he could reach Hale, a blur of brown fur shot past him. A dog leaped into the air; his jaws opened wide and latched onto Hale's arm, preventing him from detonating the dynamite.

Unable to fight the effects of the gunshot wounds any longer, the light in Julian Hale's eyes dimmed and then extinguished. His body fell over dead. The lighter rolled from his lifeless hand.

"Axle! *Aus!*" Rick commanded Axle to let go of Hale. He squatted down and rubbed Axle's head. "Where did you come from, buddy?" Rick had never been more proud of his dog than he was in that moment. "*So ist brav! So ist brav!*" Rick praised Axle over and over again in German. "Good job! Good job! You saved us, buddy!"

Stephanie rolled over, disoriented. She felt the vibration of boots stomping about her, but she was deaf from the explosion. It was like a silent nightmare. She had watched Julian's body swaying above her, his gun raised. She had squeezed her eyes shut tighter with each muffled gunshot that followed.

When she opened her eyes, she had been shocked to see Axle hanging from Julian's arm. Julian had swayed only once more before he toppled over and landed on top of her, his body limp, lifeless.

Boots stopped in front of her, and Axle licked her face. She could hear the distant echo of the word *clear* repeated over and over again. Then the weight of Julian's body was lifted off her and she could see Rick looming above her. He slit the zip ties, setting her arms and legs free. Stephanie grabbed his offered hand and he jerked her to her feet, shoving her forward, prompting her to run for the door.

It had happened so fast, leaving no time to clear her mind. The only objective was to escape before any dynamite detonated. She stumbled out into the coolness and sucked in air. She had prepared herself for death, but now she was very much alive. She tried not to fall as they rushed down the steps.

Rick swept her up into his arms and carried her far from the house. He dropped to his knees beside a tree, but he didn't let go of her. His strong arms held her to him. Burying his face in her hair, they rocked together, not speaking. His body heat warmed her, driving away the shock. She was aware of nothing around her, not the SWAT team and bomb squad members running in and out of the house, not the flashing red-and-blue lights. There was only Rick. Rick was all she saw, all she felt. She was alive and she was in his arms. Slowly, her hearing improved, and she could hear his voice.

"I've got you. You're safe. I'm never letting you go."

Stephanie wrapped her arms around his neck. Looking up into his shining eyes, she knew she was rescued. She kissed his stubble-covered chin. He tipped her face up, and his warm, soft lips covered hers.

Chapter Twenty-One

Friday
Two Weeks Later

Stephanie walked down the hallway toward her classroom carrying a stack of photocopies for the day ahead. Her principal leaned out the door of his office and called to her. "Hang on, Stephanie. Before you go, I need to talk to you for minute."

"Sure, Jim. What's up?"

She followed him into his cramped office. Photographs of the Pop Warner football team he coached lined the walls. Fifteen years' worth of elementary-aged football players grinned back at her. It was strange to think that many of those boys in the older photographs must be men by now, with kids of their own. On the edge of his desk sat a photograph of Jim's oldest daughter's wedding from the previous summer. It was a cozy, messy space, but it was still the principal's office, and Stephanie couldn't help but feel like a kid in trouble.

"Everything okay?" she asked Jim as she sat down in the hard plastic chair that he pointed her to.

"Just fine," he assured her. He picked at a hang-nail without making eye contact. "I know you've had a rough few weeks. You've had a lot on your mind. Normally I wouldn't want to bother you with this right now, but I've put this off as long as I possibly can." He sat down on the edge of his desk and folded his arms. "I need to have all of my staffing decisions set for the next school year."

Stephanie wiggled in her seat. *Here it comes.*

"I need to know for sure what you plan to do next year." He finally looked her in the eye. "I put a contract in your mailbox. If you're staying, I need it signed by the end of the school day."

The blonde woman behind the desk handed Rick his credit card. "You can have that back now," she said.

He slipped the card into his billfold and returned it all to his back pocket.

She typed with the tips of her fake red nails. Then she grabbed paper from the printer and folded it into two envelopes and handed them to him. "I believe that is all you need for now. When we confirm the final details and itinerary, I'll have more for you."

"Thanks." Rick stood and offered his hand. "I appreciate all of your help. I know this isn't something you deal with on a regular basis. You were able to get an amazing deal for these."

She shook his hand and grinned. "No, thank *you.* This was all new for me. I definitely don't get requests for that destination too often. It was quite the learning experience. But most importantly…" She winked. "It's so romantic."

Rick tapped his open palm with the envelopes and returned her grin. "That's the goal."

* * *

Stephanie slid the bookmark between the pages and closed the book. It was a cliffhanger, and now her students would have to wait all weekend to find out what was going to happen next in their story. It might be cruel, but "Leave them wanting more" was her guiding philosophy when it came to their read-aloud times. She had an innate sense for where to stop reading, knowing how to pull them in, hook them and then leave them dangling over the cliff. She waited for the begging to begin.

A collective groan engulfed her. "No. Not yet, don't stop."

There were many times in the past when she had let her students talk her into reading more. She was sure they would try it again today. The kids reveled in the victory of convincing her to abandon whatever was next on her agenda. When it came to books, she was a total pushover—anything for the sake of a great story. "I really shouldn't…" she would often say, and then they would know they had her. The kids always ate it up, and so did Stephanie.

Their school pulled its enrollment from neighborhoods where it would be tough to round up very many books at all. Yet here they were, all thirty kids completely engrossed, begging her to keep reading to them. Moments like these thrilled her and whispered to her heart, *See, your life has purpose here, too.* She glanced at her desk where the unsigned contract sat, knowing she had to decide soon.

Stephanie leaned against the back of her high stool and pulled the Newberry Award–winning book into her chest. If she wasn't so excited about what was coming next, she might be tempted to keep reading until the bell rang to go home for the weekend.

"We'll pick up here on Monday." She gave them her wickedest grin. "You'll have to wonder all weekend long what is going to happen next." More groans pelted her.

"Just one more chapter. Please," begged a boy named Jaxon.

"Sorry, Jaxon, we have to stop. We have a special guest speaker coming today, remember?"

Right on time, the door opened, and Axle trotted in, his head alert and his chest puffed up with pride. His wounds were healing nicely and he looked healthy and happy. Behind Axle, holding the leash was Rick. The sight of him sent a rush of blood to Stephanie's cheeks. She blinked. *Hello, guest speaker.* She blinked a few more times. *Stop staring, Stephanie. Your students are watching.* It was going to take time for her to get used to the idea that this gorgeous man in uniform loved her. She cleared her throat and said, "Class, these are my friends Officer Powell and his K-9 partner, Axle."

A girl named Kylie raised her hand but didn't wait to be called on before she blurted out, "Is that your boyfriend, Miss O'Brien?" Nervous giggles tittered around the classroom. Stephanie chose to ignore the question, but Rick leaned in and whispered into her ear.

"Yeah, Miss O'Brien. Am I your *boyfriend*?"

If her face was red before, it was on fire now. She led the way to the front of the classroom. Leave it to kids to be direct.

"Get out the questions you've written for Officer Powell and show me what your best attention looks like." Stephanie stood a little taller as her kids made her look good. They scrambled to follow her directions. It took only seconds before all of their desks were cleared of everything but a single sheet of paper, all their arms were folded, and thirty pairs of eyes were staring at Rick expectantly.

Rick leaned toward Stephanie's ear and whispered behind his hand, "Wow. Impressive crowd control. Sure you don't want to become a cop?"

Never in a million, trillion years. She leaned toward him and whispered back behind her own hand, "It's all in the training, Officer Powell." She shrugged and then, before turning back to the class, she winked and added, "I might be able to give you a few pointers."

Rick rewarded her flirting with a flash of his dangerous dimple. If she wasn't careful, she would forget she was standing in front of her classroom and get lost in banter with Rick. She addressed her students. "Remember class, best manners." Stephanie pointed her first two fingers at her own eyes and then turned the fingers toward the kids. "I'll be watching from the back."

The kids laughed, but held their attentive postures. A warm sense of satisfaction filled her. They were good kids, and she cared about them so deeply. Stephanie threw out her hand toward the students, "Okay, Officer Powell, they are all yours."

She sat down at the round table in the back of the room to watch. "Miss O'Brien told me to tell you some stories about my dog, Axle," Rick told the class. He stroked Axle's fur and then cocked his head, squinting his eyes as if he weren't convinced that was such a good idea. "She said you would want to hear all the good stories about how Axle is a hero, but I'm not sure if I should. I wouldn't want to scare you or anything."

The kids leaned farther forward. Stephanie giggled. *He's good. Definitely knows how to hook a room full of ten-year-olds.* She felt her own body leaning forward, captivated by Rick's charisma in the spotlight. Who was she fooling? He knew how to hook the teacher, too. Everything about Rick captivated her. This was nothing new.

The bell rang, announcing the end of another week. Her students slammed shut the journals they were writing in and shoved them into desks or backpacks, scrambling to be the first in line to go for the weekend.

Stephanie stationed herself in the doorway as she did at the close of every day. "High five, handshake or hug?" she asked each exiting student. Kylie chose a high five. Jaxon surprised her by requesting his first hug of the school year. Miguel stuck out his hand for a quick, shy shake. Down the line she said goodbye to each student for the weekend.

After the last hug, she turned back into the empty classroom. She grabbed her lesson plan book and sat down in one of her students' desks. Each day she chose a different desk to sit in before she left, praying for the student who sat in it. Today she chose Jaxon's desk. His dad was up for parole soon, and she prayed that when he came home it would be good for Jaxon. The boy had come so far this school year and was blossoming before her eyes. *Thank You, Lord, that I've been able to watch the work You are doing in his life.*

Stephanie opened her planner and traced her finger over the photograph of Moses. She really did need to ask Emily for a more current picture of him, but this was Moses as she remembered him in her heart, the age he had been the last time she held him.

She stared ahead at the whiteboard with all her notes written on it in dry-erase marker. She liked seeing the classroom from the students' point of view. It gave her perspective.

Today had felt normal for the first time since she had come back. She had wondered how long it would take for her to readjust to everyday living without the constant threat of death hanging over her head. It had happened sooner than she expected. It had been a sweet day. Rick and Axle's visit being the sweetest part.

Slipped between the pages of her planner was next year's contract. She pulled it out, fingering the paper until the edges started to curl. Stephanie clicked her pen open. The pen hovered over the paper, shaking. She squeezed her eyes tight. She knew what she needed to do. All of the doors to Liberia were closed.

For now.

With a settled heart, she opened her eyes and signed her name, making her decision firm. Liberia owned a part of her heart—it always would—but sitting here in Jaxon's desk, she knew that this school held her heart, too. Someday she would go back and serve the people of Liberia, but when she did, she would be motivated by love and gratitude, not because she was afraid of losing God's approval. She put down the pen, content. Joining Him in the work He was doing right here in the lives and hearts of her students, that was a meaningful life, too.

Rick stood outside Lincoln Elementary, leaning against his patrol car. He could see into the ground-floor windows of Stephanie's classroom. She was sitting in one of the students' desks, working. He pulled out his phone and texted her. Look out your window. Can you join me?

He felt his own phone vibrate as her answer came through.

On my way out. :)

Rick grinned as Stephanie left the building and walked toward him. Her steps were light, almost skipping. Watching her made him feel weightless. As she drew near, he saw that her smile reached her eyes. She was happy, and that made him happy. He wanted to spend a lifetime making her feel that way. He hoped the envelopes in his pocket would be his first step in accomplishing that.

"I should finish planning for the week…" she told him, glancing over her shoulder at the school.

"No, you shouldn't. You should go get some coffee with me. Besides, I brought you a present." He reached through the open window of his car and pulled out a sticker. It was a silver Seattle PD badge he kept to pass out to kids. "I think you've earned this, partner."

He peeled off the sticker's backing and stuck the badge to her shirt. "There, it's official."

Stephanie giggled. "Does that make me Deputy O'Brien?"

He mocked a heart attack. "Deputy? You're killing me. Unless you are planning on working for King County, let's try Officer O'Brien."

Her face turned red. "Oops. Guess I've got a lot to learn."

"Training starts now," he told her, pulling her into his arms.

Rick took both of Stephanie's hands in his, then he cocked his head and gave her the signature squint she found so adorable. "So, have you given any more thought about what you are going to do next year?"

His question made her realize how happy she was

to have the decision made. She nodded. "Actually, Jim called me into his office this morning and gave me until the end of the school day to make my final decision."

Rick's grip tightened on her hands. "And?"

"I signed the contract," she told him. "I finished signing right before I got your text, in fact."

He exhaled, and a slow smile spread across his face. "And you are okay with that decision?"

Axle rubbed against her legs. She leaned down and petted the top of his head, returning Rick's smile. "Rick, I'm better than okay with that."

"Good." He seemed giddy with excitement. "Because I have another present…" He held two envelopes out to her.

Confused, she opened them and pulled out travel documents, plane tickets and an itinerary. Shocked, she looked up at Rick's grinning face. Chills ran up her body. Gratitude and love washed over her as she realized what she was holding. "Are these…?"

He nodded. "Tickets to Liberia for this summer. Tickets for two."

Stephanie grasped the papers to her heart. It felt as if her chest couldn't hold all of the joy. She choked on her emotion, unable to speak.

"I've already put in for the time off." Rick said. "And I've made arrangements with your sister."

He pulled her back into his arms; it was uncomfortable pressing against his bulletproof vest and gun belt, but it was right where she wanted to be. "I love you, Stephanie. Liberia is a part of who you are, and I want to learn to love what you love. I know you wanted to go back there full-time. This is only a short-term trip for now, but it's a start."

She lifted her tear-soaked face and found his lips, hoping her kiss would say what her voice couldn't.

He pulled away. "Coffee?"

"Yes, please."

"How about every morning for the rest of our lives?" he asked her. It felt as if he was asking for much more.

Stephanie nodded, speechless.

His laugh was music. "Are you sure you are ready to be involved with a cop? You know better than anyone what that could mean, and the price you might have to pay because of my job."

She repeated his words back to him. "I love you, Rick. Being a cop is part of who you are. It's important and noble work. Let's do this—" she waved the tickets, and then tapped her police badge sticker "—all of it, together."

He clasped her hands in his. "You're sure?"

"I'm beyond sure. Are you sure?"

"I know what I want out of life, and you are what I want. But I was afraid I might be moving too fast for you."

She shook her head. "Not after all that we've gone through together. We've been on the relationship fast track. I know that you are what I want, too."

His grin was huge. "Well, in that case, Axle, give the lady her other present."

"There's more?" She wasn't sure her heart could hold any more.

Axle trotted back to her side and sat at attention. She hadn't noticed before that there was a small box attached to his collar. Her hands trembled as she detached it.

Rick put his fingers over hers before she opened it. "Not yet. Hold on." He hollered over her shoulder. "I think it's safe for you all to come out of hiding now."

Out of nowhere, the entire Watkins family appeared at her side. Haddie snuggled up to Stephanie and wrapped her sweet little girl arms around Stephanie's waist. Terrell put his arm around Joash while Val attempted to take video on her cell phone. Val was shaking and crying so much, Stephanie doubted the video quality would be worth watching. None of that mattered to her, though. All she cared about was being surrounded by these people, to bask in her rich life of love.

Rick lowered to one knee and said, "Stephanie O'Brien, will you do me the honor of becoming my wife?"

All she could do was nod. Finally she squeaked out a tearful, "Yes!"

The Watkins family erupted in cheers and whoops and hugs while Axle barked joyfully and ran in circles.

Rick stood up and pulled Stephanie to him. Their bodies melted together in a kiss of promise. She forgot about the world around her. She didn't care about the catcalls from her friends. She and Rick were lost in each other and their dreams for the future.

Joy enveloped Stephanie. She hadn't been looking for Rick Powell, but God had brought him, anyway, as a gift to her. He had given her more than she could have asked for or imagined.

She had had her plans, but God's were better. Rick lifted her off the ground, taking her breath away as he squeezed.

Much better.

* * * * *

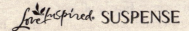

SPECIAL EXCERPT FROM

Love Inspired
SUSPENSE

*A serial killer is after a military nurse. She'll fight to
stay one step ahead of him with the help of a heroic
soldier and some brave K-9s.*

Read on for a sneak preview of
Battle Tested *by Laura Scott,*
the next book in the Military K-9 Unit miniseries,
available October 2018 from Love Inspired Suspense.

Two fatal drug overdoses in the past week.

Exhausted from her thirteen-hour shift in the critical
care unit, First Lieutenant Vanessa Gomez made her way
down the hallway of the Canyon Air Force Base hospital,
grappling with the impact of this latest drug-related death.

The corridor lights abruptly went out, enclosing her in
complete darkness. She froze, instinctively searching for
the nearest exit sign, when strong hands roughly grabbed
her from behind, long fingers wrapping themselves around
her throat.

The Red Rose Killer?

It had been months since she'd received the red rose
indicating she was a target of convicted murderer and
prison escapee Boyd Sullivan.

She kicked back at the man's shins, but her soft-soled
nursing shoes didn't do much damage. She used her

elbows, too, but couldn't make enough impact that way, either. The attacker's fingers moved their position around her neck, as if searching for the proper pressure points.

"Why?" she asked.

"Because you're in my way…" the attacker said, his voice low and dripping with malice.

The pressure against her carotid arteries grew, making her dizzy and weak. Black spots dotted her vision.

She was going to die, and there was nothing she could do to stop it.

Her knees sagged, then she heard a man's voice. "Hey, what's going on?"

Her attacker abruptly let go just as the lights came on. She fell to the floor. The sound of pounding footsteps echoed along the corridor.

"Are you okay?" A man wearing battle-ready camo rushed over, then dropped to his knees beside her. A soft, wet, furry nose pushed against her face and a sandpapery tongue licked her cheek.

"Yes," she managed, hoping he didn't notice how badly her hands were shaking.

"Stay, Tango," the stranger ordered. He ran toward the stairwell at the end of the hall, the one that her attacker must have used to escape.

Save $1.00

on the purchase of ANY
Love Inspired® book.

Available wherever books are sold,
including most bookstores, supermarkets,
drugstores and discount stores.

Save $1.00

on the purchase of ANY Love Inspired® book.

Coupon valid until November 30, 2018.
Redeemable at participating retail outlets in the U.S. and Canada only.
Limit one coupon per customer.

52615926

5 65373 00076 2 (8100)0 12382

Canadian Retailers: Harlequin Enterprises Limited will pay the face value of this coupon plus 10.25¢ if submitted by customer for this product only. Any other use constitutes fraud. Coupon is nonassignable. Void if taxed, prohibited or restricted by law. Consumer must pay any government taxes. Void if copied. Inmar Promotional Services ("IPS") customers submit coupons and proof of sales to Harlequin Enterprises Limited, P.O. Box 31000, Scarborough, ON M1R 0E7, Canada. Non-IPS retailer—for reimbursement submit coupons and proof of sales directly to Harlequin Enterprises Limited, Retail Marketing Department, Bay Adelaide Centre, East Tower, 22 Adelaide Street West, 40th Floor, Toronto, Ontario M5H 4E3, Canada.

U.S. Retailers: Harlequin Enterprises Limited will pay the face value of this coupon plus 8¢ if submitted by customer for this product only. Any other use constitutes fraud. Coupon is nonassignable. Void if taxed, prohibited or restricted by law. Consumer must pay any government taxes. Void if copied. For reimbursement submit coupons and proof of sales directly to Harlequin Enterprises, Ltd 482, NCH Marketing Services, P.O. Box 880001, El Paso, TX 88588-0001, U.S.A. Cash value 1/100 cents.

® and ™ are trademarks owned and used by the trademark owner and/or its licensee.

© 2018 Harlequin Enterprises Limited

LISCOUP14766

SPECIAL EXCERPT FROM

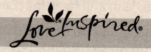

Though Texan cowboy Toby Christner was raised Amish, he has no plans to settle down in the new community along Harmony Creek. But when he meets Amish nanny Sarah Kuhns, he can't help but wonder if a Plain life with her is exactly what he needs.

Read on for a sneak preview of
The Amish Christmas Cowboy *by Jo Ann Brown, available in October 2018 from Love Inspired!*

Toby was sure something was bothering Sarah.

He thought through their conversation among her family's Christmas trees. She'd been distressed by how Summerhays and his wife paid too little attention to their *kinder*, but she'd been ready to speak her mind on that subject.

So what was bothering her?

You.

The voice in his head startled him. He'd heard it clearly and, for once, it wasn't warning him away from becoming too close to someone. Instead, it was telling him the reason why there might be a wall between him and Sarah.

Maybe it was for the best. Every day he lingered was another drawing him into the community. Each moment he spent with Sarah enticed him to look forward to the next time they could be together. In spite of his determination, his life was being linked to hers and her neighbors.

That would change once his coworker's trailer pulled up to take him back to Texas.

Sarah gestured toward the *kinder*. "They're hungry for love."

"You're worried they're going to be hurt when I go back to Texas."

"Ja."

He wanted to ask how she would feel when he left, but he'd hurt his ankle, not his head, so he didn't have an excuse to ask a stupid question.

"The *kinder* will be upset when you go, but won't it be better to give them nice memories of your times together to enjoy when they think about you after you've left?"

Nice memories of times together? Maybe that would be sufficient for the *kinder*, but he doubted it would be enough for him.

Don't miss
The Amish Christmas Cowboy *by Jo Ann Brown,*
available October 2018 wherever
Love Inspired® books and ebooks are sold.

www.LoveInspired.com

Love Inspired®

Inspirational Romance to Warm Your Heart and Soul

Join our social communities to connect with other readers who share your love!

Sign up for the Love Inspired newsletter at **www.LoveInspired.com** to be the first to find out about upcoming titles, special promotions and exclusive content.

CONNECT WITH US AT:

Facebook.com/groups/HarlequinConnection

 Facebook.com/LoveInspiredBooks

 Twitter.com/LoveInspiredBks

LISOCIAL2018